BY YIYUN LI

Kinder Than Solitude
Gold Boy, Emerald Girl
The Vagrants
A Thousand Years of Good Prayers

KINDER THAN
SOLITUDE

KINDER THAN SOLITUDE

A NOVEL

Yiyun Li

RANDOM HOUSE

NEW YORK

Published in the United States by Random House, an imprint of The Random House Publishing Group, a division of Random House LLC, a Penguin Random House Company, New York.

RANDOM HOUSE and the HOUSE colophon are registered trademarks of Random House LLC.

Library of Congress Cataloging-in-Publication Data
Li, Yiyun.
Kinder than solitude : a novel / Yiyun Li.
pages   cm
ISBN 978-1-4000-6814-2
eBook ISBN 978-0-8129-9602-9
1. Friendship—Fiction. 2. Accidental poisoning—Fiction. I. Title.
PS3612.I16K54 2013
813'.6—dc23   2013017307

Printed in the United States of America on acid-free paper

www.atrandom.com

2 4 6 8 9 7 5 3

Book design by Victoria Wong

To Dapeng, Vincent, and James

You can't both live and have lived, my dear Christophe.

Romain Rolland, *Jean-Christophe*

KINDER THAN
SOLITUDE

1

Boyang had thought grief would make people less commonplace. The waiting room at the crematory, however, did not differentiate itself from elsewhere: the eagerness to be served first and the suspicion that others had snatched a better deal were reminiscent of the marketplace or stock exchange. A man shouldered him, reaching for multiple copies of the same form. Surely you have only one body to burn, Boyang laughed to himself, and the man glared back, as though personal loss had granted him the right to what he was not owed by the world.

A woman in black rushed in and looked around for a white chrysanthemum that must have been dropped earlier. The clerk, an old man, watched her pin it back onto her collar and smiled at Boyang. "You wonder why they can't slow down," he said when Boyang expressed sympathy for what the clerk had to endure. "Day in and day out. These people forget that those who rush to every sweet fruit of life rush to death, too."

Boyang wondered if the clerk—whom no one wished to meet and, once met, became part of an unwelcome memory—found solace in those words; perhaps he found joy, too, in knowing that those who mistreated him would return in a colder form. The thought made Boyang like him.

When the older man finished his tea, they went over the paperwork for Shaoai's cremation: her death certificate, the cause of death
lung failure after acute pneumonia; the yellowed residence registration card with an official cancellation stamp; her citizen's ID. The
clerk checked the paperwork, including Boyang's ID, carefully, his
pencil making tiny dots under the numbers and dates Boyang had
entered. He wondered if the clerk noticed that Shaoai was six years
older. "A relative?" the clerk asked when he looked up.

"A friend," Boyang said, imagining disappointment in the old
man's eyes because Boyang was not a new widower at thirty-seven.
He added that Shaoai had been ill for twenty-one years.

"Good that things come to an end."

There was no option but to agree with the old man's comfortless
words. Boyang was glad that he had dissuaded Aunt, Shaoai's mother,
from coming to the crematory. He would have been unable to guard
her from strangers' goodwill and malevolence alike, and he would
have been embarrassed by her grief.

The clerk told Boyang to come back in two hours, and he walked
out to the Garden of Perpetual Green. Shaoai would have scoffed at
the cypresses and pine trees—symbols of everlasting youth at a crematory. She would have mocked her mother's sorrow and Boyang's
pensiveness, even her own inglorious end. She, of all people, would
have made good use of a life. Her distaste for the timid, the dull, and
the ordinary, her unforgiving sharpness: what a waste that edge had
rusted, Boyang thought again. The decaying that had dragged on for
too long had only turned tragedy into nuisance; death, when it strikes,
better completes its annihilating act on the first try.

At the top of a hill, older trees guarded elaborate mausoleums. A
few birds—crows and magpies—prattled close enough that Boyang
could hit them with a pinecone, but he would need an audience for
such a boyish achievement. If Coco were here, she would know how
to poke fun at his shot and to look impressed when he showed her the

pine nuts inside the cones, though the truth was she had little interest in these things. Coco was twenty-one, yet already she had acquired the incuriosity of one who has lived long enough; her desire—too greedy for her age, or too meager—was for tangible comforts and material possessions.

At the end of a path a pavilion sheltered the bronze bust of a man. Boyang tapped the pillars. They were sturdy enough, though the wood was not the best quality, and the paint had faded and was peeling in places; according to the plaque the pavilion was less than two years old. A bouquet of plastic lilies laid underneath looked more dead than fake. Time, since the economy had taken off, seemed to move at an unreal pace in China, the new becoming old fast, the old vanishing into oblivion. One day he, too, could afford—if he desired it—to be turned into a stone or metal bust, gaining a minor immortality for people to laugh at. With a bit of luck, Coco, or whatever woman replaced Coco, might shed a tear or two in front of his grave—if not for a world without him, then for her misspent youth.

A woman appeared over the rise of the hill, and upon seeing Boyang turned so abruptly he barely glimpsed her face, framed by a black-and-white patterned scarf. He studied her black coat and the designer bag on her arm, and wondered if she was a rich man's widow, or better, a mistress. For a moment he entertained the thought of catching up with her and exchanging a few words. If they liked each other, they could stop at a village on the drive back to the city and choose a clean countryside restaurant for some rustic flavors: sweet potatoes roasted in a tall metal barrel, chicken stewed with so-called "locally grown, organic" mushrooms, a few sips of strong yam liquor that would make their stories flow more easily and the lunch worth prolonging. Back in the city, they might or might not, depending on their moods, see each other again.

Boyang returned to the counter at the designated time. The clerk informed him that there would be a slight delay, as one family had insisted on checking everything to avoid contamination. Contamination with someone else's ashes? Boyang asked, and the old man smiled and said that if there was any place where people's whims would be accommodated, it was this one. Touchy business, Boyang said, and then asked if a woman had come alone to cremate someone.

"A woman?" the clerk said.

Boyang considered describing the woman to the old man, but then decided that a man with a trustworthy face and gentle sense of humor should be dealt with cautiously. He changed the subject and chatted about the new city regulations on real estate. Later, when the clerk asked him if he would like to take a look at Shaoai's remains before they were ground to ashes—some families requested that, explained the clerk; some asked to pick up the bones themselves for proper closure—Boyang declined the offer.

That everything had come to an end like this was a relief as unconvincing as the pale sun that graced the dashboard as Boyang drove back to the city. The news of the death he had emailed to Moran and Ruyu. Moran, he knew, lived in America, though where Ruyu was he was not certain: America most probably; perhaps Canada, or Australia, or somewhere in Europe. He doubted that the two of them had remained in touch with each other; his own communications with them had never once been acknowledged. On the first of every month, he sent separate emails, informing—reminding—them that Shaoai was alive. He never spoke of the emergencies, lung failure once, and heart failure a few times: to limit the information would spare him the expectation of a reply. Shaoai had always pulled through, clinging to a world that had neither use nor a place for her, and the brief messages he sent had given him a sense of permanency. Loyalty to the past is the foundation of a life one does not, by happenstance or by will, end up living. His persistence had preserved that untouched alternative. Their silence, he believed, proved that to be the case: silence maintained so emphatically could only mean their loyalties matched his, too.

When the doctor confirmed Shaoai's death, Boyang had felt neither grief nor relief but anger—anger at being proven wrong, at being denied the reunion that he had considered his right: they—he and Moran and Ruyu—were old in his fantasy, ancient even, a man and two women who had nearly lived out their mortal lives, converging one last time at the lake of their youth. Moran and Ruyu would perhaps consider their homecoming a natural, if not triumphant, epitaph. To this celebration he would bring Shaoai, whose presence would turn their decades of accumulation—marriage, children, career, wealth—into a hoarder's laughable collection. The best life is the life unlived, and Shaoai would be the only one to have a claim to that truth.

Yet their foolishness was his, too, and to laugh at his own absurdity he needed the other two: laughing by oneself is more intolerable than mourning alone. They might not have seen the death notice in their emails—after all, it was only the middle of the month. Boyang knew, by intuition, that the email addresses he had from Moran and Ruyu were not the ones they used every day, as his, used only for communicating with them, was not. That Shaoai had died on him when he had least expected her to, and that neither Moran nor Ruyu had acknowledged his email, made the death unreal, as though he were rehearsing alone for something he needed the other two women—no, all three of them—to be part of; Shaoai, too, had to be present at her own funeral.

A silver Porsche overtook Boyang on the highway, and he wondered if the driver was the woman he had seen in the cemetery. His cell phone vibrated, but he did not unhook it from his belt. He had canceled his appointments for the day, and the call most probably was from Coco. As a rule he kept his whereabouts vague to Coco, so she had to call him, and had to be prepared for last-minute changes.

To keep her on uncertain footing gave him the pleasure of being in control. *Sugar daddy*—she and her friends must have used that imported term behind his back, but once when he, half-drunk, had asked Coco if that was what she took him for, she laughed and said he was too young for that. *Sugar brother*, she said afterward on the phone with a girlfriend, winking at him, and later he'd thanked her for her generosity.

It took him a few passes to find a parking spot at the apartment complex, built long before cars were a part of the lives of its occupants. A man who was cleaning the windshield of a small car—made in China from the look of it—cast an unfriendly look at Boyang as he exited his car. Would the man, Boyang wondered while locking eyes with the stranger sternly, leave a scratch on his BMW, or at least kick its tire or bumper, when he was out of sight? Such conjecture about other people no doubt reflected his own ignobleness, but a man must not let his imagination be outwitted by the world. Boyang took pride in his contempt for other people and himself alike. This world, like many people in it, inevitably treats a man better when he has little kindness to spare for it.

Before he unlocked the apartment door with his copy of the key, Aunt opened it from inside. She must have been crying, her eyelids red and swollen, but she acted busy, almost cheerful, brewing tea that Boyang had said he did not need, pushing a plate of pistachios at him, and asking about the health of his parents.

Boyang wished he had never known this one-bedroom unit, which, already shabby when Aunt and Uncle had moved into it with Shaoai, had not changed much in the past twenty years. The furniture was old, from the '60s and '70s, cheap wooden tables and chairs and iron bed frames that had long lost their original shine. The only addition was a used metal walker, bought inexpensively from the hospital where Aunt used to work as a nurse before retiring. Boyang had helped Uncle to saw off its wheels, readjust its height, and then secure it to a wall. Three times a day Shaoai had been helped onto it and practiced standing by herself so that her muscles retained some strength.

The old sheets wrapped around the armrests had worn out over the years, the sky-blue paint badly chipped and exposing the dirty metal beneath. Never, Boyang thought, would he again have to coax Shaoai to practice standing with a piece of candy, yet was this world without her a better place for him? Like a river taking a detour, time that had passed elsewhere had left the apartment and its occupants behind, their lives and deaths fossils of an inconsequential past. Boyang's own parents had purchased four properties in the last decade, each one bigger than the previous one; their current home was a two-story townhouse they never tired of inviting friends to, for viewings of their marble bathtub and crystal chandelier imported from Italy and their shiny appliances from Germany. Boyang had overseen the remodeling of all four places, and he managed the three they rented out. He himself had three apartments in Beijing; the first, purchased for his marriage, he had bestowed upon his ex-wife as a punishing gesture of largesse when the man she had betrayed Boyang for had not divorced his own wife as he had promised.

A black-and-white photograph of Shaoai, enlarged and set in a black frame, was hung up next to a picture of Uncle, who had died five years earlier from liver cancer. A plate of fresh fruit was placed in front of the pictures, oranges quartered, melons sliced, apples and pears, intact, looking waxy and unreal. These Aunt timidly showed Boyang, as though she had to prove that she had just the right amount of grief—too much would make her a burden; too little would suggest negligence. "Did everything go all right?" she asked when she ran out of the topics she must have prepared before his return.

The image of Aunt's checking the clock every few minutes and wondering where her daughter's body was disturbed Boyang. He regretted that he had pressed Aunt not to go to the crematory, but at once he chased that thought away. "Everything went well," he said. "Smoothly."

"I wouldn't know what to do without you," Aunt said.

Boyang unwrapped the urn from the white silk bag and placed it next to the plate of fruits. He avoided looking closely at Shaoai in the photo, which must have been taken during her college years. Over the past two decades, she had doubled in size, and her face had lost the cleanly defined jawline. To be filled with soft flesh like that, and to vanish in a furnace . . . Boyang shuddered. The body, in its absence, took up more space than it had when alive. Abruptly he went over to the walker by the wall and assessed the possibility of dismantling it.

"But we'll keep it, shall we?" Aunt said. "It could come in handy someday for me."

Unwilling to let Aunt steer the conversation toward the future, Boyang nodded and said he would have to leave soon; he was to meet a business partner.

Of course, Aunt said, she would not keep him.

"I've emailed Ruyu and Moran," he said at the door. It was cowardly to bring up their names, but he was afraid that if he did not unburden himself, he would be spending another night drinking more than was good for his health, singing intentionally off-key at the karaoke bar, and telling lewd jokes too loudly.

Aunt paused as though she had not heard him right, so he said again that the news had been sent to Moran and Ruyu. Aunt nodded and said it was right of him to tell them, though he knew she was lying.

"I thought you might like me to," Boyang said. It was cruel to take advantage of the old woman who was not in a position to protest, but he wanted to talk with someone about Moran and Ruyu, to hear their names mentioned by another voice.

"Moran is a good girl," Aunt said, reaching up to pat his shoulder. "I've always been sorry that you didn't marry her."

Even the most innocent person, when cornered, is capable of a heartless crime. Boyang was amazed at how effortless it was for Aunt to inflict such fatal pain. It was unlike her to say anything about his marriage. Between them they had shared only Shaoai. He had told Aunt about his divorce, but he had not needed to remind her, as he had had to remind his parents, not to discuss it. And to speak of Moran as a better candidate for his marriage while intentionally leaving out the other name—Boyang felt an urge to punish someone, though he only shook his head. "Marriage or no," he said, "I need to run now."

"And to think we haven't heard from Moran for so long," Aunt persisted.

Boyang ignored the comment, and said he would come back later that week. When he had asked Aunt about the burial of Shaoai's cremains, she had replied that she was not ready. He suspected, perhaps unfairly, that Aunt was holding on to the urn of ashes because that was the last thing binding him to this apartment. He and Aunt were not related by blood.

When Boyang got back into his car, he saw that both his mother and Coco had called. He dialed his mother's number and, after the call, sent a text to Coco saying he would be busy for the rest of the day. Coco and his mother were the two chief competitors for his attention these days. He had not deemed it worthwhile to introduce the two—one was too transient in his life, and the other, too permanent.

Going to his parents' place after Aunt's was a comfort. Remodeled as though for an advertisement in a consumer magazine, their home provided a perfect veil behind which the world of unpleasantness receded. Here more than elsewhere Boyang understood the significance of investing in trivialities: beautiful objects, like expensive drinks and entertaining acquaintances, demand that one think little and feel nothing beyond one's immediate surroundings.

They had taken some friends out for dinner the night before, Boyang's mother explained. They had too many leftovers, so she thought

Boyang might as well come and get rid of the food for them. He laughed, saying he did not know he was their compost bin. His parents had become particular in their eating habits, obsessing over the health benefits, or lack thereof, of everything entering their bodies. He could see that they would order an excessive amount of food for their friends yet touch little themselves.

The topics at dinner were his sister's American-born twins, the real estate prices in Beijing and in a coastal city where his parents were pondering purchasing a waterfront condo, and the inefficiency of their new housekeeper. Only when his mother had cleaned away the dishes did she ask, as though grasping a passing thought, if Boyang had heard of Shaoai's death. By then, his father had gone into his study.

That he had kept in touch with Shaoai's parents and had acted as caretaker when illnesses and deaths had beset their family—this Boyang had seen no reason to share with his parents. If they had suspected any connection, they had preferred not to know. The key to success, in his parents' opinion, was the capacity to selectively live one's life, to forget what one ought not to remember, to untangle oneself from lesser and irrelevant others, and to recognize the unnecessariness of human emotions. Fame and material gain are secondary though unsurprising, if one is able to choose the portion of one's life to live with impersonal wisdom. For this belief they had, as an example, Boyang's sister, who was a prominent physicist in America.

"So I heard," Boyang said. Aunt would not have kept the death from the old neighbors, and it did not surprise him that one of them—or perhaps more than one—had called his parents. If there were any pleasure in delivering the news of death it would be that call, castigation barely masked by courteousness.

His mother returned from the kitchen with two cups of tea and passed one to him. He cringed at her nudging the conversation beyond the comfortable repertoire of their usual topics. He showed up whenever she summoned him; the best way to stay distanced, he believed, was to satisfy her every need.

"What do you think, then?" his mother said.

"Think of what?"

"The whole thing," she said. "One must acknowledge the waste, no?"

"What waste?"

"Shaoai's life, obviously," his mother said, adjusting a single calla lily in a crystal vase on the dinner table. "But even if you take her out of the equation, others' lives have been affected."

What others, Boyang wanted to say to his mother, would be worth a moment of her thought? The chemical found in Shaoai's blood had been taken from his mother's laboratory; whether it had been an attempted murder, an unsuccessful suicide, or a freak accident had never been determined. His family did not talk about the case, but Boyang knew that his mother had never let go of her grudge.

"Do you mean your career went to waste?" Boyang asked. After the incident, the university had taken disciplinary action against his mother for her mismanagement of chemicals. It would have been an unpleasant incident, a small glitch in her otherwise stellar academic career, but she insisted on disputing the charge: every laboratory in the department was run according to outdated regulations, with chemicals available to all graduate students. It was a misfortune that a life had been damaged, she admitted; she was willing to be punished for allowing three teenage children to be in her lab unsupervised—a mismanagement of human beings rather than chemicals.

"If you want to look at my career, sure—that's gone to waste for no reason."

"But things have turned out all right for you," Boyang said. "Better, you have to admit." His mother had left the university and joined a pharmaceutical company, later purchased by an American company. With her flawless English, which she'd learned at a Catholic school, and several patents to her name, she earned an income three times what she would have made as a professor.

"But did I say I was speaking of myself?" she said. "Your assumption that I have only myself to think of is only a hypothesis, not a proven fact."

"I don't see anyone else worthy of your thought."

"Not even you?"

"What do you mean?" The weakest comeback, Boyang thought: people only ask a question like that because they already know the answer.

"You don't feel your life has been affected by Shaoai's poisoning?"

What answer did she want to hear? "You get used to something like that," he said. On second thought, he added, "No, I wouldn't say her case has affected me in any substantial way."

"Who wanted her to die?"

"Excuse me?"

"You heard me right. Who wanted to kill her back then? She didn't seem like someone who would commit suicide, though certainly one of your little girlfriends, I can't remember which one, hinted at that."

In rehearsing scenarios of Shaoai's death Boyang had never included his mother—but when does any parent hold a position in a child's fantasy? Still, that his mother had paid attention, and that he had underestimated her awareness of the case, annoyed him. "I'm sure you understand that if, in all honesty, you tell me that you were the one who poisoned her, I wouldn't say or do anything," she said. "This conversation is purely for my curiosity."

They were abiding by the same code, of maintaining the coexistence between two strangers, an intimacy—if their arrangement could be called that—cultivated with disciplined indifference. He rather liked his mother this way, and knew that in a sense he had never been her child; nor would she, in growing old, allow herself to become his charge. "I didn't poison her," he said. "I'm sorry."

"Why sorry?"

"You'd be much happier to have an answer. I'd be happier, too, if I could tell you for sure who poisoned her."

"Well then, there are only two other possibilities. So, do you think it was Moran or Ruyu?"

He had asked himself the question over the years. He looked at his mother with a smile, careful that his face not betray him. "What do you think?"

"I didn't know either of them."

"There was no reason for you to know them," Boyang said. "Or, for that matter, anyone."

His mother, as he knew, was not the kind to dwell upon sarcasm. "I never really met Ruyu," she said. "Moran of course I saw around, but I don't remember her well. I don't recall her being brilliant, am I right?"

"I doubt there is anyone brilliant enough for you."

"Your sister is," Boyang's mother said. "But don't distract me. You used to know them both well, so you must have an idea."

"I don't," Boyang said.

His mother looked at him, rearranging, he imagined, his and the other people's positions in her head as she would do with chemical molecules. He remembered taking his parents to America to celebrate their fortieth wedding anniversary. At the airport in San Francisco, they'd seen an exhibition of duck decoys. Despite the twelve-hour flight, his mother had studied each of the wooden ducks. The colors and shapes of the different decoy products fascinated her, and she read the old 1920s posters advertising twenty-cent duck decoys, using her knowledge of inflation rates over the years to calculate how much each duck would cost today. Always so curious, Boyang thought, so impersonally curious.

"Did you ever ask them?" she said now.

"Whether one of them tried to murder someone?" Boyang said. "No."

"Why not?"

"I think you're overestimating your son's ability."

"But do you not want to know? Why not ask them?"

"When? Back then, or now?"

"Why not ask now? They may be honest with you now that Shaoai is dead."

For one thing, Boyang thought, neither Moran nor Ruyu would answer his email. "If you're not overestimating my ability, you are certainly overestimating people's desire for honesty," he said. "But has it occurred to you it might've only been an accident? Would that be too dull for you?"

His mother looked into her tea. "If I put too many tea leaves in the teapot, that could be considered a mistake. No one puts poison into another person's teacup by accident. Or do you mean that Moran or Ruyu was the real target, and poor Shaoai happened to take the wrong tea? To think, it could've been you!"

"My drinking the poison by accident?"

"No. What I'm asking is: what do you think of the possibility of someone trying to murder you?"

The single calla lily—his mother's favorite flower—looked menacing, unreal with its flawless curve. She blew lightly over her tea, not looking at him, though he knew that was part of her scrutiny. Was she distorting the past to humor herself, or was she revealing her doubt— or was the line between distorting and revealing so fine that one could not happen without the other? For all he knew, he had lived in her selective unawareness, but perhaps this was only an illusion. One ought not to have the last word about one's own mother.

He admitted that the thought had never occurred to him. "It's a possibility, you know," she said.

"But why would anyone have wanted to kill me?"

"Why would anyone want to kill anyone?" she said, and right away Boyang knew that he had spoken too carelessly. "If someone steals poison from a lab, that person intends to do harm to another person or to herself. For all I know, the harm was already done the moment that chemical was stolen. And I'm not asking you why. Why anyone does anything is beyond my understanding or interest. All I would like to know is who was trying to kill who, but unfortunately you don't have an answer. And sadly, you don't seem to share my curiosity."

2

When the train pulled into Beijing's arched station on August 1, 1989, Ruyu, adjusting her eyes from the glare of the afternoon to the shadowed grayness of the station, did not yet know that one's preparation for departure should begin long before arrival. There were many things that she, at fifteen, had still to learn. To seek answers to one's questions is to know the world. Guileless in childhood, private as one grows older, and, for those who insist on the certainty of adulthood, ignored when they become unanswerable, these questions form the context of one's being. For Ruyu, however, an answer that excluded all questions had already been provided.

The passengers moved to both ends of the car. Ruyu remained seated and looked through the grimy window. On the platform, people pushed one another out of the way with their arms, as well as—more effectively—their bags and suitcases. Someone—though Ruyu did not know who, nor did she feel compelled to be curious—would be waiting for her on the platform. She took a pair of barrettes from her school satchel and clipped them in her hair. This was how her grandaunts had described her to her hosts in a letter they'd sent a week before her journey: a white shirt, a black skirt, and two blue barrettes in the shape of butterflies, a brown willow trunk, a 120-bass accordion in a black leather case, a school satchel, and a canteen.

The last two passengers, a pair of middle-aged sisters-in-law, asked her if she needed help. Ruyu thanked them and said no, she was fine. During the nine-hour journey, the two women had studied Ruyu with unconcealed curiosity; that she had only taken sips of water, that she had not left her seat to use the washroom, that she had not let go of her clasp of her school satchel—these things had not escaped their eyes. They had offered Ruyu a peach and a pack of soda crackers and later a bottle of orange juice purchased through the window at a station, all of which Ruyu had declined politely. They had between themselves approved of her manner, though that had not stopped them from feeling offended. The girl was small-built, and appeared too young for a solo journey in the opinion of the women and other fellow travelers; but when they had questioned her, she had replied with restraint, revealing little of the nature of her trip.

When the aisle was cleared, Ruyu heaved the accordion case off the luggage rack. Her school satchel, made of sturdy canvas, she had had since the first grade, and its color had long faded from grass green to a pale, yellowish white. Inside it, her grandaunts had sewn a small cloth bag, in which were twenty brand-new ten-yuan bills, a large amount of money for a young girl to carry. With great care, Ruyu pulled the trunk from under her seat—it was the smallest of a set of three willow trunks that her grandaunts owned, purchased, they had told her, in 1947 in the best department store in Shanghai, and they had asked her to please be gentle with it.

Shaoai recognized Ruyu the moment she stumbled onto the platform. Who would have thought, besides those two old ladies, of stuffing a girl into such an ancient-looking outfit and then, on top of that, making her carry an outdated, childish school satchel and a water canteen? "You look younger than I expected," Shaoai said when she approached Ruyu, though it was a lie. In the black-and-white photo the two grandaunts had sent, Ruyu, despite the woolen, smock-like dress that was too big for her, looked like an ordinary schoolgirl, her eyes candidly raised to the camera; they were the eyes of a child who did not yet know and was not concerned with her place in the world.

The face in front of Shaoai now showed a frosty inviolability a girl Ruyu's age should not have possessed. Shaoai felt slightly annoyed, as though the train had brought the wrong person.

"Sister Shaoai?" Ruyu said, recognizing the older girl from the family picture sent to her grandaunts: short hair, angular face, thin lips adding an impatient touchiness to the face.

From the pocket of her shorts Shaoai produced the photo Ruyu's grandaunts had mailed along with their letter. "So that you know you're not being met by the wrong person," Shaoai said, and then stuffed the photo back into her pocket.

Ruyu recognized the photo, taken when she had turned fifteen two months earlier. Every year on her birthday—though whether it was her real birthday or only an approximation of it she had wondered at times without asking—her grandaunts took her to the photographer's for a black-and-white portrait. The final prints were saved in an album, each fit into four silver corners glued on a new page, with the year written on the bottom of the page. Over the years the photographer, who had begun as an apprentice but was no longer a young man, had never had Ruyu change her position, so in all the birthday portraits she sat straight, with her hands folded on her lap. What Shaoai had must be an extra print, as Ruyu's grandaunts were not the kind of people who would disturb a perfectly ordered album and leave a blank among four corners. Still, the thought that a stranger had kept something of her unsettled Ruyu. She felt the dampness of her palms and wiped them on the back of her black cotton skirt.

"You should get some cooler clothes for the summer," Shaoai said, looking at Ruyu's long skirt.

In Shaoai's disapproving look Ruyu saw the same presumptuousness she had detected in the middle-aged women on the train. So the older girl was no different from others—quick to put themselves in a place where they could advise Ruyu about how to live. What separated Ruyu from them, they did not know, was that she had been chosen. What she knew would never be revealed to them: she could see, and see through, them in a way they could not see her, or themselves.

Shaoai was twenty-two, the only daughter of Uncle and Aunt, who were, in some convoluted way Ruyu's grandaunts had not explained, relatives of the two old women. "Honest people," her grandaunts had pronounced of the family who had promised to take her in for a year—or, if things worked out, for the next three years, until Ruyu went to college. There were a couple of other families in Beijing, also of remote connections, whom her grandaunts had considered, but both households included boys Ruyu's age or not much older. In the end, Shaoai and her parents had been chosen to avoid possible inconvenience.

"Do you need a minute to catch your breath?" Shaoai asked, and picked up the trunk and the accordion before Ruyu could reply. She offered to carry one of the items herself, and Shaoai only jerked her chin toward the exit and said she had helpers waiting.

Ruyu was not prepared for the noises and the heat of the city outside the station. The late afternoon sun was a white disc behind the smog, and over loudspeakers a man was reading, in a stern voice, the names and descriptions of fugitives wanted for sabotaging the government earlier that summer. Travelers for whom Beijing was only a connecting stop occupied the available shade under the billboards, and the less lucky ones lay under layers of newspapers. Five women with cardboard signs swarmed toward Shaoai and, with competing voices at high volume, recommended their hostels and shuttle services. Shaoai deftly swung the trunk and the accordion case through the crowd, while Ruyu, who'd hesitated a moment too long, was surrounded by other hawkers. A middle-aged woman in a sleeveless smock grabbed Ruyu's elbow and dragged her away from the other vendors. Ruyu tried to wiggle her arm free and explain that she was only visiting relatives, but her feeble protest was muffled by the thick fog of noise. In her provincial hometown, rarely would a stranger or an acquaintance come this close to her; when she was younger, her grandaunts' upright posture and grave expression had protected her from the invasion of the world; later, even when she was not being escorted by them, people would leave her alone in the street or in the marketplace, her grandaunts' severity recognized and respected in her own unsmiling bearing.

It took Shaoai no time, when she returned, to free Ruyu from the hawkers. Where is my accordion, Ruyu asked when she noticed Shaoai's empty hands. The accusation stopped Shaoai. With my helpers, of course, she said; why, you think I would abandon your valuable luggage just to rescue someone who has her own legs to run?

Ruyu had never been in a situation where she had to run away; her grandaunts—and in recent years she was aware that she, too— had the ability to make people recede from their paths. As an infant she had been left on the doorstep of a pair of unmarried Catholic sisters, and she was raised by the two women who were not related to her by blood. Like two prophets, her grandaunts had laid out the map of her life for her, that her journey would take her from their small apartment in the provincial city to Beijing and later abroad, where she would find her real and only home in the Church. Outside of the one-bedroom apartment she shared with them, neighbors and school-teachers and classmates were unnecessarily inquisitive about her life, as though the porridge she ate at breakfast or the mittens dangling from a string around her neck offered clues to a puzzle beyond their understanding. Ruyu had learned to answer their questions with cold etiquette. Still, she despised their ignorance: their lives were to be lived in the dust; hers, with the completeness of purity.

Shaoai's helpers, waiting in the shade of a building by the road-side, were a boy and a girl. Shaoai introduced them: Boyang, the stout boy with tanned skin who was roping the accordion case to the back rack of his bicycle, had white flashing teeth when he smiled; Moran, the skinny, long-legged girl sitting astride her bicycle, had already secured the willow trunk behind her. They were neighbors,

Shaoai said; both were a year older than Ruyu, but she would be in the same grade with them in her new school. Boyang and Moran glanced at the accordion case when school was mentioned, so they must have been informed of the plan. Ruyu did not have legal residence in Beijing; when her grandaunts had first proposed her stay, Uncle and Aunt had written back, explaining that they would absolutely love to help out with Ruyu's education but that most high schools would not admit a student who did not have city residency. Ruyu is a good musician, her grandaunts replied, and enclosed a copy of the certificate of her passing grade 8 on her accordion. How Uncle and Aunt had convinced the high school—Shaoai's alma mater—to admit Ruyu on account of her musical talents, Ruyu did not know; her grandaunts, when they had received the letter requiring that the accordion and the original copy of the grade 8 certificate accompany Ruyu to Beijing, had not shown surprise.

That night, Ruyu lay in the bed that she was to share with Shaoai and thought about living in a world where her grandaunts' presence was not sensed and respected, and for the first time she felt she was becoming the orphan people had taken her to be. Already Beijing made her feel small, but worse than that was people's indifference to her smallness. On the bus ride from the train station to her new home, a man in a short-sleeved shirt had stood close to Ruyu, and the moment the bus had begun to move, he seemed to press much of his weight on her. She inched away from him, but his weight followed her, imperceptible to the other passengers, for when Ruyu looked at the two middle-aged women sitting in a double seat in front of her, hoping for some help, the two women—strangers, judging from how they did not talk or smile at each other—turned their faces away and looked at the shops out the window. The predicament would have lasted longer if it hadn't been for Shaoai, who, after purchasing their tickets from the conductor, had pushed through the crowd and, as though reaching for the back of a seat to steady herself, squeezed an arm between the man and Ruyu. Nothing had been said, but perhaps

Shaoai had elbowed the man or given him a stern look, or it was simply Shaoai's presence that had made the man retreat. For the rest of the bus ride Shaoai stood close, a steely presence between Ruyu and the rest of the world. Neither girl spoke, and when it was time for them to get off, Shaoai tapped Ruyu on the shoulder and signaled her to follow while Shaoai pushed through the bodies. The shortsleeved man, Ruyu noticed, fixed his eyes on her face as she moved toward the exit. Even though there were quite a few people between them, Ruyu felt her face burn.

On the sidewalk, Shaoai asked Ruyu if she was too dumb to protect herself. Rarely did Ruyu face an angry person at a close distance; both her grandaunts had equable temperaments, believing any kind of emotional excitability a hurdle to one's personal improvement. She sighed and turned her eyes away so as not to embarrass Shaoai.

For a split second, Shaoai regretted her eruption—after all, Ruyu was a young girl, a provincial, an orphan raised by eccentric old ladies. Shaoai would have willingly softened, and even apologized, if Ruyu had understood the source of her anger, but the younger girl did not make a gesture either to mollify Shaoai or to defend herself. In Ruyu's silence, Shaoai sensed a contemptuous extrication. "Haven't your grandaunts taught you anything useful?" Shaoai said, angrier now, both at Ruyu's unresponsiveness and at her own temper.

Nothing separated Ruyu more thoroughly from the world than its malignance toward her grandaunts. To ward off people's criticism of her grandaunts was more than to justify how they had raised her: to defend them was to defend God, who had chosen her to be left at their door. "My grandaunts have taught me more than you could imagine," Ruyu said. "If you don't like my coming to stay with your family, I understand. I'm not here for you to like, and my grandaunts are not for you to approve or disapprove of."

Shaoai had stared at Ruyu for a long moment, and then shrugged as though she no longer was in the mood to argue with Ruyu. When they had reached Shaoai's home the episode seemed to have been put behind them.

Please—Ruyu folded her hands on her chest—please show me that a big city is nothing compared to you. The bamboo mattress under her was no longer cooling her off, but she refrained from moving to a new spot and stayed on the edge of the bed Shaoai had pointed to as her side. The only window in the room, a small rectangular one high on the wall, admitted little night air, and inside the mosquito netting Ruyu felt her pajamas sticking to her body. A television set, its volume low, was blinking in the living room, though Ruyu doubted that Uncle and Aunt were watching it. For a while they had been talking in whispers, and Ruyu wondered if they had been talking about her or her grandaunts. Please, she said again in her mind, please give me the wisdom to live among strangers until I leave them behind.

Ruyu's grandaunts had not taught her to pray. Her upbringing had not been a strictly religious one, though her grandaunts had done what they could to give her an education that they had deemed necessary to prepare her for her future reunion with the Church. They themselves had not attended any services since 1957, when the Church was reformed by the Communist Party into the Chinese Patriotic Catholic Association; nor did they keep any concrete evidence of their previous spiritual lives. Still, from a young age, Ruyu had understood that what set her apart from other children was not the absence of her parents but the presence of God in her life, which made parents and siblings and playmates and even her grandaunts extraneous. She had begun to talk to him before she entered elementary school. "Our Father in Heaven," she'd heard her grandaunts say when she had been a small girl, and it was with a conversation with him that Ruyu would end each day, talking to him as a child would talk to an imaginary friend or to herself, a presence at once abstract and solidly comforting. But he was neither a friend nor a part of herself; he belonged to her as much as he belonged to her grandaunts. None of the people she had met so far in Beijing, Ruyu knew, shared with her the secret of his presence: not Uncle and Aunt, who had told her that she was one of the family now and had asked her not to feel shy about making requests; not the neighbors, the five other families who had all come out to the courtyard upon her arrival, talking to her as though they had known her forever, a man teasing her about her accordion, which seemed too big for her narrow shoulders, a woman disapproving of her outfit because it would give her a heat rash in this humid weather; not the boy Boyang or the girl Moran, both of whom were quiet in front of their seniors, but who, Ruyu knew from the looks the two exchanged, had more to say to each other; and not Shaoai, who, queenly in her impatience toward the fuss the neighbors made over the newcomer, had left the courtyard before they had finished welcoming Ruyu.

Please make the time I have to spend with these strangers go fast so that I can come to you soon. She was about to finish the conversation, as usual, with an apology—always she asked too much of him while offering nothing in return—when the front door opened and then banged shut; the metal bell she had seen hanging from the door frame jingled and was hushed right away by someone's hand. Aunt said something, and then Shaoai, who must have been the one who'd come into the house, replied with some sort of retort, though both talked in low voices, and Ruyu could not hear their exchanges. She looked through the mosquito netting at the curtain that separated the bedroom from the living room—a white floral print on blue cotton fabric—and at the light from the living room creeping into the bedroom from underneath the curtain.

The house, more than a hundred years old, had been built for traditional family life, the center of the house being the living room, the entries between the living room and the bedrooms open, with no doors. The smallest bedroom, no larger than a cubicle and located to the right of the main entrance, was the entire world occupied by

Grandpa—Uncle's father, who had been bedridden for the last five years after a series of strokes. Earlier in the evening, when Aunt had shown Ruyu around the house, she'd raised the curtain quickly for Ruyu to catch a glimpse of the old man lying under a thin, gray blanket, the only life left in his gaunt face a pair of dull eyes that rolled toward Ruyu. He had said something incomprehensible, and Aunt had replied in a loud yet not unkind voice that there was nothing for him to worry about. They were sorry they could not offer Ruyu her own bedroom, Aunt said, and then pointed to the curtain that hid Grandpa and added in a low voice: "Who knows. This room could be vacant any day."

The bedroom Ruyu was to share with Shaoai was the biggest in the house and used to belong to Uncle and Aunt. Aunt apologized for not having had time to make many changes, besides installing a new student's desk in the corner of the room. The other bedroom— Shaoai's old bedroom—was not large enough to accommodate the desk, so it wouldn't do, Aunt explained, since Ruyu needed her own quiet corner to study. Ruyu mumbled something halfway between an apology and an acknowledgment, though Aunt, flicking dust off the shade of the desk lamp—new also, bought on sale with the desk, she said—did not seem to hear. Ruyu wondered if her grandaunts had considered how their plan for her would change other people's lives; if they had known anything, they had not told her, and it perplexed her that a small person like herself could cause so much inconvenience. At dinnertime, Shaoai had scoffed when Aunt reminded her to show Ruyu how to clip the mosquito netting, saying that even a child could do that, to which Aunt had replied in an appeasing tone that she just wanted to make sure Ruyu felt informed about her new home. Uncle, reticent, with a sad smile on his face, had come to the dinner table in a threadbare undershirt, but had hurried back to the bedroom when Aunt had frowned at him, and returned in a neatly buttoned shirt. From the expectant looks on Aunt's and Uncle's faces, Ruyu knew that the dinner had been prepared for her with extra effort, and, later in the evening, when she fetched water from the wooden bucket next to the kitchen for her washstand, she overheard Uncle comforting Aunt, telling her that perhaps the girl was simply tired from her journey, and Aunt replying that she hoped Ruyu's appetite would return, as it's certainly not healthy for a person her age to eat only morsels like a chickadee.

Someone walked close to the bedroom, a shadow looming on the curtain. Ruyu closed her eyes when she recognized Shaoai's profile. Aunt whispered something to which Shaoai did not reply before entering the bedroom. She stopped in the semidarkness and then turned on the light, a bare bulb hanging low from the ceiling. Ruyu closed her eyes tighter and listened to Shaoai fumble around. After a moment, an electric fan turned on, its droning the only sound in the quietness of the night. The breeze instantly lifted the mosquito netting, and with an exaggerated sigh Shaoai tucked the bottom of the netting underneath the mattress. "You have to be at least a little smarter than the mosquitoes," she said.

Ruyu did not know if she should apologize and then decided not to open her eyes.

"You shouldn't wrap yourself up in the blanket," Shaoai said. "It's hot."

After a pause, Ruyu replied that she was all right, and Shaoai did not pursue the topic. She turned off the light and changed in the darkness. When she climbed into the bed from her side and readjusted the mosquito netting, Ruyu regretted that she had not prepared herself by turning away so that her back faced the center of the bed. It was too late now, so she tried to hold her body still and breathe quietly. Please, she said, sensing that she was on Shaoai's mind, please mask me with your love so they can't feel my existence.

Later, when Shaoai was asleep, Ruyu opened her eyes and looked at the mosquito netting above her, gray and formless, and listened to the fan swirling. She had been off the train for a few hours now, but still her body could feel the motion, as though it had retained—and continued living—the memory of traveling. There was much to get used to in her new life, a public outhouse at the end of the alleyway Moran had shown her earlier; an outdoor spigot in the middle of the courtyard, where Ruyu had seen Boyang and a few other young men from the quadrangle gather after sunset, topless, splashing cold water onto their upper bodies and taking turns putting their heads under the tap to cool down; a bed shared with a stranger; meals supervised by anxious Aunt. For the first time that day, Ruyu felt homesick for her bed tucked behind an old muslin screen in the foyer of her grand-aunts' one-room apartment.

3

Celia's message on Ruyu's voice mail sounded panicked, as though Celia had been caught in a tornado, but Ruyu found little surprise in the emergency. That evening it was Celia's turn to host ladies' night. These monthly get-togethers had started as a book club, but, as more books went unfinished and undiscussed, other activities had been introduced—wine tasting, tea tasting, a question-and-answer session with the president of a local real estate agency when the market turned downward, a holiday workshop on homemade soaps and candles. Celia, one of the three founders of the book club, had nicknamed it Buckingham Ladies' Society, though she used the name only with Ruyu, thinking it might offend people who did not belong to the club, as well as some who did. Not everyone in the book club lived on Buckingham Road. A few of them lived on streets with less prominent names: Kent Road, Bristol Lane, Charing Cross Lane, and Norfolk Way. Properties on those streets were of course more than decent, and children from those houses went to the same school as hers did, but Celia, living on Buckingham, could not help but take pleasure in the subtle difference between her street and the others.

Ruyu wondered if the florist had misinterpreted the color theme Celia had requested, or if the caterer—a new one she was trying out, upon a friend's recommendation—had failed to meet her expectations. In either case, Ruyu's presence was urgently needed—could she please come early, Celia had said in the voice mail, pretty please?—not, of course, to right any wrong but to bear witness to Celia's personal tornado. Being let down was Celia's fate; life never failed to bestow upon her pain and disappointment she had to suffer on everyone's behalf, so that the world could go on being a good place, free from real calamities. Celia's martyrdom, in most people's— less than kind—opinion, amounted to nothing but a dramatic self-centeredness, but Ruyu, one of the very few who took Celia's sacrifice seriously, understood the source of her suffering: Celia, though lapsed, had been brought up by Catholic parents.

Edwin and the boys were off to dinner and then to a Warriors game, Celia told Ruyu when she arrived at the Moorlands'. A robin had flown into a window that morning, knocking itself out and setting off the alarm, Celia said, and thank goodness the window was not broken and Luis—the gardener—was here to take care of the poor bird. The caterer was seventeen minutes late, so wasn't it wise of her to have changed the delivery time to half an hour earlier? In the middle of recounting an exchange between the deliveryman and herself, Celia stopped abruptly. "Ruby," she said. "Ruby."

"Yes," Ruyu said. "I'm listening."

Celia came and sat down with Ruyu in the breakfast nook. The table and the benches were made of wood reclaimed from an old Kensington barn where Celia's grandmother, she liked to tell her visitors, used to go for riding lessons. "You look distracted," Celia said, pushing a glass of water toward Ruyu.

The woman Celia thought of as Ruby should have unwavering attention as an audience. Ruyu thanked Celia for the water and said that nothing was really distracting her. To Celia's circle of friends— many of whom would arrive soon—Ruyu was, depending on what was needed, a woman of many possibilities: a Mandarin tutor, a reliable house- and pet-sitter, a last-minute babysitter, a part-time cashier at a confection boutique, an occasional party helper. But her loyalty, first and foremost, belonged to Celia, for it was she who had found Ruyu these many opportunities, including the position at La Dolce Vita, a third-generation family business owned by a high school friend of Celia's.

Celia did not often notice anything beyond her immediate preoccupation, but sometimes, distraught, she was able to perceive other people's moods. In those moments she adamantly required an explanation, as though her tenacious urge to know someone else's suffering offered a way out of her own. Ruyu wondered whether she looked disturbed and wished she had touched up her face before entering the house.

"You are not yourself today," Celia said. "Don't tell me you had a tough day. The day is already bad enough for me."

"Here's what I have done today: I was in the shop in the morning; I stopped at the dry cleaners; I fed Karen's cats; I took a walk," Ruyu said. "Now, tell me how hard my day could be."

Celia sighed and said that of course Ruyu was right. "You don't know how I envy you."

Ruyu had been told this often, and once in a while she almost believed Celia to be sincere. "You sounded dreadful in your voice mail," Ruyu said. "What happened?"

What happened, Celia said, was pure outrage. She went away and came back with a pair of white T-shirts. Earlier that afternoon she had attended a meeting for the fundraising of a major art festival in San Francisco, and on the committee was a writer whose teen detective mysteries were recent bestsellers. "You'd think it's not too much to ask a writer to sign a couple of shirts for his fans," Celia said. "You'd think any decent man would have more respect than this." She dropped the T-shirts on Ruyu's lap in disgust, and Ruyu spread them on the table. In black permanent marker and block letters, the writer had written, "To Jake, a future orphan" and "To Lucas, a future orphan," followed by his unrecognizable signature.

Perhaps the writer had only meant it as a joke, a sabotaging wink to the boys behind their mother's back; or else it'd been more than a joke, and he'd felt called to reveal an absolute truth that a child did not learn from his parents. "Unacceptable," Ruyu said, and folded up the shirts.

"Now, what do I do with them? I promised the boys I would get them his signature. How do I explain to them that this person they admire is a jerk? An asshole, really," Celia said, and gulped down some wine as if to rinse away the bad taste. "Thank goodness Edwin picked them up from school so I didn't have to deal with this until later."

Poor gullible Celia, believing, like most people, in a moment called *later*. Safely removed, *later* promises possibilities: changes, solutions, rewards, happiness, all too distant to be real, yet real enough to offer relief from the claustrophobic cocoon of *now*. If only Celia had the strength to be both kind enough and harsh enough with herself to stop talking about later, that heartless annihilator of now. "Exactly what," Ruyu said, "will you say to them later?"

"That I forgot?" Celia said uncertainly. "What else can I say? Better for your children to be annoyed with you, better for your husband to be disappointed by you, than break anyone's heart. I'll tell you, Ruby, it's smart of you not to have children. Smarter of you to not want another husband. Stay where you are. Sometimes I think about how simple and beautiful your life is—and that, I say to myself, is how a woman should treat herself."

Had Celia been a different person, Ruyu might have found her words distasteful, malicious even, but Celia, being Celia, and never doubting the truth of her own words, was as close to a friend as Ruyu would admit into her life. She unfolded the shirts and studied the handwriting, and asked Celia if she had another pair of white T-shirts. Why? Celia asked, and Ruyu said that they might as well fix the problem themselves. You don't mean it, Celia said, and Ruyu replied that indeed she did. What's wrong with borrowing the writer's name and making two boys happy?

Celia hesitantly offered another set of T-shirts, and Ruyu asked Celia what message she wanted her children to wear to school.

"Are you sure this is the right thing to do? I don't want my children to think I lie to them."

The writer, Ruyu wanted to remind Celia, had not lied. "I'm the one lying here," she said. "Look away."

"What if the other kids at school realize that the signatures are fake? Is it even legal to do this?"

"There are worse crimes," Ruyu said. Before Celia could protest, Ruyu wrote, in her best approximation of the writer's handwriting, a message of hope and affection to the beloved Jake and Lucas. After signing and dating the shirts, Ruyu folded them and said she would get rid of the original evidence to spare Celia any wrongdoing.

A car engine was heard outside the house; another car door opened and then closed. Celia's guests were arriving, and she assumed the nervous, high-pitched energy of onstage-ness. Ruyu waved for Celia to go and greet her guests. She stuffed the two unwanted T-shirts in her bag, went into the boys' bedrooms, and placed the ones she'd signed on their pillows.

The evening's topic was a recent bestseller written by a woman who called herself a "Chinese tiger mom." As always the gathering started with the exchange about children and husbands and family vacations and coming holiday recitals and performances. Ruyu drifted in and out of the living room, refilling wineglasses and passing out food, her position somewhere between a family friend and a hired hand. Affable with the guests, many of whom used her service in one way or another, Ruyu nevertheless stayed out of conversations, contributing only an encouraging smile or a courteous exclamation. Knowing how the women saw her, Ruyu did not find it difficult to play that role: an educated immigrant with no advanced job skills; a single woman no longer young; a renter; a hire trustworthy enough, good and firm with dogs and children alike and never flirtatious with husbands; a woman lucky to have been taken under Celia's wing; a bore.

When the book discussion began, Ruyu withdrew to the kitchen. At most gatherings she would not have absented herself so completely, as she did enjoy sitting on the periphery. She liked to listen to the women's voices without following what they said, and look at their soft-hued scarves, their necklaces designed by a local artist they patronized as a group, and their shoes, elegant or bold or unself-consciously ugly. To be where she was, to be what she was, suited her. One would have to take oneself much more seriously to be someone definite — to pose as a complete outsider; or to claim the right to be a friend, a lover, a person of consequence. Intimacy and alienation both required an effort beyond Ruyu's willingness.

Celia stopped at the entrance to the kitchen. "Don't you want to sit with us?" she asked. Ruyu shook her head, and Celia waved before walking away to the bathroom. If Celia pressed her again, Ruyu would say that the topics of parenting, school options for children, and the tiger mom — who was not even Chinese but called herself Chinese for sensational reasons — held little interest for her.

Ruyu studied the flowers on the table, an assortment of daisies and irises and fall leaves arranged in a half pumpkin, around which a few persimmons had been artfully placed. She moved one persimmon farther away and wondered if anyone would notice the interfered-with composition, less balanced now. Celia's life, busy and fluid with all sorts of commitments and crises, was nevertheless an exhibition of mindfully designed flawlessness: the high, arched windows of her home overlooked the bay, inviting into the living room an ever-changing light — golden Californian sunshine in the summer afternoons, gray rain light in the winter, morning and evening fog all year round; the three silver birch trees in front of the house — birch, Celia had told Ruyu, must be planted in clusters of three, though why she did not know — complemented the facade with their white bark, adding asymmetry to the otherwise tedious front lawn; the shining modernness of the kitchen was softened by a perfect display of still lifes—fruits, flowers, earthen jars, candles in holders, their colors in harmony with seasons and holidays; and the many corners in the house, each its own stage, showcased a lonely cast of things inherited or collected on this or that trip. Celia's family, always on the run— soccer practice, music lessons, pottery classes, yoga, fundraising parties, school auctions, trips to ski, to hike, to swim in the ocean, to immerse in foreign cultures and cuisines—had done a good job of leaving the house undisturbed, and Ruyu, perhaps more than anyone else, enjoyed the house as one would appreciate a beautiful object: one finds random pleasure in it, yet one does not experience any desire to possess it, or any pain when it passes out of one's life.

From the living room, the women's voices meandered from indignation to doubt to worry to panic. Over the past few years Ruyu had got to know each of the women, through these gatherings and working for some of them, well enough to pity them when they had to come into a group. None of them was uninteresting, but together they seemed to negate one another's individual existence by their predictability. Never did anyone show up disheveled, never did any one of them dare to admit to the others that she was lonely, or sad, or suffocated under the perfect facade of a good life. It must be the isolation that sent them to seek out others like them, but in Celia's living room, sitting together, the women seemed only more bravely isolated.

Ruyu had first met Celia seven years ago, when Celia had been looking for a replacement for their live-in nanny, who was returning to Guatemala with enough money to build two houses—one for her parents, and one for herself and her daughter. Of course it crushed her heart that Ana Luisa had to leave, Celia had said when she called Ruyu, who had replied to Celia's ad on a local parenting website; but wouldn't anyone feel happy for her? Ruyu had been an oddity among the more ordinary applicants—she had no previous child-care experience, and she lived rather out of the way. But having a Mandarin-speaking nanny would be an advantage over having one who spoke Spanish, Celia had explained to Edwin before she called Ruyu.

She did not have a car, Ruyu had said when Celia invited Ruyu to the house for an interview, and there was no public transportation where she lived, so could Celia, if interested, drive down to interview her? Later, when Ruyu was securely placed in Celia's life, Celia liked to tell her friends how wonderfully clueless Ruyu had been. Who, if not Celia, would have driven one and a half hours to meet a potential nanny?

Why indeed had she agreed, Ruyu wanted to ask Celia sometimes, but the answer was not important, as what mattered was that Celia did go out of her way to meet Ruyu, and—this Ruyu had never doubted—if not Celia, there would be someone else willing to do the same.

When Celia arrived at Ruyu's cottage, which, with its own garden and views of the canyon, would have been called "a gem" in a real estate ad, Celia could not hide her surprise and dismay. There was no way she could afford Ruyu, she said; all she had was an au pair's suite on the first floor of her house.

But that would suit her well, Ruyu said, and explained that her employer was getting married in a few months, and she would like to move away before the wedding, since there was no reason for her to stay on as his housekeeper. Celia, Ruyu could see, was baffled by the relationship between the cottage and the three-storied colonial on the estate, which Celia must have seen while driving past—as well as that between Ruyu and Eric, whom Ruyu only referred to as her employer.

Curious, Celia later described the Chinese woman to Edwin; peculiar even, but all the same she was pleasant, clean, spoke perfect English, and deserved some help. Ruyu had not talked about the exact nature of her relationship with her employer, but Celia had guessed rightly that sex, with an agreement, was part of the employment. About other things in her background, Ruyu had been open

with Celia during that first meeting: she had married her first husband at nineteen, a Chinese man who had been admitted to an
American graduate school; she'd married him to leave China. Her
second marriage, to an American, was to get herself a green card,
which her first husband would have eventually helped her get, but
she did not want to stay in the marriage for the five or six years it
would have taken. She'd earned a bachelor's degree in accounting
from a state university and had worked on and off but never really
built a career, which was fine with her because she did not like numbers or money. For the past three years, she'd been working as a
housekeeper for her employer, and she was looking forward to moving on—no, she didn't mean to marry again, Ruyu had said when
Celia, out of curiosity, asked her if she was going to look for another
husband; what she wanted, Ruyu said, was to find a job to support
herself.

When Celia called again, a week later, she did not offer Ruyu the
nanny position but said that she had found a cottage, furnished,
which would be available for three months during the summer.
Would Ruyu be open to taking it—she'd have to pay the three months'
rent up front—and working for Celia on a part-time basis? She would
be happy to help Ruyu settle down, find her another cottage after the
summer, and refer her to a few other families who could use Ruyu
here and there. Without hesitation Ruyu had said yes.

The garage door opened, the noise reminding Ruyu of the im-
modest grumbling from inside one's stomach. She was fascinated,
even after years in America, by the intimate contract that sound confirmed: a door opens and then closes, yet through it neither departure
nor arrival is damagingly permanent. Sitting in Celia's kitchen and
listening to her husband's return, Ruyu allowed herself, for a brief
moment, to imagine the possibility of such a life. Not a difficult task,
in fact, as two men among the people of the world had offered her
that—yet in the end, she was the one who had left. Had she stayed in
either marriage she would have had to become one of those women

in the living room, and the thought amused her. "Your problem," Eric had said when she informed him of her moving plan only after finalizing it with Celia, "is that you don't want enough. Though I suppose that also means things will always work out for you."

Eric had been wise not to over-offer, as her two ex-husbands had, but he did indulge her, granting her all the space she needed, and making clear she should never feel bound in any way to him. Sometimes she wondered if, for that reason, she should have treated him better. But how does one treat a man better—by becoming more dependent on him, by asking more from him? All the same, what was the point of thinking of that now? A few years ago, Eric had made the local news for his involvement in a fundraising scandal during his campaign for assemblyman—so much for his wanting more.

Celia, who must have been listening also, took leave of the discussion and told Ruyu to show the T-shirts to the boys, her pitch a bit high because, Ruyu knew, of her nervousness about lying to her family. It was in these moments that Ruyu felt a tenderness toward Celia, who, despite her constant need for attention and her petty competition with her friends and neighbors, was, in the end, a woman with a good and weak heart.

A while later, with the boys in bed, Edwin came into the kitchen. In the living room, the women were still arguing about the best way to bring up a child to be competitive in a global market. A heated discussion today, he commented, and touched the stem of a wine glass before changing his mind. He poured water for himself.

Certainly Celia had chosen the right book, Ruyu said, and moved to the sink before Edwin sat down at the table. "I'll start to put things away," she said. "Celia has had a long day."

Edwin asked if he could help, though Ruyu could tell it was a halfhearted offer. Probably all he wanted was for the women debating the future of American education to vacate his house. There was not much she needed him to do, Ruyu said. Edwin kept the conversation going, talking about trivialities—the Warriors' win that night, a new

movie Celia was talking about going to see that weekend, the Moorlands' Thanksgiving plans, a bizarre report in the paper about a man
impersonating a doctor and prescribing his only patient, an older
woman, a regimen of eating watermelons in a hot tub. Ruyu wondered if Edwin was talking to her out of a sense of charity; she wished
she could tell him that it was okay for him to treat her, at this or any
other moment, like a piece of furniture or appliance in his well-kept
house.

Edwin worked for a company that specialized in electronic books
and toys for early childhood learning. Though Ruyu did not know
what exactly he did—it had something to do with creating certain
characters appealing to the minds of toddlers—she wondered if
Edwin, a tall and quiet man born and raised in the Minnesota countryside, would have been better off as a sympathetic family physician
or a brilliant yet awkward mathematician. To spend one's workdays
thinking about talking caterpillars and singing bears seemed diminishing for a man like Edwin, but perhaps it was a good choice, the
same way Celia was a good choice of wife for him.

"Things are well with you?" Edwin asked when he ran out of
topics.

"How can they not be?" Ruyu replied. There was not much in her
life that was worth inquiring about, the general topics of children and
jobs and family vacations not an option in her case.

Edwin brooded over his water glass. "You must find their discussion strange," he said, pointing his chin at the living room.

"Strange? Not at all," Ruyu said. "The world needs enthusiastic
women. Too bad I am not one of them."

"But do you want to be one?"

"You either are one, or you are not," Ruyu said. "It has nothing to
do with wanting."

"Do they bore you?"

She would not, if asked, have considered Edwin or Celia or any of her friends a bore, but that was because she had never really taken a moment to think about what Edwin, or Celia, or anyone else for that matter, was. Edwin's face, never overly expressive, seemed particularly vague at the moment. Ruyu rarely allowed her interaction with him to progress beyond pleasantries, as there was something about Edwin that she could not see through right away. He did not speak enough to make himself a fool, yet what he did say made one wonder why he didn't say more. Had he been no one's husband she would have taken a closer look, but any impingement on Celia's claim would be a pointless complication.

After a long pause, which Celia would have readily filled with many topics, and which Edwin seemed patient enough to wait through, Ruyu said, "Only a bore would find other people boring."

"Do you find them interesting, then?"

"Many of them hire me," Ruyu said. "Celia is a friend."

"Of course," Edwin said. "I forgot that."

What was it he had forgotten—that the women in the living room provided more than half of Ruyu's livelihood, or that his own wife was the angel who'd made such a miracle happen? Ruyu placed the plates in the dishwasher. She wished that Edwin would stop feeling obligated to keep her company while she played the role of half hostess in his house. In the cottage, she cooked on a hot plate and ate standing by the kitchen counter, and the dish drain, left by a previous renter, was empty and dry most of the time. In Celia's house Ruyu enjoyed lining up the plates and cups and glasses, which, unlike people, did not seek to crack and break their own lives. When she continued in silence, Edwin asked if he had offended her.

"No," she sighed.

"But do you think we take you for granted?"

"Who? You and Celia?"

"Everyone here," Edwin said.

"People are taken for granted all the time," Ruyu said. Every one of the women in the living room would have a long list of complaints about being taken for granted. "I'm not a unique case who needs special attention."

"But we complain."

Ruyu turned and looked at Edwin. "Go ahead and complain," she said. "But don't expect me to do it."

Edwin blushed. Do not expose your soul uninvited, she would have said if Edwin were no one's husband, but instead she apologized for her abruptness. "Don't mind what I said," she said. "Celia said I wasn't my right self today."

"Is anything the matter?"

"Someone I used to know died," Ruyu said, feeling malicious because she would not have told this to Celia even if she were ten times as persistent.

Edwin said he was sorry to hear the news. Ruyu knew he would like to ask more questions; Celia would have been chasing every detail, but Edwin seemed uncertain, as though intimidated by his own curiosity. "It's all right," Ruyu said. "People die."

"Is there anything we can do?"

"No one can do anything. She's dead already," Ruyu said.

"I mean, can we do something for you?"

Superficial kindness was offered every day, innocuous if pointless, so why, Ruyu thought, couldn't she give Edwin credit for being a good-mannered person with an automatic response to the news of a death that did not concern him? She had only known the deceased for a short time, she said, trying to mask her impatience with a yawn.

"Still—" Edwin hesitated, looking at the water.

"Still what?"

"You look sad."

Ruyu felt an unfamiliar anger. What right did Edwin have to look in her for the grief he wanted to be there? "I don't have the right to feel that way. See, I am a real bore. Even when someone dies, I can't claim the tragedy," Ruyu said. Abruptly she changed the topic, asking if the boys were excited to see the T-shirts signed for them.

Edwin seemed disappointed, and shrugged and said it mattered more to Celia than to the boys. "Mothers, you know?" he said. "By the way, did you grow up with a tiger mom?"

"No."

"What do you think of this fuss, then?"

If only she could, as was called for by the situation, say something witty—but rolling one's eyes and saying witty things were as foreign to her as eight-year-old Jake's contempt for his friend's family, who ate the wrong kind of salmon; or Celia's fretting over their Christmas lights, lest they seem too flashy or too modest. The freedom to act and the freedom to judge, undermining each other, amount to little more than a well-stocked source of anxiety. Is that why, Ruyu wondered, Americans so willingly make themselves smaller—by laughing at others, or, more tactfully, at themselves—when there is no immediate danger to hide from? But danger in the form of poverty and flying bullets and lawless states and untrustworthy friends provides, if not a route to happiness, at least clarity to one's suffering.

Ruyu looked harshly at Edwin. "I don't think," she said, "it is a worthwhile subject."

4

Midsummer in Beijing, its extreme heat and humidity occasionally broken by a relieving thunderstorm, gave the impression that life today would be that of tomorrow, and the day after, until forever: the watermelon rinds accumulated at the roadside would go on rotting and attracting swarms of flies; murky puddles in the alleyways from overspilled sewers dwindled, but before they entirely disappeared another storm would replenish them; old men and women, sitting next to bamboo perambulators in the shadows of palace walls, cooled down their grandchildren with giant fans woven of sedge leaves, and if one closed one's eyes and opened them again one could almost believe that the fans and the babies and the wrinkle-faced grandparents were the same ones from a hundred years ago, captured by a rare photograph in the traveling album of a foreign missionary, who would eventually be executed for spreading evil in a nearby province.

Life, already old, did not age. It was this Beijing, with its languid mood, that Moran loved the most, though she worried it meant little to Ruyu, who seemed to look at both the city and Moran's enthusiasm askance. Moran tried to see Beijing for the first time with a newcomer's eyes and felt a moment of panic: perhaps there was nothing poetic in the noises and smells, in the uncleanness and overcrowdedness of the city. When we place our beloved in front of the critical eyes of others, we feel diminished along with the subject being scrutinized. Had Moran been a more experienced person, had she mastered the skill of self-protection, she would have easily masked her love with a cynical or at least distant attitude. Tactless in her youth, she could only corner herself with hope that turned into despair.

"Of course none of them is really a sea," Moran said apologetically as she leaned her bicycle on a willow tree and sat next to Ruyu on a bench. They were on the waterfront of the Western Sea, a manmade lake, and Moran had pointed out the direction of the other seas: the Back Sea, the Front Sea, and the Northern Sea, to which Boyang and Moran had taken Ruyu the day before, as it was one of the essential places for a tourist to visit. In the past week they had taken Ruyu to temples and palaces, as they would have shown the city to a cousin from out of town.

"Why are they called seas, then?" Ruyu asked. She was not interested in the answer, yet she knew that each question granted her some power over the people she questioned. She liked to watch others feeling obliged, and sometimes more foolishly, elated, to answer her: people do not know that the moment they respond they put themselves on a stand for their interrogators to judge.

"Maybe because Beijing is not next to the ocean?" Moran said, though without any certainty.

Ruyu nodded, feeling lenient enough not to point out that Moran's words made little sense. Within days of her arrival, Ruyu knew that Moran had been placed in her new life because of the convenience such a person would provide, though that did not stop her from wishing that Moran could be kept at a distance, or did not exist at all.

"Have you ever been to the seaside?" Moran asked.

"No."

"Neither have I," Moran said. "I would like to see the ocean someday. Boyang and his family go every summer."

This was so like Moran, Ruyu thought, offering information when no one asked her to. The flowers every family kept on windowsills, Moran had explained to Ruyu when she'd caught Ruyu looking at the blossoms the morning after her arrival, were geraniums, and they were known to expel bugs. The two magnolia trees at the center of the courtyard were at least fifty years old, planted as "husband and wife" trees for good fortune. In late summer everyone would watch out for wasps because the grapevines Teacher Pang cultivated at the end of the courtyard were known for their juicy grapes. The pomegranate tree by the fence, which was now dropping heavy-petaled, fire-colored blossoms, did not bear edible fruit, though a tree in the next quadrangle, which was not blooming quite as well, produced the sweetest pomegranates. She'd explained each family's background: Teacher Pang and his wife, Teacher Li, were both elementary school teachers, and they had agreed not to work in the same school or district because it would have been boring to be around the same people all the time; only the youngest of their three children was still in school, the older two having jobs at factories, but all three lived at home. Old Shu, a widower whose children had all married, lived with his mother, who would turn a hundred next summer. Watermelon Wen, a loud and happy bus driver, had earned his nickname because he had a round belly; he and his wife, an equally loud and round trolley conductor, had a pair of twin boys not yet in school. Sometimes their mother would not differentiate them and called them both Little Watermelon. Moran's own parents worked in the Ministry of Mines, her father a researcher and her mother a clerk.

Only stupid people, in the opinion of Ruyu's grandaunts, would freely dispense what little knowledge they possessed; at times even teachers were not exempted from that category. Ruyu had always found the world a predictable place, as it was filled with people who would, with words and actions, confirm her grandaunts' convictions of the smallness of any mortal mind.

Ruyu watched Moran weave a few willow leaves into a sailboat and release it into the water. Foolishly occupied, she could hear her grandaunts comment. "Why don't you go with Boyang to the seaside?" she asked.

Moran laughed. "I'm not part of his family."

Ruyu gazed at Moran, as though she was waiting for the latter to defend her shoddy logic with more sensible words, and Moran realized that perhaps family meant something different for Ruyu. Before her arrival, Moran and Boyang had talked between themselves, but neither knew what it was like to be an orphan. Years ago, when Teacher Pang and Teacher Li had purchased the first black-and-white television set of the quadrangle, the residents used to gather in their house for any kind of entertainment. Once there was a movie about the famine in Henan province, in which a girl, who had lost both parents, walked to the crossroads and stuck a long stem of grass in her hair, indicating to the passersby that she was for sale. Moran was six then, the same age as the girl in the movie, and she was so impressed by the lofty calmness of the orphan on screen that she started to cry. What a kindhearted girl, the elders in the quadrangle had commented, not knowing that Moran had cried out of the shame of being an inferior person: she would never be as beautiful and strong as that orphan.

Moran had thought often about the movie before Ruyu's arrival. Did Ruyu know anything about her parents at all, Moran had wondered; was she the kind of girl who would sit at a crossroads, waiting to be purchased with a contemptuous smile against her orphan's fate? What Aunt said of Ruyu's grandaunts and her upbringing was vague, and it was hard for Moran to imagine Ruyu's life. Boyang, though, had brushed off the perplexity easily, as Moran had known he would.

"What I mean is—" Moran explained now. "It's his family tradition to go to the seaside in the summer."

"Why doesn't your family go?"

If only Boyang were here, Moran thought, he would have poked fun at his parents and at himself for their being a vacationing family.

None of the other families Moran knew vacationed—people only traveled when they had to, for weddings and funerals and other emergencies. The concept of moving life elsewhere for a week or two sounded pretentious, done only by idle foreigners in imported movies. "Different families have different ways," Moran said. Still, she could not help but feel a regret that she had never traveled outside Beijing. In fact, being one of the inner-city children, she could count on one hand the times she had been to the outer districts—a spring field trip in middle school to the Great Wall by train, a few bicycle outings with Boyang that consisted of riding for two or three hours to a temple or a creek, picnicking, and then riding back. "Do you and your grandaunts take vacations?" Moran asked, and at once noticed frostiness in Ruyu's eyes. "Oh, I'm sorry to be nosy."

Ruyu nodded forgivingly yet did not say anything. She had never doubted her rights to question others, but to allow another person to ask *her* a question was to grant that person a status that he or she did not deserve: Ruyu knew that she answered to no one but her grandaunts and, beyond them, God himself.

It was the first time Moran had spent time alone with Ruyu, and already she had made mistakes that alienated Ruyu. Again Moran wished that Boyang were there to redirect the conversation. But it was Sunday, and on Sundays Boyang visited his parents, both professors at a university on the west side of the city, where they had a nice apartment near campus. Their daughter, Boyang's sister, was ten years older than he. She had been a child genius, and after a total of three years in high school and college, she had won a scholarship to study with a Nobel laureate in America, and now, a few months short of turning twenty-six, she had already been granted tenure as a physics professor. "University of California, Berkeley," Boyang's parents had explained to the neighbors during a rare visit to the quadrangle to spread the news, their enunciation of each syllable agonizing Moran. She knew that in their eyes, her parents and others were people with inferior intelligence and negligible ambitions. Even Boyang, the smartest boy Moran knew, they considered insignificant compared to his sister. Moran sometimes wondered whether his parents had wanted him in the first place, as he had been raised, since birth, by his paternal grandmother, a longtime resident of the quadrangle; he had not had a chance to get to know his sister before she was sent off to America, nor was he close to his parents, whom he visited every Sunday, eating two meals alongside them and sometimes doing housework that required a young man's strength.

Four boys under ten walked past Ruyu and Moran and splashed into the water, all of them naked to the waist, the two youngest wearing inner tubes around their slippery bodies. "Do you swim?" Moran asked, glad for the distraction.

"No."

"Maybe I can teach you. This is the best spot for winter swimming. Boyang and I haven't been able to get permission to swim here past autumn equinox. In a few years, though, I'm sure we will, and by then you will be more comfortable swimming. When we are old enough—eighteen, I'm thinking, or twenty—we can all come for the swimming festival on the winter solstice."

Swifts skimmed the water's surface with their sharp tails; cicadas trilled in the willow trees. A man pedaled a flatbed tricycle along the lakefront road, singing out the brand names of beers he kept on chunks of ice, and was stopped here and there by a child running out of an alley with money in his raised hand, sent to buy a bottle or two for his elders. It was the peak of summer, and the heat had not abated in the late afternoon, yet Moran spoke of winter, and the winters to come, with the same ease with which one would speak of going home for supper. Even odder was Moran's confidence—Ruyu had noticed the same confidence in Boyang, too—when speaking of a future in which Ruyu was included. That she was here—staying in Aunt's house, attending the high school in which Boyang and Moran took great pride—had been made possible by her grandaunts, who had made her understand before her departure that in truth this relocation was God's plan for her, as it had been his plan for her to be cared for by them. That she was here by the lake . . . No doubt Moran would think of it as her own doing, as she'd been the one to ride the bicycle with Ruyu on the back, and she'd been the one to decide that, rather than going to a movie or to a nearby store for an ice pop, they were to come to her and Boyang's favorite place, a sea that was no more than a pond.

With both vexation and curiosity, Ruyu turned and studied Moran, who was pointing at the silhouette of a dwarf temple on top of the hill, behind which the sun was starting to set. There used to be ten temples around the area, and the three seas had been called the "Ten-Temple Seas," though Boyang and Moran had found only three remaining temples. "That one is dedicated to the goddess governing water," Moran said, and when Ruyu did not say anything, she turned and found herself facing a quizzical gaze. "I'm sorry, did I bore you with all this talk?"

Ruyu shook her head.

"Sometimes my mother worries that I'm too talkative and no decent man will marry me," Moran said and laughed.

Ruyu had noticed that Moran laughed more than smiled; this gave her face a look of open silliness, which seemed better suited to the role of a big sister or an older aunt. "Why don't you have any siblings?" Ruyu asked.

Theirs had been the last generation born before the single-child policy had begun, and many of Moran's classmates, and probably many of Ruyu's old schoolmates, too, had siblings. Perhaps Ruyu was asking only because it was not often that she met an only child. Humbly, Moran admitted that she did not know why, but then added that hers was not an unusual case; Sister Shaoai was also an only child.

"Do you want a sibling?"

It must have been the orphan in Ruyu who was asking these questions; it was rare that Ruyu spoke so much—around the quadrangle she was always quiet. "We're all close," Moran said. "You'll see, we are like siblings in the quadrangle. For instance, Boyang and I grew up like a brother and a sister."

"But he has his own sister."

She was older, Moran explained. She was almost from a different generation.

"Why does he not live with his parents?" Ruyu asked.

"I don't know," Moran said. "I think it's because they're very busy with their work."

"But his sister lived with their parents before she went to America?"

"It was a different case with her," Moran said, feeling uneasy, afraid of saying the wrong things about Boyang and his family. Already she felt she was betraying him in some way that she could not understand. He preferred not to talk about his parents, and his grandmother spoke of Boyang's uncles and aunts who lived in other cities more than she talked about Boyang's father, her eldest son. Moran wondered if the family harbored an unsavory past, though she would never ask, as seeking an answer to her curiosity would make her less worthy of Boyang's friendship.

"How so? Is he not their child by blood?"

"Of course he's their biological child," Moran said, worried that by simply speaking such truths she was compromising her best friend.

"Why 'of course'?"

Taken aback, first by Ruyu's insensible calmness and then by her own stupidity, Moran fell into a profound bewilderment. Growing up in the quadrangle was like growing up with an extended family, and nothing made her happier than loving everyone unreservedly. Certainly she had heard tales about neighbors in other quadrangles who did not get along and sabotaged one another's life: uprooting newly cultivated flowers, adding extra salt to a neighbor's dish where a kitchen was shared, swiping a frozen chicken left on a windowsill overnight in the winter, making unpleasant faces and noises to frighten small children the moment their parents turned away. These

stories baffled Moran, as she could not see what people would gain
from such pettiness. In the last year of middle school some of the girls
in Moran's class had become cruel, trapping other girls—the pretty
ones, the sensitive ones, and the lonely ones—with a net of mean-
spirited rumors. If there had been any harm intended for her—and
there must have been at times, though Moran had Boyang, best
friends for as long as either remembered—she'd hardly ever considered herself in a vulnerable position. Even within a family, people
could behave viciously toward one another; the evening newspapers
offered abundant evidence with their tales of domestic conflicts and
unspeakable crimes. Still, for Moran, the world was a good place, and
she believed that it would be a good place for Ruyu now that she was
their friend. Yet the ease with which Ruyu had raised the possibility
of deceit and abandonment regarding Boyang's upbringing dispirited
Moran, as though she, unprepared, had failed an important test to
win Ruyu's respect.

"Are you offended?" Ruyu asked.

Might it be natural for someone like Ruyu to doubt everything?
Right away Moran felt ashamed of her own unfriendly quietness.
"No, not at all. It's only that I'm not used to the way you ask ques-
tions," she said.

"How do other people ask questions?"

At least their conversation was not taking place in the quadrangle.
Anyone overhearing them would think Ruyu unnaturally childish for
her age, and, even if no one would admit it, Moran knew that a connection would be readily made between Ruyu's background and her
lack of tact. With a maternal patience, Moran explained to Ruyu that
normally one did not ask questions that would cause others discomfort; in fact, she continued, one did not start a conversation by asking
questions but waited for the other person to talk about herself.

"What if people won't tell you anything about themselves?" Ruyu
said.

"When people are your friends, they will tell you things. And when you're with friends, you can also tell them about yourself," Moran said. She wished Ruyu could understand that neither she nor Boyang would press Ruyu about her past. The truth was, Moran had believed—even before Ruyu's arrival—that no matter what kind of a past Ruyu had, once she lived among them, she would become less of an orphan.

Ruyu watched a bug move on the water, its slender limbs leaving barely perceptible traces. For a brief moment she found the insect interesting, but when she turned her eyes away, she forgot about it. "Why is Sister Shaoai always angry?" she asked. "She hates me being here, doesn't she?"

Moran looked agonized. "No, she doesn't. She's just upset at the moment."

Ruyu looked back at the water, but the bug was gone. She did not know the name of the insect; in fact, she had never spent much time looking at any bug, bird, or tree. Her grandaunts lived strictly indoors and only left the apartment when necessary; their home, pristinely kept, did not participate in the holidays with decorations of any kind, or in the seasons with plants on the windowsills; thick curtains, always drawn, kept the weather at a distance.

When Ruyu did not question further, Moran felt pained. She wished she could explain better to Ruyu Shaoai's situation: she had been active in the democratic protest early in the summer and was waiting for her verdict, which she'd learn once school started. She hadn't been a leader in the protest but would nevertheless face disciplinary action from the university; nobody knew whether this would be a general or a severe "political warning," a suspension of her university study, or, worse, expulsion. Moran's parents, when they talked about Shaoai, worried that her dismissiveness about her future would not help her; they did not say much, but Moran knew that they, and other neighbors too, wished Shaoai would recant the statement she had posted on the school bulletin board the day after the massacre, calling the government a breeding farm of fascists. But these things,

Moran's parents had warned her, were not to be discussed outside their house.

Moran turned around instinctively, but apart from a few pedestrians farther off on the sidewalk, she did not see any suspicious loiterers eavesdropping on them. "I know Sister Shaoai looks unfriendly sometimes," she said. "But trust me, she is a good person."

People asked her to trust them all the time, Ruyu thought, as though it never occurred to them that by so pleading, they had already proved themselves untrustworthy. Her grandaunts had never asked her to trust them, and, unfamiliar with the concept, she had once been deceived by the use of the phrase: a girl in first grade had often begged to be taken to her apartment; her grandaunts did not like visitors, Ruyu had explained, but the girl had pleaded to be trusted and promised not to tell a soul about the visit. After a while Ruyu had acquiesced, yet the day after the visit everyone in the class seemed to have learned something about her home, and even a couple of teachers came to ask her about her grandaunts' books. But to have been betrayed by someone unworthy was less humiliating than having perturbed her grandaunts. They had waited for a few days before saying, as though making a passing comment, that they did not much care for the friend Ruyu had brought home. After that Ruyu had never allowed herself to be befriended by anyone.

"How can you be certain that Sister Shaoai is a good person?" Ruyu said.

Moran watched the boys splashing in the lake. It agonized her that she could not make Ruyu see the real Shaoai: when Moran and Boyang had been the boys' age, Shaoai had been the one to take them to the lake, throwing them into deeper water to make them paddle, laughing at them when they swallowed water, yet all the time she had been within an arm's reach. Even if Shaoai was not a nurturing kind of person, both Moran and Boyang knew her to be a reliable friend. "Have you heard the saying that *the longer a road is, the more one is to learn about a horse's stamina; the more time passes, the better one gets to see another person's heart?"* Moran said. "I think by and by you will know Sister Shaoai better."

Ruyu smiled. Why would I, the thin smile said, want to know Shaoai better? Moran's face turned red: the wordless dismissal, not of herself but of someone she respected and admired, made her more diffident in front of Ruyu than ever.

"When are we going back?" Ruyu said, indicating the setting sun.

Moran was disappointed with herself. She knew Ruyu did not trust her. Why should she? Moran thought as she pedaled her bicycle through an alley, so used to Ruyu's weight on the rear rack that for a moment she forgot that it was her usual habit to chatter on while pedaling Ruyu around. Moran did not like unfinished conversations; for her, life was a series of ideal moments, all comprehensible, sometimes with small difficulties but always with a larger dose of joy. She did not like finding herself in a murky situation which she could not explain to another person, yet there was the loyalty toward Shaoai, whose trouble Moran had been told to keep to herself. If she stopped pedaling and better clarified Shaoai's anger, would Ruyu understand it?

5

When Moran's phone rang early Saturday morning, she dreaded taking the call, and listened while the answering machine clicked on. No message was left, and a minute later, the phone rang again. It was not yet six o'clock, too early for anything but calamity. Moran picked up the call and heard both her parents' voices on the other end, and for a moment she could not concentrate while her mother talked about trivialities. "And you," her father said when her mother seemed to have run out of small talk. "How are you?"

"Good."

"Your voice sounds hoarse," her mother said. "Did you catch a cold?"

"Only dry," Moran said. "I was sleeping."

"Listen," her father said, and Moran felt a twinge of panic, as he was one who preferred listening to being listened to. "We're sorry to be calling so early. But we just heard that Shaoai passed away ten days ago."

Moran asked her parents to hold on for a second, and closed the bedroom door. She lived alone in a rental, and she was used to—and she was certain her house was also used to her—carrying out a life filled with everyday noises but not human conversations. Beyond the closed door was the uncluttered space where, other than a few pieces of impersonal furniture from IKEA, a small collection of objects kept her company: a single silver vase, to which she often forgot to offer flowers; a pair of metal bookends shaped like an old man in a top hat and billowing raincoat, bending low on his cane; a stack of hand-made paper, thick, sepia-toned, too beautiful to write on; and a re-production of a Modigliani painting—a portrait of a certain Mme. Zborowska, whose eyes, under heavy, sleepy lids, looked almost blind in their pupil-less darkness. None of these objects had come into Mo-ran's life with specific meanings; she had picked them up here and there while traveling, and had allowed herself to form an attachment to them because they were only souvenirs of places that did not be-long to her, which she would never see again. In return, by quietly closing the door, she protected these things she loved from the intru-sion of an early morning phone call. Later she would not once think of them as burdened witnesses of a death from a distant past.

"We thought you should know right away," her father said.

It was not an unexpected death, she wanted to tell her parents; a relief for all, she wanted to assure them, but the words would be cli-chés her parents and their old neighbors would have already ex-changed. Her parents had called to hear different words, and yet Moran had only silence to offer.

"We thought of paying a visit of condolence," her mother said. "But what can we say to Shaoai's mother? What would you say to her?"

Moran flinched. Unlike her father, who rarely confronted her, her mother was able to turn a simple narrative into a question that demanded an answer. "I would think, for everybody's good, it's wise not to visit," Moran said, being careful with her words so that she would not open the door to more questioning.

"But that makes us coldhearted. Imagine someone in her posi-tion."

It was hard enough for her mother to have an absentee daughter;

to add, on top of that, another mother's pain of losing a daughter who'd been more than half dead the past twenty-one years? "Don't imagine," Moran said.

"But how can one stop thinking about these things? I understand that I'm more fortunate than Shaoai's mother, but what if you hadn't got involved in the case in the first place? You would have been living in Beijing, and at least our family would have stayed together. I know you think of me as selfish, but do you see my point?"

"No, I don't think of you as selfish."

"I hope you understand that a mother has to be selfish."

Ever so expectedly, the phone line, cracking just a little, spoke of her mother's tears and her father's reticence. They were in separate rooms, she knew, holding two receivers, because it was easier for them not to see each other's eyes when they were talking to her. "I don't suppose we should discuss these things now," Moran said. "See, it upsets you."

"Why shouldn't I be upset? Shaoai's mother at least knows who killed her daughter, but we've never known what took our daughter away from us."

"Nobody knows what happened to Shaoai," Moran said.

"But it was Ruyu. It had to be her. It could only be her. Am I wrong?"

Her parents must have often wondered about this between themselves, but they had never once asked Moran. Why ask now, when silence, already in place, should be left untouched; even death does not suffice as a pretext to disturb the past. "Nobody knows what happened," Moran said again.

"But you did know. You covered it up for her, didn't you?"

Moran's father coughed. "You understand, Moran, that your mother is asking not because we want to blame you," he said. "Nobody can go back and change anything, but your mother and I, you see—it's hard for us when things don't make sense."

Where does one begin, Moran thought, to make sense of any-thing? The desire for clarity, the desire not to live in blindness—these desires are not far from the desire to deceive: one has to be like a sushi chef, cutting, trimming, slicing, until one's life—or one's mem-ory of that life—is transformed into presentable bites. "Let's change the topic, shall we?" she said. "I was wondering what you'd think of going to Scandinavia for a holiday next summer. I heard it's beautiful there in June."

"We're tired of playing tourist," Moran's mother said. "We're old now. Shaoai is dead. Someday we will die, too. Is it not time for you to come home and see us?"

Not wanting to grant her parents even the vaguest hope, Moran said that she was not ready to talk about that. She promised that she would call again in a week, knowing that by then, her father would have convinced her mother to be more strategic and not to pressure her. Moran ended the phone call before her parents could protest. They loved her more than she loved them; for that reason, she would always win an argument at the end of the day.

Her parents' only child, Moran had not been back to Beijing since she had left for America sixteen years earlier. For the first six years, when she had been studying for a PhD in chemistry, she had not seen her parents once, citing the hassle for visa application and a shortage of traveling funds as the reasons for her absence. During that period a marriage, which had both distressed and embarrassed her parents, had taken place and then ended, yet that they had not crossed paths with her married life seemed to make it less real to them; at least that was Moran's hope. To this day, she suspected that they had not told anyone in Beijing about her failed marriage, and they were relieved to have not met Josef, who was a year older than her mother.

After the divorce, Moran moved away from the midwestern town where she and Josef had been living, and, when she could afford it,

she started paying for her parents to travel and meet her elsewhere—
for a bus tour through central and western Europe, on which she
dutifully accompanied them, taking their pictures with grand arches
and ancient relics in the background, making sure she herself was not
in any of the photos; for two weeks in Cape Cod, where they were an
odd family on the beach and in the ice cream shops—she was too old
to be a child vacationing with her parents, and they, having little to
cling to in an unfamiliar town, marked their days by chatting with
people their age who pushed baby strollers or built sandcastles with
their grandchildren. There and elsewhere, Moran's parents greeted
grandparents warmly, their English allowing them just enough vocabulary to express their admiration of other people's good fortune.

Moran took comfort in believing that, for what she had deprived
her parents of, she had offered other things in return: Thailand, Hawaii, Las Vegas, Sydney, the Maldives, foreign places that crowded
their photo albums with natural and manmade beauty. Over the years
they had accepted that they would never be invited to see Moran's
everyday life in America, but they had not given up hope that one day
she would return to Beijing, however short the visit might be. Always
Moran turned a deaf ear toward the mention of her hometown. Places
do not die or vanish, yet one can obliterate their existence, just as one
can a lover from an ill-fated affair. For Moran, this was not a drastic
action: one needs only to live coherently, to be one's exact self from
one day to the next, to make such a place, such a person, recede.

It took a long while after the phone call before she opened Boyang's email. The message was brief, giving the cause of death and
the date of the cremation, which had happened six days earlier. The
paucity of details felt accusatory—though what right did she have to
hope for more, when she herself had never deviated from the coldness of silence? Once a year, Moran wired two thousand dollars to
Boyang's account, her contribution to Shaoai's caretaking, but she
did not acknowledge his monthly emails. The bare bones of his life—
his successful career as a businessman in various fields, the latest in

real estate development, his unsuccessful marriage—she had learned from her parents, though her quietness in response to any news regarding him must have led them to a conclusion about her disinterestedness. They had not mentioned him when they had called about Shaoai's death.

The phone rang again. Moran hesitated and then picked it up. "Just one more thing," her mother said. "I know things are harder for you than for us. At least your father and I have each other. I understand you don't want us to interfere with your life, but wouldn't you agree that it's time to think about marriage again? But don't misunderstand me. I am not pressuring you. All I am saying is—no doubt you think this is a cliché—but maybe you should stop living in the past? Of course we respect your every decision, but we'd be happier if you found someone new in your life."

It was odd that her parents, against all evidence, thought of her as living in the past, though Moran did not argue, and promised to consider their viewpoint. She wondered which past—and which set of people associated with said past—her parents considered the enemy of her happiness: her life in Beijing or her marriage to Josef? Her parents should have known by now that her problem, rather than living in the past, was not allowing the past to live on. Any moment that slipped away from the present became a dead moment; and people, unsuspicious, over and over again became the casualties of her compulsive purging of the past.

Moran lived the most solitary and contented life she believed possible for herself. She worked for a pharmaceutical company in Massachusetts, where she occupied a small testing room alone and operated an instrument that measured the viscosity of various health and hygiene products for quality control. Despite her extensive research background in chemistry, her work did not require much skill beyond a tolerance for tedium. Yet it provided her what she needed: a stable livelihood, and a reason to be in America. What else could she ask for? She had no children, and her concerns, when she read

about climate change or carcinogens found in food or water, were
not concrete, because she did not feel eligible to worry about the future of mankind. She did not have close friends, but remained
friendly enough with neighbors and colleagues so as not to be considered an eccentric spinster. Though her life lacked the poignancy of
great happiness and acute pain, she believed she had found, in their
places, the blessing of solitude. She took a long and brisk walk every
morning, rain or shine, and again after work; twice a week she volunteered at a local animal shelter, and other evenings she spent in the
library, reading old novels that were rarely touched by others. Her job
was soothing in a way she imagined most people's work was not—she
liked the samples of manmade colors and fragrances, the unchang-
ingness of the protocols, the predictability of the outcomes. When
there were idle moments at work, she daydreamed about places and
times other than her own, in which strangers lived as vividly as she
would allow them: a girl named Grazia, who had died from tubercu-
losis at fifteen and was buried in a Swiss mountain town, forgotten by
all but her poor French governess; an aging cobbler bending over
pieces of leather and dull nails in a Parisian shop, his eyesight dete-
riorating by the day, his heart skipping a beat or two; a young shepherd in Bavaria caught in listless pining for his next-door neighbor, a
girl three years older and already engaged to the village butcher. Moran
took the precaution of looking busy, in case someone peeked into the
testing room, though she suspected that in her colleagues' eyes, she,
like the instrument she managed, was a well-tuned machine—a machine that, once trusted, could easily be forgotten. She did not hold
this against her colleagues, most of them having stoically, if not happily, settled down to a suburban life. If they felt any superiority over
Moran, she could not sense it, though this was likely a result of the
safe distance she kept herself from them; nor did she feel any advantage over the others—her colleagues, she believed, enjoyed or weathered their marriages, parenthoods, promotions, and holidays as she

herself weathered solitude. One would be foolish to consider oneself better, or even different, merely because one could claim something others could not. The crowdedness of family life and the faithfulness of solitude—both brave decisions, or both decisions of cowardice— make little dent, in the end, on the profound and perplexing loneliness in which every human heart dwells.

Moran wished now to return to her Saturday routine, which had been disturbed by her parents' calls and Boyang's email, but the news of a death, any death, was enough to prove the flimsiness of a calm life. The last time Moran had seen Shaoai was before her departure for America; by then, Shaoai had already lost much of her sight and her hair, her sinewy body taking on a dangerous plumpness, her mind no longer lucid behind her clouded eyes. What would twenty- one more years have done to that prisoner in her own body, Moran wondered, but did not force herself to answer. It was easier to imagine Grazia lying in a cabin and looking at the snowcapped mountains: a pitcher stood on her bedside table, the morning sunlight trapped in the still clearness of the water; an unfinished embroidery sampler of a Goethe poem lay next to her, reminding Grazia of the day when she, at five, had started to stitch with pink and white threads chunky alphabets.

When Moran had first arrived in America, people from local churches had paid her visits. She had replied, not as a mere excuse, though it must have seemed a glib one, that she did not have the imagination to become a believer. She knew now it was not imagination she lacked. The cobbler in Paris had lost his only son in a street battle; he did not know whom to blame, fate or revolution, and his confused tears stung Moran's heart more than her own parents' sighs. The woman in Bavaria had married without regret, unaware of her young neighbor's desolation. She'd died when she gave birth to a baby girl, and, some days, when Moran felt an icy animosity toward herself, she would let the young shepherd steal the baby girl and drown her and himself; other days, guilty about the violence she'd carelessly inflicted upon unsuspicious souls—for what reason but to make herself feel the pains that she did not allow in her life?—Moran would let the baby grow up, becoming more precious in the eyes of the brokenhearted man next door than she was to herself and the rest of the world.

Suppose one could allow oneself to be closer to the real world than to that of one's imagination. Suppose she had had someone next to her at the moment her parents called, so that Shaoai's death could be discussed. Right away Moran banged that door closed. To be caught at hoping—even if it was just by herself, but it could only be by herself—was like being caught once when she had timidly played a simple tune on a piano at a colleague's party. A child, not yet four, not old enough for piano lessons as her older siblings were, came quietly into the room, where Moran had found a moment away from the guests. Hello, Moran said, and the girl studied her with a proprietress' pity and annoyance. What right, her eyes seemed to be saying, do you have to touch the piano? Moran blushed; the girl pushed her aside and banged the keys with both hands, and despite the violent disharmony, the girl seemed to be satisfied by her performance. This, she seemed to be showing Moran, was how you played an instrument.

It was the girl whom Moran remembered now as she took her usual route to the neighborhood park, a grove that had not much to offer except an outdated playground with a metal skeleton of a train engine and a few squeaky swings, all rusty. Not everyone had the right to music, the girl's eyes said, just as not everyone had the right to claim beauty, hope, and happiness.

An old woman, tightly bundled in an oversized coat and a scarf, waited patiently for her black poodle, clad in a yellow vest, to finish investigating a rock. Moran muttered a greeting and was about to pass the pair when the old woman raised her small face. "Tell you what, don't ever forget the date of your last period."

Moran nodded. When people talked to her, she always looked attentive, as though recognizing the significance of their words.

"Every time I go to the doctor's they ask that question," the old woman said. "Like it matters at my age. If I have one piece of advice to give, go home and write it down somewhere you can find easily."

Moran thanked the old woman and walked on. Easily she could see herself lingering, listening to the woman retell the story of her long wait at the doctor's, or at the vet's office, or of a recent visit from her grandchildren, but such conversations with strangers had taken place enough times, in grocery stores and dry cleaners and hair salons and airports, that sometimes Moran wondered if her chief merit was her willingness to serve as a human receptacle for details. Sympathy and admiration and surprise she dutifully yet insufficiently expressed, and afterward the others moved on, forgetting her face the moment she was out of sight, or else they would not have seen her in the first place: she was one of those strangers people needed once in a while to make their lives less empty.

When she returned, there was a message from Josef on her answering machine. Odd that more than one person had called her today. She waited until the evening to call back. She wanted him to think that she had things to do on a Saturday.

When Josef picked up the phone, his voice was frail. Had Rachel talked with her, he asked, and Moran felt her heart sink. Rachel was the youngest of the four children of Josef and Alena; two years earlier, when Josef had retired from his job as a librarian at a local community college, he had sold the house and bought a condo a few blocks from Rachel and her husband, as they were about to have their third child. Three years younger than Moran, Rachel had been the only one of Josef's children to openly oppose her father's marriage to Moran.

"Is there something Rachel needs to tell me?" Moran asked. She remembered her panic when her parents had called earlier. She had dreaded hearing that Josef was dead.

Moran had always known that someday a phone call would come, worst if from one of Josef's children. Still, hearing it from Josef himself—about his multiple myelomas, new since they had last seen each other in June—did not make the message any less harsh. For a moment she was struck by the odd sensation that he was already gone; their conversation, a memory for the future, sounded unreal, Josef's tone apologetic, as though he had erred and unwisely contracted cancer.

How long has he known, she asked, and he said four weeks. Four weeks, Moran said, feeling her anger swelling—but before she could launch into a tirade, Josef said that the prognosis had not been dire. Survived by a caring ex-wife, his obituary would read, Josef joked when silence set in.

How long would he last, Moran wondered. How long does anyone, or anything, last? A marriage that had begun with enough affection could have gone right, love teased out with tenderness where passion was wanting, childlessness never a disappointment, as it was not a result of the age difference between Josef and Moran but of her adamant disinterest in motherhood. On holidays, Josef's children and grandchildren would visit, and friends—men and women twenty or thirty years Moran's senior, who had been Alena and Josef's friends and who had taken care of Josef after Alena's accident—would continue their tradition of seasonal get-togethers, which they'd begun long before Moran had existed for any of them.

A caring ex-wife must be the best consolation prize, Moran thought, for a man to have, or for a woman to be called. Even if Josef's children would oblige him, she would look like an awkward extra in an otherwise perfectly staged story in his obituary. For years Moran had been a regular visitor to a website that compiled obituaries from around the country. She never tired of the gently touched-up summaries of strangers' lives. Without her intrusion, Josef's life would be one of those perfect tales of love and loss: a solid upbringing in a solid midwestern town; a happy marriage to a childhood sweetheart ended abruptly by a careless driver; a beloved father and grandfather to four children and eleven grandchildren; a longtime member of the local choir, an avid gardener, a generous friend, a good man.

"I'm coming to see you," she said, deciding already that she would book the flights and the stay at her usual B&B after the phone call.

"But it's not June yet," Josef said.

During the past eleven years, Moran had visited Josef every June on his birthday, a lunch meeting rather than a dinner, because birthday dinners belonged to families, and he had children and grandchildren to celebrate with. He acted grateful for his birthday lunches, as though he did not know that they were for her sake more than for his.

June was a long while away, and who knew if he would still be here when June came again? The same thought must have occurred to Josef, and he reassured Moran that the prognosis was good: the doctors thought there was still time, at least a couple years, depending on how the treatments went.

Why, then, was he telling her at all; why not wait until they saw each other next June and spare her seven months of suspense? But she knew she was being unfair. He must have waited to break the news to other people, too—she should not expect to be among those called right away. "A plan should always be amendable," she said. "Unless it's bad timing for me to come?"

Josef said it was not bad timing at all. The hesitation in his voice— imagined or real, she could not tell—stung Moran: in death as in life she had no claim on anything. In a lighter tone she told him not to worry, as she would be out of his hair before Thanksgiving. She would book her return ticket for Wednesday, she said; other than Rachel, his children and their families would probably come and join him on that day.

"You think I'm worried about your staying through the holiday?"

"I don't want to impose," she said. Her decision to visit, she knew, was already an imposition, but Josef was too kind to point that out. Her inconsistency, which she allowed only him to see, was in itself a love she had not given anyone else, though it was not the kind of love to have done him, or anyone else for that matter, any good.

"Ever so like you," Josef sighed. "To worry about things you don't need to."

"You're bound to people," Moran said, though what she meant was that his time was bound to those around him. To think a person bound in any way—by blood, by legal documents of marriage or employment, by unsigned commitments to friends and neighbors and fellow human beings—is an illusion, though time is a different matter. In making commitments to others, what one really commits is one's time: a meal, a weekend, a marriage as long as it lasts, a final moment by the deathbed; to make the mistake of going beyond that, to commit one's true self—everyone has a story or two about that hard-learned lesson of giving more than is asked. "I can't just come and ask to be among them."

"Why not, Moran?"

"I thought you would have known by now that I don't belong," Moran said. That she had not belonged and could not blend in were the reasons she had given when she'd asked for a divorce. Blend in— what an absurd notion, as though a marriage ought to work like the hand of a masterful craftsman, slowly softening one's edges and changing one's hues until one becomes perfectly invisible. Josef, disappointed then, had nevertheless articulated that his conception of their marriage had never involved her adapting herself to his world.

But to mention his world, Moran knew, was to gain an unfair advantage. Having come into the marriage by herself—she had cited visa difficulties for her parents' absence at the wedding—she had only herself to account for, while Josef had his family, which in the end had been used as part of her excuse to exit the marriage.

Of course, Josef said now, he understood her concern. She wished he would not say that; she wished he would be less accommodating.

She would get in touch once she had the flights booked, she said. He said okay, though his voice sounded defeated. Why couldn't she be kinder to him?

After a moment of hesitation, Josef said there was one more thing she needed to know before she came: these days Rachel drove him around.

During her previous visits, Moran had not seen Rachel, and she'd wondered if Josef concealed their annual lunches from his children and friends. In their minds, she had been the calculating one: marrying Josef for security when it was needed for a new immigrant, divorcing him the moment she got her citizenship and a job offer. She imagined his having to plead with Rachel to drive him to meet Moran, guilty as a man caught cheating yet stubborn in his helplessness. "I'll rent a car," she said. "That way I can drive you anytime, if you need."

Josef thanked her. "Till then, Moran?" he said.

A dread of the immediate silence made Moran breathe in sharply. "Josef," she said, feeling, against all reason, widowed.

"Yes?"

She wanted to say that someone she knew from a long time ago had died, but it was selfish to unburden the news onto a dying man. She wanted to beg him not to let go of his hope, even though, had she been in his position, she would have easily chosen resignation. She wanted to apologize for things she had not done for him, and things she had done wrongly to him. But now, as he waited patiently on the phone, she knew that these words, true to her heart, would sound melodramatic once said. "Are you all right?" Josef asked gently.

"Of course I'm all right," she said, and added that if she had any talent worth boasting about, it was to always be all right.

Josef ignored the meanness—to herself more than to him—in her words. He had never been a fan of sarcasm. "Is there something upsetting you, Moran?"

Was he asking if her heart had been broken by another man? He would, of course, offer solace, as he had once consoled Rachel when she had broken up with her college boyfriend—but how could Moran explain to him that what was broken was not her heart but her faith in solitude? When she had asked for the divorce, she had told him that only a small part of his life would go to waste. There were his children and grandchildren, his friends and his house, all of which had crossed paths with her minimally, all of which would remain his, as they had never been hers. Considering how excruciatingly long a life was, she had said, the five years they had spent together were no more than a detour. What she had not told him was that, giving up the marriage, she had decided to live in a more limited way: all she wanted was to have her mind and her heart uncluttered, and with discipline she had since maintained a savage routine that cleansed her life to sterility. But today, two calls had come, announcing one death and another impending, and what filled the uncluttered space but pain that the most stringent cleansing would not alleviate? She missed Josef; she missed people.

"What's the matter, Moran?"

Nothing was the matter, she reassured him. It had perhaps dawned on him over the years that she was no longer looking for a companion, though she could tell that he continued to hope otherwise, counting on the day she could no longer travel for his birthday because she had someone else's feelings to consider. "I'm sorry I am nasty to you," she said.

"You surely aren't," Josef said.

"Let's not argue over this," she said, though who else would she argue with? She told him to take care of himself, and she would see him soon. When the call was disconnected, she felt pressed in, as though his voice had left a crack through which loneliness flooded into her room. She remembered a story she had read when young, about a Dutch boy finding a hole in a dam, and putting his finger into the hole to stop the ocean. In the story, the sea, which had once been a frolicking friend for the boy, murmured sinister seduction into his ear as the numbness from his finger expanded to his arm and then to his whole body. Why not, Moran said to the boy and to herself, let go of your heroic resistance and see what happens next?

But nothing happened. The silence, unlike the murmuring sea, did not engulf and drown her, and the woman in Modigliani's painting watched on, merciful in her insouciance.

Moran put on her coat and then wound a scarf around her neck, and a minute later emerged into the street. Dusk was falling, the wind picking up, sweeping leaves along the sidewalk. Lamps lit up people's windows, and here and there could be heard the opening and closing of a mailbox, the sound of a car engine coming to a full rest after the rumbling of a garage door, the buzzing of an erratic street lamp. The sound track of a suburban evening could be as deceivingly idyllic as that of a mountain village in Switzerland: the cars driven home were as eager to reach the end of their journey as were the sheep and cows trekking homeward; the barks here and there of dogs that had spent the day alone and now heard their owners' approaching steps were as exuberant as those of the sheepdogs who, after a day of working, smelled warm fried food upon nearing the cottages. Behind each door, beyond the gazes of strangers curious or insensitive, another day's happiness and unhappiness converged, adding or subtracting, modifying or concealing, leading or misleading those susceptible hearts to a place different, however imperceptibly, from yesterday's.

Once upon a time, cooking in the kitchen where for years Alena had made meals for her husband and their four children, listening for Josef's car but not really waiting for him, Moran had made up a life for herself apart from Josef, as she later would make up lives for Grazia and the cobbler and the heartbroken shepherd. It was not disappointment in her marriage, as Josef had thought, that had led her to do that, but her belief in the imperativeness of not living fully in any given moment. Time is the flimsiest surface; to believe in the solidity of one moment till one's foot touches the next moment, equally trustworthy, is like dream-walking while expecting the world to rearrange itself into a fairy tale path. Nothing destroys a livable life more completely than unfounded hope.

The life imagined in the kitchen of Josef's house was not far from what Moran conducted now: loneliness and solitude had been rehearsed while she chopped vegetables. It had been her only defense against having her heart moved to a strange place, by Josef, by their marriage, by time. Sometimes when she did not hear the garage door, or her mind was lost in the hissing of cooking oil under a closed lid, she would be startled by the sudden reappearance of Josef. Who are you, and why are you here in my life, she had half-expected him to ask her, half-wondering whether he, catching in her eyes a momentary hostility, had been waiting for her to ask him the same question.

In her adult life, Moran believed, she had not failed to foresee what was going to happen: her migration to America, her marriage to and later divorce from Josef. People would say that she was simply living toward what she thought she had seen, but that was not true. One could have wrong visions, one could have vain hopes, but deceiving oneself is more difficult than deceiving the world. Impossible, in Moran's case.

The odd thing, though, was that her clarity of vision did not apply to the past. Early in their relationship Josef had been curious about her life in China. She had been unable to share as much as he had wished for, and he had felt hurt, or at least saddened, by her evasiveness. But how does one share the memories of a place without placing oneself in it? Certainly there were moments that would stay alive for as long as she did. Her mother, before pulling Moran out of her fortress of quilts and blankets in the winter mornings, had rubbed and warmed up her own hands while singing a song advocating early rising for a healthier life. Her father's bicycle bell, a rusty one that sounded as though it had caught a perennial cold, had been stolen one day; who, the family had wondered, wanted an old bell while there were plenty of shiny ones that rang clear and loud? Neighbors' faces came to her, those who had died appearing vividly alive, those who had aged remaining young. In first grade, the district clinic had come to check the blood counts of the schoolchildren; she'd told Boyang to massage his earlobe so his blood would flow better, and he, trusting her as ever, was yelled at by the nurse afterward, because his red earlobe did not stop bleeding after it was punched by a thin needle.

But how could anyone, Moran wondered now, warrant the trustworthiness of one's memories? The certainty with which her parents spoke of Ruyu's culpability was the same certainty with which they believed in their own daughter's innocence. Those seeking sanctuary in misremembering did not separate what had happened from what could have happened.

Moran had not believed—still could not believe—that Ruyu had meant to do anyone harm. A murder needed motivation, a plot, or else it needed a moment of despair and insanity, as, in her own imagination, the young shepherd had experienced when he drowned his own love along with an innocent child. Moran had not known Ruyu well when they were young; even in retrospect she could not say that she understood Ruyu: she was one of those who defied being known. She had shown no remorse or concern when Shaoai was found poisoned. Had that made Ruyu more culpable than others? But the same could be said of Moran's own divorce: many among Josef's friends and family believed her manipulative, saying she'd got what she wanted from the marriage and discarded it the moment she had accomplished her goal. The excuse she had given Josef was half-hearted, the reticence she had maintained in front of others defiant, which made her guiltier than if she had asked for forgiveness.

Yet forgiveness Josef had given her. "Survived by a caring ex-wife," his words returned to her. Josef was dying, and Shaoai was dead: for the former, it was insufficient to watch from afar; for the latter, it was painfully confusing even seen from a distance. Moran quickened her steps. In three days she would be in Josef's city, closer to him even though he was closer to death than ever.

6

Much of Ruyu's existence in Beijing required explanations: Whose daughter was she? Where did she come from? What was she going to do with her life now that she was here? These questions, mixed with less demanding ones about her first impressions of the city and her previous life, were tiresome: either people asked questions they had no right to, or else they asked questions not worth answering.

When Ruyu could not produce satisfying answers, Aunt seemed to be both protective of her and embarrassed on her behalf; people would comfort Aunt, saying that Ruyu was still new among them, that she was shy, that by and by she would talk more. Ruyu tried not to stare at people when they said such things in her presence. She did not understand what they meant by her being shy, as she had never felt so in her life—one either had something to say to people, or did not. This idea, though, seemed unacceptable to the neighbors in the quadrangle, where life, from breakfast on, was lived in a communal manner, everyone's business pertinent to the next person; nor did her silence please the old people who sat in the alleyways, in the shadows of the locust trees before the morning breeze was replaced by the unrelenting heat of the season, and who, tired of old tales, looked up at the unfamiliar face of Ruyu, hoping that she would break the monotony but not the serenity of their days by offering something fresh and forgettable.

Soon she became known in the quadrangle and around the neighborhood as the girl who liked to sit with a dying man. There was nothing morbid about watching a man die slowly, though this, Ruyu knew, was not something others would understand. The strangers who had quickly claimed her as one of their own—a friend, a niece, a neighbor—looked for an explanation for her disturbing preference and regained their equanimity when they found one: the girl, anemic, unapproachable at times, was an orphan after all. In time, they would instill in her some normalcy and transform her into something better, but until then they would have to treat her with extra kindness, as one would when looking after a sick bird. In this group effort, almost everyone in the quadrangle was enlisted—everyone but Shaoai, who was mostly absent, and her grandfather, so close to the end that the only thing desired from him, it seemed, was a speedier death than he could offer.

The bed-bound man was quiet most of the time, but when he was hungry or thirsty or needed the pad underneath him to be changed, he gathered what strength was left in his body and gave out wild shrieks; when help was not instantly delivered, he banged his upper body against the bed, producing a terrible noise. Accustomed, Ruyu imagined, to such violent communications, Uncle and Aunt were unhurried in their response, patience their only protest against a deterioration that had lasted too long. When the neighbors talked about the old man, they spoke of him as a skillful repairman of watches and fountain pens, and of his fondness for his two-string fiddle and tall tales, as though he—the man lying in the room, no more than a bag of bones—was only playing at being alive and should not be confused with the real man.

Whenever she found an opportunity, Ruyu snuck into the old man's bedroom. A homemade wooden shelf stood at the end of the bed, empty but for a coil of bug-repelling incense, a jar of ointment for bedsores, and a framed family picture taken years ago: Shaoai, a toddler with pigtails, sat between her grandparents, and her parents, young and docile looking, stood behind. A folding chair—in which Aunt and sometimes Uncle would sit to feed the old man—leaned against the wall. A small window high up on the wall was kept open, though the air smelled constantly of stale bedding, wet pad, smoky incense, and pungent ointment.

The room, unlike the rest of the house, was not cluttered, and oddly it reminded Ruyu of her grandaunts' place. They were pristine housekeepers, and Ruyu knew that they would not find it flattering to be associated, even in her most private thoughts, with the unseemliness of sickness and decay in Grandpa's room. But her grandaunts would never ask for her opinions on such things, so they would not know what was on her mind.

Ruyu had not found the silence of her old home extraordinary until she arrived in Beijing; here words were used as a lubricant of everyday life, and the clutter in people's lives—meaningless events, small objects—offered endless subjects for a chat. In her grandaunt's apartment, there were no potted plants to leak muddy water or to drop stale flowers as Ruyu had seen in Aunt's house; there were no stacks of old brown wrapping paper to collect dust, no strands of plastic strings to get tangled, awaiting reuse. Twice a year—once before the summer, and again before the winter—her grandaunts brought out their sewing machine. During the next few days, the apartment took on a busy chaos that Ruyu never tired of: old skirts and blouses were carefully unstitched at the seams with a small pair of scissors, then rearranged and chalked, on top of paper samples, to become parts of new clothes; the small drum that dripped oil into every joint of the machine made soothing tut-tutting sounds when you pressed it; spools of thread, in different hues of blue and gray, were lined up to match the fabrics; when one of her grandaunts pedaled the sewing machine, the silver needle took on a life of its own, darting in and out of the fabric. But even during those festive days of sewing, Ruyu had

learned the importance of calm and order. She helped her grandaunts thread their needles; she cleaned up small pieces of fabric and
thread, and, when allowed by her grandaunts, sewed them into a
small ball—yet her relish in doing these things she knew to hide:
making their own clothes was, more than a necessity, a way for them
to differentiate themselves from a world to which they did not con-
form; finding happiness in one's duty was, to say the least, an act of
arrogance before God.

And it was God who had led her to Grandpa's room, which made
Ruyu feel at home: its emptiness was inviting more than oppressive,
its quietness keeping the world at bay.

At first Ruyu only stood at the entrance, ready to leave if the old
man expressed any displeasure. Sometimes he turned his murky eyes
to her, but most of the time he did not acknowledge her—she was
never the one to come with food or drink or a pair of caring hands.
When he did not protest in any noticeable way, she felt more at ease
and began sitting next to the bed. She would bring a bamboo fan with
her as a pretext, and a few times when she was found in the old man's
room by Aunt, she was cooling him down with the fan's gentle movement.

"You're very good to Grandpa," Aunt said when she came in one
evening with a basin of water and a wash towel. "But I can't say that I
like you to spend so much time with him."

"Why?" Ruyu said. "Does Grandpa mind?"

"What does he know?" Aunt said. "I don't think it's good for you."

The old man's eyes showed little expression at the exchange. The
fact that he was closer to death than anyone Ruyu had met made her
wonder if he knew things that others did not; that he could not speak
elevated him in her eyes, as the speechlessness must be a punishment
for what he had gained in life. Watching Grandpa, she felt an inexplicable kinship: he, like her, must have the power to see through
things and people, even if his silence was by now unwilling, and hers
always a choice.

When Ruyu remained quiet Aunt sighed. "You're still a child. You shouldn't spend so much time ruminating."

Ruyu moved over so Aunt could place the basin on the chair. "I don't mind sitting with Grandpa."

"Your grandaunts did not send you here to nanny an invalid," Aunt said.

Ruyu, rather than a poor relation imposed on Aunt and Uncle, was a paid guest. Before she had left, her grandaunts had explained that they would be paying a hundred yuan a month for her upkeep, more than either one of the couple earned. That hosting Ruyu was a substantial financial gain for the family was not directly stated, though she could see that it was what her grandaunts wanted her to understand. "I'm not really doing anything for Grandpa," Ruyu said. "I'm only sitting here."

"A young person should be with her friends," Aunt said. "Why don't you find Boyang or Moran and go out for a bike ride?"

Ruyu did not know how to ride a bike—nobody, not even the nosiest neighbors back at home, would expect her grandaunts to run after a youth barely balanced on a bike, ready to catch her when she skidded and fell. This deficiency seemed to have perplexed Moran and Boyang at first—they were the real children of this city, growing up on bicycles as the children of Mongolian herdsmen were raised on horseback. For them, the buses and trolleys and subways were for the very old and very young, and for the unfortunate ones who, for whatever reason, were deprived of the freedom of a bike.

Ruyu had spent much of her time with Boyang and Moran in the past weeks. Knowing the city by heart, they took Ruyu on the rear racks of their bikes in turn, riding through side streets and alleyways so that they would not be caught by the traffic police—two people on one bike was illegal. When they could not avoid a stretch of thoroughfare or boulevard, the two of them would push their bikes and walk beside Ruyu, pointing out old seamstresses' shops and hundred-year-old butcheries and bakeries along the road.

Ruyu did not mind being left alone, though others—Boyang and Moran, and the neighbors—seemed to find her ease with aloneness unnerving. To Aunt, any time Ruyu spent by herself bore an accusation of sorts. The desperateness of the world to make her less of herself made her look at it askance. Why, she sometimes thought, are people allowed to be so stupid?

When Ruyu did not reply, Aunt said that it was unfair of her to think so, but compared with other kids her age, Ruyu had spent too much time with old people. But Boyang lived with his grandmother, Ruyu said, and Aunt said that it was different with him, meaning, Ruyu guessed, that Boyang had his parents. The fact that Ruyu came from parents unknown to her was on the mind of everyone who knew her story, because, to the rest of the world, a child had to be born to a pair of parents. A child could not sprout like a small plant from a crack in the road; but Ruyu wanted the world to believe that she was rather like that—a life dropped in the crack between her two grand-aunts. That this was the most natural thing that had occurred to the three of them would never be understood by a person like Aunt.

Ruyu turned to the old man, who had half closed his eyes out of boredom or exhaustion. She wondered if he understood that all the people around him but herself would be relieved, if not happy, when he died; she might be the only person to feel a sense of loss, though she did not know him at all.

Someone told a joke in the courtyard and laughter erupted, accompanied by clapping hands that hunted bloodthirsty mosquitoes in midair. In the last light of the day, early-rising bats darted around, their high-pitched screeches, both faint and shrill, unlike any other noise made by a living creature. Ruyu had never seen bats before, and considered these strange animals, with their blind and frantic flights at dusk, one thing she loved about Beijing. Even inside Grandpa's small cube, one could occasionally catch a glimpse of a bat or two changing directions the moment when they were about to bump into the window, so abruptly yet so confidently, never making a mistake.

Aunt replaced an old coil of incense with a new one and lit it, the red tip the only live light in the room. Neither she nor Ruyu moved to turn on the light, and the old man's gaunt face became less harsh in the falling dusk.

"I've never really asked you," Aunt said after a moment, her voice dry, as if she were not certain of her right to have broken the silence. "Your grandaunts, how are they doing?"

"Good."

"Have you written them?"

When Ruyu had first arrived, Aunt had pointed out the envelopes and stamps in the drawer of Ruyu's new desk, though apart from a telegram she had sent her grandaunts about her safe arrival, she had not sent a letter: it was not expected of her. She did not want to admit any absence of communication now, so she only nodded vaguely, wondering if Aunt or Shaoai would monitor the numbers of stamps and envelopes in her drawer. Did she get a letter of reply from them, Aunt asked, and added that they—Uncle and Aunt—had written but had not heard from Ruyu's grandaunts.

Ruyu said that she had not received a letter from her grandaunts, either, and found it annoying that Aunt seemed more disappointed by the silence from the province on Ruyu's behalf than on her own. "They always know what they are doing. I'm sure they trust that you're settling down well," Aunt said. "Or the letter could've been held up somewhere. You never know."

"It's all right," Ruyu said.

"Is there a phone stand near where they live? Will the people at the phone stand take messages, or will they be able to get your grandaunts for you? I can ask Uncle to take you to the post office to make a long distance call to them."

"I don't think they like to be phoned," Ruyu said. They would not

like to be written to, either. At the entrance of their apartment building, letters and postcards and newspapers were twice a day jammed
into a wooden box painted green. The building's residents, other
than Ruyu and her grandaunts, would stop and flip through the mail,
reading headlines or stealing a glance at other people's postcards,
which, drab colored and stamped with the green emblem of the post
office, cost less to send than letters, and were preferred when privacy
was not a concern. Once, in first grade, Ruyu had felt an urge, with
her newly gained reading skills, to peek into the box. The letter on
top of the pile was for a family on the third floor, but apart from that,
she saw little. The younger of her grandaunts, who was walking up
the stairs in front of her, stopped and studied her. There was no re-
proach in the old woman's eyes, nor was anything said, but right away
Ruyu understood that what she had done out of pointless curiosity
was beneath what her grandaunts had raised her to be. "It's really all
right," she said now. "My grandaunts will write if they need to."

Aunt sighed and said certainly Ruyu knew them better. There was
a tone of defeat in her voice, though Ruyu had inherited her grandaunts' belief that people, especially the feebleminded, liked to see
themselves entangled in minor pains and useless bewilderments; she
had not the words to appease Aunt's worry.

The old man, all the while breathing shallowly in the semidarkness, lost his patience. A deep grumbling threatened to become a full
protest. Aunt switched on the ten-watt fluorescent tube dangling from
the ceiling on two metal chains; the light made the bare room, its
occupant, and its two visitors look ghastly pale. With the back of her
hand, Aunt tested the old man's bathwater, no doubt colder than
lukewarm—but what difference would it make if it was not the perfect temperature? "Now you go and find your friends," Aunt said.
"Let me clean Grandpa before he gets irritated with me."

Ruyu looked into the old man's eyes once more before taking her
leave, seeking an understanding she imagined to be there. She believed that he, like Ruyu herself, pitied Aunt, whose conversations

with Uncle were often one-sided, with him nodding or mumbling agreement but never offering much in return. When Aunt talked to her daughter, Shaoai replied in a most unpleasant manner—if she replied at all—though Aunt seemed more resigned than offended by Shaoai's sullenness. Why speak at all, Ruyu thought, when the people you were speaking with were either unfeeling walls or all-encompassing voids?

"Sometimes you wonder," Aunt said to Grandpa when she heard the house door close behind Ruyu, "how that girl would've fared if her parents had left her at an orphanage instead."

The old man listened. Living now with words locked away inside him, he liked to listen to his daughter-in-law talk. She knew it because on the days when she was not in the mood for talking, he would become agitated. Once upon a time he had not concealed his contempt for her chattiness, even though he'd been the talkative one in his own marriage. Nobody's going to sell you off as a mute, he had often said to her, and had more than once told the neighbors that his son had married a woman afflicted with the *talking consumption*. But his own quiet, uncomplaining wife had long since died, his three married daughters were the caretakers of their own in-laws, and his son, who had inherited his mother's reticence, was a poor companion: all he would do was clean and feed his father in silence. Sometimes Aunt felt vindictively joyful that she had not let her father-in-law shut her up. "I know, I know," she said to him now. "It's pointless to think that way. But still, wouldn't you want to see a child like her be just a bit more normal?"

The old man made some noises in his throat, disagreeing.

"Of course you like her that way. What other child would have the patience to sit here with you?" Aunt stripped the old man of his undershirt and started to wipe his upper body, taking caution not to rub too hard on the half-dead skin or hurt the protruding bones underneath. Despite years of being a target for his mockery, she was fond of him, feeling a kinship that she had not felt toward her mother-in-law: quiet people kept her both in awe and perplexed. "And of course her grandaunts like her that way, too. They don't bother to worry what she'll be like when she goes out in the world because they won't be around to see it. Just like you spoiled Shaoai, and now it's me who's to suffer the consequence."

The old man closed his eyes, but Aunt knew he was listening.

"Why, you don't want to hear it? All the same, where do you think Shaoai got the idea that she was free not to follow the rules? You didn't teach your own children that, did you? You raised your daughters to be obedient," Aunt said. She wondered if she, too, would one day instill some mischievous thoughts in her grandchild, so that together they could be conspirators against the child's parents, but at once she chased away that fate-taunting thought like an unwelcome gnat. "Don't think I'm chastising you for no reason. Do you remember the last time Shaoai came in to sit with you, to talk to you? For all I know, you and I and even her father don't exist for her. Being a good daughter and granddaughter? Fulfilling her filial duties? What rotten ideas for her."

The old man refused to open his eyes. Aunt took off his pants and underpants, and cleaned him gently around his crotch while holding her breath. When she finished, she told the old man that she would now turn him around. He did not make a sound, and she saw wet lines left by tears traveling from the corners of his eyes to both temples. Her heart softened a little, but right away a bleakness snuck in. She shushed him; it did no one any good to be sentimental. "Don't you dare think too much of it. We must have done something awful to Shaoai in our last lives, so she's here to make us suffer. Who knows? You might have done that girl Ruyu a favor in your last life for her to care about you," Aunt said. "She must have done some good deed in her last life, so she has her grandaunts to see about her future rather than being left in an orphanage."

But what kind of future would it be, Aunt wondered, shaking her head while putting an arm under the legs of the old man, who seemed to get lighter each day. She wished she had someone to talk to besides her husband and neighbors about Ruyu's grandaunts, but to them the two women were only her distant cousins. That she had once been arranged to become their sister-in-law she had not told anyone.

The two sisters had been born to the third concubine of a successful silk merchant. Their mother had died while giving birth to their younger brother, and the two girls, aged twelve and ten then, had more or less raised the boy, fighting, without their mother's shelter, to maintain as much of their status as they could within the large family, where four other wives and fifteen siblings vied for attention and wealth. As teenagers, they had converted to Catholicism, and Aunt had suspected that the Church, because of its connection to the West and with the power beyond the local government, had factored beneficially in their battle for themselves within the family. When their brother reached age fifteen, the two sisters gained independence and moved back with their brother to the home village of their mother. How they had managed to do this no one knew for sure, but when they had moved back—two spinsters with money but no prospect of marrying, and a boy handsome and educated yet too sophisticated for country life—the villagers treated them with suspicion and awe. Soon, the boy was enrolled as a cadet in a military academy in the capital, but before he left, the two sisters arranged an engagement between the boy and a cousin twice removed.

Sometimes Aunt wondered why she, among her sisters and cousins, had been chosen. At nine, she had not been the prettiest, nor the most gifted at needlework. Relocating, with a small bag of clothes and a pillow, to the sisters' house across the village had not been too difficult a change—she was to celebrate her good fortune, her parents had explained to her. From the departure of a few playmates who had been sent to other villages as child brides, she knew things could have been worse. Living with strangers one did not understand could be a harsh experience for some children, but she had been known as the most cheerful and thick-skinned of her peers. She had never felt unhappy with her new guardians. Strict as they had been with her, they had also been fair, and had taught her to read, which had made everything possible when she had later decided to go to nursing school.

"*The foolish are assigned the good fortune of the fools, the weak, the good fortunes of the weaklings,*" Aunt said now, thinking of her own mysterious lot. These must be nonsensical words to the old man, but it comforted her to quote other people's wisdom when she herself was perplexed. Her engagement to the young man had lasted five years, during which time she had seen him only twice when he had been on leave from the academy: shortly after graduating, he, serving as a cannoneer, had to flee to Taiwan when his side lost the civil war.

Compared to his sisters' loss, hers had been negligible, even though some older villagers had shaken their heads at her fate, wid-owed before wedded. When it became obvious that the separation across the Strait could be lifelong, the sisters told her that it was point-less for her to stay with them. Not wanting to cling to them, yet not being able to stop thinking of herself as part of their life, she had moved on but had never entirely forgotten them as they had expected her to. Once a year she wrote to them; after her marriage and later Shaoai's birth, she'd enclosed a picture of her family each year. They wrote back to her too, courteous letters bearing their goodwill toward her and her family and dutifully recounting changes in their lives— their taking up residence in a provincial city and joining a neighbor-hood workshop to produce embroidered silk scarves so they could be part of the working class, their retirement, and, a year later, their dis-covering a baby left at their door. The years she had lived with the sisters, she serving them partly as a handmaid, they in turn educating her, had never been brought up in the letters, the man who had con-nected her to them left unmentioned. Once, during the sixth year of the Cultural Revolution, a provincial official, one of those traveling investigators with menacing power, came to the clinic and asked to talk to Aunt. Had she heard anything about the women's brother, who had fled China, he wanted to know, indicating that it was a serious matter, with some Taiwanese or American spies involved. Aunt had denied any knowledge; her lie to the stranger had hurt her conscience less than her decision not to speak of the stranger's visit with her in-laws and her husband: a minor secret too late to be revealed could expand its roots. For a while Aunt had difficulty sleeping: the two sisters and her childhood spent with them taking up too much space in her heart, until she started to take sleeping pills to drive out old memories.

How the two women managed to pull through the many revolutions unscathed Aunt did not know—though who could be certain that they were unscathed? In their letters they did not mention any hardship, and after a while, when they continued to write to her once a year, she was happy that they had not been thrown into a prison somewhere and left to die. Perhaps their god had truly ensured their safety in a hostile world. When she had lived with the sisters, they, no longer having a church to attend in the village, had been carrying out their own rituals of worship; twice a year they traveled to meet their old priest, though his god certainly had not looked after him well, as he had been executed right around '49 as a counterrevolutionary by the new, Communist government. What the sisters had taught Aunt about their faith had been partially absorbed as a superstition by her, so she would never say no, in her heart, to the possibility of a deity from above. Imagine, she could have been converted by them, had her fiancé not fled China; imagine, on top of being the wife of a Nationalist officer, she could have been a counterrevolutionary by being a religious person!

There was little sense in such brooding. Still, buttoning the old man's shirt and tucking him under the blanket, Aunt wished she could tell him that it was his good fortune that she was taking care of him now, that she would be the one to see him off when it was his time to exit this world. She could have been married off to a young Nationalist officer and left the country with him; her siblings and cousins would have been questioned during the Cultural Revolution, and they would have thought it their misfortune to have a sister who was an enemy of the country. I could've been another person, she thought of saying to the old man, but he had already been upset once this evening. She patted his cheek and told him to rest before she came back with the evening meal.

7

The dead did not fade when they remained unacknowledged. For the first time, Boyang considered the necessity of a funeral. He had been to a few, all of them arranged in the most extravagant manner, and he had laughed then at the gesture of glorifying the mortal. But funerals are not for the vanity of the dead, he realized now. The dead are gone, and the living need witnesses—more so at funerals than at weddings. Happiness and grief on these occasions both explode like fireworks: happiness, if not on display, retains some value for later; grief turned inward only becomes toxic.

Neither Moran nor Ruyu replied to Boyang's email, and the void in which he was left, waiting, despite his reluctance to admit it, threatened to give Shaoai's death more weight. Where's your good sense, Boyang asked himself; do you need to put up a wanted poster, and how large does the reward money have to be? But laughing at himself did not, as he had hoped, ease his agitation. Endured alone, a death becomes a chronic illness one has to hide from others.

A week passed, and Boyang did not visit Aunt as he had promised. If she asked about Moran and Ruyu, he would not have anything new to tell her; but would she? Perhaps rather than avoiding the question, he was only dreading the silence in place of the question: if Aunt did not bring up Moran and Ruyu, he would feel lonelier and angrier. His own mother, after their one conversation, seemed to have dropped her curiosity, and it would be unwise if he talked to her again about the case. Certainly she would not mind watching him return to the topic like a hesitant fish circling back to the bait; perhaps she was waiting for that, with a fisherman's astuteness.

Why was it, Boyang thought one evening, that with so many people crowded into his life, the only ones he could not stop thinking about were those two who had kept to their vows of absence? Their silence granted them a power over him, but people, unless forced into silence, must have chosen it for the exact reason of possessing that power. A vanishing act is an old trick; nevertheless it works on hearts of all ages: could it be that we will never be rid of that child in us, who, panicking about never seeing a beloved face again, is still screaming to this day?

Listless, Boyang looked through the contact list on his cell phone and toyed with a new app, which assigned icons to different contacts. To the men with whom he could have a drink and exchange lewd jokes, he gave an icon of a wineglass or a curvy female body; to the women he wouldn't mind touching with subtle affection in a dark karaoke room, that of a lipstick. When he reached Coco's name, he hesitated and looked up at her; she was leaning on the armrest of a chair and watching him, tight lipped. Didn't he remember, she had said earlier, that they were going to meet her friends at a karaoke bar to celebrate her birthday? Boyang had said he was not in the mood to go out, adding that it was ridiculous to start celebrating a birthday a week in advance; who did she think she was, he asked, Jesus Christ or the Queen of England?

"Aren't you going to be late for your friends?" he said now. He knew he had agreed to spend the night with her, thinking that a group of mindless girls in a noisy place would be the perfect antidote to the silence. But there was no point apologizing: a man unable to extricate himself from the mercy of others has to find some balance in those who put their lives at his mercy.

In a dry voice, Coco asked him if everything was all right with his business. Would he like her to make a cup of tea for him, or would he like her to give him a massage?

What he needed most, he said, was some space to breathe and think—and please, no tears, no questions, he added, sinking heavily into the depths of the sofa.

He was not a good actor, and the boorish role he had taken on was no more convincing than the part of the obedient son he played for his mother, whose interest in Boyang, far from maternal, was dissecting. Had Coco had his mother's wisdom, she would have easily sabotaged his role with mocking incredulity, but Coco did not dare to stray from her script, in which she was a young and pretty woman from a provincial city who could not afford to look for love in this big city but, with her cunning, could get many other things. She slid off the armchair like a melancholy cat. "Would you like me to call tomorrow, then?"

The question, Boyang knew, was asked in the hope that he would want her to spend the night with him. Coco shared a two-bedroom apartment in a decrepit building with three other girls her age. She'd been the first one to find a lover with a good apartment in the city; two of the other girls had followed, though the three had continued to rent, as none of their invitations to the second nests was permanent. The one roommate who had not succeeded in the way the others had, Coco said, was pretty enough but not so smart: she was dating a boy their age who did not have anything to his name but an entry-level job at an advertising agency. Generously, the three other girls allowed the boy to spend a night in the apartment now and then. Boyang wondered if today would be one of those days. He had not been to Coco's apartment, but he did not have any trouble imagining the place, where the girls, when necessary, withdrew behind their curtained corners and nurtured alone their wounds of being used by the world; inevitably they would regain their spirits and venture out afresh, as that was what their roles required of them. Life is a battle that the lesser ones do not have the luxury of quitting midway.

"Sure, call me tomorrow," he said, and wished Coco a good night of fun.

Coco struggled with her boots and then her gloves at the door, and Boyang, from where he was sitting, unchivalrously enjoyed her fumbling, feeling too spiteful to offer help. To send Coco back to the cramped apartment where a young couple in love, without any future in the city, clung to each other for a night of meager pleasure, was to teach her a lesson about life, even though it was a lesson she had time and again refused to learn. A week short of turning twenty-two, Coco was already showing signs of fatigue, deeper than could be released by restful sleep or hidden by makeup.

Boyang had met Coco two years earlier at a party. She'd been enrolled in cosmetics school, she had told Boyang; her goal was to find a position as a makeup assistant at a wedding photography studio, and once she had enough experience, to work in the film or TV industry. Do you know any producers, she had asked Boyang, and when he said he might, she stayed at his side for the rest of the party. Who's paying for your training, he had asked, and she had said her parents, but she had been lying to them, telling them she was enrolled in a nursing program. "Who wants to take care of the old and the sick when she grows up?" she had said to him, wrinkling her nose in a childlike way.

What do you want to be when you grow up, Boyang sometimes wanted to ask Coco, but the line did not belong to that of a sugar daddy: he should feel no responsibility for her misspent youth. Shoo, Boyang said in his mind now, shoo, shoo, while waving at Coco, who, even in her resentment, did not forget to blow him a kiss—a kiss which, sadly, unbeknownst to her, landed nowhere in this indifferent world.

Boyang was glad that no child had been produced in his failed marriage. He would not have been able to protect his child from the harm of the world unless he raised him or her to be the first to inflict pain; he would also have had to become more successful at his business, so that his child could have a chance to at least become a decent person without being trampled by others. But imagining a child—his child—being a good person was as upsetting to Boyang as imagining that child being evil. Of course there was a wide range between good and evil, but could one be both callous and kind—callous enough to be immune to worldly hurt, yet with enough kindness to be spared the possible divine repercussions for that callousness?

Boyang had not hidden his disinterest in having a child from his parents, and as far as he knew, they were fine with it: his sister had—as efficiently as befitted their parents' standard—given birth to a pair of brilliant twins. His ambition, he knew, sufficed only to provide himself a comfortable life and allow him to be near his parents as they grew older. He did not feel stuck in the middle of the ladder; if anything, he felt lucky because of his track record of doing the right thing at the right time. He had taken his second year of college off to start a printing company when digital printing had just emerged in the country; after college, he had spent a couple of years working on a software program that input Chinese characters into computers, which he had sold to a big company when he became bored with programming; the stock market and the real estate market he had entered earlier than his peers, and now, with a real estate development project under his name and a couple of unrelated businesses he backed—an organic lavender farm on the outskirts of the city, with single-story vacation rentals nearby to attract trendy urbanites, and an oxygen bar in the central business district, where condensed air imported from Japan was offered at a high price to those who could afford its cleanness—Boyang felt complacent enough. He could see himself climbing a few more rungs, but he did not feel the urge to be in a different place from where he was now: purposefulness, in his view, was overrated. He had none of the potentially bad habits for a man of his status: he drank but not excessively; he was not into drugs;

he kept a girl he could be rid of easily; he had little interest in anything with ideology behind it—he had declined to support a group of underground documentary filmmakers, and he had not bitten, either, when a so-called independent artist approached him for a photography project that involved placing naked men and women in orgiastic poses in various heavily contaminated industry sites.

A beep brought a text message from Coco. "Do not go out and find another woman," it said, followed by a laughing emoticon, a scowling one, and a parade of kisses.

Poor Coco, already learning to turn everything into a joke at an age when living should be a more serious business for her. At Coco's age, the girl Boyang had been dating, who would later become his wife and then someone else's lover, had still been holding on to a belief in love and loyalty. At least Boyang should give his ex-wife credit for earning the right to laugh at her own past, as she had gone through the proper stages of dreaming, wakening, and being disappointed by a world that would never meet a young person's expectations. What would Coco laugh at in ten or twenty years—her own inept jokes? Or worse, would she have to constantly focus on things that were laughable in others, so that she did not have a free moment to dwell upon her own foolishness? Boyang did not think Coco was heading toward a promising future, but there was little for him to do. He himself would not be in that future, and besides, he was not her savior.

His ex-wife had suffered remorse after the divorce. He was lucky to have not loved her sufficiently, luckier to have provided more than sufficiently: the apartment he had left her, unless the city's real estate market completely crashed, would offer her enough if she was hit by hard times, and that alone had cleared him of any unease. Boyang did not mind being seen as a cad, but he would have liked to avoid inflicting unnecessary pain on others. He would have liked to be, as the old saying goes, a bandit with principles.

And now, what a perfect message Coco had sent. All day he had been hesitating, going over the pros and cons of making a phone call to a stranger—a woman Coco's age, a girl really. But now the message arrived, a plea masked as a warning that sounded to him more like an encouragement. Without further delay, he dialed the girl's number.

After four rings, the girl picked up, sounding younger on the line than in person. He heard only her thin voice; there was no noise in the background. Where was she—in the small art shop not many people visited, or already off work, spending a quiet night in a rented room somewhere? Boyang gave her his name, and added that he was the one who had come into the shop the day before and bought, upon her recommendation, the double-dragon kite. "Or maybe you sold many kites yesterday," he said. "In that case I'm one of the people who you convinced to buy a kite."

"No, I remember you," the girl said. "I only sold one kite yesterday."

"Sold more today?"

"Not really," the girl said, her voice low, as though apologetic. Or perhaps she was beginning to feel suspicious about the call? The day before, when she had gone into the storage room to find a matching case for the kite, Boyang had grabbed her phone from the counter and made a quick call to his phone, so he'd have her number. He wondered if she had noticed that. He did not know her name.

"Um, listen, I'm calling to see if you'd be interested in flying the kite this weekend," Boyang said.

"But I don't know how to fly a kite."

A kite seller, Boyang wanted to say, should at least pretend to know how to fly one. He wanted to make a joke that she should deliver a more complete service package but decided it would sound too familiar, off-color even. The girl, as he remembered, had not responded well to any kind of glibness. He had noticed that she had the habit of looking into people's eyes when she listened; her pupils, dark, rarely out of focus, made her look at once innocent and composed.

It didn't matter that she did not fly kites, he told her. He himself was good at it; he only needed a helper. The girl hesitated and said she wasn't sure. She had agreed to go to see an art exhibition with a friend on Saturday.

"What kind of exhibition?"

"Oh, nothing big," she said, sounding embarrassed. By what, he wondered—by being caught lying, or by being chased, which she was not used to? "It's only a small show about ancient architecture, and I thought it would be good to see it for work."

The day before, between a business lunch and a meeting at a bar near the Front Sea, Boyang had wandered into a side alley where he knew there was a quaint old house, part museum and part retail space, associated with a folk arts and crafts organization. Possibly it would be a good place to look for some birthday presents for his mother, and, walking off the wine from the lunch, he could not find a better way to kill an hour. Boyang did not care much for ancient folk art, nor did his mother, but, as far as he could tell, she already had everything he'd normally offer. Vaguely he imagined finding her a useless replica of a pottery figure from the Han Dynasty, or a cast of miniature poets drinking at a famous party from the Jin Dynasty, carved exquisitely from walnut shells—something his mother would appreciate only because he had gone out of his way to get it for her. Love measured by effort was the only love within his capacity.

The salesgirl had been the only one in the shop when Boyang entered, and when he said he was looking around, she asked him if he would like a tour of the exhibition of artisan kites. She had memorized the material and at times invited him to come closer to inspect one kite or another, to appreciate the fineness of a dragonfly's transparent wings on a small, palm-sized silk kite, or to see the calligraphy

on another—wild, dancing characters, which, if not for the girl, Boyang could not have deciphered. Secretly he slid a piece of chewing
gum into his mouth, feeling bad for the girl, who had to pretend that
he did not reek of alcohol. The girl's hair was not dyed, and Boyang
could not remember the last time he had seen such natural black in
a girl's hair. Coco's was dyed reddish blond.

"Are you one of the artists?" Boyang asked as they exited the exhibition, pointing to a poster of names on the wall, a list of the folk
artists belonging to the organization.

The girl said of course she was not. Why not, Boyang asked, and
the girl said that most of the artists were men, because they came
from prominent families in which the secret of their trades could
only be passed from father to son—and in rare cases from a father-in-
law to a daughter-in-law—to ensure the purity of the art. "The rule is
to teach a son but not a daughter, to teach a daughter-in-law but not
a wife," she said, no doubt quoting from her textbook. She sounded
ridiculously serious and reverent of the rule.

"Then why are you here, if they are not letting you in on their
secrets?"

She had been hired because she had studied the history of ancient
folk art in college, the girl said. He could see that she was no more
than a well-educated salesgirl, and he was also certain, from her
clothes and her outdated cell phone, that she was not paid well.
"What does one do after getting a degree in art history?" he asked.

"Nothing, really," she said, slightly dejected. She was lucky to
have a job, she added.

"What do your classmates do now?"

All sorts of things, the girl said, though he could see that she was
not keen for the conversation to go in that direction. He would know
more about what her classmates were doing than she did: those from
well-connected families had gone on into a different phase of their
lives, their education the perfect decoration on their résumés; then

there were those who, like the girl in front of him, would have to become another Coco, or stay a salesgirl. "Why did you go to school for it if there are no good jobs?" he asked.

"But I like it," the girl said, looking up, as if surprised by the irrelevance of his question.

"I see," Boyang said, though he did not see. She must have been asked that question all the time by her parents and relatives; was that the only answer she could come up with?

Somewhere at the back of the house, a microwave dinged, and then a door was opened and banged closed. He imagined the girl's days, spent in a shop that was out of the way and never advertised. Did she find this a lonely job, or did she enjoy the companionship of the objects more than that of people? Perhaps it did not bother her when no one came in, but people must inevitably stop by, an idle man like Boyang, with nothing or too much on his mind, or the old men on the artists' roster, who would clasp her young hands in theirs while talking at length about their glamorous histories. What kind of a future did the girl envision for herself? "Maybe you can become the daughter-in-law of one of those people, to learn the secrets of a trade," Boyang said. You are one of those girls old men love, gentlemanly or otherwise, he thought.

"But I don't want to be locked into one trade," the girl said with a seriousness that made him feel he had to either laugh at her or feel bad for her. Had he not drunk a bit too much at lunch, had he not just taken a sentimental walk by the lake he had often visited with Moran and Ruyu, he would have dismissed the girl as ludicrous. But he had been touched by her obstinacy, enough that he had bought the most expensive kite in the shop and later had made a secret call from her phone to his so that he could carry with him something that belonged to her.

"I could tag along with you and your friend to the show if you don't mind," Boyang said now. "And we can go out and fly the kite afterward."

"But my friend won't like it."

"You mean you don't like it?"

"No, my friend won't like to have a stranger to come with us. She might want to talk about things she doesn't want you to hear."

"What about Sunday?"

"I have to work on Sunday."

That seemed to have concluded their conversation; Boyang felt the girl waiting for him to hang up. He could not tell if she was alarmed or annoyed by his call, but her voice indicated neither suspicion nor impatience. "What's your name—may I ask?"

"Wu Sizhuo."

"What time do you get off work on Sunday?"

The girl paused and said seven o'clock.

"Can I come and meet you when you're off?"

"Seven is too late to fly a kite."

"But not too late for a simple dinner—if you don't already have plans?"

The way Sizhuo said okay, without hesitation or curiosity, made Boyang's heart sink a little. He'd been prepared for a courteous rejection, which would not have stopped him from stepping into the store a few minutes before seven on Sunday evening and saying he had reserved a table nearby, just in case she had changed her mind. Used to elusiveness and evasiveness in interactions—at least at the beginning of a game, whether it involved money or women—Boyang, like many, considered chasing and being chased the only validation of a person's value. Slightly disoriented, he could not think of more to say when the girl confirmed the time and said good-bye.

Boyang tried to recall whether there had been any enthusiasm or readiness in Sizhuo's voice that could have given him an excuse to cancel the dinner, but there was none. "But I like it," he remembered her saying, looking up at him with a candidness that was at once transparent and unreadable. Oddly, he felt as though he had returned to his second-grade physical education class on the day they had been

practicing hurling hand grenades. When it was Boyang's turn, he pe-
rused the long row of hand grenades, all an old Soviet model with
wooden shafts and black metal heads; he chose one carefully, and
with all his might hurled it. He had been a tall boy then, athletic, and
he had expected to set a class record with his throw, but the metal
head, loosened after years of use in training children to become mili-
tants, dropped behind him with a thud, while the wooden shaft made
a less than confident trajectory across the sky, flipping and falling
before its intended target. It was the first time Boyang had understood
the meaning of *overreach*, not in his twisted eight-year-old shoulder
but somewhere inside of him, an unfamiliar befuddlement, and that
was how he felt now: he had not known—or had not had the desire
to know—what he had wanted when making the phone call, and
now it seemed too late to go back and figure it out.

Boyang wished he had someone next to him at this moment with
whom he could talk while thinking—not about the girl on the phone
but about the memory of his failed grenade throw. What do children
throw in their physical education classes these days, he wondered—
baseballs, or a different kind of hand grenade in the shape of angry
birds? He could ask Coco about it, but she would make it into a joke
about something else. No, Coco was the last person with whom he
could share that memory. He wanted someone to see the seriousness
behind the giddy chaos: the teacher had turned pale at the accident,
though, luckily for her and everyone else, the metal head had not
landed on and cracked open a child's skull; the children had gotten
overexcited, as though an unexpected holiday had befallen them;
Moran had looked concerned as she gently tapped his arm and shoulder to assess how much he had hurt himself, then all of a sudden
broke into uncontrollable laughter. Yes, he wanted someone to see
his past with him, the children in blue gym uniforms—the most unsavory kind of blue, not light enough to be associated with anything
delightful, not dark enough to confer dignity; he wanted someone to
laugh with his childhood friend and himself but not *at* them, ugly

ducklings who, not knowing their lots, wholeheartedly embraced everything coming their way. But beyond that, he wanted someone to understand that a moment, even a trivial one, could in time accumulate weight and meaning. Looking back, wasn't it a befitting role for him to be the hero whose only real accomplishment was to sacrifice himself, and those around him, too? The intention to do good, the intention to do the right thing—who could say with certainty that these were separate from the intentions to do harm, to diminish? In allowing a bedridden woman not only to exist in his life as a secret kept from his family, but to dictate how he treated the world—with distrust and aloofness—he had pushed his ex-wife into another man's arms. In turning away from Aunt now, when she was completely alone in this world, he must be crueler than Moran and Ruyu, who had turned away long ago.

"Remember the disassembled hand grenade in second grade?" he imagined starting an email to Moran—with an appeal to nostalgia she could not possibly ignore. Would she feel the obligation to write him back if he did not mention Shaoai or Ruyu but made the note about him and her? Once upon a time—if he tried to convince himself, could he convince her, too?—there had been a tale, or a tale in the making, about them: did she forget that? No, she couldn't possibly.

Violently he erased the maudlin note from his mind. To have treated someone badly and to have refused to acknowledge that mistreatment—Boyang wondered if in his friendship with Moran he saw the nascent self he would eventually turn into: selfish but not enough to be immune to the pains caused by his selfishness; adamant in refusing to suffer yet not blind enough to others' suffering.

Boyang had known, even when they were young, that Moran's feeling toward him had been more than a friend's or a sibling's. That he had never encouraged her was his excuse to forgive himself; all the same, when the poisoning had happened, when madness and loss had overtaken their lives, he had not suppressed his urge to hurt

Moran—to punish her for her love, for being alive, healthy, and for being a good person.

What kind of man would it make him if he insisted on bringing the past into fresh focus? Boyang had not been in touch with Moran's parents over the years but had heard from old neighbors that they were well traveled, so Moran must have had a solid life elsewhere with enough good things—a husband, a career, two or three children (as she had loved children, and had always been patient with the younger kids in the neighborhood)—to prefer not to share his retrospection.

On Sunday, Boyang decided to arrive a few minutes late for his date with Sizhuo. He had taken a taxi, not wanting to risk having to drive the girl home—or to his place. The latter was unlikely, he decided: the right thing was to see her off to her place. Coco had left plenty of traces in his car as she had done in his apartment, an animal marking its territory. It would be a hassle to have to clean up for a first date.

Boyang asked the driver to drop him off on the opposite bank of the Front Sea. He took a walk near the water, then crossed the arched stone bridge, where a tour guide was speaking a memorized script, explaining in heavily accented English to a group of foreigners the origin of the bridge's name—Silver Ingot—with such seriousness, as though it mattered to those pale-skinned foreigners that the bridge had been built in the Yuan Dynasty, when the Mongolians ruled Beijing, and not (as usually and mistakenly thought) in the Ming Dynasty.

To whom did the dynasties matter now? Boyang thought of pointing out to the tour guide the misjudged faith in her audience. For Coco and her friends, what happened twenty years ago was as ancient as the events of two hundred or two thousand years ago.

In middle school, Moran and Boyang had become intensely interested in their city. They had combed through the used-book market near Confucius Temple and had pooled their allowances to buy all the books they could afford on the subjects of Beijing's history, architecture, and generations of anecdotes. Some of the books were fifty or sixty years old, some over a hundred, their thin yellow pages brittle to the touch; many bore personal stamps or signatures of their former owners inside the covers. Moran and Boyang had been eager to know their city in a way that their peers would find strange, or even *perverted*, as the youthful slang had it then, yet they had been proud of themselves, as though they alone had discovered the city, and they alone lived in it. After school, they would hide in Boyang's bedroom and tell everyone they were doing homework, while they were reading through the old books, relishing the illustrations of different decorations on old, latticed windows, memorizing histories and tales associated with streets and plazas and temples. To whom had those books belonged before they had come to them, Boyang wondered now. He was surprised such a question had not occurred to them at the time; they had taken the books as their own with the same ease— perhaps known only to youthful minds that are not tainted by self-doubts or corrupted by the distrust of the world—as they had taken the histories and beauties of the city as their own.

The summer Ruyu arrived seemed the perfect time for them to show off their expertise: they brought her to see the execution crossroads, where a hundred years earlier people had gathered to watch a public beheading, applauding when the feat had been completed; they showed her a run-down temple where two pine trees, nine hundred years old, had grown into a pair of inseparable twins; they pointed out the earthen sculptures at the eaves of old houses, different patterns indicating the different statuses of the owners. And above all, they spent long afternoons under the willow trees here on the waterfront of the Front Sea or Back Sea, talking—about what, Boyang had no recollection now. What could have made them think that Ruyu would one day love what they had passionately loved? What had been on her mind that summer when she had come to them? Pompous, incurious, he and Moran must have made the mistake that almost every young person makes at one time or another: they had never for a moment seen Ruyu as anything other than what they wanted her to be, an orphan whom they would adopt with their friendship. They had both been enchanted by her, captivated even, and they had been in a rush to offer all they had—the long history of the city, the short history of their own existence—because they could not see any other way to be of consequence to her.

First love is at times dangerous, opening in our hearts an abyss of uncertainty and despair; or else it is uncomplimentary—how many of us can look back at our first loves without laughing at our foolishness, or else cringing at our insensibilities? But most first loves peter out without dragging a life down with them. A death, though twenty-one years too late, had nevertheless become part of his first love; it was like having died from losing one's virginity—Boyang thought with sarcasm—unfortunate to the extreme of being comical.

A young couple walked past him, a Chinese woman hanging on to a white man's arm with both hands, he keeping his hands stubbornly jammed in his coat pockets. The woman said something to the man, looking up at him with the eagerness of a child seeking approval, and the man only nodded absentmindedly. In the light of the street lamp, she looked not much older than Coco, and she looked very much like Coco, with her hair dyed blond, her face and neck powdered too pale, and her facial expressions exaggeratedly dollish. Boyang had a friend who ran an unofficial agency that pimped foreigners to businesses needing a white face or a cluster of white faces to impersonate potential collaborators and funders from abroad. At least he should give Coco credit for not being so stupid as to bet her future on some useless white man mining for gold in this city—though, to think about it, what difference did it make, since Coco had put her stakes on someone both she and he knew was not to be trusted?

Even though Boyang himself had foreseen the development of this place long before it had taken off, he felt resentful looking at the lakes and surrounding areas, which had become a sort of cultural magnet, where chic white-collar workers, expats of all nationalities, tourists, and imitators of every kind converged—youths with boldly dyed Mohawks or dreadlocks, fashionable women toting designer bags and openly assessing the authenticity of one another's possessions, an avant-garde artist dressed in a gray monk's robe and wearing a long beard, looking sagely ancient, except that he made sure to always be seen with two or three beautiful young women fluttering around like butterflies. What draws you here, Boyang wanted to grab someone's shoulder and ask; what makes you leave your country, your city, your neighborhood, and come here to be part of this display of self-importance? Once upon a time, this had just been another neighborhood where people lived out their minor tragedies and comedies. Now it was called the sexiest spot in Beijing, as Boyang had read in tourist brochures. He wondered what Moran would have thought, had she come back and seen their childhood place transformed into the center stage of a masquerade party. But she must have been to other places like this, participated in the same nonsense shows elsewhere. He imagined her sitting in a plaza in Rome, or at a sidewalk café in Paris: she would have read enough about those places, and would idly tell an anecdote or two to the person next to her, laughing more than smiling because she was not the kind of woman who constrained her joy just to look elegant. To passersby, she would be the face of the carefree, and in someone's memory of that city she would live on. Why not come back then, Boyang wished he could ask her now. Why not sit by the Front Sea and tell a visitor about the princess whose arm the emperor had cut off when the rebels entered Beijing because he could not stand the thought of her falling into the hands of savage creatures? He had meant to kill the fifteen-year-old princess, but she had raised an arm in defense and had begged for her life; at the sight of her gushing wound he had cried and said it was her misfortune to be born into the imperial family. Boyang remembered Moran telling the story to Ruyu that summer. They had been standing next to the tree where the emperor had hanged himself when he could not bring himself to kill his favorite daughter. *The end of the Ming Dynasty,* he remembered the exact words Moran had used, her solemnness too sincere even for him to laugh at her now. Ruyu had acted nonchalant; all the same she had reached over the perimeter fence, trying to pick a leaf off the ancient tree, but it was too far for her to reach.

Why not come back now, you two deserters? One life has ended because of you and you—and yet, Boyang knew, he himself could not be exempted. One life had ended, and none of them was innocent. That must be something, no? How many people by the waterfront had murderous thoughts now and then, dark ghosts casting shadows on their minds, from which they had to look away? How many had succeeded in a murder?

Boyang walked for an extra few minutes to calm himself and turn his attention to his upcoming date. When he finally approached Sizhuo from the unlit side of the street, he could see that she had already locked up the shop. Standing right outside a pool of orange light from a nearby street lamp, she was not sending text messages on her cell phone; nor was she impatiently looking left and right for his late arrival. From her posture—straight backed, still as a statue, her eyes looking ahead although they must be seeing little in the darkness—he could not tell if she was used to waiting for others, or if she had never been in that position, waiting not having worn out her patience.

8

"Please know that every day I live for when I come to you. Please let the strangers around me remain strangers. They don't know you, and they pity me because they don't know you."

Ruyu stopped, sensing something had gone awry. She used to love this last moment of her day, when nothing stood between God—her future—and herself: even her grandaunts, who had retreated behind the curtain to have their private conversation with him, did not matter for the time being. Ruyu did not know, however, that believing was the only way for her grandaunts to maintain their dignity in a life that had taken too much from them: the death, too early, of a weak-willed mother, the disappearance of a brother for whom they had exhausted their love and hope, properties confiscated, privilege of belonging to the Church deprived. The world was a bleak stopover for the sisters, in which they, armed against it with a religion that had become more of their own making as time passed, were either unaware of the shadow they had cast in an orphan's life or else regarded it as irrelevant; she, in turn, her pupils adjusted to a perennial dusk, deemed what she perceived in their formidable shadow the only life worth living, sterility mistaken for purity, aloofness for devoutness.

Since Ruyu had come to Beijing, however, the calm brought by her conversation with God had vanished. Could it be that he was keeping himself distant just as a test? Or was it possible that he had stayed behind, leaving her among strangers? Pleas made to him, love and loyalty expressed repeatedly and desperately—these, unacknowledged, were strewn around her, corpses of unwanted words like those dead flies when summer ended. How odd, Ruyu thought now, that other insects would disappear when winter came, but flies would drop dead on windowsills or at the corners of a room, not allowed to escape, even in death, their ugliness displayed publicly.

Perhaps there's a reason for that, as there's a reason for anything; her grandaunts would say God alone knows what it is. But if God could forsake the flies and deprive them of private deaths, how could she know if she was different in his eyes from those flies? Her grandaunts had never had doubts in God, but what if they had made a mistake—what if he, like her parents, found little merit in her to keep her?

A panic hit Ruyu with such violence that she felt as though she were being attacked by a physical force, her breath taken away by an acute pain. She opened her eyes and unclasped her hands, yet nothing had changed in her surroundings: the lamp on the desk was shining steadily; the gloved hands of Mickey Mouse on the clock face moved forward by even leaps. She was alone in the bedroom she shared with Shaoai, her back to the entrance, the curtain undisturbed. Uncle and Aunt had already gone to bed. Grandpa had been fed the sleeping pill that would keep him quiet through the night. Shaoai and a friend of hers from college were in the living room watching TV with the volume turned low. From the open window, Ruyu heard the startled cry of a cicada, with desperate urgency, before it went silent. The first autumn crickets chirped in the grass, their night song melancholy.

Ruyu ordered herself to focus. Any minute now, Shaoai and her friend Yening might turn off the television and come into the bedroom. Yening had returned from her hometown on a late-afternoon train for the new semester at the university, and she was going to spend the night with them before moving back into her dorm. It had seemed natural to all that the bed Ruyu shared with Shaoai—a double bed—would be just fine for the three girls.

"Please forgive me, and please give me courage to be worthy of your love," Ruyu started again, though her fear that she was a nuisance to him was growing more intense. She remained in the same position without opening her eyes, waiting for the fierce pain she was experiencing to pass, all the while knowing that the pain could be nothing but his punishment. He had seen all there was to see, and he would be seeing to it that all would be well for her. Why, then, was she still asking him every day for strength, which she should have had by now? Wouldn't he be irritated by her failure to live up to his standards; wouldn't he be burdened by her neediness; by her love, which she did not have a way to show; by her constantly asking more from him, always asking, always?

Soundlessly someone entered the room, but only when she dropped a pillow on the bed did Ruyu sense her presence. Ruyu turned around abruptly to face Yening, who was sitting on the bed, her eyes fixed on Ruyu yet unfocused, perhaps seeing nothing but phantoms in her own mind. At dinner, Ruyu had noticed that Yening, a tall and wispy girl, had been courteous toward everyone but had not eaten or talked much. Aunt had not bombarded her with questions, nor had she pushed more food onto the guest; though, nervous, with her incessant chattering, Aunt had been stupider than ever. Ruyu had noticed—and having a visitor among them confirmed her observation—that Aunt seemed superstitiously fearful of quiet, as though any moment not filled with some kind of back-and-forth indicated a failure on her part, or worse, some sort of impending disaster.

"I thought you were watching TV with Shaoai," Ruyu said when the older girl did not speak or avert her stare. There was something in Yening that Ruyu found unsettling, but she was too young to know the reason: the older girl occupied the same impertinent role in life as Ruyu did; the hardest loss is to be defeated by one's own strategy in others' hands.

Yening shrugged. From the living room they could hear Shaoai change channels. "What were you doing when I came in?" Yening asked.

"Nothing."

"You can't be doing nothing."

"I was only sitting here and thinking."

"Thinking of what? Or whom?"

Ruyu shrugged, then realized that she had just learned the distasteful gesture from Yening.

"Were you, by any chance, talking to your god? Shaoai said you conversed with your god more than you conversed with us mortals," Yening said, choosing her words with a malicious care.

Ruyu stared back. Yening waited, and when no reply came, she pointed to the accordion case in the corner of the room with her chin. "Is that your accordion?"

"Yes."

"I heard no one around here could make you condescend to play."

Ruyu wondered if Shaoai had sent her friend in to humiliate her. Why else would Shaoai even talk to her friend about Ruyu? Shaoai did not like Ruyu, that much was clear: she seldom talked to Ruyu, which was, in fact, fine because Shaoai rarely talked to anyone these days without making sharp comments. But at night she never seemed to tire of putting on a show of hostility and disgust. She waited until Ruyu went to bed and then would turn off the light while continuing to read with a handheld lamp, furiously turning pages and sometimes ending her reading by throwing the book out of the mosquito netting so that it dropped on the floor with a thud. Ruyu, who got up as early as possible—fortunately, Shaoai never woke up early enough to trap Ruyu with another round of confrontational displays—sometimes stole a glance at the book on the floor if the cover was facing up. For several days in a row it was a book called *The Second Sex* by someone named de Beauvoir; the book's title made Ruyu uncomfortable, and once she knew its yellow spine and dog-eared look, she avoided looking at the title even if it was staring back at her from the floor. There were other books too, thinner, all with disagreeable titles: *Nausea, The Flies, The Plague*. One book, though, had caught Ruyu's attention — *The Confessions of a Child of the Century*; she would like to know what the book was about, but she dared not move a page for fear that Shaoai would wake up and catch her.

"I played the piano at your age," Yening said. Ridiculous, Ruyu thought, her speaking as though they were from different generations. "I practiced all the time. I didn't have enough time, though, and wouldn't have minded having forty-eight hours a day for piano. I'm surprised, according to our friend out there, that you haven't touched your instrument since you came."

"The accordion is a loud instrument."

"All instruments are loud."

"I don't want to disturb Grandpa."

"How do you know you can even disturb him?" Yening said, and then softened her voice. "I'm worried that you'll lose your touch if you don't practice every day."

"I can wait until school starts. Moran said there's a music room in the school."

"Still, your neighbors must think you're too haughty to play for them."

"Nobody thinks that," Ruyu protested.

"How can you be so certain?" Yening asked, opening her eyes innocently before narrowing them again. "You're too young to know anything. You don't know half of what people think of you," she said with the dismissive gentleness people reserve for crippled animals and dead babies.

Ruyu flinched. Indeed, quite a few neighbors had asked her to perform an evening concert for the quadrangle. She'd shaken her head politely at the requests and wondered why people were persistent in their efforts to make her do things that she had made clear she would not do. She neither liked nor disliked the accordion, which had been chosen for her by her grandaunts. In fact, the instrument suited her poorly. Its bulky body felt like an inelegant extension of her chest. Sounds coming from it were too loud, the music she played — polkas and waltzes from places she imagined as being perennially sunny — too cheerful. Back home, she sometimes practiced by pressing the keyboards without unbuttoning the bellows; only then could she see herself as a musician, the silent tunes an extension of her thoughts, heard by nobody, heeded by no one.

"What charming, endearing innocence," Yening said, smiling to herself as if savoring the comment, but before Ruyu replied, she started to pat her pillow. "Which side of the bed do you take?" she said, her face all of a sudden frosty, as though she had exhausted her goodwill and wished to be left alone.

Later, lying awake, Ruyu heard Shaoai climb into bed between her and Yening. Neither of the girls was pleasant, and Ruyu wondered how they'd become friends. Or perhaps that was how things had to be for those two, one person's edge constantly cutting into the other person's edge, those who hurt others seeking likewise to be hurt.

Much later, Ruyu was awakened by an angry exchange of whispers. She did not know what time it was or how long the quarrel had been going on. She stayed as still as she could and kept her breathing even, and soon it became clear that the two girls were arguing about a boy.

"Let him go off to be a monk," Shaoai said, "if he doesn't have the courage to stand up for himself."

"It's not a question of courage. The question is, what's better for him?"

"Or should we ask what's better for you? Certainly it'd be harder for you to seduce him if he shaves his head and lives in a temple."

"That's distasteful, Shaoai."

"I don't think truth ever tastes good to anyone's palate."

"But you're unfairly harsh toward him because you're jealous of him."

"Jealous is the wrong word," Shaoai said. "He's not worthy of my jealousy."

"Of course not," Yening said. "Any boy I lay my eyes on is a low creature for you. All you want is for me to love no one, and to be stuck with you."

"If it feels that way, you are welcome to get yourself unstuck any time."

"Certainly you'd say so, now that you have a cute and dumb girl sharing your bed."

Both girls were quiet for a moment, and then Ruyu felt a slight breeze on her cheek as Yening lifted the mosquito netting. "Where are you going?" Shaoai asked. Yening did not answer, and a moment later Ruyu heard her tattered slippers going off toward the living room. She waited for the bell on top of the door to jingle, but it did not.

"Have you eavesdropped enough?" Shaoai said, her voice low but not whispering.

Ruyu stayed still.

"I know you're awake," Shaoai said. "Just so you don't misunderstand the situation: the boy we were talking about used to be a friend of mine, too, but now he's worried about disciplinary action against him for what he did in the protest. His parents arranged for him to leave the university and go to a temple for a while. Imagine that. To be exempt from secular matters."

Please make her stop. Please make her vanish, because she doesn't matter to you, and so she doesn't matter to me.

"I guess all you need to know is that Yening and I disagreed about his decision," Shaoai said. "She thinks it's a good idea. She thinks any idea that saves his ass is a good idea. But then she feels miserable about letting him go into a world where she has no right to be. Wouldn't it be nicer if she could be his personal temple?"

The bitterness in Shaoai's words was too much. "I didn't ask you to tell me," Ruyu said.

"I'm telling you to spare you the extra time you'd spend dwelling on it," Shaoai said. "Now you know the whole story; you'd better forget it tomorrow."

Yet there was more to it, Ruyu knew, but that mattered little to her because it was not her position to discern the true from the untrue: secrets of any kind breed ugliness. Ruyu felt an uncleanness clinging to her the way she had read in books a leech attached itself to a body.

"Though, to think about it, maybe it wouldn't be a bad thing for you to know a little more about how the world works," Shaoai said. "Who knows what your grandaunts have done to taint you?"

"You don't even know them," Ruyu said.

"Do I want to know them?" Shaoai retorted. "From how they've brought you up, I would advise that a young person should run the moment she sees them."

Back home when Ruyu had seen people exchange mocking looks behind her grandaunts' backs, she had learned not to feel bothered: none of those people understood her grandaunts, and, more important, her grandaunts did not need the understanding of others. She wished she could now treat Shaoai's chatter as one of those irrelevant voices, but Shaoai seemed to have made up her mind not to be dismissed. "Now let me explain to you what I mean," Shaoai said. "What do you think of Yening? Is she a good person in your eyes? Would she be a good person in your grandaunts' opinion?"

"She's your friend," Ruyu said. "Why do you need my opinion?"

"See, your answer proves my exact point. Before she's my friend, she is a being *out there*, a *fact*; anyone should be able to form an opinion of her. My mother thinks her eccentric. My father probably thinks of her as a spoiled child, as I am. Our very cowardly friend—the would-be monk—thinks she is wickedly attractive and wants her to wait for him to finish his stint in the temple so he can marry her. But you, what's your opinion? All you do is look at her coldly and say to yourself: she has nothing to do with me. And then she becomes nothing to you. Do you see that? There is a human being there, whom you, with whatever absurd logic your grandaunts have given you, turn into a non-being."

Ruyu felt as though she were being swept into an abyss by Shaoai's words, which were ludicrous yet had the irresistible force of insanity. "But it's true that Yening and I have nothing to do with each other," she said, but realized her error right away. To give up a position of silence, to allow oneself to be engaged—already she was allowing Shaoai what she did not deserve.

"You missed my point," Shaoai said. "I am only using her as an example. Or maybe she is the wrong example. But those people shot dead in Tiananmen Square? Have you found yourself thinking, for even a moment, about them or their families? Have you asked Moran or Boyang about what they have seen or heard? No, and no, because those dead people have nothing to do with you; hence, they are nothing to you. Rest assured, you are not the only one who maintains that stance. More and more people will choose that attitude now that a revolution has been crushed, but that does not exempt you. In fact, I have to say, you must have been born a heartless person, or else you must have been thoroughly brainwashed by your grandaunts. Either way, I find your lack of interest in anything but your own little faith to be more than horrifying. Of course you can shrug your dainty shoulders and say, what does your opinion have to do with me?"

Ruyu did not speak when Shaoai finished her monologue. Her silence seemed to infuriate Shaoai even more. "Well?" she said. "Have you made up your mind not to condescend to answer me?"

"What do you want me to say?" Ruyu said.

"It's not what I want you to say. It's what you want to say for yourself. Come on, defend yourself. Defend your grandaunts. Let's at least have some fair play."

"My grandaunts don't need me to defend them."

"And you yourself?"

"I'm fine with your thinking of me as anything, or nothing," Ruyu said, and was relieved to hear Yening's shuffling steps nearing the bedroom. Before Shaoai could find more words, Yening entered the room. "Why the silence all of a sudden?" she said to the dark room, laughing lightly. "I thought you two were having a good time."

The next day, Shaoai helped Yening move back into her dorm, and when she did not return for dinner, Aunt wondered aloud if she had missed Shaoai saying that she was going to move back into the dorm that day, too. "You'd think I wouldn't miss something so important," Aunt said to Uncle, who comforted her, and said he himself had missed it too, if that indeed was Shaoai's plan.

When Aunt asked Ruyu, she said she didn't know of any such plan, either. Perhaps in Shaoai's eyes, Ruyu was like one of those birds that occupied another bird's nest; but the thought did not bring Ruyu any remorse, nor did it diminish her relief that soon Shaoai would move out of the house, and she would have a bedroom to herself.

Just as the dinner was ending, Shaoai returned and with a stern face announced that she had decided to commute for the new semester. Uncle and Aunt exchanged a nervous look. "Did any school official talk to you?" Aunt asked.

"No."

"Does that mean everything will be all right?"

"Nothing is ever all right, if you ask me," Shaoai said.

"But the school—will they . . . will you . . ." Aunt tried in vain to find the right words.

"You're worried that I'll be expelled? And I won't graduate and won't have a job and will remain a burden to you forever?" Shaoai said. "Let me say this: there are worse things in the world than not graduating with a useless degree in international trade and relations."

Aunt and Uncle watched as Shaoai stormed back to her bedroom. Had there been a door, Ruyu thought, Shaoai would have banged it

shut as befitting her drama, and, as though the same thought had occurred to Shaoai, she came out of the bedroom and said that it was
stuffy in the house and she was going for a walk. Aunt glanced at the
clock on the wall and was about to say something, but Uncle shook
his head discreetly at her. A moment later, the door was slammed
shut; the bell on top, unconstrained, swung back and forth furiously.

No one said anything, but when Aunt looked up and caught
Ruyu's eyes, she sighed and said she wished that they could offer her
a more peaceful stay, and that Shaoai were a better companion. "Had
your grandaunts known what kind of failures we are as parents, they
might not have sent you to us," Aunt said, looking dejected.

"Every family has a book of challenging fate written out for them,"
Uncle said, solicitously looking up at Ruyu, pleading for her to agree
with the cliché, so she did, saying that Aunt should not think too
much, and that everything would turn out all right in the end. Eager
to believe someone—preferably someone other than her husband—
Aunt seemed to have found comfort in Ruyu's words, and repeated
the saying herself as though to further console the other two in the
room. When Grandpa made the noises demanding his supper, Aunt
sprang into action. With a tender sadness, Uncle watched Aunt fill a
bowl of gruel, adding soft, fermented tofu on top. At least they had
each other, Ruyu thought, just as her grandaunts had each other.

When Aunt was out of the room, Uncle said to the half-empty
platters on the table, "It's kind of you to be understanding."

For a moment Ruyu wondered if Uncle, who so rarely initiated a
conversation, was in fact talking to her. She looked at him, but he
only smiled at the unfinished dishes, the same way he smiled when
the neighbors teased someone in the yard, or when Aunt complained
about the weather. Ruyu did not know if he expected an answer from
her.

"Shaoai has been headstrong from the very beginning," Uncle
continued. "A difficult baby, you would say. We talked about having

another child after her—Aunt wanted another one—but I was so frightened that I could not imagine having to go through everything a second time."

"But you might have had a different child," Ruyu said. "I've heard people say that siblings from the same parents can have opposite temperaments."

Uncle sighed. "Many told us that, too, but I didn't believe them. To be honest, I now regret my stubbornness. If we had had a second child, he or she might have made it easier for us now, don't you think? At least Shaoai would have learned how to be nice to someone younger than she. We're sorry that she doesn't really consider you part of the family."

Ruyu shook her head as though to say that these things did not matter. Had Uncle and Aunt had another child—a boy, for instance—her grandaunts might have thought the household unfit for Ruyu. She would then have been sent to another place to live, with a different set of people . . . but it was useless to pursue such thoughts. She stood up and said she would put the leftovers away if Uncle had finished his meal.

The last days of summer were always sunny. The August heat, already abating, was still intense enough to create an illusion of never-endedness—of a moment, a day, a season. Cicadas, stubborn creatures, having spent long years underground, would not forsake their posts in the trees; yet their days were numbered: dusk muted their singing and brought, along with the first breeze of the evening, the autumnal song of the crickets.

One leaf drops and you know autumn is here; on the morning of the last day of August, Ruyu heard Boyang's grandmother exchange the cliché with a neighbor in the courtyard. The season's end seemed to have brought out the sentimental side of people, as though everyone was preparing for a small part of himself to die with the summer lives. Watermelon Wen, upon hearing the old woman's words, chanted in a drawn-out falsetto an opera passage about an old general's grief over a tree that had aged during his fifty-year war career; Wen's twin boys imitated their father from behind the screen door and then fell to giggling, cutting the performance short and diluting the sadness.

Wait until you fall in love with the autumn in Beijing, neighbors kept telling Ruyu, or else they would say, wait until you fall in love with Beijing this autumn. The notion that someone would fall in love with a place or a time was new to Ruyu; she might have tolerated it better were it not for the certainty of everyone about how she should feel. A season was a season for her—no more, no less, because that was the way time was for her grandaunts, each day a replica of the previous day; a place, any place, was merely a spot for resting during one's migration from beginning to end. Only in a drama would an old man lay his hand on the coarse bark of a tree and mourn in advance his own death; in real life, a man's grief for himself was as wordless as the dim light in Grandpa's eyes, the passing days pooling into a stale puddle around his dying body.

On the morning of August 31, Boyang roped Ruyu's accordion onto the back of his bicycle, and Moran sat astride her bicycle, balancing it with both legs and waiting for Aunt to finish talking with Ruyu so that she could hop onto the rear rack. It was the day the entering class was to register at the high school. In addition to a general admissions letter, Aunt handed Ruyu a note directing her to meet the music teacher after registration.

The school, No. 135, occupied an old temple. Its spacious, park-like yard was dotted with ancient elms and mulberry bushes, the well-designed garden in its center long since taken over by wildflowers and ivy. Several rows of rudely constructed, single-story brick buildings had been added as classrooms and dorms, giving the campus the look of a hastily planned people's commune. The temple itself, which was occupied by the administrators and the teachers, had been split into two levels and divided into offices with thin walls, though signs of the original architecture—the high ceiling, the round wooden pillars, and the long narrow windows—remained visible. Inside, it was perennially dark: the walls and the ceilings retained their wooden panels painted a deep brown; the floor was the original brick one, gray and uneven and in places repaired with a patch of cement. Fluorescent tubes buzzed in the hallway and inside the offices. There was nothing to love, Ruyu reflected, about this new school.

Moran and Boyang seemed elated that all three of them were assigned to the same homeroom. After registering, they took her to meet Teacher Shu, the music instructor. The music room was in a cottage at the far end of campus, which Boyang said once served as sleeping quarters for the monks' visiting family members. Ruyu imagined Shaoai's friend Yening in a similar cottage at another temple, the boy she was in love with wearing a long, drab robe and counting his beads silently while she poured her heart out. How odd, Ruyu thought, finding oneself in a place that had no relevance to one's life but was necessary for the time being: her grandaunts would not have any idea that she would be schooled in a former Buddhist temple.

Teacher Shu was one of the ugliest men Ruyu had ever met. Short, bald, with an unevenly shaven face and a pair of round eyes that were so wide open they seemed never in need of blinking, he reminded her of an owl with ruffled feathers, more clueless than menacing. When he smiled, he did so with unadorned glee, showing teeth that had been yellowed by smoking. "I've been waiting for you," he said when Ruyu presented herself, and waved a dismissive hand at Boyang and Moran, who dutifully left the music room but lingered on the porch, leaving the door ajar.

Ruyu played "The Song of Spanish Bullfighters" and "The Blue Danube"; when asked to keep on, she played a couple of polkas. She had not practiced for a month, and her fingers, though not uncertain, stumbled a few times at places they had not before. Teacher Shu nodded with a pensive look, and when she stopped, he asked to take a look at her accordion.

The instrument, a 120-bass model made by Parrot Accordion—the most coveted model of the best brand name, for which Ruyu's grandaunts had paid a black market price when she had turned nine—seemed to impress him more than either Ruyu's performance or her grade 8 certificate, which she had brought to show him. He touched the head of the golden parrot with a finger, and then wiped his fingerprint away with his sleeve. Could he have a try, he asked. Yes, Ruyu said, and refrained from looking at his cigarette-stained, stubby fingers as he buckled the instrument and loosened the straps.

"How long have you played?"

"Six years."

Teacher Shu said that six years was not bad for a girl her age. "Do your parents play any instruments?" he asked, but before Ruyu could think of a proper reply, he launched into "The Song of Mongolian Herdsmen," his unsightly right hand moving up and down the keyboard like a showy dancer, his left hand pulling and pressing the bellows with an effortless rhythm. In the middle of his performance, a tall, sinewy woman approached the entrance. Moran and Boyang, who had been leaning against the door frame, quickly straightened and made way for the woman. She took a seat in a nearby chair and watched Teacher Shu, her face softening without showing a definite smile. When he finished the song, she introduced herself as Headmistress Liu. Later, when Ruyu got to know Teacher Shu better, he would tell her stories about Headmistress Liu when nobody was around, how she had remained unmarried to fulfill her ambition of becoming a top educator, how underneath her stern and intimidating appearance, she was a kind woman without many people close to her.

"See, that's how you play the accordion. It's a one-man band, and you have to be a bit of everything yourself. You have to know how to sing and whisper and bellow and talk and croon and even weep," Teacher Shu said, unstrapping the accordion and handing it carefully to Ruyu. "Imagine yourself as one of those bullfighters, and a giant bull is charging at you. What feeling does it give you when you launch into the song?"

Ruyu stared at him. She did not know if it was a question requiring an answer from her.

Teacher Shu scratched his head. "Well, that may be asking too much of you. All right, you can't be a bullfighter. But picture yourself in a long, sweeping dress being waltzed around a ballroom in Vienna," Teacher Shu said, and hummed a few measures of the "Blue Danube" and swirled himself around, his arms held up properly, his chin lifted. Boyang laughed, but was right away stopped by Moran.

"Now, how does your body move in a dance like that?" Teacher Shu said when he circled back and stopped in front of Ruyu.

"I don't know how to dance."

"You don't have to know. Just imagine. Think of yourself as Princess Sissi. Think of yourself as Romy Schneider in Sissi's shoes," Teacher Shu said. "Do you know the movie I'm talking about?"

"No."

Teacher Shu paused, and then made a gesture of resignation.

Ruyu wondered if she had failed her interview. Apart from Teacher Shu and her former accordion teacher, an older man her grandaunts had paid to teach her twice a week, she had not met another musician and had not given much thought to music or to those who played it. She neither liked nor disliked music, as liking or disliking anything in life was beside the point. She could just as easily have become a chess master or a painter or a ballet dancer—anything that would have differentiated her from her peers in the provincial city. That music had been chosen for her, that the accordion had been the instrument—these things Ruyu had accepted because they were part of the necessities of her life. She did not see the point of imagining herself into a princess's body.

Teacher Shu nodded to Headmistress Liu, and they withdrew to a small office adjacent to the music room. Moran beckoned to Ruyu, and she hesitated and then moved closer to the door, carrying the accordion case with her. "Isn't Teacher Shu the most fun person?" Moran said.

"Is he?" Ruyu said.

Moran blushed. "Oh, he may look off-putting at first, but trust me, he's really one of the best teachers."

"Just so you know," Boyang whispered to Ruyu, "Moran has had a crush on Teacher Shu for three years now."

"Hey," Moran said. "Hey!"

"And Teacher Shu is not married," Boyang said, still addressing Ruyu but grinning at Moran, who was about to say something when Teacher Shu and Headmistress Liu came out. He handed a folder of music sheets to Ruyu and told her that he would teach her every Tuesday at four, starting the following week. She was welcome to leave the instrument there, too, he said, and handed her two keys, a small one for the security room where all the instruments were kept, and a big copper one for the cottage door.

Ruyu's grandaunts had not said anything about accordion lessons, and she wondered if she would have to explain to Teacher Shu that she did not have money to pay him. Would that affect her status at school? Later she voiced her doubt to Moran and Boyang. "Why would you pay him if you're a student at the school?" Boyang said.

"Why else should he teach me?" Ruyu said, and explained that at home her teacher was paid ten yuan every time he taught her, plus round-trip fare for the bus.

"Doesn't Teacher Shu get a salary from the school?" Moran said.

"But is the school going to pay him extra to teach me?" Ruyu said. "I could've not come here. He would've earned the same salary without the bother of teaching me, no?"

Moran turned to look closely at Ruyu, but her face was inscrutable as always. Ruyu's concern sounded sensible, but Moran could not help but think something was wrong with Ruyu's logic. There was more to life than money, Moran wanted to explain to Ruyu, and in

her mind she could do it well, patiently, as when she had had to resolve a conflict between two neighborhood kids. Like the other families in the quadrangle, Moran's family was not well-off, but their
struggles were the same ones experienced by most people they knew,
of having to calculate well to make ends meet, of spreading the ration
of eggs, meat, and other food wisely throughout the month. Even so,
Moran's parents never failed to make extra dumplings to give to
neighbors or to share the fresh fruit her father sometimes got free
from working with those in the quadrangle. This kindness was returned by others, too, and the life Moran knew, which took place as
much within her family as outside it with neighbors and friends, was
not one in which wealth, or the lack of wealth, was much thought of
as an important factor. But even as Moran went over this argument in
her mind, she knew it was not merely Ruyu's monetary concern that
unsettled her. To envision Teacher Shu's life without her seemed
natural for Ruyu; it must be equally easy for her to imagine a life
without Teacher Shu, or, for that matter, without Boyang and Moran
herself. Moran, who did not know what was out of her reach, unconsciously moved closer to Ruyu, as though looking for reassurance.

"If you ask me . . ." Boyang said.

"But nobody is asking you," Moran snapped, taking both of them
by surprise.

"All right, even if you're not asking me, I say let's not worry ourselves about this," Boyang said. Things, he added, would work out
one way or another, and instead of standing in front of the school gate
like three idiotic new students, how about going to the Back Sea,
renting a boat for the rest of the afternoon, and enjoying the last day
of summer before going back to the cage?

"The *cage*?" Moran said. "If your parents heard you talk about
school like that, they would take you into their charge."

"Then I'd be in trouble for real," Boyang said, pantomiming a
caged monkey and emitting bitter screams.

Ruyu watched his performance, and when she did not smile as Moran did, Boyang asked Ruyu if she was still worrying about her accordion lesson. She shook her head. "How do you know you're not in a cage here and now?" she asked.

"Ha ha, you've got me," Boyang said. "The best jokes are always told by people like you, who don't even smile when they say funny things."

Moran glanced at Boyang, and brought up the boating proposal again. The day, with its bright sun still high in the cloudless sky, had taken on an unreal quality. The glimpses Ruyu had seen of their coming school life, when Boyang and Moran had shown her the campus, seemed strangely distant from what they were used to in the summer. Classrooms, newly painted, with chairs still resting on top of the desks, their legs pointing upward and forming a small metal forest, had looked familiar yet unwelcoming; the science annex, where in one room Bunsen burners clustered on a bench next to the door, and in another a few new posters covered up old ones, the insides of frogs and human beings vividly portrayed, had felt cold and lifeless; next to the track field, a gym teacher had been hosing down a few cement Ping-Pong tables; at the far end of campus, the students who boarded at the dorms had already moved in, and a few colorful blankets were airing out on the clotheslines; two girls had been standing at the entrance to a dorm, looking perplexed: one of them had placed her thermos a little too close to the edge of the steps, and it had fallen, almost soundlessly, hot water pouring down the steps, steaming along the way.

All excitements were pointing to tomorrow, when actions and interactions would decide who each of them would be in a new grade, among a new group of people; today thus became a vacuum, having turned into nothing before its time.

Listlessly, Moran looked at Ruyu, hoping she'd agree to the impromptu outing, dreading that she would say no. Spending the day alone, at least for Moran, seemed unimaginable: rarely was a day in her life passed without Boyang; yet with or without their companionship, Ruyu seemed undisturbed all the same.

"Another day by the lake?" Ruyu asked, though her tone was as vague as her face, and Moran could not detect any preference.

Moran and Boyang could easily cycle to their favorite spot by the lake, hop into a rowboat, and spend the rest of the afternoon afloat, listening to the cicadas in the trees, watching the peddlers in the alleyways, and talking about trifles, but this prospect, which a month ago would have been the perfect picture of a summer day, with its familiar mindlessness, now felt incomplete, as though by entering their world, Ruyu had made it smaller. Already the three of them felt, at least to Moran, more of a unit than just Boyang and herself. "Do come along," Moran said, and the begging note in her own voice made her shiver slightly in the shade of the trees.

9

Twice Moran had read through her employees' manual, but an ex-spouse's sickness, however terminal, was not listed as a legitimate reason for an extended leave. This was not unexpected, though it reminded her again that, when a death was pending, all connections but those defined by blood or marriage were dismissed as inconsequential. She wondered what other options there were. Or perhaps the idea of a leave was too greedy: deaths, like memories, required one's entire heart, leaving little space for negotiation.

On a piece of paper, Moran listed things that she needed to look into, possible expenditures, and resources available. She had some vacation time saved—other than the annual holiday trip with her parents, she rarely took time off. The lease to the house would expire at the end of next August, but if she was unable to sublet the place, she could keep making payments from afar. Her savings account would last her two years or longer; she had always lived simply, and would continue to do so after the move. Her portfolios had posted some minor gains, as she was a conservative investor, unambitious and thus mostly unscathed by the recent financial recession. Her company's stock, which she had accumulated some shares of over the years, she would hold on to as emergency backup. These concrete things— numbers and columns and lists—calmed Moran, as they gave this evening a purposefulness that was absent on other evenings. She would keep her car, a secondhand Saab; and she would keep her clothes and those few things she had grown attached to. The house could be cleaned out more or less with a weekend tag sale; what she could not sell she would drop off at the Goodwill store downtown. Back in the Midwest she would not need a place the size of her current rental; she could easily get by with a studio apartment. Already she could envision the place; no, not the place in its physical reality, but its imperturbable solitude, which had become a necessity for her, a habitat.

It comforted Moran that many things could be done, and they would be done without complications or difficulties. Sixteen years earlier she had come to this country with two suitcases, in which she had packed everything she had imagined necessary to begin a new life: clothes, a quilt and a pillow pressed and bound tightly to make space, two bowls, a pair of chopsticks, a folding knife, a meat cleaver, two tins of tea leaves, an umbrella, two packs of sanitary napkins, and a Chinese-English dictionary. What she could not fit into her luggage—her Sony Walkman and her many cassettes, her books, a few girlhood diaries, and the single photo album her mother had put together, containing pictures and snapshots from different stages of her life—those her mother had promised to keep safe until she came home the next time. But she had not gone back to reclaim them—*people rarely reclaim what they have lost,* somewhere she read that; *they only replace them.* Her parents, when it had become clear that she might never do so, had brought with them the photo album and the diaries on one visit to America. Moran had put them away without taking a look inside.

After the divorce, Moran moved again with the same two suitcases and an even smaller collection of things. All that had mattered she'd left behind. Her ring she had returned to Josef; the thought that he had two pairs of rings to discard, or to keep, made her heart ache, yet she did not know what to do—nor did she want—to alleviate her own pain, as it must have hurt Josef more. The wedding photos and the snapshots taken on their honeymoon—a week off the coast of South Carolina (Josef had proposed the Bahamas, though Moran's Chinese passport at the time had made it hard to travel anywhere outside the States)—she had asked Josef to keep with his family pictures. You travel so lightly, he had said when he dropped her off at the airport, his blue eyes filled with gentle sadness, though what he had meant, what had really let him down, was that she *took* everything so lightly. Blame that on the mental state of an immigrant, she had said, a ready excuse she had used again and again as she continued to live in a state that in Josef's and other people's eyes should have been transitory but had acquired a permanency over the years. To be able, at any moment, to pull up roots minimally put down, to be able to exit without being noticed or missed—these things gave her an odd sense of virginal freedom. *Anything concerning the heart leaves it in confusion;* she had found this motto in one of the Buddhist books she had read after Shaoai's poisoning; *to desire nothing is to have no vulnerability.*

But how many hearts could truly succeed in keeping themselves immune to all that would make them susceptible? With discipline Moran had lived in unperturbed calm since the divorce; no, even in her marriage she had longed for nothing but placidity. But peace like that was only a locked gate, and more than anyone, Josef had been gently pointing it out to her, not pushing it, yet not pretending he hadn't seen it, either. Was that why she had broken her wedding vow? Moran had married Josef for all she could inherit from his past—his friends, children, and grandchildren—so that she would not have to build a life of her own; she had thought the crowdedness of his world would allow a young wife to exist quietly, and his first marriage, long and happy, would provide enough of a sheltering shadow for her to be nothing more than a replacement. Yet she had been proven wrong. Josef had not taken marriage as lightly as she had. Life, fair as it is, unexpectedly so at times, sets up trapping webs for even the most inconspicuous creature: Moran, panicked at the predicament in which she had found herself—love offered where she had asked only for kindness—would not have spared a limb or two in her scrambling to get herself untangled, and in doing so she had left a few scratches on Josef's life, too. Any wound deeper than that she would not allow herself to believe. The thought that she could be ruthless was too much for her to bear: ruthlessness was a trait she associated with Bo-yang, and before him, Ruyu; before her, no one, as in those days, blinded by her eagerness to love, Moran had found the world a loving place.

Moran had met Josef at the county jail the first year she'd been living in America, on a tour organized by a local church group to introduce international students to the American legal system. The group had sponsored other gatherings—potlucks in the park, free English lessons on Tuesday and Thursday nights, and a fundraising concert for the church—but Moran had not gone to any of them.

There had been only four students—two boys from India and a young couple from Thailand—when Moran arrived at the jail. A man, pudgy, bald, and dressed soberly in a dark-colored jacket, came in a few minutes later and introduced himself as Josef. He said that the woman who was in charge had come down with the stomach flu, so he'd had to step in to help.

The sheriff hosting the tour seemed undeterred by the less than promising attendance. His initial remarks in the lobby lasted almost an hour, during which he gave a detailed account of his being shot at by a teenager, of the psychological trauma he'd had to overcome, of the everyday challenges a law-enforcement officer had to face, of America and its justice.

The Thai couple smiled and nodded, their hands clasped behind their backs. The two Indian boys gallantly volunteered when the sheriff produced handcuffs with which to demonstrate the more painful and the less painful way of being arrested, depending on one's willingness to cooperate. Moran wondered if she could slip away, but Josef, standing behind his charges, dutifully blocked her way to the exit. Once again she read the visiting hours posted on the wall, which she had already memorized. It was a Saturday, the only day that the inmates were not allowed visitors. A needle of pain pulsed in Moran's head, but surely there was more in life for one to endure than an afternoon in a county jail, which would, at some point, come to an end.

Once the sheriff unlocked the metal gate, both a relief and a hushed reverence settled over the foreign tourists. Through the barred door of a low-security cell, they saw a few men in orange outfits sitting around a table playing cards, none of them looking up at the procession in the hallway. All sorts of reasons, the sheriff answered when the Thai couple guiltily asked what had brought the inmates here. In an unoccupied cell the sheriff showed them a metal toilet with neither a lid nor a seat, and a brown mattress folded up in a corner. With a tape measure he demonstrated the size of the window, not wide enough for the skinniest man to climb through, yet offering a plentiful view of the world outside: the bare tops of the trees, the low, lead-colored clouds in the sky.

One of the four high-security cells was occupied, and the sheriff stopped in front of the door to give an introduction. He unlocked the inspection window and peeked inside before locking it again. A woman's voice could be heard, whimpering, then screaming, then lowering again to a whimper. A metal basket affixed to the door frame held a toothbrush and a tiny tube of toothpaste.

The Thai couple looked away, as though embarrassed on the sheriff's behalf. When he asked if anyone wanted to have a go at a straitjacket, which had been left outside the cell, neither of the sanguine Indian boys volunteered. A detour led them to the office, where the sheriff gave yet another long speech. By the time the group was released onto the chilly, empty sidewalk, it was dusk. In the orange light of the street lamps, big flakes of snow fell soundlessly, and already the world was covered by an undisturbed layer of whiteness.

It was the first time the Indian boys and the Thai couple had seen snow, so they all perked up, as though the afternoon had been a test they'd had to pass to earn this marvelous sight. The two parties soon disappeared, one trudging uphill, the other heading to the lake. For a moment, neither Moran nor Josef moved, both frozen in the dread of their separate loneliness. Then he asked her if she was all right, and suggested a cup of hot chocolate to recover from the dreadful tour.

At the café, Josef asked Moran where she had come from, what she was studying at the university, and whether she had experienced any cultural shock in America; Moran had a stock of ready answers to these questions, replies that would deter further questioning. When Josef ran out of questions, he told her that he did not belong to the church group, but that a couple who were longtime friends of his had been trying to interest him in the group's activities. "I hope you've enjoyed others more than today's," he said.

Moran said she had not been to any other event.

"So you wanted to see a jail?" Josef said. "But not a football game? Not Oktoberfest?"

Moran did not have an answer prepared, so she only shook her head, as though she, too, were baffled. She had made acquaintances in the new town but had been unwilling to befriend anyone; another girl from her college had come to Madison, too, for engineering school, but Moran had declined when the girl had asked her to be her roommate. When Josef continued waiting for an answer, she said that perhaps she had a negative view of life, and was drawn to the dark side of the world. She did not say that Oktoberfest and college football games did not interest her because they were things you went to with other people.

Josef looked at her more attentively. She wondered if he would ask for explanations, which she could not, and would not, give him. But Josef only gestured at her name tag and asked if Lara was a common Chinese name.

She'd decided to give herself an English name when she'd arrived in America because she thought it might be hard for Americans to pronounce her name, Moran replied, though that was only partially true. In the program where she was studying for a PhD in chemistry, she was known as Moran; in the Westlawn House, a three-story building offering rooms to women in science and technology, where Moran had a bedroom and shared a kitchen, bathroom, and living area with eight other women—two from Poland, three from Ukraine, two from Jordan on an exchange program, and one Canadian Korean—no one had any trouble saying her Chinese name. She used Lara only with strangers, like the young man managing the grill at the student cafeteria, and the cashier at the grocery store who had a hook for a hand and who so loved waving at Moran that she could not avoid checking out at his register. He had once been an alcoholic, he told Moran; he had lost both children to his ex-wife when they divorced, but before that he had lost his arm when he drove his car into a wall. Never touched a drop after that, he had said cheerfully, and always wished Lara a good stay in America as he punched her total into the register with his good hand.

Josef asked her something, and Moran, having missed the question, asked him to repeat it. "How did you decide on the name Lara?" he said again.

"I wanted something simple."

"But why Lara? Why not Lily or Nancy?"

Moran wondered if Josef was one of those tedious people who could grasp only things for which there were ready explanations. In college, Moran had halfheartedly dated two boys, and both had bored her with their efforts to reduce the world to a heap of things in need of sorting out. Moran wondered if Josef, in his youth, had likewise exasperated girls his age, but the man, unaware of Moran's scorn, waited patiently, his eyes limpid. It was the first time Moran had seen a pair of blue eyes at close distance.

"I borrowed the name from a Russian novel," Moran said.

"Not by any chance *Doctor Zhivago*?"

Moran looked up, surprised. "I wondered when you said your

name," Josef said, and started to hum "Lara's Theme." His voice, just loud enough for the two of them to hear, astonished Moran: its beauty and sadness seemed to belong to a different era, when men were handsome and women were beautiful and romance was accompanied by its own tune and a well-timed fade-out was the only trace of death.

"A song from my youth," Josef said when he finished.

"From mine, too," replied Moran. In her bedroom in Beijing, there was a box of novels, *Doctor Zhivago* among them, that she had been unwilling to sell but that she knew she would never go back to reread. The books had been her loyal companions for the last two years of high school. By then, Shaoai and her parents had moved away from the quadrangle. Ruyu, still attending the same high school, had become a boarding student and never said a word to Moran when they saw each other at school. Boyang's parents had taken him away, sending him to the high school affiliated with their university; on weekends, when he came to the quadrangle to visit his grandmother, Moran would either make up an excuse to be absent, or else stay in her bedroom, burying herself in one of the bulky novels translated from Russian or French. She had never been much of a reader of fiction before, but those novels, whose characters bore long and unmemorable names, had comforted her: even the most complicated stories offered a clarity that she could not find in the world around her, and each character came to an uncomplaining end, Doctor Zhivago giving up his life when he could not catch up with Lara in the street, Lara giving up happiness.

"You're still young," Josef said.

Moran wanted to retort that only a fool would look at age in such a simpleminded way. But the stranger was being kind, and being true to his observation. Moran was two months short of twenty-three. To be admired for one's youth when one had seen the dead end to which youth led—one might find solace in the admiration, yet it was not a sufficient diversion. Josef, at his age, could withdraw to the sanctuary of his memories, but Moran still had years, decades, ahead of her. She wished she were as old as Josef—having to live on when one had lived enough made one a weary impersonator of all that she was not.

Moran wiped the tabletop around her cup with the paper napkin, thinking that there must be a right reply to Josef's comment; only she did not know what it was. When she looked up again she realized that Josef must have said something, but the look on his face said that he didn't want to embarrass her by repeating it. To fill the silence, she asked him if he had been to a jail before.

It was his first time visiting a jail, Josef said; he and all the people he knew were law-abiding citizens. "Not that there's much worth to it," he added.

A man like Josef would find amusement in looking into another world, feeling complacent in a life safeguarded by sensibility. But life was never as secure as he thought. A crime could be committed, or worse, half-committed, and an unfinished murder could be worse than a murder plotted out and accomplished coldheartedly. But all this Moran had not said to Josef then, or later.

After a moment, Josef started to talk about Alena, of his and her being crowned as the Bohemian prince and princess at a Czech festival in 1952; of her winning the state championship at an accordion contest the year after. Accordion? Moran murmured, not saying more, and Josef nodded and said accordion indeed, not your everyday instrument in this country, but both he and Alena played the instrument, like every child of Czech immigrants. Their grandparents had come to the new continent from nearby villages; their fathers had been drinking buddies, both fond of pickled cow tongue. The marriage between Josef and Alena, Moran could tell, had been a good one, children raised with their best interests in mind, friends maintained with loyalty, the history of the older generations treasured, decades of memories dutifully deposited in family albums. When Josef spoke of Alena's accident, Moran watched his eyes dampen. Certain things are easier to share with strangers when one feels the nearness of farewell; death casts less of a shadow in the heart of a passerby.

Before they parted, Josef asked Moran if she had any plans for her first Thanksgiving in America. She said no, and he asked her if she would like to join his family for the holiday. He had not mentioned that it would be the first one for him and his children without Alena, but Moran had guessed it. Had she accepted the invitation because other people's wounds had always been more of a calling, a reason for her to be? After the divorce, Moran acquired the habit of looking at everything in their relationship with scrutiny. After all, their two years of dating and three years of marriage—a story preserved completely as though in amber, which had no connection to her life in China— was the only one for which she could find a beginning and an end; yet even this simple tale made little sense when she studied it closely. What if she had found an excuse to decline Josef's invitation, as she had always done with similar invitations in those days, and ever since?

But back in that coffee shop, it had felt only natural to say yes to Josef, because it had been good of him to think of inviting her, a newcomer in a foreign land. When she gave him her phone number, she told him her real name.

"Which name would you prefer to go by?" Josef asked.

"It doesn't matter," she said, though she knew it did.

"Well then, we'll call you Moran," Josef said, and she noticed that he had included his family in the sentence. "Does your name have a meaning? I heard every Chinese name has a meaning to go with it."

There could be many different Chinese characters for a name like hers, she explained. The characters her parents had chosen for her meant quietness. "Silence?" she tried again, sounding out the word, but then said the meaning was more like reticence. "It means for someone to choose not to express an opinion, to refrain from speaking."

What an odd name to give to a child, she waited for Josef to say, but he only nodded, as though there were nothing strange about it. She wished, then, that she had insisted on Lara, who would have been a different person: attractive, impertinent, mysterious.

When Moran had left China, she had known that she would never return, though this she had not told her parents; nor had she revealed it to Boyang, when she had asked him to arrange for her to see Shaoai a few days before her flight. They had been strangers to each other then: Moran had chosen to go to a university in Guangzhou, the farthest she could get from Beijing; Boyang and Ruyu had enrolled at the same university in Beijing, though in their second year, Ruyu had abruptly given up her study and married a man to go to America.

Uncle and Aunt must have been told about Moran's visit that day, as they had both left before her arrival, leaving Shaoai in the care of Boyang, who helped her move around with his strong arms and coaxing words. The chemical, having destroyed much of Shaoai's brain, had left her near blind and with the intelligence of a three-year-old. Unable to see well, Shaoai had come to where Moran was sitting on the edge of a chair and put her face close, as though she could only see a mouth, a nose, or a patch of skin at a time. Shaoai's mumbling was incoherent, and her mood swings—from laughing to crying to whimpering—seemed neither to embarrass nor to distress Boyang. His face, having a harshness Moran did not remember seeing before, was no longer boyish, and she felt intimidated by what she sensed behind his tender authority toward Shaoai and his flawless courteousness toward Moran herself: this was someone who had found all the solutions he needed for his life, and she, among others, would be sacrificed if she hindered him in any way.

The visit had not lasted long. Shaoai's dangerous plumpness, and the unexpectedness of her bumping from one corner of the room to another, made Moran jumpy, and she could see that Boyang had no intention of helping her; rather, he seemed to take a kind of vicious pleasure in Moran's discomfort. Years ago he had given her the ostensible reason for the end of their friendship: she had loved him more than as a childhood companion, and in doing so she had been the one most responsible for an unresolvable crime.

Had Moran been a different person she would have confronted his injustice in that apartment: it is easier to hold a person accountable for a tragedy than to hold fate, which defeats everyone impartially, accountable. But pride held her back. She did not want to be seen as begging for forgiveness.

When he saw her to the door, he slipped her his business card. "Don't ever forget us," he said slowly, and before she said anything, he closed the door behind her.

He had known her well enough to put such a curse on her, and all she could come up with in her own defense was not to think about what she could not forget. If forgetting is the art of eliminating a person, a place, from one's history, Moran knew she would never become a master at it. Rather, she was like a diligent craftsman, and never gave up a moment of vigilance in practicing the lesser art of not looking back, not thinking about the past.

But it would have been different for someone named Lara, who would choose what to forget from her past, and what to carry on for a better life. Long after the divorce, Moran maintained the habit of giving her name as Lara to the Starbucks baristas. She had once met another Lara at Logan airport, both of them waiting for their coffees, both stepping forward when summoned. The other Lara said her parents had gone through a period of thinking that everything Russian was holy, and had named her Larissa—Lara—after the heroine of a Russian novel. Later, her parents left their hippie-hood behind and gave her younger sisters more normal names: Jennifer, Molly, Aimee.

It was odd, Moran thought as she buckled herself in and waited for the plane to take off, how one could become a collector of irrelevant memories. Easily she could recall the other Lara from the airport: her full head of red hair, her tired eyes when she talked about her parents, who were "wintering"—Lara's word—in Florida. She was not particularly close to them, Lara had said; none of the four siblings was. "A psychologist friend keeps telling me: the refrigerator is empty; stop going to it," Lara had said, gulping down her coffee with a hungry vehemence.

10

Sister Lan and Brother Zechen,

Your two letters, written respectively on August 5 and August 17, have reached us safely, and we have read them with care. We thank you for receiving Ruyu into your family, and all arrangements are more than satisfactory to us. We have sent two hundred yuan for October and November via postal order. Do not feel obliged to telegraph unless the money does not arrive.

Ruyu has written us, and we believe she is happily settled. As you said, she is an easy child to care for, but we would appreciate it if, from time to time, you remind her of her goal. Regarding her future, nothing matters more to us, and thus to her, than that she goes to America; we would be grateful if you ensure that she spends enough time studying and practicing the accordion. We are not particularly interested in the so-called well-roundedness of a person's character, as the schools these days seem to advocate, but we must stress that good grades and special talents in music are essential in her case.

We thus conclude our letter with our best regards. Seeing our words is like seeing us in person.

Sister Wenlu and Sister Wenshu
2nd of September, '89

Ruyu,

Your letter, written on August 24, has arrived safely, and we have read it with care. We are pleased that you have settled down, and that Aunt and Uncle and Shaoai are nice and caring, and that you have made friends.

Once again, we would like to remind you that, since the day you were sent to us, you have been a chosen child of God. We trust that you understand your purposeful journey henceforth, and that you know how to live discerningly among people who do not understand this about you.

All is well here; hence no need for you to worry about us. Seeing our words is like seeing us in person.

Grandaunts
2nd of September, '89

In separate rooms, Aunt and Ruyu read the letters that had arrived in the evening post. Both put the letters away afterward, yet neither was able to shake off the mood brought about by the correspondence. Instinctively Ruyu knew that the last—and the only—letter she had sent to her grandaunts had disappointed them. It was the first real letter that Ruyu had written—if one did not count the school assignments to write holiday greetings to conscripts at the local military camps or the House of Glory, where veterans from the Korean War and earlier conflicts aged and died. She would not have written had it not been for the repeated urging of Aunt.

Ruyu had not known what to say to her grandaunts, as they had never relied on her words to know her. In the end, she had sung the praises of her hosts and neighbors and asked about her grandaunts' well-being, as she imagined a letter should. But her grandaunts' words succinctly reminded her of her place in life, as they had always done when she had been younger and had been caught in an excessive expression of her feelings. With a gaze or a shake of the head, they would stop her from laughing or fussing or crying; any emotion—be it happiness or sadness, anger or contentment—was a sign of human arrogance. Think about how you appear to the eyes above us, they would say, neither gently nor harshly, and afterward they would direct her to a quiet corner. A moment of reflection, they said, was not a punishment but an opportunity for her to learn to put some distance between her and whatever triviality had made her laugh or cry. One is always watched, they explained to her; one's life is lived under all sorts of eyes, but only one pair counts.

That she modified her behavior according to her surroundings, and wrote a letter that could only be written by someone like Moran, who seemed to consider it a paramount goal to please everyone around, must have dismayed her grandaunts. Ruyu wished she had had a stronger mind than a foolishly impressionable one: everyone she met in Beijing seemed keen to change her somehow, as though what mattered was not what she was but the possibilities she offered for others to imagine another person. Even Watermelon Wen's twins had told her that she would look exactly like the young actress in a popular TV program for children if she smiled more. Sister Ruyu, maybe you could be a TV star and we could go on the program with you, the boys said aloud, and Ruyu wondered why not a single grownup in the courtyard would stop their nonsense.

But there was no need to fret about her grandaunts' letter, as to dwell upon their reaction was to live again in human eyes. The truth was that what *they* thought of her mattered no more than what others thought of her. Their goal, her grandaunts had repeatedly told her, was to bring her to God; if she could stop living for them, suppose she could stop living for him, too? This notion, having never occurred before, took her breath away. Instinctively she closed her eyes, asking for his forgiveness.

At dinner, Ruyu was especially remote, and her silence, combined with Shaoai's sullenness, unnerved Aunt. She had not shown her husband the letter from the two old women; she had to at some point that night, but she needed time to recover from their words. She could not really tell which sister had penned the letter, as both sisters, she remembered, had the same unfeminine penmanship in the old style of the Wei Dynasty. She herself had been trained, when she had been under their charge, to practice the same style of calligraphy by copying out the words inscribed on ancient tablets. She had not been a brilliant student; she had looked foolish in their eyes, ineducable. Earlier, when she had opened the letter, she had felt her heart race; the severe handwriting on the envelope, each stroke carrying the weight of disapproval, had made her feel small again, intimidating her into a mindless daze.

"Did you read your grandaunts' letter?" Aunt asked Ruyu when the silence had become unnatural. "Were they happy to get your last letter?"

Ruyu nodded but did not offer anything more to continue the conversation.

"I do think they sounded happy," Aunt said. "At least in their letter to us."

Shaoai made a sound as though laughing through her throat, but Aunt did not yet want to turn her attention to her daughter. Since the beginning of the new school year, Shaoai had been to the university only a few times. It was the fourth year of her study, and she should be getting an assignment for an internship soon. Her parents' fear, though, was that the school would not assign anything to Shaoai, thus disqualifying her for graduation and making it impossible for her to secure a permanent job.

"They asked about you," Aunt said to Ruyu again after a thoughtful bite. "I think you like the school, no?"

"Yes."

"And the coursework—is it heavy? Can you follow everything all right? If you have questions, ask Boyang and Moran. Well, Boyang is probably a smarter bet if you have questions about your studies, but Moran can help with everything else."

Ruyu said all was fine. The first week of school had been a whirlwind; half of her classmates, like Ruyu herself, were new to the school, but Moran and Boyang—coming straight from the middle school section and knowing the school well—had been hovering around her the whole time, making certain that she would not feel left out. The school was about a thirty-minute walk away, but it seemed never to have occurred to Moran and Boyang that Ruyu would prefer walking to school by herself. Every morning they left the quadrangle together, three of them on two bicycles, and every evening returned the same way.

"And the accordion practice? Your grandaunts asked especially about that."

She had had a lesson with Teacher Shu, Ruyu said, and he liked her playing all right. She had hoped to stay in the music room for practice as long as she could after school, but within a week, Headmistress Liu had gathered the incoming high school students and briefed them about an urgent political assignment: on the night of October 1—the fortieth birthday of mother China—the students were to participate in a celebration at Tiananmen Square with four hundred thousand of their fellow citizens. To prepare for this assignment, Headmistress Liu continued, all students were expected to stay after school for two hours each day, practicing group dancing and later attending dress rehearsals at the levels of subdistrict, district, and city.

"Do you have enough time for the accordion?" Aunt asked.

She practiced every day for half an hour after lunch, Ruyu said, and she hoped that after the month of dancing practice, she would have more time in the afternoons.

Shaoai raised one eyebrow. "So you are going to be one of the lucky citizens to celebrate our Communist victory? What an honor."

Aunt looked at Uncle pleadingly. When he did not speak, she sighed. "Don't speak in that manner, Shaoai," she said. "Ruyu doesn't have a choice."

Shaoai leaned toward Ruyu as though she hadn't heard Aunt's words. "Have you thought of boycotting it?" Shaoai asked.

"I don't understand what you mean," Ruyu said.

"You know, skipping practice here and there, or, maybe better, skipping the celebration altogether," Shaoai said. "My mother can get you an excuse note for a sick leave—don't you think, Mama?"

"It's a political assignment," Aunt said. "I don't want you to give Ruyu wrong ideas about things."

"I'm teaching her to use her own brain to think," Shaoai said. "She'll never learn that from school."

Uncle sighed and placed his chopsticks next to his bowl, adjusting them so that they were perfectly paired. "Let me ask you a question, Shaoai," he said. So rarely did he participate in the dinner conversation between Shaoai and Aunt that the room seemed to suddenly take on an unfamiliar mood. "There will be four hundred thousand people at the Square for the celebration. According to your estimate, what percentage of those people have the ability to think independently?"

"Zero, if you ask me," Shaoai said. "The ones who do will find ways not to go."

"So suppose Ruyu listened to your advice and did not go to the celebration. How could her absence affect the celebration?"

"I know where you're leading me. No, if she did not go, nobody would notice. But what if those four hundred thousand people all had the guts not to go?"

"Practically speaking, what is the probability of that happening?"

"Well, if not four hundred thousand, how about four hundred, or four thousand?"

"Let's say four thousand boycott the celebration. What difference do you think their action would make? The live broadcast would still show four hundred thousand people gathering to celebrate. Yet those four thousand would probably face disciplinary actions afterward. Who do you think their action would harm but themselves and their families?"

"Yes, you're absolutely right. We should all stay obedient, follow orders, and let cowardice direct our lives," Shaoai said, adding after a moment of hesitation, "just like you."

Aunt's face looked intense. She opened her mouth as though she were about to say something but caught herself just in time. She left the table to close the only open window in the room, and then brought out a fan from her bedroom and switched it on.

Uncle's face, calm as always, seemed unaffected by Shaoai's words. He looked down at his chopsticks and readjusted them. "When I was a little younger than you, the civil war was still going on, and there was no telling which side was going to win. I remember going to teahouses with Grandpa, and on the wall of every teahouse was posted this single rule: *Do not talk about politics.* Grandpa pointed it out to me and said it was a lesson any responsible person should learn. Now, if you think about the different governments and revolutions he has been through, what better lesson could he have given his children?"

"But have you thought that it's people like him, and people like you, who have made this country impossible for our generation? That's why we have to do the fighting: because you haven't."

Ruyu felt all of a sudden tired. Bored. She wished she could tell Shaoai to stop being a clown who took herself too seriously. At school when Headmistress Liu had announced the political assignment, some of the students had bemoaned the loss of time for playing basketball or Ping-Pong after school, but Headmistress Liu had no patience for any of the complaints. "When we talk about a political assignment, we're talking about a political assignment, not a children's game," she had said. "Be positive. Consider it an opportunity to get to know your new classmates. Enjoy the dancing for the sake of dancing." Oddly, those who had complained the loudest seemed to have come to enjoy dancing the most. Indeed, just as Headmistress Liu had predicted, the dancing practice after school became a daily party for the three hundred first-year students, the outer circle of boys and the inner circle of girls rotating in different directions, giving the boys the opportunity to hold each girl's hands.

"Every generation recognizes easily what they are owed by the last generation," Uncle said. "Every generation thinks they can achieve what the last generation have not. We've had enough revolutions in our lifetime because of that thinking."

"But this is going to be our revolution. It's going to be completely different from yours. All your revolutions came from following the lead without thinking."

Uncle nodded, looking exhausted. When he did not speak up again, Aunt said tentatively, "Of course we understand what you're saying. But young people tend to forget about their own welfare. As your parents, we consider it our responsibility to remind you not to go to extremes."

"So that you will have a daughter safe-at-hand to see that you're well taken care of when you grow old, like Grandpa has you and Baba?" Shaoai asked. "If that logic stands, it's even more reason for Ruyu to become a revolutionary. Who could be better fit for the job than an orphan?"

Aunt took a sharp breath, and Uncle frowned, but neither said anything right away. Tauntingly, Shaoai looked at Ruyu, despising her, the younger girl thought, because Shaoai had a pair of parents and she had the luxury to disregard their love. Ruyu looked straight into Shaoai's eyes and smiled disarmingly. In a courteous voice, she said that she was afraid she was a disappointment to Sister Shaoai, as she did not have an ounce of revolutionary blood in her.

Shaoai pushed her chair backward and stood up. "I don't think you'll ever understand me, nor will I accept your view, so let's forget about this," she said to her parents, though her eyes had not left Ruyu's face.

Uncle and Aunt watched Shaoai pick up her bicycle key and walk out to the yard, greeting Boyang's grandmother in a falsely pleasant voice. Watermelon Wen said something across the courtyard, and in a moment several neighbors joined in. How was the beef stew, some- one who must have seen Aunt cooking earlier asked Shaoai, and she replied that it was the same as always. Count yourself lucky to have beef to eat, Boyang's grandmother said. In 1958, her husband's family in Henan Province couldn't even find good tree bark to stuff them- selves with.

Aunt fidgeted. She looked at Uncle's bowl and said that if he'd finished, there was no need for him to wait for her. Aunt worried when she and Uncle were late to the courtyard gathering after a meal, as though their absence would be taken as a negative statement. Uncle nodded and said he would go out and represent the family in a minute. The courtyard was a stage that neither Aunt nor Uncle could imagine missing, and both made their best efforts to be good participants—he by quietly smiling and nodding, she by always talk- ing about the positive side of any issue at hand.

When Uncle joined the neighbors, Aunt seemed to relax a little. She turned to Ruyu and said she was sorry that Shaoai was sometimes unpleasant. Ruyu could tell that Aunt wanted to say more, but as she continued to watch her, Aunt balked and changed topics, asking Ruyu if the desk lamp was bright enough for her study in the eve- nings. Ruyu smiled and said that of course it was, and then pointed to the clock on the wall, saying it was late, and Grandpa must be hungry for his supper.

The girl was a better fit for her grandaunts than she herself had been, Aunt thought as she spooned mush into the old man's mouth. She had felt like a piece of defenseless sponge when she had lived with the two sisters, absorbing their criticism, and her porousness had not changed since. In contrast, Ruyu seemed immune to that fate of being perpetually bogged down by the sogginess of the world. Aunt sighed. She wondered what kind of woman Ruyu would grow up to be.

Sitting at the desk, unable to focus on her studies, Ruyu reread the letter from her grandaunts. From the defeat she had seen in the faces of Uncle and Aunt, she knew that, however outrageously Shaoai might throw herself against the world, they would love her all the same, wishing that they could offer their flesh as a cushion between her and any danger. But neither of you can do anything for her, Ruyu thought; you can never save her. This thought comforted Ruyu. Against her will she had begun to like Aunt and Uncle, yet that seemed more of a reason for her not to tolerate their foolish love for their daughter.

That night, Shaoai returned earlier than Ruyu had expected. Moran and Boyang had come into her bedroom only twenty minutes earlier—often at the end of the night they would come in, quizzing one another on the spelling of English vocabulary for the next day, or just chatting. Aunt welcomed these visits, and Ruyu had let herself become used to them, as she rarely agreed to visit the other two at their houses.

Moran stood up when Shaoai entered the room, but the older girl signaled for Moran to stay where she was sitting with Ruyu on the edge of the bed, and told Boyang not to vacate the only chair. Ruyu had noticed that both Moran and Boyang idolized Shaoai, who treated them with a respect mixed with teasing familiarity. "So, how is high school after all?" Shaoai asked, sitting on the edge of the desk.

Ruyu listened as Moran and Boyang shared tidbits with Shaoai— nicknames of teachers inherited from the older students, a strange new classmate, the construction projects planned for the campus.

"And how is it with this epic political assignment you've got?" Shaoai asked.

Moran looked carefully at Shaoai's face and then turned to Boyang, who shrugged and said it was all right. The dancing was tolerable, and in any case it was only for a month. When Shaoai did not comment, Moran added that not many students were really into it, and some of them talked about wearing all black for mourning on the evening of the celebration.

"Are they serious, or are they just being boastful?" Shaoai asked with interest.

Moran looked embarrassed, and Ruyu wondered if she had lied. Ruyu herself had not heard such conversations, but then she did not have any friends; news and gossip about the school all came from Moran and Boyang.

"Or should I ask if it's only your wishful thinking that such a thing would happen?" Shaoai said.

"Moran and I talked about wearing black as a protest with a few of our friends, but somehow the teachers got wind of it," Boyang said.

"And?"

"Headmistress Liu talked to us," Boyang said.

"And intimidated you into acquiescence?"

"Not really," Boyang said. "She only made us see how childish a protest like that would be."

"Childish? Is that the word she used?" Shaoai said.

Boyang shrugged, and said that in any case Headmistress Liu made it clear that their talk had to stop. Moran looked nervously at Boyang and then at Shaoai, and when the latter did not speak, Moran said that Headmistress Liu meant that their behavior would only hurt themselves and the school, which, Moran said, was not what they wanted.

"What do you want?" Shaoai asked.

The question seemed to put Moran into confusion. Shaoai stared at her, and then laughed cheerlessly. "I don't blame you," she said. "I didn't know what I wanted at your age. Imagine, I had thought of becoming a spy for this country."

When Shaoai did not say more, Moran explained in a lower voice to Ruyu that Shaoai had been approached once, before she had entered college, by a secret agent who had met her at the English Corner near Tiananmen Square. He said he had been watching her for a few weeks, and had been impressed by her personality; he had asked her if she would be interested in becoming a secret agent—she would have to give up going to college, but they would give her other training.

Ruyu was aware that Shaoai had been listening to their conversation, waiting for Ruyu to be impressed perhaps, but she refused to meet the older girl's eyes, and barely nodded when Moran finished the story.

"Imagine, I could've known how to drive a jeep or put a silencer on a pistol or concoct all kinds of poisons by now," Shaoai said, but before anyone could comment, she changed topics abruptly, asking other questions about school. The atmosphere in the room became more relaxed. A few times Boyang broke into laughter. Moran seemed more cautious in her cheerfulness, yet Shaoai seemed to have made up her mind to be amiable for the moment.

Later, at bedtime, Shaoai still seemed amicable. "Do you like Boyang?" she asked as Ruyu settled into her side of the bed.

"Why do you ask?"

"Just curious. You look comfortable with him."

"I like him as much as I like Moran," Ruyu said carefully, feeling her muscles tense. She never knew where conversations with Shaoai would go.

"Or do you mean that you dislike them equally?"

"Why does it matter? They don't need me to like them."

"We're not talking about what they need," Shaoai said, and leaned over to stare at Ruyu. "What I want to know is if you like them—or anyone, for that matter."

"Why should I?"

"Why indeed!" Shaoai said. "What is it like to have so much contempt for the world?"

"I don't have any contempt for anyone," Ruyu said.

"Do you feel anything?"

"I don't know why you are asking, and I don't know what you are asking," Ruyu said, and when Shaoai did not turn her stare away from Ruyu's face, she shut her eyes.

"Only because I find your unfeeling attitude toward the world most extraordinary. Do you know a person like you cannot be trusted?"

Ruyu opened her eyes and did not avert them when Shaoai continued studying her face. "I didn't ask you to trust me," Ruyu said. "So why don't you leave me alone?"

"I didn't ask you to come and live here. I didn't agree for my parents to take you in," Shaoai said, her voice all of a sudden hoarse. "Leave you alone? Why don't you spare all of us that judgmental attitude? Why don't you leave *me* alone?"

At such a close distance, Shaoai's face looked as though distorted by pain. "If you tell me how to leave you alone, I'll do it just as you would like," Ruyu said. "I didn't know I was in your way. Your parents told my grandaunts that you would be living in the university dorm during the school year."

"So the fault is mine?"

"I don't have another place to be."

"You've left me no place to be."

For a split second Ruyu had the impression that Shaoai, enraged implacably, would strangle her. She willed her body to stay still and said in a calm voice that she was sorry if that was how Shaoai felt. And it was late, she said, and she had a weekly exam tomorrow morning. Before Shaoai could reply, Ruyu switched the light off. She had not yet had a moment of free time to pray, but she was too tired to worry about that now.

For a while Ruyu stayed awake, and she knew that Shaoai was awake, too. Ruyu was vaguely aware of a power she held over the older girl, but what it meant she did not want to understand; to some extent she preferred to believe that it was the same power she held over Boyang and Moran, though the latter two were transparent, while Shaoai was, despite being a nuisance, a mystery. Yet the mere thought of understanding that mystery struck Ruyu as sordid. Besides, she would never allow herself to be outwitted in what she excelled at: the habit of being opaque allowed her to be a mystery in people's eyes. To want to know any person better requires one to give up that position and to become less inscrutable.

11

Three days passed, but the conversation Ruyu had begun to dread, in which Celia would request an explanation as to why Ruyu had told Edwin but not Celia about the death of a friend, had not occurred. The person who'd died wasn't close, Ruyu would have said, but that would not have sufficed. For Celia, any death, be it that of a stranger she'd read about in the newspapers, a passing acquaintance's distant relative, or an aged neighborhood pet, was relevant, the grief she felt on other people's behalf leaving her constantly bruised yet acutely alive. To deprive Celia of an opportunity to mourn was to deny her the right to feel.

Wickedly Ruyu wondered if she should have told Celia about the death: no other stranger would feel the waste of Shaoai's ambitions and desires or imagine her imprisonment in her body for twenty-one years as unreservedly as Celia would. Why not be lenient and let the loss of Shaoai be acknowledged? Who else would do that for Shaoai if not Celia? Certainly Shaoai's mother must be suffering. Boyang had not mentioned Aunt in his email, but Ruyu knew she was alive: when Uncle had passed away a few years earlier, Boyang had emailed with the news. All mothers, though, mourn the deaths of their children, and a mother's grief, like a mother's love, offers little redemption. The world would be a kinder place if mothers, and mothers alone, were the judges of their children. Everyone would be absolved of her sins before her heart repents, everyone but *you*, Ruyu thought with a sudden rage: you—lonely, vicious, remorseless orphan.

Shaoai's death had not taken Ruyu by surprise. Had she not been, by keeping an email address available to Boyang and by checking it regularly, waiting for Shaoai to die all along? Had he been waiting too, she wondered; had Moran? Little had bound them together but the waiting, which, all over now, would finally release them into a void, where even the keenest ears could not discern that they, like three unconnected music phrases, had once been in the same piece. Ruyu wondered what ripples the death had left in the other two hearts, but perhaps they had become immovable over the years, which she hoped, for the sake of their happiness, was the case.

Ruyu had not seen Moran or Boyang since she had left the country, but instinctively she knew that they had not forgotten her. Would it be a solace to them that they had not been forgotten by her, either? Other people in her past—her grandaunts, her two ex-husbands, Eric—she did not think about often. When she did, she thought of them incuriously, their lives, and in the case of her grandaunts, their deaths, affecting her little. But at least she had enough mercy for Moran and Boyang: sometimes she allowed herself to wonder about their current lives. It was their bad luck to have met her, their bad luck to have stumbled onto a battleground where they had had no reason to be. But to whom had the battleground belonged? Once upon a time Ruyu had thought that the battle was between herself and Shaoai, but the latter had not deserved to be her equal; it could have been between Ruyu and God, but she had been unwilling—was still unwilling—to grant him that position.

Suppose one could head into a battle without a definite enemy, and one could, with a blind resolution, leave a trail of corpses behind. If that were her lot Ruyu saw no point questioning it now. Moran and Boyang had been her casualties, yet in some way their lives must have been enhanced by her, too. This view, no doubt heartless to the world, comforted Ruyu: they had not been extraordinary people to start with. Years of living—quarreling with the surroundings, making do with small triumphs—would have worn out their innocence in the most banal way. Though it wasn't innocence betrayed that made them interesting—innocence is always betrayed—but that neither Boyang nor Moran understood how to carry a burden as enduring as Shaoai, or why it was theirs.

God should have had mercy for Moran and Boyang, Ruyu thought; God should have let Shaoai die a long time ago. Willfully, wishfully, he changes his mind and adjusts a few minor details, but revision of the script—of any script whose creator is cursed with all-seeing eyes—must amount to little gratification. Does that make him feel lonely, abandoned even? Or bored, and enraged by his boredom?

You, Ruyu said in her heart to the god she had long stopped believing in, *you have my sympathy.*

Only once in her life had Ruyu been surprised—by Shaoai's fingers and tongue, probing where they had no right to; and by her own paralytic silence, which must have been interpreted by Shaoai as acquiescence. Had that been in God's script, too? If he'd intended other schemes for Ruyu, she had not let herself be caught again. He had beaten her that one time because he was God, and she had been young.

The bells on top of the door jingled. Ruyu tried to suppress her vexation—a customer was coming into the store, wanting something, or worse, not knowing what he or she wanted, demanding recommendations and later approval from Ruyu. Yet when she looked up it was only Edwin, who, both hands occupied with take-out bags from a nearby deli, walked sideways into the shop. Jamming his foot between the door and its frame, he let the door close gently so that the bells would rattle less.

She should have stood up to greet him, but for a moment Ruyu did not move, watching the door close behind Edwin in slow motion and wishing that someone would rush in, instantly bursting the bubble of stealthy quietness that was now enclosing the two of them.

"Hello," Edwin said.

"Oh, it's you," Ruyu said. Why would anyone mute a bell that was supposed to ring?

"Are you closed?"

"No," Ruyu said, trying to recover from her momentary frustration. "Did Celia send you not only to buy dinner but also to get treats?" she said. It must be one of those days when Celia couldn't find enough inspiration to cook a dinner both aesthetically and nutritionally satisfying.

They were celebrating a coworker's fiftieth birthday the following day, Edwin said, and he thought he would bring some sweets. Ruyu nodded at the display and told him to take his time. She should have been more accommodating, making recommendations, chatting about the children and their schoolwork, but the silenced bell had come back to her—not from this cozy boutique in the suburban town center that looked like a quaint Old West main street, but from the Beijing quadrangle half a lifetime ago. More often than not, the bell above the door to Shaoai's house did not have a chance to jingle before Aunt hurried to cover it with an anxious hand. What was the point of having a bell if one had to constantly prevent it from ringing, Ruyu had thought then. Had she asked Uncle, he would have said that it was Aunt's nature to want to save the bell from unnecessary wear, or that she did not want to disturb the bedridden Grandpa, but Ruyu knew Uncle only wanted to believe his answers. To have or not have a bell in the house: neither seems wrong, but to mute one that has been given a place is an act of inconsistency, to want comings and goings to be known and yet remain unknown at the same time. The furtive eagerness with which Aunt raced to reach the bell when she heard someone's steps approach the door—Ruyu remembered it now, and shuddered with a violent resentment—was it not a kind of greediness, to be there, always there, to be the first person to greet those who came and the last person to say farewell to those departing?

"What do you think, Italian or French?" Edwin asked, studying the truffles. "Or you recommend neither?"

"Belgian," Ruyu said, knowing that anything Edwin chose would, in the end, bear signs of poor judgment in Celia's eyes. "How's Celia?" she asked.

Concerned, as always, that their Thanksgiving dinner would not be a smooth success for her visiting parents, Edwin said. Ruyu nodded with sympathy. Last year Celia had been hurt when her parents decided to spend the holiday with her sister's family. Two years in a row, Celia had said; not that she wanted the hassle of hosting them, but shouldn't they give an explanation?

Edwin placed two boxes on the counter and watched Ruyu ring them up. "How are you feeling these days?" he said, his tone too casual to sound natural.

Ruyu looked up. Really, she thought, spending unnecessarily on two beautiful boxes of truffles just to ask a question like that? She placed the golden stickers with the shop's logo on top of the boxes and smoothed them with her fingertips. That Edwin had refrained from relating their conversation to Celia could have been an oversight on his part; at least that was what Ruyu preferred to believe. "Why do you ask?" she said.

"I remember you said your friend died," Edwin said. "I hope you're feeling better."

Why on earth had she slipped and told him something so irrelevant? Worse, why had Edwin, who seemed a sensible person, chosen not to forget a conversation that should not have happened in the first place? To turn something into a secret—the way Edwin had with Shaoai's death—is like inflicting a wound on one's own body. To let the harm be known—to walk into the shop and ask about the death again—is to thrust the wound into someone else's sight. A secret that never heals makes a person, however close, a stranger, or worse, an intimate, an enemy.

"I'm doing just fine," Ruyu said. "Thank you for asking."

Edwin mumbled something, and his face turned beet-colored. Ruyu sighed. As a shop assistant, she was neither impatient nor untalented when it came to small talk. People came into the store out of idleness, and idly they studied the pretty objects on the shelves: imported toffees and chocolates in exquisite wrappings and packages, handmade mugs bearing witty or cloying or nonsensical images and words, flimsy china teacups arranged around a teapot like well-behaved orphans perpetually begging to be filled with love, tin windup toys that were neither sturdy nor attractive to children today but nevertheless gave the store an old-world feeling. None of the objects for sale was essential to anyone, but because of their non-essentialness they continued to be, and continued to be cherished: much of life's comfort comes not from the absoluteness of happiness and goodness but from the hope that something would be good enough, and one would find oneself happy enough. Perhaps it was for that reason people would walk in—La Dolce Vita was one of those stores one entered without knowing what one wanted, thinking that it would provide a clue, a solution, or at least a moment of distraction. It was Ruyu's job to convince a customer that someone—be it a friend or a family member or even the customer herself—deserved decadence. That she spent part of her time in a store that mattered little to anyone did not bother Ruyu; these places—the shop, Celia's kitchen, the soccer field where once in a while she drove Ginny's son to practice and waited among a group of women who watched their children with tireless love—allowed Ruyu both to be among people and to treat them as though they were the pair of kissing Dutch dolls next to the cash register. Given enough distance, she could even let herself feel a fondness toward these men and women and children; yet out of that obliterating mist had come Edwin, who, for whatever reason, insisted on his right to be regarded as real and indispensable. "I didn't mean to sound harsh," Ruyu said. "I just don't want to make a fuss about something trivial."

"A friend's death is not trivial."

Ruyu looked at Edwin, uncertain as to whether she despised or pitied him, a man foolishly falling victim to his own kindness. The concern in his voice was that of a needy soul; acting as though he was agonized by her loss, he was asking her to acknowledge his right to feel her pain. "She was not a close friend," Ruyu said, trying hard to maintain the evenness in her voice. It was his bad luck to have stepped onto that old battleground, but today she saw no need for another casualty.

"I thought you looked sad the other day."

"Then I'm afraid you made a mistake," Ruyu said. "She was one of those people I would not want to see or hear about ever again, and I feel no pain whatsoever about her death. No, let me take that back. The only pain I feel is that she didn't die soon enough. Now, are you reassured that I'm going to survive just fine?"

Edwin flinched, trying to find words, and Ruyu, her mercy for him gone, stared at him, not offering any assistance in his struggle. Time, be it old or new, lived or yet to be lived, was merely a body she carried inside her heart, its weight growing less conspicuous by the day, its coldness more acclimated to, and its possessiveness easily taken, or mistaken, for composure. And then there was Celia—all the Celias of the world—who made it easy for Ruyu to be who she was: their eyes looked neither at nor through her, but looked instead for themselves in her face. Hadn't Edwin learned anything from his marriage? Why would he come here trying to resurrect what was beyond revival? "Are you religious?" Ruyu asked.

Edwin shook his head. Baffled, he explained that his grandparents and parents had been, and they had raised him according to their faith—but no, he was not religious now.

"Then don't try to be good to strangers," Ruyu said. "It's pointless."

"I don't understand."

"An easy example: at this moment, shouldn't you be worrying more about your family's dinner getting cold than about a dead person you've never met?"

Edwin's face turned red again. "I'm sorry," he said. "I shouldn't have intruded."

Something softened in Ruyu's heart. The urge to embarrass and the urge to humiliate were as treacherous as the urge to be kind, as any sentiment granted another person the status of being less hypothetical. "Let's forget this altogether. The person has no place here, and let us not complicate life with death," Ruyu said, gesturing to the door, where the bells were dutifully waiting to bid farewell to Edwin. "Do send my love to Celia and the kids."

Later Ruyu walked home in the moonlight. The fog from the bay had drifted inland, and across the canyon, orange lights lit up people's windows, just smudged enough to appear dreamy. Three nights a week Ruyu stayed at the shop until closing. The walk uphill, if she'd shared it with another person, would have been beautiful in people's eyes; but companionless on these walks, she must cut a lonesome figure to those who knew her by sight. But loneliness is as delusive a belief in the pertinence of the world as is love: in choosing to feel lonely, as in choosing to love, one carves a space next to oneself to be filled by others—a friend, a lover, a toy poodle, a violinist on the radio.

All her life Ruyu believed she was able to fend off love and loneliness, her secret being that the present would be let live only its allowed duration. The person who dusted the shelves at the shop was as solid and real as the person who nannied two Pomeranians when their owners went to southern France or Italy for the holidays, or the person tutoring an unmotivated teenager in Mandarin. A born murderess, she had mastered the skill of snuffing out each moment before releasing it to join the other passed moments. Nothing connects one self to another; time effaced does not become memory.

Crickets chirped in the bushes, pausing with the approach of Ruyu's steps, so that, at any given moment, she could hear only those in the distance. These autumn lamenters, even in chorus, were slyer than nightingales, bleaker than owls. It was nearly Thanksgiving, but the season was a particularly mild one, even for northern California. In Beijing, the last of the autumn crickets would be frozen now by the first cold front from Siberia.

Certain things come unannounced, like crickets, like the darkness of the season: by the time one notices them, one has already fallen victim to their wicked charm. Ruyu watched as her shadow was turned by a nearby bush into something too strange to belong to her. Instinctively she stepped back and hid from the sole street lamp behind a tree. Something slid into the bushes behind her, a squirrel or a raccoon. Nature makes one look for one's own species, but what would one's species do but make one lonelier?

Half a block before she reached her cottage, her cell phone rang. It was Celia, and Ruyu picked up the call: one should not neglect the mortal.

"Where are you?" Celia said.

"About to open my door."

"Edwin said you looked unwell. What's wrong?"

Was belated honesty a form of deception? "Nothing is wrong," Ruyu said.

"Did you catch a cold?" Celia said. "Your voice sounds funny."

"Maybe it's the signal."

"Or maybe not," Celia said. "Listen, you don't have to tell me, but if talking it out helps, I'm all ears."

"All ears for what?"

"Edwin seems to think that someone important died," Celia said. "Why didn't you say anything?"

"I would've told you if it *had* been someone important," Ruyu said. "The fact that I only randomly mentioned it to Edwin but forgot to tell you—shouldn't that be enough to prove that nothing is the matter?"

"Was it a woman? Edwin thought it might be one of your exes' lovers?"

Perhaps there was nothing but true compassion in Edwin's curiosity, but Ruyu could not help feeling resentful: passive-aggressively, he had enlisted his unsuspicious wife to ambush Ruyu. She sighed. "Let's talk about this later, Celia."

"Can you come for coffee tomorrow? Before you go to the shop?"

Ruyu looked at her watch. She had fewer than twelve hours to come up with something reasonably good to stop Celia from pursuing the topic. Yes, Ruyu agreed. She would come after Celia dropped the kids off at school.

But by the time Ruyu had settled in for the night, she could no longer follow through with her resolution to prepare a tale for Celia. Any planning required her to imagine the future—a day or a month to come—but the moment she set such a task for herself, her mind stubbornly vacated itself. People went to yoga studios and meditation retreats to achieve the same effect; too bad she could not share her secret with the world, Ruyu thought, feeling already lethargic. She had noticed that since the news of Shaoai's death arrived, she had become more prone to feeling tired. All that arguing with a god from the past must have affected her more than she had expected.

Ruyu had long ago realized that her grandaunts, religious and pious as they had believed themselves to be, had only held on to a faith that had been more of their own creation, and the god they had given her, too, had not been the god in other people's prayers. But what did it matter if they had given her the wrong faith, now that she had gone astray from that faith? All the same, Ruyu knew that she had to credit her grandaunts: by giving her a god they had given her a position of superiority, when an orphan like her could easily be devoured by the world; by leaving them and their god behind, she had gone beyond destructibility.

Ruyu filled the bathtub and then turned on the CD player, which contained the piano concerto she had been listening to earlier, by whom at the moment she did not care to remember.

In the warm steam, she drifted off a little; here and there a phrase from the concerto caught in her head, and she seemed able to see it printed clearly on a music sheet before the notes swam away like tadpoles. One easily lost tadpoles, as one could lose anything. Once, at eight, Moran and Boyang had gone to a nearby pond to catch tadpoles, which they had carried in wax paper tubes filled with pond water and secured on both ends by vines; they thought of running back to the quadrangle and depositing the tadpoles in the giant barrel in which Teacher Pang kept two koi fish, but for one reason or another, they took a detour to visit a classmate, and for a while the three of them bounced up and down in the classmate's bed, the tadpoles completely forgotten by their captors.

They never dared to ask the classmate about his bed, Moran had said when she told Ruyu the story. The poor tadpoles, Boyang had said guiltily; and the poor friend, Moran had added, the voice so clear and close to Ruyu's ears that she opened her eyes abruptly. The steam had not dispersed. She must have dozed off for only a moment, yet she felt confused; she thought she had seen and heard Moran and Boyang, not only as the teenagers retelling the story, but also as eight-year-olds, carefree children who should have been strangers to her, yet they had looked familiar in her dream, if, in fact, it was in her dream she had seen them.

Why they had told her the story Ruyu had no recollection. They had told her all sorts of things, but little remained in her memory. The last thing she would ever want to dwell upon was other people's childhoods, yet Moran and Boyang had seemed, a moment ago, so vivid that she could almost feel their astonishment at losing the tadpoles.

Ruyu did not remember what she had looked like at that age; of course she remembered her grandaunts well: their voices and gestures, their neatly plucked eyebrows and well-combed buns, which never blurred when she saw them in her mind's eye. But she could not see herself then, or at any age when she had been in their care. Had her grandaunts had a mirror in their apartment? Ruyu remembered an oval one, not larger than a hand mirror, standing on a metal stand on top of a tall dresser, which her grandaunts would consult before leaving home. Had she ever been handed the mirror, Ruyu wondered, and she could not answer with any certainty. The dresser, she remembered, was extraordinarily tall, with eight levels of drawers, two on each level. It was one of the few of her grandaunts' possessions that had survived multiple visits by the Red Guards: unlike the smaller items, the dresser could not be hidden, yet the revolutionary youths had spared the heavy furniture, perhaps deeming it too heavy to move downstairs and throw into the fire, or not having the right tools to ax it apart. By the time Ruyu could reach an object on top of the dresser, she must have been nearly ten, she calculated. No, she did not remember looking into a mirror; there must have been times when she had been allowed to do so, but what difference would it have made? She had already missed the opportunities—no, she had not missed them, because they had never been granted her in the first place—for a normal childhood. There was no disappointment in that: disappointment is for those who begin with a plan, those who sow seeds and refuse to accept the barrenness of life.

Much more had been planned for her, much more expected from her at one time or another, and her achievement—could this be her only one?—was to have sabotaged everyone's good script. But why not? She had never asked to be part of anyone's interior life, but people, with too much confidence or perhaps too little, seemed ill at ease unless they found some way to change that.

Ruyu's first marriage had ended when the man to whom she had been married for two years had lost control and beaten her. She had not defended herself other than to shield her face from his fists, and afterward she had watched with equanimity as the man broke down and cried, calling her a monster who had turned him into a wife beater like his father. What had she done but remain the same person he had seen only twice before marrying her, she had thought later, studying her bruised body in a mirror so that she could have a better sense of the pain she should feel. When she had, through an acquaintance, met the man nine years her senior, it had not been for the prospect of a good life or a happy marriage in America, but for an exit from her grandaunts' charge and her own Chinese life. When he, with only two weeks of vacation time and the goal of finding a wife, had decided to marry a stranger, a girl not yet twenty, shouldn't he have prepared himself for all that could possibly come? Surely he had thought of practicalities: his bank account he had never shared with her, each week allocating her an allowance of twenty dollars on top of the grocery money; he had given her the choice of pursuing a degree in either accounting or biostatistics, both of which would allow her to find a job easily and make a substantial contribution to the household; he had, at the beginning of each university semester, registered her for her classes, so that he would know her exact whereabouts at any moment of the day, and he never enrolled her in evening classes, because in the evenings she was expected to waitress at an all-you-can-eat Chinese buffet, which hired immigrants on student visas who had no legal right to work and would work for less than minimum wage. If their marriage was a transaction, Ruyu had accepted his terms, offering, in return for lodging and food and tuition money, her consent to be wifely. To be wifely, to sign over her future for a one-way plane ticket: she had never agreed to love, and had not expected his love; yet it was in the name of love he had raged, and called her the coldest person he had ever met. Even a chunk of ice would have melted after his two years of trying, he had said, calling her names she had not imagined him able to. She wondered if his father had used the same names for his mother.

When he finally calmed down, Ruyu said that she would not call the police—with his PhD almost finished and a job offer from a former colleague of his advisor's, he could not afford a criminal record, which would eliminate his dream of obtaining a green card in this country. In return, she said, she wanted a divorce and enough money for the next two years of tuition and living expenses. He did not have that kind of money, the man said, and Ruyu replied that she lived simply and did not need much; if he would not agree, she said, she would have to take care of matters by other means.

Scheming, he had called her in an email after their divorce, listing all the things she had done to ensnare him. The sincerity of his fury made Ruyu wonder about the difference between what one was and what one appeared to the world. She had not thought of herself as a calculating person, not because she was better than that, but because she did not find anything in life worth scheming for. She had asked little and would have been fine given less, but to want less, to want nothing, was, in the end, a kind of greediness her husband could not live with.

Ruyu had not thought of marrying again after that. She had gone on to finish her degree in accounting, as she had seen no need to change course. When she graduated, it became clear that she would either have to be ambitious and find a job with a big firm that supported a working visa, or find a legal way to stay in the country so she could work at a job that was less demanding.

Sometimes Ruyu wondered if her second marriage could have lasted longer, even forever, if circumstances had worked out for them. If anyone had the right to complain about her scheming, it could only be Paul, whom Ruyu had met before graduation and had decided to date wholeheartedly for her future stay in this country: the wedding had taken place before her one-year post-degree stay in the country expired.

Paul had grown up in North Dakota, and had on a whim transferred to a state university in California after two years at a local college; he'd wanted to see a bigger world than his hometown of two thousand people. After graduation, he had found a job at the height of the dot-com bubble in Silicon Valley, but, neither brilliant nor ambitious enough, he had been unable to find another job after the bubble burst. By then, Ruyu had gotten her green card through the marriage and was working part-time as a bookkeeper for a few local businesses. Unlike her first husband, Paul had never considered her work essential to household finances; his dream was to make a decent amount of money when his company went IPO, and then to have three or four children to keep Ruyu busy at home. But when that dream had broken, he could not build another dream. And then there were his parents, always there, always hoping that one of their children—all four had gone away, all to big cities—would come back to be part of the family business, which sold kayaking equipment and managed tours for adventurous vacationers.

It was a painful decision for him, too, Paul said; he hoped that she understood in the long run it would be the best for them.

Homecoming of any sort struck Ruyu as a sad comedy. Her first year in America, her ex-husband had brought her to see the university's homecoming parade, and one float, with a group of older men dressed up in matching suits and waving and grinning under the school banner, made her feel embarrassed for both the men on the float and those who had to watch them with cheers. Human beings are bad actors, but the worst are those who offer more than is required of them: heroes in the shoes of extras. But perhaps that is what people cannot stop doing—inventing consequences because our smallness is too heavy for us to bear. Afterward, in class, Ruyu would sometimes study her classmates and wonder who, among those boys who did not take off their baseball caps and did not stop chewing gum when the professor spoke from the podium, would grow up to be the men on the float.

Ruyu had flatly refused to join in Paul's homecoming. His picture of their future was claustrophobic for her. There would be the creeks he had waded and fished when he was young, the ice cream stand where he had bought a cone for a high school girlfriend; Ruyu did not mind that he had a past, but she refused to be absorbed into his, or anyone else's, history.

Compared to her first divorce, the second was more subdued, less dramatic. She had been fond of Paul, even if she had not loved him; she had learned to be among people—his friends and colleagues—and to dress in a way that made him proud, and to be witty, even flirty at times. If anything, the five years of marriage had taught her that she could fit into any role if she made an effort, though nothing satisfied her more than staying at a distance, watching people until she could see through them. Paul's dream to become a millionaire, unrealized, had not saddened her. She had not minded seeing his folly confirmed; she felt pleased, even, as she would feel when she saw any mortal's falling.

The water in the bathtub had turned lukewarm, and reluctantly Ruyu pulled herself out of it. The concerto had long since ended, but she had not noticed the quiet until then. In the vast world out there, those who had crossed paths with her were living in their safe cocoons; and those who had died—her grandaunts, for instance, or Uncle, or Shaoai—what had become of them?

Ruyu did not miss her grandaunts in the sense she had never missed her parents. The four of them had taken enough from her; what had been left was to be either cherished or else discarded with an insensitiveness that matched theirs. Uncle's death had caused, however transient, a ripple of melancholy in Ruyu's heart, followed by relief: Uncle had been one of those whose lives were saturated by unwarranted sadness, and what could be a kinder antidote to sadness than death itself?

Shaoai's death, granted mercifully at long last, must be an antidote, too. Despite sounding ruthless, Ruyu had meant it when she told Edwin that Shaoai's death had come too late, not only for the one waiting for death but for those around her. With each year's passing Ruyu was a year older than Shaoai, whom she had known only as a young woman. A strange feeling stirred in Ruyu when the thought occurred that Shaoai had been young at the time; innocent even, but was it real innocence when it could be—and had been—used to taint another person? And then, the worst battle, Ruyu thought, is fought between the innocent: not knowing how to spare themselves, they don't for a moment feel mercy for the other.

12

The celebration in Tiananmen Square on October 1 came and went; eventless, Moran could not help thinking with disappointment, as she had wondered if people would find ways to protest the event, which took place only four months after the bloodshed there. But bloodshed, even if it hadn't been forgotten, cast little shadow on this day. There was no one climbing up the pole of the streetlight to shout out slogans, nor was there any organized sabotage—a homemade explosive tube thrown into the crowd not to hurt people but to cause havoc, a false alarm message to deceive people into an evacuation—as she and Boyang had wishfully imagined.

The only drama of the day happened earlier in the afternoon. When they gathered at the school, Headmistress Liu distributed two lipsticks to every homeroom, saying it was a district order that the girls look more festive. No one pointed out that wearing makeup was prohibited in school, as was clearly written in the students' manual. When it was Ruyu's turn, she passed the tube to the next girl in line without applying it.

"But why?" asked the class monitor. "It's not poisonous."

Moran bristled, ready to defend her friend. Ruyu was not one to make trouble and attract undue attention to herself, even though she had not put on a festive dress as instructed. She had on, for the day, a long-sleeved cotton smock, greenish gray, one of those she had brought with her from home; the only color about her, bright against her anemic skin, was the red gauze required for the dancing, which — unlike the other girls who wore the gauze as a scarf or a headband or even as a flower on their chest—she wound around her wrist.

It's not hygienic, Ruyu replied. The class monitor stared at her, horrified by such an impertinent comment, but Ruyu only half-smiled; her contempt, which she had no intention to hide, contrasted with the class monitor's fury, her face flushed, her chest heaving, words partially formed and sputtering out.

The class monitor was not a likable girl, and already Moran could see that she would grow up into someone who would not hesitate to mistreat those who were less fortunate than she was. Still, Moran felt bad for her, fearing that in Ruyu's eyes Moran herself occupied a position not much different from the class monitor's. Moran sighed, and stepped in between the class monitor and Ruyu. "Let's not make a big fuss," said Moran to the monitor placatingly. "It would make Headmistress Liu think you can't do your job well."

Everyone seemed to enjoy the night. The students milled in tight circles, as the loudspeakers blared across the ocean of people the fourteen songs they were to dance to. Every thirty minutes there was a fifteen-minute break for fireworks.

When the boom-booming shook the ground, Moran watched her schoolmates cheer, their upturned faces lit by the flashing in the sky. A boy climbed on top of another boy and hailed the crowd: "Look at me!" Few looked, but when the boy jumped back down, he raved about the number of people. Four hundred thousand, he said, you don't get noticed by four hundred thousand people every day of your life.

A classmate, whose father was said to be the Party branch leader of a photography agency, came over with an expensive-looking camera and asked to take a picture of Ruyu and Moran. Moran suspected that the boy had a crush on Ruyu; several boys in the class did, and through their eyes, Moran felt she could understand more about

Ruyu than she could through her own eyes. Without any reciprocal affection, Ruyu would nevertheless allow them to seek her out at recess, asking them questions and listening to their answers with an attentiveness that must have been both flattering and unnerving for the boys; sometimes they blushed or stammered, unable to stand her scrutiny.

The boy had Ruyu and Moran stand together. He squatted to adjust the angle and the focus of his camera and then positioned himself lower to the ground. Where did he want them to look, Moran asked, and the boy said to look forward, so they would appear as though they were women warriors.

Unlike the boys, not many girls in their class seemed to like Ruyu, and none had befriended her. It must not matter much to Ruyu, but Moran felt both offended on Ruyu's behalf and lucky that she herself had been allowed to be, however limited, a friend.

A boom, and the sky lit up. A split second before the shutter clicked, Boyang jumped into the picture, his hands on the shoulders of both girls to balance himself. In the final print, Moran was facing forward, as directed by the boy photographer, looking more astonished than heroic; Ruyu had turned to look at the intruder, the photo capturing only the side of her face, behind which Boyang was laughing with wild triumph; on top of all three heads hung full blossoms of red and orange and purple and silver.

Eventually the boy photographer, unhappy with his altered masterpiece, would reluctantly make prints of the picture, though by then—Shaoai was already poisoned—Moran would feel differently toward the photo. She would be probing alone, half-blindly as though she were looking for a lost companion in a heavy fog: when at last she located a shadowy figure, when she reached a hand out, what she touched would be a shop window coldly reflecting her blurry image.

They returned from the celebration near midnight, tired, thirsty, yet lively, like all young people coming back from a party. On the back of Boyang's bicycle, looking unusually flushed, Ruyu told the other two that this was the first time she had seen fireworks at such a close distance. Back home, her grandaunts chose not to participate in any festivity on the eve of Lunar New Year, their curtains always pulled closed before night fell; one time, though, someone had pointed an eight-flash-booster toward their third-floor window—it had exploded a window pane, and their curtain had caught fire.

"How terrible," Moran said. "Did your grandaunts catch the person who did it?"

Ruyu shook her head and said it didn't matter who had done it. She remembered the momentary fear she had felt, though her grandaunts had never lost their composure, even as they put out the fire. Through the broken window, the freezing air of the January night had rushed into the apartment. No one had stepped out of the festivities to admit the wrongdoing. As she helped her grandaunts nail a piece of cardboard over the window, she'd looked below and wondered if the people down there were laughing at her and her grandaunts. She had no doubt the accident was more than accidental.

"Why would someone do that?" Moran said. "It was dangerous."

"People are idiots," Ruyu said. Moran looked at Ruyu, the contempt in her face the same as when she had told the class monitor earlier that the lipstick was unhygienic. Boyang, having not discerned the coldness in her words, replied that had he been there, he would have lit and stuck a two-banger into the villain's sleeve.

The families around the quadrangle had turned in, but waiting lamps had been left burning in the windows of all three houses for their return. When they were about to say farewell to one another, something moved in the darkness under the grape trellis. A feral cat was Moran's thought, but when Boyang went closer to investigate, he found Shaoai sitting on an overturned bucket and sipping from a bottle of yam liquor.

"Did you all have spectacular fun?" she said, enunciating each word with care, which made her sound more drunk.

"Are you all right, Sister Shaoai?" Moran asked.

"You're celebrating with the masses, and I'm celebrating here by myself," Shaoai said. "The nation needs young people like you, and the dead and the forgotten, alas, have only me." Pointing to the sky unsteadily with the bottle, she started to recite a poem by Li Po.

Amongst the flowers is a pot of wine
I pour alone but with no friend at hand
So I lift the cup to invite the shining moon,
Along with my shadow we become party of three

The moon although understands none of drinking, and
The shadow just follows my body vainly
Still I make the moon and the shadow my company
To enjoy the springtime before too late

The moon lingers while I am singing
The shadow scatters while I am dancing
We cheer in delight when being awake
We separate apart after getting drunk

There was no moon in the sky, and the flowers in the courtyard had long passed their prime. Moran looked around, fearful that Shaoai would wake up the neighbors. None of the houses seemed to be stirring—or could it be that everyone was listening, hiding behind the curtains? There was something intrusive about Shaoai's drunkenness, melodramatic even. Moran wished she had been the only one to have seen Shaoai in this state; she wished she could put a veil over the whole scene—to protect whom, though? Shaoai never needed protection, and Moran could not help feeling embarrassed for her own timidity. Shaoai had always been the one to say what was on her mind, to do what she deemed the right thing. Uneasily Moran turned to her friends, and caught sight of Ruyu, who, standing apart from her and Boyang yet close enough to see Shaoai, looked on with an icy light in her eyes.

"You three!" Shaoai said, turning her face toward Ruyu. "Why not come here and join me?"

After a pause, Moran poked Boyang, so he shook his head and said that it was late, and they all needed to go to bed soon. Shaoai snickered and mumbled something. The three friends walked back quietly, the festive mood of the night gone, exhaustion overwhelming them like a flood.

Moran's mother had stayed up waiting for her, and when she entered the house, her mother brought her a bowl of millet porridge with chestnuts. "What happened to Sister Shaoai?" Moran asked, and her mother only pointed at the bowl and said to finish it before it got cold.

Moran was not hungry, but she knew she would never get any news out of her mother if she did not convince her mother that she was well fed. At the table, Moran's mother watched attentively her daughter's every morsel; when she saw that Moran had eaten enough, she revealed the news that Shaoai had been expelled from the university. The notice had been mailed to her parents a week earlier, but Shaoai must have intercepted it. Earlier that day she had gone back to the university dorm and returned with two traveling bags of belongings. Only then had she told her parents the news. "Shaoai's mother fainted and bumped her head on a table corner," Moran's mother said. "Good thing it was not too serious. Teacher Li and I spent some time with her this evening."

"How is Aunt now?"

"Better, I think. It was just a moment of overwhelming distress that went to her head," Moran's mother said. "You know she's not the weak kind who can't live with a little disaster. None of our generation is that weak."

"What will they do?"

"Who?"

"Aunt and Uncle."

"What can they do? Shaoai was expelled for political reasons—which work unit would dare to hire her? I told her mother at least she had not been shot dead on the Square. At least she had not been arrested and thrown into a prison somewhere. You ought always to look at the positive side."

Moran laid the spoon next to the bowl. Her mother sighed. "Between you and me—and really, don't say this to Aunt or the others—but don't you think Shaoai is partially responsible? What's wrong with recanting? Ninety-nine out of a hundred people would have done that. It's her parents' bad luck to have such a stubborn daughter."

"But isn't that what makes Shaoai a better person than most people?" Moran asked. Shaoai would have scoffed at the lipstick assigned to them and called it demeaning; she would not have put on a silky dress, as Moran had that evening, to follow the official order to look pretty.

"Being good means little. Trust me, being good means nothing in this country. Being right, and being on the right side of any conflict, is the only way to stay safe. An egg never wins when it hurls itself against a rock. Now, don't you go to school and say anything to your classmates. It's better to keep your mouth zipped—you know that, don't you?"

Moran nodded. She didn't have the heart to argue, though she knew she disagreed with her mother. It pained her that Shaoai was in such trouble; it pained her also to imagine Aunt and Uncle suffering. "What is Sister Shaoai going to do now?"

"Do? Nothing for her to do. Stay around. Be an *unemployed-and-stay-at-home* youth. Thank goodness Aunt agreed to host Ruyu for that extra bit of money."

"I thought Aunt was a relative of Ruyu's grandaunts."

"Relative, yes, but can you just send a girl to another family for free? No. Whoever Ruyu's grandaunts are—see, I don't know them, so really I don't have the right to criticize them, but between you and me, I don't like the sound of those ladies. All the same, they are to be commended for how much they pay for Ruyu's stay."

Moran wondered how much it was. If she asked, her mother would tell her, though what difference would that make? She was late in understanding many things about the world, which must have always been less opaque to Ruyu.

Moran's mother shook her head and launched into her favorite monologue about the responsibilities of parents and children. Any news or event might offer an opportunity. "Now, parents feed and clothe a child and provide an education. To repay that upbringing, a child should always bear the parents' well-being in mind when making any decision. If you don't excel in school, you're not only destroying your own life but your parents', because how can you repay your parents if you don't get a good job? You marry the wrong person, and you're not only being irresponsible to yourself but bringing distress to your parents. Anything you do, think of your parents first. Other than the Monkey King, nobody comes out of a crack in the rock."

Had Shaoai been there, she would have erupted into argument, but Moran only said of course, she knew these things by heart. Moran had long accepted that she was not a special person; in fact, she was commonplace in many ways: she was not one of the top students in school, and there was never going to be anything brilliant about her career. She was not as feisty or as sharp-minded as Shaoai; at her age, Shaoai had led her debate team to the city championships twice in a row. Had Moran been a boy, she would have been more convenient to her parents when they needed someone to mend the roof or haul in the three hundred kilos of bok choy—their only vegetable for the whole winter—at the beginning of November. What she was not she could make up only in ways available to her: she was a model child who treated her parents and all the grownups around with respect; she smiled at everyone, neighbors or strangers alike, not because she wanted to be praised for her cheerfulness but because she truly believed that any bit of sunniness she could offer the world would be a comfort; she was a loyal friend, a reliable babysitter, and a good person. What else could she be but a good person? Yet being good, in the end, means little in this world. Sitting by the table and listening to her mother, Moran felt defeated, though when her mother finished, she compelled herself to smile. How lucky she was to have the porridge after such a long day, she said, and her mother said of course, who else but one's own mother would take care of her daughter with such love.

In another house, in the middle of the night, motherless Ruyu woke up, startled by unfamiliar sensations: a hand moving ever so clandestinely underneath her pajamas, her lips pried open by a wet and warm tongue; a foreign body on her own, the weight not heavy but enough to pin her down as one could be pinned down by a nightmare, and, as in the case of a nightmare, one would afterward forever question why one had not awakened in time, why one had not protested.

Ruyu opened her eyes and saw Shaoai's eyes hovering near hers, too near, but how could she see in the darkness, how could anyone see? There must be a lamp somewhere—or was a house, a city, the world, always lit, complete darkness a luxury available only to the dead and the unseeing?

Please make her stop, Ruyu said in her heart, though to whom? No one came to stop the hands and the tongue, nor did she believe that anyone could stop the insanity behind those unclean organs that clung to her: the inconvenient knees and elbows, the slippery fingers, the greedy lips, the unrestrained desire, unrestrainable, consummating itself and in doing so making its object abandon existing as herself—neither a girl nor a woman Ruyu felt, but a being as blind as the force driving her predator. As poisonous.

In one's hoping for help, one becomes small; smaller yet when no help comes. Only then does one understand that this moment is al-

ways there, waiting, preying, in disguise, or even in arrogant open-
ness. How could she have misread life with such foolishness?

Yet that was not the worst. The worst is not a moment robbed
from one's life, but what's left in place of the moment: an abyss where
all the other moments could slip in easily. One does not wake up
from a nightmare unhaunted.

Clammy, cold, Ruyu did not remember falling back to sleep,
though when, again, she woke up with a start, she realized that she
had dozed off. Shaoai was next to her; still? Ruyu thought with dismay, but then, why not? There was no place for either of them to go,
now, or ever.

"If you're waiting for me to give you an explanation," Shaoai said,
"I can tell you that you're hoping in vain."

Ruyu wondered if Shaoai had been waiting for her to wake up, to
beg for an explanation that Shaoai alone would have the power to
deny. "Nor will I apologize," she continued.

Is this what people do after any sort of unnatural happening—
prattle, so that all will become normal after a while? Time, refusing
to become memory, demands one's attention with a suffocating grip,
yet one can do nothing about time, nor can one do away with time.

"Someday you'll be grateful to me," Shaoai said. "I know you may
not believe me now. If you're angry, you can stay angry for as long as
you're able, but this is what I think you should know: you have a
brain, which you are responsible for filling with meaningful thoughts;
you have a life ahead of you, which you should live for yourself. You
have not been taught to think or to question by your grandaunts. For
heaven's sake, you have not even been taught to have human feelings. Since they haven't done that for you, someone else must."

Do murderers expect gratitude from the murdered souls for setting them free from their earthly burdens? If Ruyu went to Grandpa's
room now, could she put her hands gently on his brittle neck and
liberate him from the humiliation of being half-dead?

"You are the most unbending girl I've ever met," Shaoai said, all of a sudden possessed by an anger that Ruyu did not understand. "Why do you think you have the right to be like that?"

"I don't understand what you are asking," Ruyu said. "I don't see how the kind of person I am has anything to do with what happened."

"Of course it doesn't in your mind, but that's what I'm talking about. Live like a real human being. Bring yourself down from the clouds. Open your eyes."

Yet there was nothing to see, Ruyu thought, but could she be wrong? Suppose ugliness is worth seeing, too?

"Just so you know: I don't want you to think too much of what happened. As a matter of fact, nothing much has happened between you and me. Someday, you may even shrug it off and laugh at it," Shaoai said, and after a moment she added bitterly, "If you don't believe me, go ask Yening. She may have wisdom to share with you."

Ruyu wondered if Shaoai had said that out of the hope of being contradicted. Perhaps Shaoai wanted to know how permanently she had marked Ruyu's life because she had failed to make Yening her possession. Ruyu shifted her body and felt the mosquito netting brush her face. Aunt had said earlier that day that the netting would be kept up until the end of the week. All the mosquitoes would be gone by the second week of October, she had said with cheerful assurance. One nuisance out of one's life, Ruyu thought, feeling a dull ache behind her eyes. Was this how people felt when they wanted to cry? Ruyu could not remember the last time she had cried.

"Why don't you say something?" Shaoai asked.

"Do you do that to Moran, too? Do you want to do that to her, too?"

Shaoai seemed taken aback. "Of course not."

"Why of course? Why not?" Ruyu asked. Though she knew the answer already. Shaoai's desire would never bring her to Moran, because Moran, with her idolization of the older girl, held no meaning for Shaoai, just as Ruyu herself, and her grandaunts also, meant nothing to God. Bad things happen—wars, plagues, parents abandoning their children, the heartless preying on those with hearts—and no one, not a human nor a god, will ever intervene.

Shaoai seemed baffled. "Moran, she's only a child," she said after a moment.

Moran did not sleep well that night, perhaps because of the day's excitement. When she woke up at daybreak, she could no longer stay still. She got out of bed and washed quietly at the washstand, and through the window she could see Shaoai, who'd risen early also, lingering under the grape trellis. Had Shaoai stayed outside overnight? Moran wondered; but having few words of comfort for her, Moran found herself unwilling to go into the yard, as she would have done on any other morning.

13

On their second date—five days after their dinner on Sunday—Sizhuo asked Boyang his age, and whether Boyang was his real name. Why, he said with amusement, and placed his citizen's ID on the table. They were in a teahouse near his parents' place, which he'd planned to stop by afterward, hoping it would seem to his parents as though they were on his mind often enough to warrant an unplanned visit. But the thought of seeking their approval, however unconsciously, made him decide at once to skip seeing them after all. On the most fundamental level, they were the best parents he could ask for: they caused him no conflict, either internal or external, while with each day's passing he was made more aware, by his guilty glances at the calendar, that he had not visited Aunt since the day of Shaoai's cremation. It was more Aunt's fault than his own, he insisted to himself, turning defiant as people do when their limits are shown in unsparing light: unlike his parents, she reminded him of all the complications he was incapable of dealing with in life. Who had granted her the right to do that to him?

He had told his secretary that he was taking the afternoon off—Sizhuo worked five and a half days a week, Friday afternoon and Saturday being her time off. Other things he had gathered on their first date: she'd grown up in a village in the northeast, near the border of Russia; her father was the only teacher in the village school, teach-

ing six grades in one room; her mother ran a seamstress' stall; she had
a younger brother at a provincial university with two more years of
study; his major was marketing, and Sizhuo hoped she could help
her brother come to Beijing after graduation.

"You're older than I thought," Sizhuo said after studying the ID.

"What does that even mean?"

Sizhuo pushed the ID back across the table. "My friend said if
you were over thirty-five I should not see you again."

"Wait a minute, who's this friend, and how old is she?" Boyang
said, feigning indignity. From Sizhuo's background—and she had
not shied away from giving details when he had asked the previous
time—he had calculated that she was twenty-two or twenty-three,
more or less Coco's age.

Sizhuo shook her head, as if to say the questions were not important.

"And what makes her so prejudiced against men my age?"

"She said men *that* old"—Sizhuo stopped, but there was neither
apology nor coyness in her pause—"men at your age want different
things than I do."

The friend might not be wrong, Boyang thought, but what did
he want from this girl whom he knew he should have left alone
altogether? There were plenty of people in his life to cater to his
sentiments, and his sentiments had a reliable pattern—reliable
enough—so that he did not worry about unpleasant surprises, nor did
he wait for joyful ones. For mindless pleasures, he could go to Coco,
with whom there was a cleaner contract, less befuddlement. For in-
tellectual intrigue, he could talk with his parents—his mother more
than his father, who had started to show early signs of dementia; or
even with his sister, to whom over the years he had grown closer than
when they'd been children, but perhaps it was more accurate to say
that in adulthood they found each other, as she had been launched
into the world not as a child but as a mind of genius that had to dwell
in a child's body for some time. If ever he wanted to develop affection

for the young there were his two nieces for him to dote on from afar. If he wanted to play games with people—did he ever want that? no, not really—there were plenty of opportunities, challenging rivals, and profitable gains if he wanted to make scheming more a part of his life. In thus looking at his life, Boyang could not find a place to fit the girl. She's miscellaneous, he thought; others belonged to that category, too, the unsettled and the unsettling: Moran, Ruyu, Shaoai— she had been the center of that category for so long that it was impossible to think of her as absent now—perhaps even Aunt; and of course he himself, too, at listless moments, when people in his life failed to entertain or distract him. But to put Sizhuo into that space that he rarely allowed himself to visit—was it an alarming sign?

"What does a girl your age want?" Boyang asked. Easily he could list all the things Coco wanted, none of them too expensive. He could list a few things Sizhuo desired: to hold on to her job at a time when many young people were jobless after graduation; to find a way to move up in life—by what means? he wondered, and decided that marriage was the only possible way—and purchase a small apartment, outside the Fifth or the Sixth Ring Road; to know a few of the right people so that her younger brother could get a foothold, however unsteady, when it was time for him to enter the job market; to work with her sibling to establish some sort of settlement in Beijing, so that eventually their parents could come and live with them. Marriage and children would ensue, and by the next generation the family's migration from the countryside to the metropolis would be complete. A familiar story, and Boyang could see that he could come in handy in that narrative. Was that why the girl had agreed to a second date? At their previous dinner, he had only vaguely spoken of his profession; he had made certain that for both dates he had dressed with impeccable but not extravagant taste, though he wondered if she could recognize the subtle difference. On so many levels, she was not like Coco, which was part of the reason that he felt unequipped to come to any conclusions yet. When one has enough protocols set

up for life, anything that does not fall readily into an available protocol makes one suspect that he has been underplayed. Treacherous
was not what he would call Sizhuo, yet he was treading less familiar
waters, which, thrilling as it was, could also be perilous.

Sizhuo looked pensive. "I suppose I want . . ." She paused and
looked up again. "Do you have a child?"

"I'm not married," Boyang said. "Listen, many men my age might
be monsters in your eyes, but if I had a wife, I would give her enough
honor not to chase young girls around."

"But that doesn't mean you didn't have a wife before, right? So it
is possible you have a child?" Sizhuo said. He wished that she were
being coy or even flirtatious, but her unsmiling expression made the
conversation seem like a logic debate.

"Yes, it's possible. But no, I don't have a child. If I had one, I
wouldn't hide the fact from you."

"But how do I know if you're lying or not?" Sizhuo asked. "I don't
know you, so the only way is to go by your words."

Boyang laughed. "What are you, miss? A private detective?"

"No, certainly not," she said, leaning back so the waitress who had
brought them their tea could place the set between them. When the
waitress finished pouring, she lowered her eyes and said she hoped
they'd enjoy the tea. Sizhuo thanked her, her eyes never leaving the
girl's face. Boyang wondered if Sizhuo was aware that his eyes had
not moved from her face. When they were left alone again, Sizhuo
said that people lied sometimes, and she would like to know when
and why they did.

"Do you not lie?" Boyang said.

The girl thought and said she did not lie so much as she would
avoid situations in which dishonesty would be required of her.

"I'd call you a lucky girl if you've been achieving that," Boyang
said. "For instance, here's a question for you: you like me enough to
see me a second time, is that right?"

Sizhuo blushed. Her inexperience—no, her innocence was what

made him lose his head and become less tactical, yet innocence also brought her into this dilemma. It was one lesson, Boyang wanted to say, that she had yet to learn: innocence can be one's weapon only when it's not seen by the world.

"I don't have an answer to your question," Sizhuo said.

"That's the most conventional answer people use to dodge a question," Boyang said. "And that's even worse than lying."

"But if it works? Why can't I use it if others use it successfully?"

Because he hated to see her as one of the others, but Boyang did not say that. "One thing that makes my age more advantageous," he said, "is that it's easier for me to catch someone lying than when I was twenty. But in any case, I'm going to tell you this and it's not a lie: I was married once. Not anymore." Under forty, divorced, no children, with an excellent income and spacious housing in the city, Boyang was one of the most desired men on the marriage market, a *diamond bachelor.* "Now, not only am I too old, but now you know that I'm divorced. Does that add to my disqualification as a suitor?"

Sizhuo looked uneasy at the term *suitor* but quickly regained her countenance. "No, I think it's expected for someone your age."

"What is expected?"

"A divorce. My friend says the only thing worse than a man over thirty-five is a man over thirty-five who has never married."

Boyang laughed, but Sizhuo only watched him with unaverted eyes. He felt his heart sink a little. What was she doing with him — making him a specimen for her girlish study of men and their characters, so she could afterward discuss him with her friend? "Now, who is this friend of yours?"

"Someone you don't know."

"But she's someone I must know!" Boyang said. "I'll offer her a position screening job candidates for me."

Sizhuo's face froze for a split second, and he wondered if girls always felt jealous when another girl was being praised. "But she's employed already," she said.

"I can give her a better offer."

Sizhuo shook her head and pretended to study the tea set. She had insisted on meeting elsewhere, away from the area around the Front Sea and Back Sea; why, he had asked, and she had said there were too many tourists, and they had made the place impossible to breathe.

"What are other things on your friend's list that you're to find out about me?"

"I'm the friend," Sizhuo said.

For a moment Boyang did not grasp the words. Sizhuo smiled and said there was not another person she consulted with. She herself was the friend she was speaking of.

"I see," Boyang said, but he could not see where the conversation was going. What he noticed was that the girl looked sadder and older when she smiled, a pity in a young, good-looking woman; a smile — unless it was the kind Coco and her girlfriends perfected in front of a mirror with a fashion magazine for a textbook — should be a woman's best adornment.

"Had I been my own best friend, I'd have wanted to know the answers to those questions," Sizhuo explained again, and he recognized a hint of placation in her voice. "Does that make sense? I wasn't really lying."

The girl had too much patience with the world, Boyang thought; she must never have been in a situation where impatience was an option for her, or she had never considered it her due. "So, what's this best friend inside you whispering to you now? That I'm a bad choice for you?"

"Can I ask you a question — are we on a date?"

The easiest response would be to make a joke to defuse the girl's uncanny persistence, but would that suffice? Would that make him a lesser person to her? Sizhuo's eyes, when Boyang looked at them, seemed to indicate a resolve to never let a single detail pass without being seen. He wondered if that tenacity came to her naturally. "Traditionally speaking, this should be considered a date."

"But what if we're not traditionally speaking?" Sizhuo asked.

"Why do you ask?"

"Because I want to know how you think about these things."

"Me, or men in general?"

She seemed torn; each option put her in a situation with which she had to reconcile: in wanting his personal opinion she risked putting him in a weighty position in her life; in casting him back into an ocean of men, she would question her own unfairness.

A tenderness stirred in him: he had already known her more than perhaps he was willing to. Every question to which one seeks an answer will inevitably come back, a boomerang to cut into one's flesh. She was not armored against that danger as she might have thought; no, she was not protected at all: only those who do not seek answers are safe from being touched.

"I'm asking," Sizhuo started to answer, then paused to reconsider. "I suppose I'm asking about what you, yourself, think."

Boyang felt a surge of satisfaction, as though he had won a hard battle against a battalion of men, their indistinctive faces retreating fast. "I think of myself as a conventional man in this aspect, and so of course I take it that I've asked you out on a date," he said, keeping his expression thoughtful. "However, you're asking for more honesty, so I'll give you more: only very tentatively do I consider this a date."

"Why tentatively?"

"Because such a conversation should not be happening on a date, don't you think? When people are wholehearted about any kind of business, they don't analyze and question why they are there in the first place."

"I see," Sizhuo said, and Boyang thought she looked a little defeated. During their first meeting, she had seemed to enjoy herself more, though their conversation had been less demanding then: she had talked about her work and her childhood in the northern village; he had asked her questions, and in turn gave a few harmless details about his own life.

Neither spoke. The conversation seemed to be going off in an unexpected direction, though Boyang could not decide if he was disappointed. There was no reason for him to be in this girl's life, and he should be glad that she had the good sense to question his presence. All the same, he wanted to hold on to her a little longer; he even wanted to confide in her—but confide what? he thought, alarmed. The girl seemed to have a center, perhaps unknown to her, like a mysterious vacuum, which effortlessly drew him toward her. Could it be youth, or innocence, that was doing the trick? No, that must not be it. He thought of the other girl from years ago, the orphan who had made a fool of him. There was nothing youthful or innocent in Ruyu even back then; still, the same vacuum, dangerous in that case, had been there to draw him in. Boyang raised the teacup to calm himself. People don't vanish from one's life; they come back in disguise.

"Suppose we aren't really on a date," Sizhuo said. "Then what do we do now? We shake hands and say good-bye, right?"

Boyang pointed at his watch. "We've only been sitting here for twenty minutes," he said. "Don't you think it's a bit rushed to say farewell now?"

"But is it?" She gazed at him.

"Did you come today just to find out if we're on a date?"

"Perhaps."

"And now that you know the answer, you're ready to take off," he said. "Not even inclined to stay for a friendly chat?"

"What's the point of a friendly chat when we're not even friends?"

Indeed, they were no more than strangers who had caught each other's eye by happenstance—a smile, a nod, eyebrows raised in surprise or marvel or bafflement, but what one should not ask for, and thus should not be granted, is the right to linger. To breach the contract of transience—whether to indulge oneself in the belief that much more could happen, or to have merely an undisturbed moment to ponder the impossibility of making something out of this, or any kind of, encounter—is to overreach, to demand clarity from life's muddiness. Certainly Boyang's ache for permanency, his ache to make sense out of the nonsensical, should have been cured by now. Why couldn't he simply agree with the girl, wish her a happy life without him, and part ways amicably? Yet he was not ready to let her go. She seemed to be living in a universe of her own making, but how could she—how could anyone—live so seriously and so blindly? Where did her fallibility hide itself? Her lack of corruption reminded him of the folktale in which a child could turn a rock into a piece of gold, yet remained oblivious to the fact that this capacity—more than it would make him rich—would launch him into an unredeemable life: my child, the world is a much worse place than you can ever imagine.

Boyang did not know whether he was jealous of Sizhuo or angry at her on behalf of the world that had already gone bad. It was not exactly an urge to protect that made him linger, nor a desire to destroy, but if she was destined to lose that universe of her own making, he wanted to be the one responsible—he, the corruptor who beat all other corruptors. "It takes time and effort to find a friend in this city, no?" he said. "Why not give us some time?"

"Friendship happens," Sizhuo said.

"But not love?"

"Love happens, too."

"So neither is something we can strive for? Or should I say, I'm given no hope in either category?"

Sizhuo looked at Boyang quizzically. He wondered if he had been unwittingly aggressive, but he had little—or too much—to lose: in either case, one was allowed a deviation from the protocol. "How about this?" he said, pointing to the window; across the street, on the side of a building, was a billboard for a fitness center. "I have a membership to the gym there. There are six badminton courts on the second floor, and we can go there once a week to play badminton. We don't even have to talk if you don't want to."

"I don't know how to play badminton," Sizhuo said.

Boyang wanted to kick himself for his oversight. Certainly she, growing up in the village, would think of badminton as a luxury sport, but could he explain to her that he and Moran used to play in the alleyway, dodging people on foot or on bicycles, often having to climb up to the rooftop to retrieve a stray birdie? Could he tell her that in the summers, he and other boys would hunt for the fat, green larvae of cabbage butterflies, put them into birdies, and launch them straight into the sky with their racquets? The poor worms always plunged back to the earth with nothing to meet them but a solid death, yet there had been nothing ominous to him, or even to Moran, about those random executions. Would Sizhuo protest if he told her the story? Coco would have screamed and called the action sick, but Sizhuo had grown up in the countryside where lives were probably butchered or maimed every day. "How about Ping-Pong?" he said.

She smiled, which again made her look resigned. Did the village school where her father taught have a crude concrete block that served as a Ping-Pong table in the yard, as his elementary school had? His childhood, even though it had been a city childhood, had come almost a generation earlier, and could not have been too different from Sizhuo's.

"I don't know how to play Ping-Pong."

"How about racquetball?" he said. "Now, hold it—give me the pleasure to say I don't know how to play it, either. I've watched people play, and the ball sure goes fast. We'll be too occupied with learning the game to feel awkward about not talking."

"Why do you want to play racquetball with me if you don't mind not talking?" she said.

Any activity would be an excuse for him to continue seeing her— this she had no reason not to understand. "I suppose I'm interested in getting to know you better," he said. "So I'm scrambling to find anything you'll agree to do with me so I have an opportunity."

"Is this how a man of your status courts a woman?"

He looked into her eyes but could find neither malice nor irony in them. "What kind of status are you referring to?"

"You have a car and an apartment, so you must also have a good career?" she said, asking more than stating, and he nodded to confirm her guess. "Does that mean when you court a woman, you can always find something to do with her?"

"To do?"

"What if you lived in a basement with three other provincial boys, and you did not have any savings? You worked six and a half days a week, and yet you knew you would never be able to afford the cheapest apartment in this city. What if all you possessed was your being, and there was nothing you could do but be yourself? Would you still be courting a girl?"

No, he thought; this was not a welcoming world for young men without any means. A few weeks ago, a woman in her early twenties had said in a TV interview that she would prefer an unhappy marriage with a BMW to being in love with a young man who could afford only to carry her on his bicycle. Boyang mentioned the name of the young woman—already her bold practicality had made her a national celebrity—and asked what Sizhuo thought of the woman's preference.

Sizhuo looked agonized. She crossed and uncrossed her fingers, the first time he had seen her lose her equanimity. "I wish she were completely wrong about everything. I don't think she was, though," she said. "This is not the kind of world I thought I'd grow up to live in, you know?"

She was not the first to have realized that, he wanted to point out. What made her different from other disillusioned souls? All young people start with untainted dreams, but how many would retain their capacities to dream? How many could refrain from transforming themselves into corruptors of other untainted dreams? We are all wardens and executors biding our time; what's taken from us, what's killed in us, we wait for our turn to avenge. Such wisdom, had Coco ever been interested, Boyang would not have hesitated to share: he would have sneered, laughed, enjoyed his position the way a cat gently plays with its prey. But what made Sizhuo different—what made him pensive now—was that he wanted a better answer for her; he wanted a better world to offer her. Was this how a father would feel toward a child? He made a face, the question conjuring the most farcical: paternal, he thought, a paternal sugar daddy.

Sizhuo did not take her eyes from his face. "You must find my ranting laughable," she said, though her face showed no sign of unease due to self-consciousness. "Sometimes I think so, too, but the moment I think that way, I know I'm wrong."

"I'm not laughing at you," he said. "More at myself because, you know, I'm one of those people who have made the world a bad place for you, and in turn I'm asking you to like me, even to fall in love with me."

"What do you do that for?"

"To ask you to like me?"

"To help make the world a bad place, if what you said was true."

"What else can I do?"

Sizhuo looked baffled, as though he were asking her for an answer.

"Nobody can refrain from doing things," he said. "You see, a child can get by with just being, but we aren't children forever. We must live by doing things. And either we do harm, or, if we are extremely lucky, we do some good. The problem, as you know, is that the world is an unbalanced place, and it requires more bad than good to maintain that unbalance. If you want to do one good thing—say, if you give money to a beggar child—no big deal, right? But no, it's not that simple. To be able to do that, you have to deceive yourself into believing that a bill dropped in her basket is going to help her, to give her one more morsel of food, to spare her one beating from her parents. While in reality, you and I both know that she might have been stolen or rented or sold to the begging ring; by giving her money, instead of doing anyone any good, what you're really doing is contributing to criminals, helping them profit from doing damage, and encouraging more criminals to steal and sell babies into that trade. So what do I do? I either give her the money, or I don't, all depending on my mood that day. But either way, I have no illusions about doing anything good for her, or for anyone. I'm sorry, is this too bleak for you?"

Sizhuo shook her head. "Why is the world unbalanced?" she said. "Why does it require more bad than good?"

He could give her his hypothesis about the connection between human hearts and entropy that he sometimes played in his head, but he would have to be drunk to go on with such nonsense. Already he regretted that their conversation was going off on a tangent. He was here to woo a woman. He was not here to be baffled and defeated by the world alongside her. "Why that is," he said, "I truly don't know."

"Do you want to know?"

No, he did not, he thought, though he knew that was only wishful thinking. The real question was, can anyone afford to know? "Do you?" he asked.

"I do," she said. "That makes me a fool in people's eyes, I know, but I don't mind being a fool."

"What *do* you mind?"

"Not knowing, and making do with not knowing."

14

After the celebration on October 1, life went back to the old routines, nearly normal again, though Moran no longer knew what kind of normalcy she was thinking of. There was little hope in the case of Shaoai, who no longer belonged to any school or work unit. Neither Moran nor Boyang had the courage to ask Shaoai about how she spent her days. In the evenings, she could be seen in the house or in the courtyard, moody and distant.

Uncle was no more reticent than before, bearing his trademark smile without fail, and Aunt was as chatty as ever. Yet their stoic efforts could not dispel the despondent fog hanging over their faces. They looked older now, and were sometimes distracted when they tried to follow the neighbors' conversations. More than before they seemed intimidated by their daughter.

Hardships in lives, Moran was raised to believe, are like unpleasant weather, which one endures because bad weather will break as inevitably as bad luck will run its course. Hope is the sunshine after the storm, the spring thawing after the bitter winter; the goddess of fate, capricious as she is, has nevertheless an impressionable mind, as any young female does, who would smile at those who have perseverance.

Moran's nature was to find hope for others before she could feel hopeful herself. To stay silent was the first step in resigning oneself to

hopelessness, so armed with inherited and wishful thinking, she repeated the stale wisdom to Shaoai when they found themselves alone
in the courtyard. It was a Saturday afternoon, a half day at school, and
both Boyang and Ruyu disappeared around noon. Moran wondered
if Ruyu had a rehearsal; as for Boyang, he must have gone to a basketball or soccer game with other boys.

"Things will become better, Sister Shaoai," Moran said. "Don't
lose heart. Remember the tale in which the man lost one horse only
to find that it brought another horse back to the stable?"

"Since when did you turn yourself into a mouthpiece for the wise
and the optimistic?" Shaoai said, looking at Moran askance.

Moran blushed. "I don't want you to feel alone in your situation,"
she said.

"You don't want me to feel alone, huh? And I bet you want many
things for others, too, right?"

Moran shook her head confusedly. Too young to know that her
affection was the kind that made a child revolt against a mother, she
was disheartened by Shaoai's punishing words.

"It's ambitious of you to want things for me," Shaoai said. "But let
me give you a solid piece of advice, the same I've given my parents:
don't waste your feelings on an unworthy person."

Moran stammered and said she admired Shaoai as always.

"My dear Moran, in this case I wasn't talking about myself. Sure,
my parents should've known by now not to spend their energy worrying about me," Shaoai said. "And you, don't you think you're a bit
childish, following your two other friends as though you can't see
they'd prefer to be left by themselves?"

It took Moran a moment to understand what the older girl was
insinuating, and by then Shaoai had unlocked her bicycle, leaving
Moran in an abyss. Slowly she turned toward her house, fumbling for
the key.

There was no reason not to believe Shaoai. Moran wondered if
others—her parents, for instance, or Boyang's grandmother—had

wanted to warn her, too. Since childhood, Moran had seen, in the approving eyes of their elders, a future for her and Boyang. She had refrained from naming it because he had not named it. Loyalty to that future was all she had, yet loyalty to a future, unlike to the past, is a feeling both blind and arrogant. What begins with a label bears an expiration date; by defining something only after its disappearance — a sibling, a friend, a childhood sweetheart—Moran would one day understand that the loss, limited for him because he must have long ago dismissed it with a name, was for her a continuing void.

Moran slipped into bed with her school uniform still on, and under the cover of the blanket she shed quiet tears. A small shift in the past few days, which had been so minute that she had been uncertain whether it was only in her imagination, came back to her with new significance. It used to be that Ruyu would hop on whichever bicycle was closer to her, though one morning last week she had walked around Moran and sat behind Boyang, and ever since had chosen his bicycle.

The next day Moran proposed to Boyang that the three of them use his room rather than Ruyu's for their night study. To give Sister Shaoai some space, Moran said. After a difficult night she had decided that her friendship with the other two should not change, but she did not want her bravery—or foolishness—to be seen by Shaoai.

Boyang readily agreed. He must have found it hard to be around Shaoai these days, too; Moran wondered if Shaoai had embarrassed Boyang by commenting on the relationship between him and Ruyu. Moran did not detect any change in him toward herself, and Ruyu was distant but no more than before. Perhaps Shaoai had been in such a bad mood that she wanted to hurt others; what she had told Moran might not be true. This thought made Moran hopeful again, and it cast a pitying shadow over her sympathy toward Shaoai. Like anyone with a youthful mind, Moran, too occupied with her own prospect of happiness, had little capacity for real sympathy—the kind that is not perfunctorily expressed out of one's duty toward another person's misfortune. But how many people are strong enough to give—or to receive, even—real sympathy? In distress and in catastrophe, one often looks for the strengthening forces not in people closest to one, but in the perfect indifference in strangers' faces, who put one's woes back to where they belong—irrelevant to the extent of being comical.

"Every generation has to learn this lesson," Moran's mother said at dinner when the topic turned to Shaoai. "Public protest will never do in this country. Unfortunately, some pay more dearly than others. Now that you're not a child anymore, use your brain better."

Moran mumbled an answer. The neighbors did not discuss Shaoai's situation. All had gone through the political "recheck" over the past few weeks, none but Shaoai with a harsh outcome. They all treated her with the same respect and patience, but behind closed doors, they must have exchanged critical words about Shaoai, as Moran's parents had.

A moth fluttered into the lamp above the dinner table, and Moran's father waved his chopsticks as though the gesture alone would make the distraction go away. Moran watched the moth, its wings dusty and gray, its flight purposeless. These moths, no larger than ladybugs, seemed to have become a permanent fixture in the house. They came from the straw-colored worms that lived in the bags of rice her parents had scrambled to buy out of fear of the ever-worsening inflation; it was Moran's job to winnow out the wiggly worms before cooking the rice. Unlike the mosquitoes and flies her mother hunted down with a single-minded determination, the moths, doing no harm, were left to live and die on their own.

Moran sighed, and her mother, as though she had been waiting for the opportunity, launched into a speech about why a young person like Moran felt she had the right to sigh. Moran listened with an obedient expression. These days, the moths, along with supplies her parents had stored in their battle against inflation—bars of alkaline soap, drab yellow and wrapped in straw paper, boxes of matches that had become damp and became harder to strike by the day, toilet paper, laundry detergent, inexpensive tea in the form of crude bricks, all growing stale, collecting dust—these made Moran's heart despondent: every time she turned around, she seemed to bump into another pile of things, stirring another moth from its repose into a frenzy of blind flight. The world had become smaller, dimmer, but was it for her alone?

Such despair Moran had to hide from her parents. Hadn't her mother survived an impoverished childhood among six siblings, supported by the meager earnings of their father as a pedicab driver? Hadn't her father weathered years of humiliation as the son of a petit bourgeois?

The same gray moths fluttered in other houses, too, yet Boyang and Ruyu never seemed to be bothered. Why would they be, if life was generous and granted them all the good qualities that Moran herself lacked? But such a bitter thought made her feel guilty: certainly Ruyu had experienced bigger loss; certainly she deserved more kindness, better love.

After the last class of the day, Ruyu went to the music room to practice the accordion. Sometimes, when she played on the porch, Moran came over to watch. She did not want to go into the low-ceilinged cottage, which was gloomy, and indeed she had no right to be in there; besides Ruyu, there were a few other student musicians Teacher Shu supervised—four violinists, two boys who played four-hands on the piano, and a middle school girl who played the xylophone and belonged to a fifty-member, all-girl xylophone ensemble in Japan, where she was the only Chinese student. How the girl could join a Japanese ensemble Moran did not know, and some days, sitting on the porch and listening to the instruments, each preoccupied with its own music, she wondered about the things she had missed or would miss in life. She had no talent for creating anything beautiful— the only music she could make was to whistle a simple tune, wobbling with uncertainty, and even that drew disapproving looks from her mother because it was unladylike to whistle; her drawings and her handwriting were childish, and she had few skills in any art; even her body and face were nondescript.

Moran turned to study Ruyu—it was one of the best autumn days in Beijing, the sky blue in a crystal way, and Teacher Shu had driven all his charges, other than the two pianists, onto the porch to practice. In the shade of the eave, Ruyu moved her fingers up and down the keyboard in a distracted way, yet when Moran closed her eyes, she could not tell the difference between a halfhearted performance and a dedicated one, as she could not tell the difference between Ruyu's confidence and her impertinence.

"This must be boring for you," Ruyu said when she finished a piece. "You shouldn't feel obliged to wait for me."

"No, it's not boring at all," Moran said. "What is it that you just played?"

Ruyu turned over the sheet of music as though she had not heard the question. "I can walk home," she said after pausing to read the next sheet. "Or else I'll catch a ride with Boyang."

Three days a week, Boyang played basketball, and on the other two days, he played soccer or just hung out with a few boys by the bicycle shed, exchanging tall tales. Sometimes Moran joined them, as they were all friendly with her, though their favorite topics— Michael Jackson, breakdancing, Transformers—did not interest her. Once in a while, she played Ping-Pong, but she was not a great player, and would step aside when the games became competitive. Three girls with whom she had been close in middle school stayed after class, too, talking more than doing anything; Moran's friendship with them had not continued as easily as she'd expected: there seemed to be a dangerous undercurrent, a triangle of complications in which Moran often got lost, and their words, seemingly pregnant with meaning, sometimes sounded too assiduous or simply silly.

"I don't mind waiting," Moran said. "In fact, I like to watch you play."

Ruyu looked at Moran with a cold scrutiny. "Do you mean you like to watch people play music? Or do you mean you like to watch me?"

Moran blushed. What right, Ruyu seemed to be saying, did Moran have to sit next to Ruyu, claiming to be her friend? "I don't know. Maybe I just like to listen to real music being played on an instrument."

"Why?"

"Because I don't play music?" Moran said, wavering under Ruyu's steadfast gaze. "No one I know plays music."

"Do you want to?"

Moran looked at the girl on the xylophone, who was practicing with such abandon that even when her eyes were open—and they were huge, almost inhuman eyes, mysteriously deep—she seemed to be seeing nothing. Years later, the girl would transform herself into the drummer for the first female rock band in China, and Moran would see her photo in a magazine: clad in a layer of shiny black leather, she had the same abandon, or exaggerated despair, in her eyes.

Ruyu glanced at the girl. Moran wondered if in Ruyu's eyes the girl was simply a pretentious actor, or worse, a nuisance. Yet the girl could travel with her instrument on an airplane to Japan, showing her passport to the officials in both countries. Apart from Boyang's sister, Moran had not known another person who had left the country; none of the people in the quadrangle was even qualified to apply for a passport.

With wordless contempt Ruyu turned to look at Moran, as though to ask her if she wanted to be the girl at the xylophone. "I do wish I could play music," Moran said. "But not everyone can afford to."

"Why not? I'm an orphan, and even I can do it."

It was the first time Ruyu had used the word *orphan*. Moran did not have words to comfort Ruyu, but the claim, with its haughtiness, had been thrown more as a dagger at the world, and Moran, unable to reply, offered herself as the target.

Ruyu returned to her practice and launched into a maddeningly paced polka. Moran understood that she was not a welcome companion on the porch. Pride would have required her to apologize and to absent herself, but whether she left or not seemed to matter little. Of course Ruyu could do many things that no other person could do: it was not because she was an orphan—had Moran been an orphan, she would have been one of those shivering and begging by the roadside; it was not because Ruyu was beautiful—she was, but there were other girls more beautiful, better built than she, yet at times they, too, were susceptible to the uncertainties that Ruyu was immune to; no, Ruyu could do anything she wanted, to others, to the world, because she knew she was someone destined to be special. She felt no burden to prove it to herself or to anyone, nor had she any tolerance for those who were not chosen as she was. What was Moran like in Ruyu's eyes? Years later, it would strike Moran as either the most fortunate or the most unfortunate happening in her life that the first time she looked at herself through someone else's eyes, she had chosen Ruyu's: who was she to Ruyu but someone so ordinary that neither her joy nor her pain would amount to anything but the dross of everydayness?

A few days later, Boyang told Moran that Ruyu had asked to see the university where his parents taught. "Saturday afternoon," he said. "Shall we go together?"

The university, on the west side of the city, was not far from the Summer Palace, and its campus had been, in its previous incarnation, a residence for the closest cousins and allies of the emperors of the last dynasty. It was said to be one of the most beautiful places in Beijing, yet in all the years Moran had known Boyang, she had never once visited the campus. It was part of the world he did not want to share with her; nor would she have found herself at ease near it. His parents, she knew, had little regard for her and her parents and people like them.

Ruyu's request did not come as a surprise. Still, it agonized Moran that what was forbidden for her was something ordinary for Ruyu, who had only to ask to be handed the entry pass. Was Boyang aware of the difference? She looked at him, and he seemed excited by the plan. "Of course we'll put her on a bus and we'll meet her at the university. But do you think she'll handle the bus ride all right? She'd have to change to another route midway. Alternatively, you could ride the bus with her. But then we won't have the two bicycles, and it's an awfully big campus to walk around." Boyang stopped. "What? Did you already plan something else for Saturday?"

"No, not at all," Moran said. She sounded too eager, she thought, but she did not want to disappoint him.

"Would your parents be okay if we have dinner there? Not with my parents. Ruyu asked if we could see my mother's lab, and I thought we could have dinner in a dining hall and then go there after hours, so we won't have to deal with talking to people."

"Will your mother be there?"

"Oh silly, don't you worry. She wouldn't stay for us. She wouldn't change her plans for the prime minister."

Despite Moran's misgivings, as the day came nearer, she, too, started looking forward to the outing. There was little doubt that Boyang would attend his parents' university—he was a top student and would not even need to claim family privilege to get in. He had always believed that Moran would attend the university, too, though she wasn't so sure herself. She would have to improve her academic standing and score perfectly on the entrance exam, but when she voiced such doubts to Boyang, he only teased her for being overcautious. Of course things would work out, he told her; she was better than she allowed herself to think. Imagine the freedom they would have when they went to the university, he had said, and she had seen no option but to trust his enthusiasm, and had, up till now, enjoyed his vision.

"So," Shaoai said on Friday evening at dinner. "Did I hear right about some visit to a university tomorrow?"

Ruyu did not raise her eyes to acknowledge the question. These days, dinnertime was a torment for her, worse than bedtime, because by then she had an open battleground separating her from Shaoai. Only once after that night had Shaoai tried to touch Ruyu again, but she had, with the most even voice she could manage, told the older girl to leave her alone. No more words had been said afterward, no more advances made, and every night Ruyu wrapped her blanket tightly around herself and stayed alert by only sleeping shallowly.

Ruyu had sworn, and had so far kept her word, that she would never lay eyes on Shaoai's face again. The presence of Aunt and Uncle, though, made things harder. At dinner, with the older girl sitting across the table, Ruyu had to either look into her bowl of rice or, when Aunt talked to her, look up at Aunt, yet willfully blur her peripheral vision.

"What university?" Aunt said, bristling. *University* was one of the words they did not want to bring into the household lately.

"Ruyu here," Shaoai said, "is going to check out where she's going to spend her bright future studying."

What was worst was that there was no way for Ruyu to shelter herself from the noises the other person made: the clinking of chopsticks, the scraping of chair legs on the floor, the grunts in place of answers to Aunt's questions, and the various comments hurled at Ruyu to provoke a reaction.

Aunt looked at Ruyu, was about to ask something, but then changed her mind.

"And I just heard that our dear old Yening got an internship at Sino Oil and Gas," Shaoai said.

When no one responded right away, Aunt sighed and asked what kind of job Yening would be doing.

"Learning how to be a charming and accommodating young woman in the real world," Shaoai said. "What else would she be doing?"

If only Shaoai would shut up, Ruyu thought, but these days it was Shaoai who led the dinnertime conversation, as though her topics were harmless, everyday subjects. No doubt she was aware of—perhaps even enjoying—the pains she was inflicting on her parents, who were unable to stop her from tormenting them. Already Ruyu could see Shaoai slowly losing her place everywhere but in her parents' hearts—not a prospect for a job, less sympathy from the neighbors, fearful looks from Moran and Boyang. But why should one feel sorry for Shaoai's parents? It was their doing, bringing a person like that into the world, and they were not to be spared from living under her despotism long after she ceased mattering to the world.

"Are you all right, Ruyu?" Aunt asked.

From the look on Aunt's face, Ruyu knew that she must have missed a question, asked by Aunt to avoid carrying on a difficult conversation with Shaoai. Ruyu apologized, and said she was wondering if she had forgotten to bring an important test prep kit home.

Aunt looked worried; Ruyu wondered if secretly Aunt welcomed the opportunity for a manageable misfortune. "Do check your school bag," she said. "If it's not there, Boyang or Moran must have theirs with them. Is it something you have to finish tonight?"

Ruyu said she would check and excused herself from the dinner table. In the bedroom, on the narrow desk, was the folder of the test kit, and mechanically she picked up the top page and started to read the first question; halfway through she got lost, but she kept looking engaged, lest Aunt look in. On the chair was her book satchel, a new one that Aunt had insisted on buying, as she said no high school student should use a child's satchel like the one Ruyu had brought from home. In the corner of the room was an old chest of drawers, the bottom two drawers belonging to Ruyu. A glance at the top drawers, where Shaoai kept her underclothes, made Ruyu recoil violently, tearing the paper.

Her grandaunts' willow trunk was under the bed, and Ruyu had covered it with an old shawl to keep the trunk free of dust. Her accordion was at school, locked in a place that looked as if generations of monks' ghosts visited at night. These were all the things she owned in life—not much, but enough for her not to be a disposable being. When her parents had left her on the doorstep of her grandaunts, had they thought of the possibility that she might have died of hunger or cold before the two sisters discovered the bundle? In her grandaunts' eyes, God had made them find her before bad things had happened, but Ruyu understood now that their god had no more wisdom than whatever words they put in his mouth. If Ruyu packed everything and left at this moment, she would leave no trace in these people's lives, yet she would have no place to go but to jump into the river with the trunk. If she killed herself, her grandaunts could ask and ask, but neither their god nor any mortal would have the simplest explanation.

Yet people do not die until they are made to. An infant for whom no love can be found in her parents' hearts, if left in the wilderness, will cry until her voice grows hoarse; it is not in our nature to expire quietly.

The next day, Ruyu took the bus to the west side. It was the first time she had ridden a bus since the day she arrived. Just a little over two months, but already so much had changed. The men and women around her could not harm her because she had learned the secret of willing herself out of their sights and thoughts. Invisible, she felt indestructible.

Halfway to the destination, two children, a boy and a girl, not older than ten, came up and stood next to her. Neither reached for the back of a seat but swayed back and forth, keeping their balance. They were talking about rocks, using the terms *sedimentary* and *igne-*

ous and *metamorphic* with such ease, as though they had no other reason to be in the world at that moment than to understand how millions of years had made one piece of rock different from another. A few stops later, they got off the bus. Through the window Ruyu watched them cross the street, threading between honking cars that did not slow down for them. That must be how Moran and Boyang had once looked. So much confidence in their ability to keep the dangerous world at bay; so little doubt about their futile efforts.

The university campus was indeed as beautiful as Boyang had boasted: a tree-lined lake, where the supple branches of weeping willows, their leaves barely turning yellow, reached for the water's surface to touch their own reflections; a boat carved out of stones, forever moored next to an island; a pagoda, a temple, an ancient bell sitting on a hilltop; a bronze statue of Cervantes as a skinny man holding a broken sword; a few graves of famous people, both Chinese and Western, who had died long ago—neither Moran nor Ruyu had heard of any of them, though what a place to be buried in, their ancient solitude pleasantly interrupted by the hustle and bustle of the college students on foot or on bicycles. Toward the end of the day, many students were heading toward the dining halls, spoons clanking in the metal pails they carried in their hands or in the carriers wired to their bicycles.

Moran felt shy sitting at one end of the long table in the dining hall, with Boyang and Ruyu across from her. Some college boys whistled at them, finding them laughable in their high school uniform perhaps, yet this did not seem to bother Boyang or Ruyu. Once in a while someone would come over and pat Boyang on the back, girls and boys alike—they were his parents' students, he told Moran and Ruyu. His mother had left the keys to her lab with one of her graduate students, he said, who would meet them at the entrance of the old chemistry building.

"Is there a new chemistry building?" Moran asked, but Boyang, who was saying something to Ruyu, did not hear.

Ruyu turned to Moran, waiting for or daring her to repeat the question, but Moran looked away as though she was studying a young couple at the other end of the table, who were gazing at each other without touching their food. The hunger in their eyes made Moran feel like an intruder—and perhaps she was, there and elsewhere. She thought about the people who welcomed her as an audience: Bo-yang's grandmother when she reminisced about the famines in '41 and '58; Watermelon Wen's two boys, who mimicked the quirks of the neighbors with exactitude; strangers in the alleyway, who had this or that complaint to make; her parents, who never tired of repeating the lessons they had learned from living humbly. If only it were that easy to be around those she wanted to be closest to; but they, it seemed, only wished her to be absent: Ruyu did not like her around when she was practicing the accordion, and now, sitting across from her friends, Moran wondered if Boyang was only trying to be nice by including her.

The laboratory was on the top floor of a three-story building. The hallway was cramped with old equipment, rolled-up posters, three-legged chairs leaning on rickety tables, and other nameless things that seemed to have been sitting in the dust for years. The graduate student with the keys looked introspective, and he said a few words about locking up before disappearing down an unlit hallway.

Boyang unlocked the door and turned on the fluorescent lamps. "Not much to see, really," he said. Still, he walked the girls through the aisles, opening a cabinet here and there to show where the chemicals and supplies were stored, flipping on the switch for the fume hood to show off the toxic signs with grinning skulls on a few brown bottles.

Later they sat in the office adjacent to the lab. Boyang boiled water on a hot plate to make tea. It was oddly formal, as none of them drank tea at home. Still, it seemed to make him happy to play the host. There were two chairs in the office, a tall spinning one for his mother and a small wooden one. Moran hesitated when Boyang asked them to sit and took the wooden chair. Ruyu sat down behind the desk and looked at the titles of the papers in front of her.

"I wouldn't touch them if I were you," Boyang said.

"Why?" Ruyu said. "Will your mother notice?"

"Notice? There is nothing she doesn't notice."

"Will she mind?"

"No, she won't. Rather, you might give her the wrong idea that I'm into her research now, and who knows, maybe the next time I see her, she'll give me a whole folder of papers."

"What kind of research does she do?" Ruyu said.

Boyang shrugged and said it was too complicated a subject to be interesting to anyone but his mother.

"Will you study chemistry when you go to college?" Ruyu asked.

"No," he said. "Too boring."

"What subject will you major in?"

"I don't know. Something useful. Engineering. Or something with computer programming. What will you study?"

Ruyu did not answer, and turned to ask Moran what she was planning to study. Until recently, Moran had thought she would major in whatever Boyang chose. It had seemed sensible, as he knew these things better, but now it would sound ridiculous if she said engineering or computer programming. "Maybe chemistry," she said. "I don't mind boring subjects."

Boyang laughed and said that statement alone would set his mother off. "But since when have you thought about studying chemistry?"

Moran shook her head confusedly, aware that Ruyu was watching her with an intensity she did not understand. She changed the subject and asked Boyang a few questions about his mother's graduate students, but she could see that his heart was not in the topic. He was uncommonly quiet.

Their conversation lagged a little, though neither Boyang nor

Ruyu seemed in a hurry to leave. The sun had set, and from the only window in the office they could see the slanted roof of the neighboring building, its terra-cotta tiles, once painted golden and green, all faded now. A crow croaked in a nearby tree, and immediately someone cursed loudly the bad luck a crow's cry would bring.

Something about the evening—the dinner away from home, the closeness of the world that carried on its mundane business outside the window, their freedom unintruded upon—made Moran feel as though at long last she had arrived at the threshold of her real life, for which she had been rehearsing as a diligent child. Trust and loyalty, disappointment and resignation, happiness and sadness, friendship and love—in this new life, unlike in a rehearsal, everything was in place, and nothing would stop the play from moving toward curtain fall. Moran looked at her friends: confident, they appeared better prepared.

What if nothing could be changed, and she would always be given that minor role? What if there was nothing in her that made her lovable? But there must be something lovable in every one of us, or else why would we go from one day to the next? In her despondence, unknown to herself, Moran held out seeking hands to her friends: a smile, an affectionate gesture, a wordless affirmation—it does not take much to save one from despair, but they, untouched by the urgency devouring her, watched the dusk fall in their intimate obliviousness.

Moran wished she could be part of that quietness; her own, forced upon her, only made her heart ache for words. But if she spoke, she would be a thoughtless crow, disturbing a dream, gaining nothing but a silent curse.

Ruyu stood up and said she would be back in a moment, and Boyang nodded, saying that the ladies' room was down the hallway. When she left, Moran turned to him, but he was still looking at the roof across the yard, and she knew that he had something on his mind. She wished she were the same person she used to be, the one who would not hesitate to ask him. There had never been secrets between them.

"Isn't she a special person?" Boyang whispered, turning to Moran with a pleading look, as though by not mentioning Ruyu's name, she would be kept a treasure.

Moran smiled and agreed.

"Do you really think so, too?" Boyang asked eagerly.

"We've never met someone like her," Moran said.

Boyang looked happy. "I wonder what she would study at the university."

"I think she wants to go to America."

"I know. We can go, too."

It both comforted and pained Moran that, like a sibling, she was still included in every plan he made. "And then what?" she said.

Boyang seemed not to detect any change in her mood. "We could rent a house together," he said. "Imagine that, a real house, with a yard and an attic. I know you can do that in America."

Innocently—yet with the cruelty that only the innocent can execute—Boyang had made Moran see herself as a chair in that house, a poster on the wall, a curtain half-pulled. They were good matches for each other, she thought, both handsome, smart, both special in ways that she herself would never be. She should count herself lucky to be invited into their lives in any manner, but when the time came, there would not be a place for her in that house. She had enough pride not to be a piece of furniture or a decoration in anyone else's life, but it would not be her pride that separated her from them but the truth he was unable to see now: when the time came, she knew, he would have forgotten that he had ever issued the invitation.

Listless, Moran stood up and said she would be back in a minute. Again Boyang pointed the way to the ladies' room down the hallway, yet this time he seemed to be doing so in a dream, his eyes looking for something outside in the dusk. The sky had turned from the bright colors of sunset to a deeper gradient of red, magenta, and blue. Love can make an ordinary evening poetic. Sadness, too, can do that.

When Moran exited the office, she saw Ruyu standing next to the fume hood, and when she heard Moran's steps, she turned to face her, both hands in her pockets. Instinctively Moran glanced at the brown bottles in the hood. The light and the fume switches were on. "Have you two had a good talk?" Ruyu said, and turned the switches off. "I didn't want to disturb you, in case you needed some private time."

Flustered, Moran said that they had been waiting for her.

Later in the evening, Moran waited at the bus stop for Ruyu. Boyang had gone to his parents' apartment, but before he left, he had said several times that Moran was to meet Ruyu's bus so that the latter would not get lost on the way home. How could she? Moran wished she could ask; the bus stop was only a ten-minute walk from the quadrangle, and it wasn't late enough for any real safety risk. But she had agreed, promising that she would make sure all went well.

Ruyu looked tired when she stepped down from the bus, yet when Moran asked her to hop onto the back of her bicycle, Ruyu only shook her head. "Go ahead and ride home," she said. "I'll walk."

Moran said she was not in a hurry in any case. She pushed her bicycle and walked next to Ruyu, knowing that she must be a nuisance in Ruyu's eyes. After a moment of silence, Moran asked Ruyu what she'd thought of the university.

"What do you think?" Ruyu said.

"Beautiful campus, isn't it?" Moran asked. When Ruyu did not say anything, Moran added, "It'd be wonderful if we could all go there after high school."

"Do you really think so?" Ruyu asked, and stopped to look sideways at Moran.

What she thought of anything was a question she could no longer answer with confidence. It dawned on her that when people asked for her opinions, they were not truly interested in hearing them. "Why did you want to see the lab?" Moran said.

"Why do you ask?"

"I don't know. I thought you would be more interested in seeing the campus. I didn't know you were interested in chemistry labs."

"But we saw the campus, too."

Yet Ruyu had not asked to see where Boyang's father, who was a specialist in high-energy physics, did his research; this, though, Moran did not want to say just for the sake of contradiction. They walked across an alley, stepping on the crunching leaves with the same rhythm.

"Where do you think people go after they die?" Ruyu asked when they turned into another alleyway.

Moran paused and turned to look at Ruyu. Her eyes were limpid enough, and there was not the coldness Moran dreaded in them. She sensed that Ruyu was in a mood to talk about something, but Moran felt tired; all she wanted was to go home and curl up in her bed. "I don't think they go anywhere," she said. "They're cremated, and that's all."

"But that's only according to you atheists."

"Do you—" Moran recalled the question she had never before dared to ask. "Are you religious?"

"Why, because my grandaunts are religious?"

"Why else did you ask the question? Where do you think people go after they die?"

"Nowhere," Ruyu said, the weariness in her voice reminding Moran of an older woman. She had seen the exhaustion in people like Aunt and her own mother, defeated by a shortage of money and food or by unfairness at work and beyond. "Are you all right?" Moran said.

"Why wouldn't I be?"

"But something must have made you ask the question," Moran said. "About people dying."

"People die all the time. Shaoai's grandfather will die sooner or later. One day my grandaunts will die, too. Anyone could die anytime. Even young people. Even you and I. Today. Tomorrow. Who knows?"

Moran shuddered. They had both unconsciously come to a stop under an old locust tree, its canopy of leaves — it was too dark to tell what colors they had turned or how soon they would fall — sheltering them from the deep, clear sky. Autumn crickets sang in the grasses and in the cracks of the alley wall. From a house in a nearby quadrangle, they could hear a TV commercial for Maxwell House instant coffee, a brand that had just begun to be imported into the country. It would be followed by another commercial for Nestle's instant coffee, also newly introduced. If she closed her eyes, Moran could see the steam rising from the mugs in both commercials, the actresses taking deep, dreamlike breaths. But what did coffee smell like? No family in the quadrangle would squander their money on a jar of either brand, and it occurred to Moran only then that she had never thought about what made the actresses look blissful. How many people watching the commercials would know the fragrance of coffee? Perhaps that's what happiness is like, looking more real when it is scripted and performed by others.

The theme song of a popular TV drama came on after the Nestle commercial. Moran's parents would be watching it, and they would be wondering what in the world could have made her miss the show. "Did you," Moran started the sentence, and then wavered before she could gather the resolve. "Did you take something from the lab?"

Ruyu looked calm as she studied Moran. "You must have been brought up well, not to use the word *steal*," she said finally.

"You did, didn't you?"

"Did you see me do anything?"

"No, but I thought . . ."

"If you didn't see with your own eyes, you can't say what you think," Ruyu said. "What you think or what anyone thinks does not count."

"But won't you tell me?"

Ruyu shook her head. "What's the point of telling you anything?" she said in a quiet voice, yet rather than sarcasm, which Moran had braced herself for, the words seemed to contain a sadness she had not imagined Ruyu would be capable of showing to others.

"What did you take?" Moran asked gently.

Ruyu looked down at the tips of her shoes, and when she looked up again, the melancholy had vanished. "Are you going to report your suspicion to Boyang?" Ruyu said with half a smile.

Moran felt an acute pain she had not known before. If it were yesterday, she would have ridden into the city to find the last telephone stand open at this hour and dialed the number of Boyang's parents; she would have weathered their questioning just to talk to him, to tell him her worries, but all, after today, had become impossible. What could she say to him, that the girl he had fallen in love with had stolen from his mother? But why, he would ask, and how did she know?—and Moran would not be able to answer. Ruyu was right. Moran had not seen anything, and she had no right to claim knowing anything. Boyang would shake his head to himself, too generous to say that he was disappointed in her, that her unfounded suspicion came from nowhere but that unkind place where jealousy fed dark imagination. The thought of living with people's disappointments, his in particular, made Moran panic. She looked pleadingly at Ruyu. "I won't say anything to him if you prefer that."

"But whether you say anything to him or not should have nothing to do with me," Ruyu said. "You can't say you have done or not done something only for my liking. Isn't that true?"

Moran felt overwhelmed by queasiness. "I won't tell him. It's my decision," she said.

"Then that's that," Ruyu said. "Shall we go back? It's late."

"But wait. We can't just yet," Moran said. "Why did you take something from the lab? What are you going to do with it?"

"If I say I never took anything, will you believe me and forget about it?"

Moran took a deep breath but could not sense any relief. "No," she said. "I can't."

Ruyu smiled. "People want things for different reasons. Some want money to buy things; others want money that they never spend. Some want people to be their properties; others want to be properties of other people," she said. "If your imagination were right, have you thought that I only wanted something that could make me feel better?"

"But how?" Moran said, seized by the fear that either she was losing her mind or Ruyu was. "You're not thinking of killing yourself?"

Ruyu's eyes, unfocused for a split second, narrowed with derision. "I don't know how you came up with that silly idea, Moran."

Only that morning she had been a different person, Moran thought; she'd felt sad, but the sadness was no more than a young girl's mood. Even sitting in the office next to Boyang, watching the sky change its hue, she had still been that person, sadder but never for a moment uncertain about the world. Between then and now, what had been was no more, but why and how this change had happened she did not know.

"Are you worried?" Ruyu said. "Are you going to talk to all the grownups so they can be alarmed? The truth is, if anyone ever wants to destroy herself, there's nothing you can do. But at least you should know that it's a sin, according to my grandaunts, to commit suicide. There's no redemption for people like that."

Words like *sin* and *redemption* did not exist in Moran's vocabulary. She did not know half of what Ruyu knew about life, and now, was it too late? "Are you feeling unhappy?" Moran asked, trying to steer the conversation in a less treacherous direction.

"You know, I notice that you always ask people if they're happy or not."

Did she? Moran wondered. She had not been conscious of it, but perhaps she did have the habit. Sometimes she ran into one of the younger kids in the neighborhood, and if he or she was crying, the first question she would ask was *what made you unhappy?*

"I don't think people ask that question," Ruyu said.

"They don't?"

"No one has ever asked me that question," Ruyu said. "You're the first one, and the only one. And if you think about it—I don't mean to hurt your feelings, Moran—but if you think about it, that's the most pointless question. If the person says yes, I'm happy, then what?"

"I would be happy for them."

"And if he's not happy?"

"If the person is unhappy, I'll make an effort to change that," Moran said.

Ruyu looked at Moran as one would look at a baby bird maimed by a feral cat, sympathy and disgust seeming to blend into something less distinguishable. Without another word, Ruyu began to walk.

To be brought to an understanding of her own foolishness like that was like walking into a wall she had never known to be there. The pain was so acute that for a moment Moran felt the urge to gasp.

15

Josef asked only for a cup of black coffee, and even that he did not touch while watching Moran eat her eggs and toast. She knew that her overthinking had fallen short again. The evening before, when she had called Josef from the airport, he had suggested a simple dinner, and she had flatly refused because she had not come to be hosted or taken care of in any way. She asked him what his next day would be like, and he said he had a visit to the hospital in the morning. She would pick him up and drive him to his appointment, she said, deciding for both of them as she had decided all the birthday lunches.

The hospital cafeteria would be too depressing at this hour, Josef had said, and she had agreed to go to a small café nearby for breakfast. But now—too late as always—it occurred to her that he could not eat anything: today he would have another chemo infusion; with all her consideration, how could she have forgotten that for a town this size, one would never need to leave for an appointment two hours ahead of time?

Josef, though, watched her eat as though nothing was out of place. His suit hung loosely; his cheeks, once round and flushed and called affectionately by her his "Buddha" cheeks, were sallow now, creased skin on sharp bones. He moved much more slowly than before, though with dignity. She wondered if his bones and joints troubled him, and whether it was a result of the illness or the chemotherapy—

though did it matter? His back was straight when he sat next to her in the car, and he did not let himself slouch after the waitress had brought them their orders. He was one of those people who would meet death with an impeccable manner, shaking hands, thanking death for taking the trouble to come and fetch him, and, having put his affairs in order ahead of time, bidding farewell to his family and friends before journeying onward. "It's ridiculous to sit here and wait," she said, disturbed by the thought that his final departure was no longer hypothetical. "Next time we'll leave for the hospital just in time."

"This is the only time I go while you're here," Josef said. "So don't worry about next time. By the way, Rachel said to thank you for your help today."

That, Moran thought, was his cue for her to ask about Rachel, her children, and her siblings and their children. In the past, Moran and Josef had been talkative at his birthday lunches, each picking up a new subject before quietness set in: he would speak of the local orchestra concerts he'd attended, various construction projects in the city, his children and grandchildren; she would speak of new products at work, the colors she'd painted her bedroom, the pots of herbs she was cultivating on her windowsill. What she had failed to do in their marriage she seemed to have managed since, at least once a year: to assign interest to small matters. It takes courage to find solace in trivialities, willfulness not to let trivialities usurp one's life. Trivialities, though, could wait now, or could be done away with forever. "There," she said, "will be next time. I'm moving back."

"Back, Moran, to where?"

Did she detect suspicion or even panic, however fleeting, in his eyes? The house she had known to be theirs—and before that, his and Alena's—had been remodeled and sold two years earlier. Josef's move to the condo, she had known at the time, would be only the beginning of a series of moves, each confining his world more. Indeed, back to where? But a more apt question would be, back to when? Over the years she had failed to offer Josef evidence of settlement: a new marriage, a love interest, an affair, anything to end their birthday ritual. It was kind of her to come, he said every year, his happiness and gratitude genuine because she was the one to rearrange her life once a year for him. But Moran wondered if he was only acting for her sake—his life would have been the same otherwise, children and grandchildren providing a solid reality for his memories of Alena, polished into perfection by time. Had Josef not preserved a place for her to alight, Moran would be a hapless bird lost in migration from one year to the next. Indeed, back to when: the moment she had asked for a divorce, or earlier, when she had convinced herself that a man with a loving heart would offer her a place in life, or even earlier, when they had first found affectionate companionship in each other?

"Don't worry. I won't install myself in your living room like an uninvited guest. I won't be in your way when your children come to see you. Oh, no, don't you worry, Josef," Moran said, feeling her stomach tighten. She had meant to find the best time to tell him her plan, but five minutes into the breakfast, she was already losing her strategy. She could not bring herself to say that there must be times when he needed a driver, a hand to hold on to when he walked on the icy sidewalk, someone to listen to him reminisce while sleep eluded him, a lover of his good heart.

Josef was quiet, then said that it was comforting to know that, with a bit of food in her, Moran was her old self again.

He meant that impatience and irritation came easily to her when she was with him, part of herself that no one else was allowed to see. To the world, she was not unlike Josef: poised in an old-fashioned way. She liked to imagine that she carried with her something good from him, though at times she suspected she was one of those people who would latch on to what was not in their nature and set about making it their own: once upon a time, it had been Shaoai's romantic vehemence about injustice and Boyang's lack of concern for all things troublesome. (How had those two traits mixed in her? she wondered, but it seemed too long ago for her to understand.) There had been Ruyu's imperviousness, a most alien quality, yet for years Moran had striven for it, as though by aligning herself with Ruyu, she could claim at least a small part of Ruyu's impunity. But how does one tell where one's true self stops and makes way for all the borrowed selves? To this day, Moran still sometimes woke from dreams in which she had laughed jovially. Often Boyang was in those dreams, and sometimes Ruyu, too, and the backdrop, however vague, was unmistakably one of her favorite corners of Beijing; in the first moment of wakefulness, the unconstrained happiness, like the lingering aftertaste of the locust blossoms they ate as children, was intensely real, until she remembered that she was no longer a person who had things to laugh about, or people to laugh with. Extreme disappointment seems a lesson one can never master: no matter how many times it had happened, the realization would still hit her like a fierce bout of physical illness, and for a moment she would be dazed, asking herself how it could be that her life had not turned out to be a place for that happiness.

"Did I offend you?" Josef said.

Always quick to admit wrongdoing, always ready to apologize—it was the same for both of them. How could two people like that make a marriage, which required a certain degree of irrationality, work? "I mean it, Josef," Moran said. "I'm moving back to town."

"Why?"

"That"—she stared at Josef—"is a stupid question."

"But what will you do about your job?"

She could say she had arranged a leave to make him feel better, but the truth was she never lied to him. It wasn't much, she knew: one can withhold many things and build a wall around oneself; one can have a graveyard of dead memories without speaking a word. But at least she was adamant about giving him the kind of love she had not given others: it is rare that one meets a person to whom one chooses never to lie. "I'm giving it up," she said. "Don't, please, Josef, don't try to convince me otherwise. It's only a job."

"And what are you going to do here?"

"That can be decided later," Moran said. "Unless you oppose this move with all your heart."

Josef sighed. "This is a free country," he said.

"Would it leave you in a difficult situation with your children? Would they oppose it?"

"You can't change your life at this moment just for me."

"Why can't it be for me, too?" she said, though her voice was low, and she was not sure if he heard her. What he'd called her life was only a way of not living, and by doing that, she had taken, here and there, parts of other people's lives and turned them into nothing along with her own.

The café was filling up, the warmth of people and their everyday contentment pressing in. It was a Wednesday. This must be the day of the week for the four gray-haired ladies two tables away to meet up and laugh, and for the two young mothers by the window to compare notes on motherhood, their infants sleeping in carriers next to them. A few couples had come in, all of them Josef's age, and Moran had dreaded recognizing them as his friends, though he had only smiled and nodded at them in the friendly way one smiled and nodded at strangers. Other than two college-aged girls, who were doing some intense work over their coffee, the café seemed to be a place for people who were either at the beginning of their stories or, more befittingly, at the end. Even the college girls, in a way, were only starting out. What one did not find at this place was someone in the middle of a story—but perhaps those people, like Moran herself a week earlier, did not have the luxury of idleness on such a morning. They would be sitting in a cubicle somewhere, secured and entrapped; sometimes they look up at the ceiling, a forgotten memory from their childhood or a glimpse into their old age passing through their minds like the fleeting shadow of a bird flying by, before their thoughts are reined in to the immediate present. No, to be in the middle requires one to be practical: one does not walk away from a stable job; one does not take a sojourn from life. Yet was it her true position to be in the middle—without a future to look forward to, was she, despite her age, already at the end?

"Are you going to look for a job here?" Josef asked.

"Only if it's flexible enough," Moran said. "Though maybe not for a while."

"Then how are you going to spend your time?"

"I'm coming back to be near you. Unless—" she paused, a sudden fear hitting her. "Unless you have a lady friend now. I wouldn't want to be in the way."

"I would've told you," he said. They had circled the topic in the past, but had always managed, at the end of each meeting, to inform each other of their love lives, or of the lack of love in their lives. He had gone out with a woman for a while, but by the time Moran came for his next birthday, the relationship had fizzled. There had been other interests, though nothing fruitful had come of them, disappointments for him perhaps, but she had felt relieved each time, and guilty about her relief.

"Then what prevents you from saying yes to my proposal?"

"Wouldn't you say no, too, if you were in my shoes?"

"No."

"But you would, Moran," Josef said gently. "You know you would."

"There's this old tale in China. An ironsmith boasted that he had built the sharpest spearhead—one that could pierce all armor; then he boasted that he had built the sturdiest armor that no spearhead would be able to pierce."

"So he was asked to test his own products on each other?" Josef said.

"Very good thinking, my dear Josef," Moran said. "But the lesson is, I think, that each and every one of us has flaws in our reasoning, and we should not take advantage of that in another person. What I would do if I were in your shoes doesn't matter. What matters is what I would decide in my own shoes."

"Of course it would be . . . wonderful to see you more."

"Then why don't we settle on this?"

"But I won't be here forever."

Of course it was like Josef to remind her of a fact that she never forgot. "Shouldn't that be more of a reason for me to come back?" she said, and abruptly asked the waitress walking past to bring them the check.

"We still have some time," Josef said.

"Can't you see that I don't want to be a fool and cry in here?" she snapped, and leaned her face into her hands, warning herself not to fail her first test. He did not need a weepy woman; facing death, he was more defenseless than she was.

The waitress came with their check. Moran did not change her posture and let Josef take care of it. When he asked if she was ready to go, she took a deep breath and looked up. The effort to ensure that her eyes stayed dry had exhausted her, but she was glad that the dam inside her had not broken. "Now, don't look so worried," she said. "I'm not here to bring a scandal to your name."

"Man in seventies bullies visiting ex-wife into tears in public," Josef said. "No, no, we don't want to see that in the paper."

"But that ex-wife is not visiting anymore," Moran said. "The big news is, she's moving back to haunt him."

Josef made a gesture of being caught in a spotlight, his hands raised halfway in an effort to shelter his face, which was flushed by the sudden movement. Momentarily they were back in a better time, when he had made her smile with a few unexpected improvisations. Were these moments, she wondered, enough to be called happiness this late into their story?

Later, when she dropped Josef off at his place, he asked if she would like to go up and sit for a while. She hesitated, and then said she would let him rest. She wanted to make a few appointments to look at some rentals before everyone headed out of town for Thanksgiving.

"Moran, enough fooling around. Let's drop the subject."

"Why?" she asked. In his voice she'd detected the weariness that belonged to people who were too tired to feel responsible for how they spoke.

"You and I both know that you should not leave your job."

She wondered if the visit to the hospital had made him change his mind. He had introduced her to the nurse as a friend, and the nurse had asked about Rachel and her family before they left. Could it be that there was a settled rhythm to his life that he did not want her return to disturb? Or that his time, already limited, had little extra to spare for her?

"Will it be too much for you? Will I be taking you away from your family and friends?" she asked, tightening her grip around the steering wheel, even though she had parked the car, perfectly centered between the two lines, just as he had taught her.

"You know that's not the reason."

"Then what is?"

"You still have half a life to live."

"Why can't moving back here be part of that half?" she said. His face looked ashen, much sicker than it had earlier; he must be exhausted from spending the morning with her. What if she, despite good intentions, was only toxic for him?

"You know it means the world to me that you came," Josef said. "It's too flattering by half that you're talking of moving back. But we ought not to indulge ourselves."

"You may need someone," Moran said, though she knew that the role of caretaker could easily be filled by another person: Rachel, for instance, or his other children; down the line, it would probably be a hired nurse, or else he would be moved from the condo to a facility. Many stories of his generation would end that way, and he would argue that there was no point in being different.

"You're being stubborn," Josef said.

She exited the car and opened the passenger door. "Come," she said, bending down and reaching for his hand. "I'll walk you up after all."

Moran had not been in Josef's condo before, but a place, like the person who inhabits it, can become close to one at the first encounter. Of course there were the things from the old house: the framed pictures of the children and Alena; the oil painting of a lone, white-washed farmhouse dwarfed by the rolling green hills behind it, which used to hang in the family room; the sofa and the coffee table, both of which, Moran had once calculated, must be about her age, if not older. But more than these objects, it was the unclutteredness that reminded her of her own house. One could easily trace a life lived in solitude. The footprints, though invisible, were not hard for her to see: the steps to the kitchen, the bathroom, the bedroom, all taken out of necessity.

Moran asked Josef if he would like to lie down, and he said it would be better that he sit on the sofa. On the coffee table, five pills of three different colors lined up on a coaster, next to a glass of water. She asked if he needed to take the medicine now, and he said yes, and thanked her when she handed the water and the pills to him.

She imagined he had picked them out of different bottles—he must do this every time he left for the hospital, lest he forget or feel too sick to do it afterward. Perhaps there is a line in everyone's life that, once crossed, imparts a certain truth that one has not been able to see before, transforming solitude from a choice into the only possible state of existence. Moran had always thought she had crossed that line long ago—but when, she asked herself, and she could not come up with an answer. It could have been when she extricated herself from Josef's life, or earlier, when she had sat in that dingy apartment in Beijing, paralyzed and ashamed by the sight of Shaoai's oversized body and mindless giggling. But she would have been too young for that crossing to count as real experience, and her solitude, which had not chosen her but had been chosen *by* her, was different from Josef's solitude: hers was a protest, his a surrender.

Josef dozed off on the sofa, his mouth slightly open, his breathing shallow. She picked up an old blanket from the sofa and laid it softly on him. His eyelids, too pale—as though they were a naked part of a body that should be kept out of sight—made her look away. If she left now, he would wake up to the empty room, thinking she was only a phantom in a dream. If she stayed, he would open his eyes and be momentarily disoriented; but however meager her offer was, it must be better than a dream.

Moran walked to the window, which overlooked the parking lot. A man, the manager of the building judging by his looks, was unloading bags of rock salt from his pickup truck. Earlier, at the café, two or three tables of people had been discussing the coming snowstorm, which the forecast said would hit the area hard by the end of the week; would it affect holiday traveling, the people at the café had wondered, worries about their children's homecoming lining the old women's faces. The nurse, too, when saying farewell to Josef, had said glumly that they were going into another long winter, as though, in her tired eyes, last year's stale snow was still sitting in gray piles by the roadside, never melting with time.

Moran remembered the delight in the eyes of the Thai couple and the Indian students from years ago upon seeing their first snowfall; back in their home countries, the news must have left ripples of marvel in many hearts. She herself had not shared their relish. One can always go back to another moment in history to negate the present; only the impressionable and the inexperienced—in that case, the people from the snowless tropics—are liable to christen a moment *memory*. The snow-covered hills west of the Back Sea; her bicycle tires skidding on rutted, hard-pressed snow before crashing into Boyang's; a squad of snowmen they had lined up in the courtyard during one of the biggest snowstorms—if she wanted, she could always assign more meaning to those memories, diminishing others.

Yet her connection to the Midwest had begun with snow. Before she met Josef, she had been in Madison for two and a half months, but those days, like the time since she had left Josef, had been willfully turned into the footprints of seabirds on wet sand, existing only between the flow and ebb of the tide. Is it possible for one to develop an attachment to a place or a time without another person being involved? If so, the place and the time must make a most barren habitat. Beijing in her memory had remained two cities, the one before Shaoai's poisoning and the one after, yet in both places she had not been alone. Guangzhou, where she had gone to college for four years, had been marked by the absence of any communication between her and her old friends in Beijing, but even that lack had been meaningful: people, absent, could claim more space. The Massachusetts town Moran had lived in for the past eleven years, however, did not offer a memorable emptiness; in shunning people, she had turned the place, with its abundant sunny days in the summer and its beautiful autumn colors, into a mere spot on the map, the time she'd spent there collapsed into one long day of not feeling. No, solitude she did not have; what she had was a never-ending quarantine.

The snow on the day when Moran had first met Josef had been light and flaky, and in the parking lot he had swept a layer of it off the windshield with his gloved hands. He had offered to drive her back to the Westlawn House, and she had not known how to decline, even though she would have preferred a long walk in the snowy dusk.

It was time to get a new scraper, he said, and when he saw her puzzled look, he asked if things were all right.

She said everything was all right, though he looked concerned still, and wanted to know if her headache was bothering her and if she needed some medicine. She would not have said anything more, but she knew that if she did not tell the truth, she would make a good-hearted man worry unnecessarily. She reassured him that she was perfectly fine; except that she did not know what he meant when he talked about a scraper.

Their relationship—a friendship before it evolved into love or companionship—had begun where little common ground could be found between them. It was a matter of paying attention that had brought them together. For Josef, the objects and sights that had been familiar to him had become less so. For Moran, it was making an effort to find new things—and there were plenty in a new country—so that she could stop looking inward for an explanation that could make her recent history less puzzling.

Sitting in Josef's car that day, for the first time Moran had looked at the world from the passenger's seat. The traffic signs and lane dividers lit by the headlights as though they were taking turns becoming visible; the rushing and swirling of snowflakes toward the windshield at an angle and speed she had never thought possible; the dashboard, with its circles and numbers in pale neon green—all these made her look at the world more closely, as she had not done for a long time. At Westlawn, several of her housemates had cars, but Moran preferred walking, and had arranged her life within a walking distance radius and occasionally a bus ride: she walked to school and to a nearby grocery store for food, and on weekends she rode the bus to town to look at the shop windows and the people who shopped behind the windows. Once she had taken a more adventurous route, climbing up a hill and then trekking down a long, grassy slope, stirring up insects, which had reminded her of her intrepid younger days, hunting for crickets and katydids with Boyang. To stop herself from reminiscing, she ran downhill, and when she reached the edge of the state highway, she waited for over five minutes, until no car was in sight in both directions, before sprinting across the six lanes to the other side, where a spreading Wal-Mart had amazed her with its abundance of everything one needed—or would never have imagined one would need—for a life in America.

"Is this the first time you've seen snow?" Josef asked as they were waiting for the red light to turn green. She must have looked wide eyed, leaning forward.

She said no, and then asked him what was making the clicking sound.

"The engine?" he said, and turned off the car radio, which had been tuned to a classical music station at low volume. He listened. Strange, he said, he couldn't hear anything. He had just had the car checked at the mechanics' a few weeks earlier, he said, and all had seemed well then.

It turned out to be the blinking of the turn signal, for, after the light changed and the car turned, the sound went away. When the small mystery was solved, Josef seemed genuinely shocked, while Moran was rather happy. At the beginning of the semester, she had taken a ride with her lab-mates to a welcome picnic; sitting in the backseat among the more talkative Americans, she had felt baffled by the clicking sound, though she had been too shy to ask.

That winter—long, brutal, as everybody had warned Moran— seemed to be forever connected to the joint effort between Josef and Moran to understand each other through the gap between their ages, and between their origins. Nothing could be left unsaid or unexplored; everything deserved a closer look. Snow, which was simply *snow* in her mother tongue, gave rise to a new vocabulary, as Josef patiently explained when the season brought different forms of snow: as flakes, as powder, as sleet, as drifts. What the snow trucks and plows spread was a mixture of sand and salt, he explained, a novel practice to her, since back home the only way to tackle snow was to brandish a shovel, and sometimes a whole work unit or school had to pause for half a day to clean the road.

All she did was ask questions: anything else she said would have had some connection to Beijing, and it was to forget the other place that she had welcomed Josef's friendship. The graininess of the sand and rock under her soles did not go away, even between snows, and the coarseness gave her an odd impression of a boldly announced uncleanness. Back in Beijing, winter brought another kind of uncleanness: dust, never settling and hurled everywhere by wind, gave the sky a tinge of yellow and covered everything with a layer of gray; on the days of dust storms, she had to cover her whole head with a gauzy scarf, and even then, when she arrived home, the first thing she would have to do was rinse her mouth and wash the dust off her face. Once, when she and Boyang had gone to a science exhibition, she had been both amused and appalled when, reaching their destination, even the folds of their eyelids were filled with fine dust. But such memories would have made no sense to Josef, and she always redirected the conversation when he asked her about China. She preferred being told about things she did not know, and in retrospect she wondered if her interest in even the most mundane details had been good for Josef that winter. He had not been a talkative person; all the same, it must have made a difference for him to have been listened to with such attention.

As the winter drew on, the town started to take on a grimier look. People, though tired of the snow, never seemed to tire of talking about it. At a café where they had gone a few times, the owner, Dave, joked about putting up a sign that said "no whining."

Moran asked Josef to spell the word "whine" for her, and asked for the meaning. He thought for a moment and then took on a high-pitched voice: *"Everybody crowds round so in this Forest. There's no Space. I never saw a more Spreading lot of animals in my life, and all in the wrong places."*

She looked at him: the first glimpse of his jocular self changed him into a different person. When he asked her to guess to whom the lines belonged, she shook her head.

"Here's the clue. I only did that to give you a sense of a whiny voice. What he really sounds like is this—" Josef pulled both sides of his face downward with his hands and lowered his pitch into a grumbling voice. *"There are those who will wish you good morning. If it is a good morning, which I doubt."*

Moran smiled. There was a mischievous light in his eyes when he made his face morose.

"Have you heard of Eeyore?" Josef asked when she could not guess the answer.

"Eeyore?" she said.

"Or Winnie-the-Pooh?"

Moran shook her head again, and Josef seemed to be at a loss for words.

It must be a boring business for him when every subject needed an explanation, Moran thought, feeling self-conscious. So much could be left unsaid between herself and Boyang, as must have been the case between Josef and Alena, though the analogy made Moran uneasy. Neither she nor Josef had designated these weekend meetings—movies and coffees and sometimes a visit to a local museum—as anything consequential. She liked to believe that she was an international student he was helping to get to know America better. She could see, when she and Josef ran into his friends in town, that they approved of this side project of his because it was a distraction from grieving.

Josef explained that Winnie-the-Pooh was a character from a children's book. He had read it so many times to his four children at bedtime, he said, that he could not help memorizing many parts. She imagined him acting out the book, though she could not envision him as a young father, nor his children at a young age. At Thanksgiving she had met his family, three sons and one daughter: Michael, whose wife's name was Sharon, and whose children were Todd and Brant; John, who had come with his fiancée, Mimi; George, by himself; and Rachel, the only one still in college. They, including the two boys, both under age five, had intimidated Moran. She had tried to explain to herself that it was only her diffidence about her English that had made her ill at ease, though she knew that was not the only reason.

"If you like," Josef said now, "I can bring the book to you next week. Or else we can stop by the bookstore to get a copy for you."

How befitting, she thought, and all of a sudden felt angry. In his eyes, she must be a young woman raised in an underdeveloped country, exotic but also pitiable in her ignorance. Do you have chocolates in China? a friend of Josef's had asked her once, with perfect kindness; or else: Did your parents bind your feet when you were young? Will they arrange a marriage for you?

Moran said that if Josef wrote down the title of the book, she could find it in the library. She did not know if he could detect the change in her voice.

Josef found a pen in his jacket pocket and wrote the title and the author's name on a napkin, doodling a plump animal at the bottom. She watched him, both annoyed by him and ashamed at her annoyance. Her graduate advisor had been lending her the picture books his two children had outgrown—the best way to improve her English was to start with children's books, he had said, and added that when he had been in graduate school, a woman from China in his lab, who had since become a professor at Arizona State, had read through the entire children's section at the local library.

Moran had not minded her advisor's giving her the exquisitely printed cardboard books. He was a good man, she knew, and he wanted her to thrive in this country. But to be offered a children's book by Josef seemed a different matter. What happened to *Doctor Zhivago*, she wanted to ask. In her backpack was an English translation of the novel, which she had checked out from the university library; the last stamp had been from nine years ago. On the previous Sunday, they had talked about the novel. She had told him that there was a line toward the end of the novel that she had underlined many times in the Chinese translation, though when he had asked her what it was, she could not answer, and said she would look for it in the English translation.

"He tried to imagine several people whose lives run parallel and close together but move at different speeds, and he wondered in what circumstances some of them would overtake and survive others." Reading it for the first time in English had been a bit of a shock. The words had lost their meaning; the line she'd underlined in her Chinese translation was, in English, an ordinary sentiment; or else something had caught her attention at seventeen but had lost its impact. Still, she had brought the book to show the words to Josef, though she wondered, after Winnie-the-Pooh, if it was pointless to do so. To start a life with a new language is like being returned to childhood—no one is really interested in your thoughts; all the world wants is for you to be contentedly occupied or else safely tucked away. Perhaps Josef was no different.

He seemed not to notice Moran's change of mood. He asked her if she had plans for the Christmas break; she said no, and he said that if she liked, he would bring her to his friends' house—a couple—as they always had the best gatherings on Christmas Eve, everyone singing Christmas carols at the end of the evening. Would his children come to the party, too? Moran asked, and Josef said that Thanksgiving was their family holiday. John and Mimi were planning to spend the week in Hawaii. Michael and Sharon were taking the children to see Sharon's parents in Memphis. George and Rachel? Moran asked, and Josef said that they might or might not come. "I don't want them to feel that they have to spend the holidays at home for my sake."

Each member of the family, Moran thought, had a position in the world, and everything they did—working, raising children, partying, vacationing—added more assurance to that secured place. Even Josef, who hadn't yet recovered from the most difficult year of his life, could rely on the consistency of his days—staff meetings at the library, choir practice, dinners with friends, and a meeting with Moran on Sunday afternoons. At Thanksgiving dinner, Moran had been impressed by the certainty of everyone in his family; no matter what the topics had been—college basketball, Bill Clinton's second term, the different ways to cook a turkey, Rachel's internship applications—the family members all seemed to have opinions, none of them shy to state his or her own. At times the back-and-forth had become a verbal game among the siblings or between a couple, and the ease with which they had carried on had given Moran an unreal sense that they lived in a TV show. But it must be her misimpression: what's wrong with a family gathering around a table full of food and conversing in a lively way? In a parallel world, if things had happened differently, Moran herself could have belonged to such a scene: she would have remained friends with Boyang, and they would have bantered as easily—she dared not imagine them as a couple, but they would remain affectionate as siblings. In a parallel world Shaoai would have made a brilliant career for herself, as government permission was no longer required for working; Ruyu—what would have happened to her?—perhaps she would have moved out of their lives as abruptly as she had come in, but Boyang and Moran might not have felt the loss acutely: even someone like Ruyu could be replaced or forgotten, if one made the effort.

But there was only this one world, in which Moran had no position to claim as hers. This was not because she was a new immigrant; some of the other Chinese students she ran into on campus seemed as confident about America as they were about China. To have a position—any position—requires one to have opinions: Moran had none of them. What she did have were observations and questions— those that she asked Josef, to which he would provide answers, and those that she kept to herself, each unanswerable one pushing her further away from the world: sometimes she felt as though she was living from a long way off. Why couldn't anyone detect the hollow echo of her voice when she spoke?

There was no reason not to accept Josef's invitation to the Christmas gathering; perhaps she could play the role of a happy audience. When they left the café that day and reached Josef's car—a Ford Taurus, as he had pointed out to her when he had learned her birthday, which made her a Taurus, too—Moran kicked the mudguards of both wheels on the right side. Chunks of frozen slush dropped to the ground with dull thuds, which strangely cheered her up. She had noticed other people doing that, and sometimes when she saw a car with too much accumulation behind the mudguards, she had an urge to give them a kick.

Josef looked at her oddly. "I'm sorry," she said. "Is it a bad thing to do?"

Of course it was not, he said, though he looked distracted. She wondered if the action was unladylike in his eyes, but he did not know her: he would never envision her riding a bicycle down an empty stretch of road in Beijing with both hands off the handlebars, or pedaling alongside Boyang, whistling a John Denver song in duet: *Country roads, take me home, to the place I belong*—years later, when a colleague of Moran's whistled the song in the hallway, Moran would quietly weep into her hands, because a heart is always short one piece of its armor.

Josef drove quietly, and sensing his moodiness, Moran wrapped her scarf more tightly. He turned the heater up a notch, and then, without Moran's prompting, he said that Alena used to do that, too. She could not stand even the smallest gathering of mud or slush, and it used to baffle him that she could feel so strongly about something trivial.

"Did you ask her why she did it?"

"Yes, but she didn't know, either. She said she couldn't help it."

Moran had seen pictures of Alena at Josef's house, looking down at one of her children, or, in a photo from their wedding, laughing away with a childhood friend. Had she kicked the mudguards for the simple satisfaction of getting rid of something unsightly, or had there been something within her that could only be expressed by a violent yet harmless action? Thinking about another woman's past when the woman was no more had made Moran ashamed. That secret had belonged to Josef and, before that, to Alena.

A phone rang somewhere in the condo. Josef shifted on the sofa but did not wake up at once. Moran found the phone on the kitchen counter. She wondered if it was Rachel, and after a moment of hesitation, she took the call.

Rachel sounded flustered. "Oh, good, you're still there with Dad," she said.

"He's taking a nap."

"Will you be able to stay with him for a while? I promised I would come over, but the school just called. I think Willie is coming down with some sort of stomach bug."

"I'm sorry, Rachel," Moran said. "Go ahead and take care of everything. I'll be here."

When she turned around, she saw that Josef had woken up. Was everything all right, he asked, and she repeated Rachel's words. He nodded and said that Rachel had been stretched thin since his diagnosis.

If Moran tried again to talk about her plan to move back, it would be taking advantage of his guilt, though what if she talked to Rachel instead? Would her approval change his mind? But the thought of stepping from her hiding place behind Josef and speaking to Rachel made Moran uneasy. During her marriage to Josef, she had gotten along all right with his three sons, who had been living farther away; Rachel, who had stayed, had never liked Moran. Of course there were reasons for Rachel's animosity: the protective instincts of a daughter toward her widowed father; her loyalty to Alena; Moran's age—she was only three years older than Rachel; and Moran's foreignness. Josef had only hinted at these things, though Moran had not needed him to spell them out; he had said that by and by Rachel would come around, and all they needed was a little patience.

To accept these reasons was to agree that everything could be explained by a few generalized statements: a stepmother is evil, a foreigner is not to be trusted, a dubious woman taken in by a good man will repay his kindness like the viper in Aesop's fable, roses are red, violets are blue. But Moran found it hard to fit herself, or anyone for that matter, into a space secured by such unwavering convictions.

"You look pensive," Josef said. "What's on your mind?"

"Rachel," Moran said honestly.

"She's not what you remember from before."

The last time Moran had seen Rachel, she had been engaged to Matt; the prospect of a happy life had made Rachel more resentful of Moran's pending divorce from Josef. Certainly she was the only one who knew this was how things would turn out, Rachel had said then; her dad and her brothers had all let themselves be deceived. There had never been any scene between Rachel and Moran, but all the same, Rachel's words had made Moran wonder if indeed she had used Josef, mistaking him for the starting point of a new story, abandoning him when that script had failed—one's life could have only one beginning, and that happened at birth. When people talk about starting over, it's only wishful thinking: what came before, what happened yesterday, did not come or happen in vain.

"How's Rachel these days?" Moran asked. Earlier on the phone, she could hear in Rachel's voice the weariness of middle age setting in. "And her family?"

It made Josef happy to talk about his children and grandchildren. Apart from George, his children had all settled down in the Midwest: Michael worked in hospital management in Omaha, and Sharon, after the two boys had started school, had gone back to graduate school and become a middle school teacher; John, who had trained as a child psychologist and had become the headmaster of a private school in Chicago, had three children with Mimi, and together he and Mimi had overcome some rocky patches in their marriage; Rachel and Matt had their own optometry business, where Matt worked as the optometrist while Rachel ran the business. Even George, who had moved away to Portland, Oregon, to be the co-owner of a food truck and who had stayed single, seemed to make Josef proud, if only because he found George's life a little mysterious.

"So you see, everyone is in good shape. I'm lucky that way," Josef said.

There was a solidness to Josef's children that Moran felt attached to from afar, the way a traveler feels drawn to a fireplace seen from outside a window and between half-pulled curtains. Every time Moran walked past a party, she could not help but take a look: people in twos and threes chatting or smiling or sipping from near-empty glasses. Moran did not want to be there, but she held on to the belief that they were happier than she herself was. Of course there were dramas known only to themselves, but she believed that if they were troubled or distressed, they had sound reasons to feel that pain: when Rachel had broken up with her college boyfriend, it had been a volatile period filled with tears and then parties that had made Josef worry, but it was at one of those parties that she had met Matt, and all of a sudden things had been better; the six-month separation between John and Mimi, after Mimi could not continue her career as a vocalist when she had moved with John for his job, had for a while been disheartening, but she had since found enough to do with the church choir and an after-school program that she now felt *fulfilled*—no doubt Mimi's word, as Josef had explained to Moran at one of his birthday lunches.

"You certainly should take some credit," Moran said now. "Are you hungry? Do you want some food? Or a cup of tea?"

Josef looked at her as though he had not heard her questions. "Except—what do we do with you, Moran?"

"What's there for you to worry about?" she said, and regretted right away that her voice sounded stern.

"You're slow to move on, you know?" Josef said gently.

Moran wondered if he was speaking of her inability to move on from their divorce—or could it be that he was speaking of his own death? To ask a person if she could survive one's death indicates a kind of arrogance, or else a love so deep that no one but a dying man would admit it.

"Moving on? That's an American thing I don't believe in," she said. If one starts without a position, it's meaningless to think about the next point in time and geography. The last Thanksgiving that Moran had been Josef's wife—in 2001, not long after 9/11—the subject at the table had been *moving on*. Moving on—to where, or to what? she had thought to herself. She had seen the phrase often in the newspapers around that time and had found it more than baf-fling, though only Moran seemed to have doubts about what it meant for the country, for its people, to move on.

So much confidence, and where could one find evidence to prove that their optimism was justified? Even Alena's senseless accident had not cast a single shadow of fatalism in her family's hearts. When Josef had married Moran, his friends, despite their doubts, must have been comforted by the fact that he had moved on; after their divorce, moving on would have been part of what people had said to Josef—or had not even needed to—to make her stop mattering to him.

16

On the Sunday after their visit to the university Moran woke up with a start, as though something had happened and she was already late. The night before, she had told her parents that she was exhausted and gone to bed right away, but for a long time she could not sleep. The emotions that had stormed through her and left her mind a devastated land came back to her now, all pointing to that unmistakable fact: Boyang was in love with Ruyu.

But why not? Moran tried to reason with herself. He was right to choose Ruyu, and why should she be surprised? One's mind, fooled by pride, does not recognize the wisdom that comes from sorrow. Prematurely one rushes for the remedy of dignity, not knowing that dignity, rather than rejection, turns one's heart into a timid organ, pleading for protection.

In the first light of day the quadrangle stirred to life, the doors opening and releasing people from their houses into the open air: someone brushing teeth and rinsing with loud gurgles next to the spigot, Teacher Pang watering his flowers while humming an operatic tune, Watermelon Wen's wife snapping at the twins, who had been working keenly to trap a cat visiting from the neighboring quadrangle. A moment later Moran heard Boyang's grandmother asking if the visit to the university was fun, and Ruyu replied that it was. A different place than this, isn't it? Boyang's grandmother said, and

Ruyu must have acknowledged the question with a nod, as Moran did not hear her reply.

Boyang was in love, but was Ruyu, too? Her disturbed mood and uninterpretable behavior of the previous night did not belong to someone in love. Could it be that she had no reciprocal feeling toward him? That hope, too precarious to be further explored, nevertheless left a door ajar in Moran's heart. Boyang was one of those people who could get anything he wanted, but there must be a point when that luck ran out. Heartbroken, perhaps he would notice another heart broken for him.

After breakfast, Watermelon Wen's wife asked Moran to look after the twins. The woman complained that once again it was her turn for the weekend shift on the trolley route, even though everyone in the quadrangle knew she asked for it whenever she could. She and her husband were a loving couple but both had quick tempers: on the weekends when they were home together they tended to get into fights, about children, grocery shopping, or simply some disagreement over a TV drama.

Moran was relieved to have something concrete to do. Already she had tipped over a bowl of porridge at breakfast. It threatened to be a long day, and she waited eagerly for Boyang's return, yet she dreaded it, too. Loyalty required her to be happy for him, but she was not a good actor; and then, loyalty to whom? The separateness between them had not occurred to Moran until that moment. Since when had they reached the point where what was good for him was for her no longer so?

Ruyu came over to the table under the grape trellis and watched Moran teach the twins paper cutting. The boys complained when what they made turned out crooked. They poked each other with miniatures of Transformers, and asked to be let go so they could battle it out. Moran told them to stay in her sight. There was a trembling in her voice, but she hoped that Ruyu did not detect it.

Ruyu picked up a piece of finished work, and said she did not know Moran could do paper cutting. Ruyu's effort at making small talk surprised Moran. There was a calmness in Ruyu's eyes. Moran wondered, her heart sinking, if she had made a mistake: perhaps Ruyu was in love, too.

"I'm not very good at it," Moran said, and explained that Boyang's grandmother was a gifted paper-cutter, and she herself had tried to learn but could only do a few simple patterns. To bring Boyang's name into the conversation felt like a challenging gesture, or else a surrender, but Ruyu did not acknowledge it as either, as though he did not, this morning, deserve a place in their conversation. Moran picked up a children's book from the top of a stack, an adventure of two friends, one named Little Question Mark, the other Little Know-It-All.

"We used to joke that Boyang was Little Know-It-All," Moran said.

"And you were Little Question Mark, of course?"

Moran was about to say yes, but then felt self-conscious that she would be unfairly boasting about a connection that Ruyu did not have with Boyang. "How are you feeling this morning?" Moran asked instead.

"You sound as though I've been ill."

Had Ruyu forgotten the night before? "You looked wretched last night," Moran said. "You talked about . . ."

"Never mind what I said."

"How can I not?" Moran asked. "Are you less unhappy today?"

"There's your question about happiness again," Ruyu said. "Why are you trying so hard?"

"At what?"

"At being good," Ruyu said and stood up.

"But wait," Moran said, urgent in her pleading. "Don't go yet."

"Why?"

Moran looked around and lowered her voice. "Can you tell me what you took from the lab yesterday?"

"When will you stop asking questions, Little Question Mark?"

"I worry about you."

"But who asked you to worry about me?" Ruyu said and left before Moran could reply.

There was no one Moran could turn to for advice: to talk to any grownup, or to talk to Boyang, would be to break her promise to Ruyu. If only Shaoai had not been in so much trouble herself. She might even know what Ruyu's real mood was. But to bother Shaoai now, with a crisis perhaps only imaginary, would be inconsiderate.

Loneliness comes with secrets; secrets in turn become the badge of honor for loneliness. Lingering in Moran's heart was the wish, childlike, childish, for a transparent world, and to be barricaded in her loneliness by Ruyu's secret—murky, inexplicable—gave Moran the first taste of a life violated. Sometimes she felt feverish; other times she shivered: loneliness, when not understood by its possessor, becomes a hallucination.

An odd thought occurred to Moran: that her life, compared with Shaoai's or Ruyu's, was so dull that it must not be a worthwhile one in the eyes of the other two girls. Even Boyang seemed to have a story elsewhere, his parents and his sister forming a world that had not much of an overlap with the quadrangle; he could have a conversation with a graduate student, and without any difficulty he could see himself in a house in America. *Keep your eyes open, or else you won't know how marvelous the world is,* said a slogan for a travel program on television. The program was the first of its kind, and indeed the world appeared marvelous through its lenses: intrepid bungee jumpers on a cliff in New Zealand; a carefree young couple punting on the River Cam; the empty inner courtyard of Karl Marx's birthplace, geraniums blossoming on the windowsills; green ivy climbing the redbrick buildings on the Ivy League campuses; the Golden Gate Bridge in the morning mist; Times Square flashing at night.

She could keep her eyes open all the time, but what Moran saw were those around her: her father going over the family accounting book item by item to make sure they had done their best to save a few extra yuan for a refrigerator; Aunt and Uncle plagued by the fear that Shaoai would be forever kept out of the *system*; queues for rationed food; gray moths living and dying without a purpose. If the world was indeed marvelous it must be so for those whose imagination was livelier than hers. To see, it seemed to Moran, required much more than to open one's eyes.

But what did Ruyu see of the world? Moran did not know. She could not even say with any confidence what Boyang saw now, though that was because these days his eyes were turned to Ruyu constantly. Perhaps two people in love, having made an entire world by themselves, do not have to look elsewhere. There were songs and poems written about that, but no songs or poems had been, or would be, written about queues or ration stamps or the pettiness of worrying over the price of pork. Moran felt old. What if she would never have anything poetic in her for people to love?

These thoughts, circling and leading nowhere, often left Moran in a trance, and on Thursday morning she was caught in politics when her mind lost its track. When the teacher called her name, she stood up, vaguely aware that she had been asked a question.

"Can you give us an example, classmate Moran?" the teacher prompted her.

When she did not answer right away, Boyang, who sat behind her, whispered, "Bok choy."

Moran said bok choy, and there were titters here and there.

"Hmm, that is rather a . . . unique example," the teacher said. "But can you give us some better ones?"

"Cooking oil?" Moran ventured. "Maybe sugar? Rice? Flour?"

The classroom broke into roaring laughter. Moran turned to look at Boyang, who nodded and held up a thumb. Whatever the teacher had been talking about, Moran certainly had diverted the course of the conversation in a less serious direction. She was not a mischievous student; rarely was she caught in any kind of spotlight, but she was not remorseful about putting herself momentarily in the shoes of the class clown. For one thing, standing rather than sitting, being the cause of such glee, had jolted her out of her foggy mood.

The teacher signaled for Moran to take her seat. "All concrete examples," she remarked when the class calmed down. "I wouldn't disagree with you, though I was hoping for some better ones: the production and distribution of steel, for instance, or coal mining, or railway construction." She looked at her watch, and then went on to summarize the lesson on Soviet versus Chinese models of planned economy.

At recess Boyang told Moran that the teacher had been asking for examples that demonstrated the advantage of a planned economy, and it had been brilliant of Moran to give her a list of rationed food. For the rest of the day some of the boys mouthed "bok choy" whenever Moran walked past them, though she knew they did not mean ill. She laughed when one of them told her that she should think of applying to the school officials to start a bok choy club; they would all join if she were to be the chairwoman, he said.

It was odd how a small incident like this had cleared her turbid mood. Moran remembered the couplet Teacher Pang and Teacher Li had hung in their living room: *The world, unspectacular, does not offer complicacy; only the foolish complicate their lives with self-inflicted befuddlements.* The world, like her parents and her neighbors, had never treated her unkindly; in return they expected her to act as a person in her position would do: pleasantly, obediently, sensibly.

When they left school that day, Moran decided that she must genuinely appreciate being close to Ruyu and Boyang. They were two extraordinary people, and how lucky she was to be their friend. One day she would look back and miss these days, and right away she chased the sentimental thought from her mind.

They stopped at a department store on the way. It was Aunt's birthday, and Ruyu said she wanted to buy a present, and she already knew what it would be. Aunt used to carry a glass container as a tea mug in a net crocheted with colored nylon. The bottle, sturdy, its orange lid bearing the trademark of Tang, had been given to Aunt by her colleague when the latter finished the contents. A few days earlier, when Aunt had been buying pickles, she had put the bottle on the counter, and within a minute someone had stolen it.

None of the families in the quadrangle had tasted Tang, the powdered orange juice imported from America. It had been appointed by NASA as the official drink for astronauts, the TV commercial informed its audience, with a slow-motion single drop of liquid rebounding from a glass of juice, which was in a color so intense that Moran could not help but cringe at the contrast between that orange on the screen and the dinginess off the screen. More and more her life reminded her of the watercolor sets she had had in elementary school, a new set at the beginning of each school year. They were of the cheapest kind, with twelve ovals in a narrow box and a tiny brush. The only time the set looked beautiful was before she opened it: the colors, no matter how diligently she applied and reapplied, were pale to nothing on the paper, and afterward the ovals dried and caked and then fell off in small chunks and fragments. Still, she had never asked her parents for a more expensive set, like the ones some of the other schoolchildren proudly carried. Her parents, if asked, would have scrambled to buy her a good set, Moran knew; they would have skipped a few meals with meat, but she had feared that she could not prove herself worthy of a better set.

But the day Ruyu bought the bottle of Tang was not one of those gloomy days of faded watercolors. Aunt was overwhelmed by the extravagance of the present. It had cost eighteen yuan, more than a month of Moran's lunch money; the sales assistant, a middle-aged woman, had looked with critical curiosity at Ruyu when she produced two ten-yuan bills, and when she had turned to the register for the change, she had mumbled to a colleague that she wondered what kind of parents would have spoiled a child with such luxury. Moran had fidgeted, yet Ruyu had stood still as though she had not heard the remark, loud enough and meant for her to hear.

In the evening, Boyang and Moran came over to see Aunt try her birthday present. Shaoai had not come home for dinner that day, and Ruyu could tell that Aunt had felt both sad that Shaoai was not there for her birthday and relieved that the meal, which Uncle had cooked for Aunt, had gone smoothly, without the usual tension.

Aunt lined up several mugs, and solemnly scooped the fine orange powder into each, while Uncle added water from a hot water kettle. Not boiling hot, Uncle explained, as a too high temperature would be detrimental to the vitamin C in the powder. Why not just add tap water, Boyang suggested, and Aunt said that cold water was not good for stomachs. "You all need to learn to take care of your bodies," Aunt said. "You won't always be this young."

It took no time for the powder to dissolve, and the color in each mug was as intense as promised by the TV commercial. "Now go ahead and bring a mug to every family," Aunt said to Moran and Boyang. "Don't forget to tell them this is a present from Ruyu."

"Why? Don't we get to try it first?" Boyang asked.

"You'll have yours when you come back," Aunt said, and asked Uncle if they had more mugs.

"Hold your generosity," Boyang said. "That bottle will be gone in no time."

In a rare good mood, Uncle said that Aunt would be happy to see the powder gone, as she would have a new Tang container to carry around proudly. "And this time she can even brag about having drunk the whole bottle ourselves," he said.

Aunt faked anger and told Uncle to stop poking fun at her. Boyang laughed, and carried two mugs, holding the door open for Moran, who followed him with two in her hands. Ruyu picked up a mug and said she would save it for Sister Shaoai in the bedroom. And don't forget Grandpa, Ruyu said to Aunt, which made her pour a small portion out of her own mug and bring it to Grandpa.

It was a cloudless night, and the moon, a day short of being full, cast a layer of silver on the courtyard. When Moran finished her deliveries—the two families had sent compliments and good wishes back with her to Aunt—she found Boyang waiting for her under the grape trellis. A few days earlier Teacher Pang had harvested the grapes to share with the neighbors, but a few clusters, not quite ripe, had been left behind.

Boyang reached for a cluster and handed half to Moran. "See, she *is* a good-hearted person," he said in a hushed voice.

The comment, coming out of nowhere, startled Moran. For one thing, she wanted to say that she had no idea whom he was talking about, though that would be dishonest. "Who has ever said she's not?" Moran asked.

Boyang looked sternly at Moran. "Then why are you hostile to her these days?"

"Am I?"

"Maybe others can't tell, but you know you're treating her a little differently from before," Boyang said. "Is it because of what I said to you last Saturday?"

Perhaps love allows perceptions that one does not possess otherwise. Like many boys his age, Boyang had not been observant. That boy has a mind like a sieve, his grandmother used to remark about his inattentiveness.

"Is it true that I'm hostile?" Moran asked. "How can you tell?"

"There's really not anything that we don't know about each other."

Is there, Moran wondered, or should there be? "Do you think Ruyu feels that way, too?"

"That you're being unfriendly? I hope not, though even if she feels it, she won't say anything," Boyang said. "You know how she is. She has grown up holding everything in."

Moran sighed. "I've been trying to be a good friend to her."

"Have you really?" Boyang asked. There was an unfamiliar edge to his voice, which made Moran's heart ache.

"Why? What's wrong?"

"I think you are jealous of her."

Moran felt grateful that they were in the dark, and even the bright moonlight would not reveal the coloring of her face, which was burning with shame and anger and a helpless despair. The line between innocent and heartless, if indeed there is one, must be so subtle that only those most experienced with human nature can perceive it. Moran, herself having not outgrown the age when innocence and heartlessness often go hand in hand, felt herself shrinking in front of Boyang. To appease him and to defend herself were equally impossible. There are moments in life when to speak at all is to speak wrongly.

"If you'd met someone special I would be very happy for you," Boyang said. "I don't understand why you're not happy for me."

"But I am happy for you!"

"You know you're not, and I know why you feel that way," Boyang said. "You're like a sister to me, and I thought you and I had the purest friendship."

Was there ever a pure relationship between two people? Moran wished she could tell Boyang about the chemical Ruyu had taken from his mother's lab, but the right moment of telling—if there had been one—had passed. "Let's go back," Moran said, feeling a sickness in her stomach.

A door opened, and Uncle, stepping out of the house, looked up at the moon for a long moment before trying to discern the figures in the shadow of the grape trellis. "Is that you two?" he asked. "Hurry before the Tang turns cold."

The next morning Moran woke up with a high fever. "Must be an early flu," she overheard Boyang's grandmother saying when her mother told Boyang and Ruyu to go to school without Moran.

She spent the day in bed, sleeping on and off, welcoming the physical illness because she was now exempted from thinking. Her mother had moved the radio from the living room to a chair next to her bed, and had left a kettle of hot water underneath the chair. She would ask Boyang's grandmother to check on Moran at lunchtime, her mother said, but Moran said she had better not; if she did have the flu she would rather not have anyone come near her, she said.

Ever so sluggishly time moved forward. Moran had forgotten to wind her wristwatch the night before, so it had stopped sometime before daybreak. She watched the slanting angle of the sunlight entering the window, leaving a path of floating particles in midair. In her Chinese textbook there was the poem about a lifetime passing like a white horse leaping across the narrowest crevice; the ancients had not been wrong if a thousand years had passed easily between their writing and her reading the poem, but had they also felt the weight of a never-ending movement when they had written those lines?

The radio, kept on at a low volume, proceeded from the morning news to the weather forecast and later the preschool children's sing-along program, though they all sounded unreal in her feverish half dreams. Moran thought about the people who would be listening to the radio on a morning like this: pensioners, shop owners sitting behind counters and waiting for the first customer of the day, a bicycle repairman at a roadside shed pulling out a punctured inner tube, someone outside the *system* like Shaoai, having no place to be.

Toward the end of the day Moran heard people come back from work. Her fever had not broken, which gave her the excuse to stay isolated. Later, Moran heard Boyang's voice from the living room, and her mother explaining to him that he had better stay away. Could he just say hi, he asked, and Moran's mother said she would check to see if Moran was awake. Moran closed her eyes, and when she heard Boyang leave, she wept quietly.

It took Moran a week to recover, and except for the weekend

when Boyang went to his parents' apartment, he came over every evening to chat with her, and once Ruyu came with him, too. When Moran was feeling less sick, she would prop herself up with a pillow, and he would sit astride a chair placed at the entrance of the bedroom. They had been polite with each other at first, but soon Boyang returned to his usual self. Several other classmates had caught the flu, too, he said, but he and Ruyu had been lucky not to have it; the midterm was in two weeks, but there was no need for Moran to worry about the missed classes, as he would go over everything with her once she felt well enough; in biology lab the next day they would be dissecting frogs, which he knew she would not like to do, so she might as well stay sick and skip it; and, by the way, did she know that Sister Shaoai was also sick, so when everybody was at work or at school she and Shaoai could keep each other company.

"What happened to Sister Shaoai?" Moran said, surprised that her parents had not told her about it.

Boyang said it was probably the same virus. Remember when they had the measles together, he asked, and she said of course she did. In third grade Moran and Boyang had been caught by a measles epidemic, and his grandmother had set up her house for the two to be quarantined from the rest of the quadrangle; every morning and evening she would feed them dark, bitter liquid brewed from herbs, but otherwise they had been left alone with a chess set and a radio. Moran was a terrible chess player. Every time she was about to lose Boyang would switch sides with her, and it amazed her that however badly she opened her game he was able to change it for the better; sometimes they would switch sides several times in a game, until she would lose almost all the pieces for both red and black, and there was nothing to do but to call it a draw.

Those had been the happiest days, she thought, but did not say so to Boyang, for whom happier days were to come.

Unlike Moran, who was recovering by day, Shaoai deteriorated. By the time Moran was allowed to go back to school, little was on her mind but Shaoai's illness—she had gone into a coma a few days before. The doctors were baffled, as the flu-like symptoms had quickly given way to other, more serious problems: hair loss, vomiting, seizures, and loss of much of her brain functions; all the tests run had offered few clues.

Before Boyang left for his parents' home for the weekend, he told Moran to call him if there was any news about Shaoai. Every day Aunt and Uncle took turns being at the ICU with Shaoai; neighbors had offered to take a few shifts so the couple could rest, but they had declined, saying it was best if they could be there before the doctors could give a definite diagnosis.

After lunch on Sunday, Moran went to Shaoai's house and looked for Ruyu. Earlier in the morning they had studied for midterms together. Uncle was taking a nap, and Ruyu was feeding Grandpa some rice mush. These days Ruyu spent much of her free time taking care of Grandpa, who alone was spared the worries that had shrouded the quadrangle like a dark fog. For each day Shaoai stayed in coma, it seemed one more person started to lose heart. At breakfast that day, Moran's mother had wondered aloud if they should hope now for a different scenario: "For sure Shaoai cannot recover as a normal healthy person again—sometimes you don't know if it'd be easier for everyone if her parents let her go."

In the small cube of Grandpa's bedroom Ruyu looked pensive. After she fed Grandpa and cleaned his face and neck with a towel, she told Moran in a low voice that she would be sitting here with Grandpa until he fell asleep. I'll sit with you, Moran whispered back. Ruyu glanced at Moran, and she knew that Ruyu did not welcome her company. Still, Moran could not help but feel less uneasy if she could keep an eye on Ruyu; during the weekdays Boyang was always around, but on a Sunday like this, when everyone's attention was elsewhere, Moran was particularly unwilling to leave Ruyu alone.

Neither spoke. Grandpa looked exhausted, and dozed off soon. The only window high on the wall was open, and Moran watched the blue sky beyond, and listened to a few sparrows pecking on the roof. Autumn would soon be over, and when winter came the peddlers would set oil drums aflame on the street corners and later roast sweet yams and chestnuts in the hot ashes. In the past winters, Moran and Boyang used to stop by one of the oil drums and pick up the biggest yam, its purple or brown skin charred and wrinkled. Easily she could see, in her mind's eye, Ruyu and Boyang divide a yam into halves, smiling at each other through the steam rising from the golden inside of the yam.

Moran stopped herself from pursuing the thought, ashamed that she was so selfish as to dwell upon her minor pain while Shaoai's life was in danger. Moran did not believe Shaoai would die, and these days before her recovery reminded Moran of the time when she had fainted in a municipal bathhouse as a child. The air, hot with thick steam, had been oppressive, and grownups, comfortable in their nakedness, gossiped loudly; their voices, mixed with the running of showers and the splashing of the bathwater, had sounded as though they had come from far away; when Moran's legs turned cottony, the last thought on her mind had been to hold on tight to the bath soap because fragrant soap was not cheap.

Any day now, any moment, Aunt or Uncle would come back with some good news—a diagnosis, or better, a retreat of the virus, and Moran would breathe freely again, as she had found herself awake in the cold air of the locker room, though the soap had slipped away, and had never been recovered. One day the neighbors in the quadrangle would refer to this time as the days when Shaoai had been mysteriously sick, as they would speak of the May afternoon when an army tank was overthrown and burned down at a nearby crossroads, or the day in June when Teacher Pang's cousin pedaled three bodies on his flatbed tricycle from the Square to the hospital. Perhaps Moran would even think of these days as the beginning of a love story between Boyang and Ruyu. Life, in retrospect, can be as simple as a collection of anecdotes, and anecdotally we live on, trading our youthful belief in happiness—and at that age happiness almost always means being good, being right, and being loved—for the belief in feeling less, suffering little.

The gate to the courtyard opened, and it was clear from the neighbors' gathering that Aunt had come back. Moran looked at her wristwatch—it was two o'clock, not yet time for Uncle to change shifts with Aunt. At once Moran felt hope arising—for sure by now the doctors would have found out how to treat Shaoai, though that hope was dashed when she heard Aunt's voice.

"No, she's the same," Aunt said to the querying neighbors. "But one doctor asked me if she had been in contact with any chemicals recently. I told him that she was an international trades and relations major, but he said her symptoms more and more reminded him of a poisoning case he had seen in the seventies."

"Poisoning?" several neighbors gasped. "But how could it be?"

"I don't know," Aunt said. "We don't know how she's been spending her time these days, or what kind of people she has met. I was coming back earlier because I thought we might find the phone numbers of her old classmates and ask them."

Moran turned to look at Ruyu. The latter was watching Grandpa's shallow breathing as though she found it mesmerizing. Moran hesitated and then grabbed Ruyu's elbow. "Come," Moran said. "I need to talk to you."

Ruyu did not resist, and led the way to her bedroom. She sat down on the bedside and looked up, her eyes lucid. Moran pulled over the chair and sat down, feeling as though she herself had committed a crime and had to enlist Ruyu in a cover-up. "Where is the chemical you took from the lab?" Moran asked.

"Gone."

"Gone where?"

"I don't know," Ruyu said. "I put the test tube in my drawer, but it was gone."

"Since when?"

"I'm not sure. A few days now," Ruyu said, and looked irritated. "I'm not like you, Moran, and this is not my home. Nothing I have really belongs to me. If someone takes something from me, what can I do but shrug and say, suit yourself?"

Taken aback, Moran did not know what to say.

"You think I poisoned Sister Shaoai?" Ruyu said, looking into Moran's eyes with a taunting half smile. "Are you interrogating me now?"

"No! But did you hear what Aunt just said? The doctors thought it might be some chemical poison."

"The doctors said it was meningitis earlier. And they may say something else tomorrow."

"But why didn't you say anything when Sister Shaoai got sick?"

"About what? Everyone got the flu last week. And then they were talking about bacterial infection."

"Do you think it was Shaoai who took the chemical?"

"I don't know."

"Did she ask you about it?"

"You think people will ask your permission when they take something from you?"

Moran felt an urge to shake Ruyu. There was a life they had to save before it was too late. "What did you take from the lab, do you remember?"

Ruyu shook her head. "I never did say I took anything."

"Do you understand that this is a serious matter? Can you come with me to tell Aunt and Uncle what happened? We need to call Boyang and his mother."

"Do you think," Ruyu said, raising her eyes, "that Sister Shaoai would like it if indeed it was her intention to commit suicide?"

"But we can't sit here, doing nothing."

"Why? What's wrong with doing nothing? The world would be a much better place if people did less," Ruyu said. "Why do you all think you have the right to change someone's life only because you want to?"

Ruyu's anger baffled Moran. It was useless to go on arguing. Moran stood up, and realized that her legs were shaking.

"Where are you going?" Ruyu asked.

"I'm going to talk to the grownups," Moran said. "Are you coming with me?"

There was something unreadable in Ruyu's eyes, a mixture of pity, derision, and curiosity. In the years to come Moran would return to this moment to study Ruyu's face, searching for panic or guilt or remorse or fear — anything that would make Ruyu comprehensible — yet once and again Moran would see none of those, only a chilling tranquility, as though Ruyu had foreseen all that would come. But how could she have? To grant that prescience to a fifteen-year-old was to give her a mystic power beyond her capacity. Still, in every revisiting of the moment, that look had again manifested itself as Ruyu's tepid effort to save Moran from taking a wrong turn; unseeing, unthinking, Moran had not heeded Ruyu's admonition. Don't tell, that look had said, warning more than pleading; stay still, that look had said; rehearse your lines before you put yourself on stage; those who have not the words for themselves will be the only ones found guilty.

Over the years Moran never stopped imagining that alternative of *not speaking*. It comforted her at times to think how things would have turned out: without the belated injection of the antidote — Prussian blue, a name belonging more to a painter's easel than to a doctor's cabinet — Shaoai would have died young, a heroine whose death could be explained only by fate, which was both unjust (letting a senseless tragedy befall a young woman already wronged) and merciful (it could've been worse, dragging on and making everyone suffer unduly, people would console themselves). A secret would have stayed alive between Ruyu and Moran for some time, though like other adolescent episodes, it would be put aside one day, presumed to be buried, and never let out to light again. Perhaps something good would eventually have come out of the love between Boyang and Ruyu, or else it would have taken the natural course as all first loves do, blossoming and fading and leaving no permanent damage. Either way, Moran herself and Boyang would have remained friends, and one day, when things stopped mattering so much, she would tell him the secret. They would shake their heads then, baffled or resigned, but too removed from the tragedy to feel perturbed. Life had been kind to them, they would tell each other, even with its mysteries unsolved and unsolvable.

"Go ahead," Ruyu said. "It's your decision to talk, not mine."

The moments and hours and days that followed became an elongated tunnel, in which Moran was the lone traveler, carried forward not by her own will but by the unforgiving current of time; if that tunnel had ever ended she would not have noticed it. One day, when she arrived in America, she would see a commercial for a local support group for autistic children, in which a girl in a lilac-colored dress sang and acted out a story about the futile battle of an itsy-bitsy spider against the rain. Moran was not the only person in the living room of Westlawn then; her housemates were around, waiting for the opening game of the football season between the Badgers and a visiting team. None of them would notice Moran's tears, and she would never again sit among them to watch television. She was not the only one trapped by life. She was afraid of meeting another person like her, but more than that she was afraid of never meeting another person like her, who, however briefly, would look into her eyes so that she knew she was not alone in her loneliness.

The blood tests confirmed Moran's words and what had been taken from the laboratory, and Prussian blue saved Shaoai's life but not her damaged brain. Ruyu must have stuck unwavering to her side of the story, which Moran could only piece together, over the years, by herself—she could not bring herself to ask others, and even if she had, no one would have told her anything: yes, Ruyu would say, she had stolen the chemical out of despair; no, there was not any concrete reason for her despair, but only a passing mood; no, she wouldn't call herself unhappy, though she wouldn't say she was happy, either; she had not felt she needed to worry when the tube of chemical was gone, as she had thought someone might have tossed it out while cleaning the room. Again and again she had to answer the questions, asked by grownups in the quadrangle, the high school officials, the university security committee, the police: no, she did not know who had taken the poison; no, she had not had a plan to kill Shaoai; no, Shaoai had never spoken of suicide with her; had she spoken of that with Shaoai? no, though she had talked about it briefly with Moran; perhaps Moran had told Shaoai; perhaps Moran had rummaged through Ruyu's things and looked for the tube, or Shaoai had done that; had Moran ever spoken of suicide, no, of course not; would Moran want to kill Shaoai, no, she did not think so, though she could only speak from what she knew, and she did not know anyone well in this city; no, she had no reason to want to harm anyone; no, she did not do anything to harm anyone.

Moran did not know how much the world had trusted Ruyu's words; though people must have trusted her enough, as eventually the investigation stopped, leaving too much space for everyone to come up with his own conjecture: could it be that there had been two suicidal souls under one roof? Or could it be that the thought of suicide was like a virus—it did not matter how it had started, but in the end it had caught both girls, and by mere chance one was spared? There had been reasons for Shaoai's despair, and evidence: her being expelled from the university, her uncertain future, her dark mood, her one drunken episode that many had witnessed; quite a change from the ambitious and outgoing girl she used to be, people would agree. Less sense could be made out of Ruyu's situation, though she was an orphan sent to live with strangers, and she was at an age when hormones could easily induce untrustworthy moods; who knows, the neighbors sometimes thought—there was no way to find out how her life had started: suppose there had been genes of madness to start with, in the parents' lines? Their abandoning a baby girl could be more than being irresponsible; any orphan could be a host of dark secrets and unseemly history.

Ruyu's grandaunts had been telegraphed and phoned; they, citing the inconvenience of travel at their age, did not come, though they did send a telegram, in which they said that they had raised Ruyu as a God-fearing child, and they believed that she would not lie. The telegram arrived in the middle of another crisis, when Grandpa was found unconscious; he was rushed to the emergency room, and never returned to the quadrangle.

Moran's mother had signed for the telegram. Months later, when Moran found an excuse to stay home on a weekday—she felt sick, she told her mother, who let her skip school without further questioning—she looked around to see if her parents had saved anything related to the case, but the only thing she found was the telegram. Her mother must have conveyed the unkind message to Aunt and Uncle subtly, or did it matter even if she had not said anything? By then all was over: Boyang had been transferred to the high school affiliated with his parents' university, and was allowed only to visit on weekends to see his grandmother; Ruyu, with Teacher Shu's help, had become a boarder at school, and her stay in the quadrangle, barely four months, was never brought up by the neighbors afterward; Grandpa had passed away, and Shaoai's family, having relocated to another district, had not come back for a visit again, though they were not forgotten: each year the neighbors pooled their money and sent a donation to Shaoai's parents for her caretaking.

The vacated house had stayed empty for more than a year; bad feng shui, people would say, with two disasters hitting the family in a short time. Eventually a young couple moved in. They had been married for three years, but had been living in separate dorms assigned to them by their work units, which they had had to share with others. They were so happy to have a place assigned to them that the neighbors could not bring themselves to ruin their mood. By and by, however, the story would reach their ears, as in this city no secret would stay a secret, no history could be laid permanently to rest in peace.

After the case was closed, Moran's parents never spoke to her about it again. They must have learned how she had wept in front of strangers because unlike Ruyu, Moran could not answer the questions. Why had she not alerted anyone about the theft? people wanted to know; had it happened before that she had witnessed other illegal actions but had refrained from telling? Why had she not said anything to any grownup when her friend had talked about suicide with her? Had she worried about her friend's safety? Had she considered herself a responsible friend?

Moran did not know if Ruyu had been suicidal, or murderous; could it be that a person could not be one without being the other? The more she tried to understand Ruyu, the murkier her own mind became. All the same she did not protest when, in the end, blame was laid on her more than on the two other girls, as her silence could not be acquitted as their potential madness would be. People were lenient not to say this to Moran — that is, all but Boyang, who, as always, came up with his quick conclusion, and did not hold back. "You never really liked Ruyu, did you?" Boyang said to Moran in their last real conversation. He had moved away by then, and had written and asked to see her on a Tuesday afternoon. She had skipped school and met him near the Back Sea.

But that was not true, she argued weakly for herself.

"Why didn't you say anything, then? I understand your decision not to tell a grownup, but why not tell me?"

Nothing she could say would appease Boyang's fury now, or ever. He had lost too much — his first love, two friends, and his childhood home.

"Did you think I would love you if Ruyu had been taken out of the picture? Did you think if she killed herself we could go back to where we were?" Boyang asked.

When Moran broke into tears Boyang did not seem to soften his opinion. Angrily he sped away on his bicycle. Look at what you've done, a voice said to Moran, though she did not understand that it was her future self speaking: look at how you've destroyed everything.

17

"So," Celia said the moment Ruyu entered the house. "What's going on with you?"

"Nothing much."

"Then who was this woman who died?"

"That," Ruyu said, "is a long story."

"Just as I thought, but the question is"—Celia paused and studied Ruyu's face before handing her a clothes hanger for her raincoat; it was a drizzly morning, the fog dense, threatening to stay all day—"are you going to tell me the story? See, I knew something was up when you came over the other night. I asked Edwin, and he said he couldn't tell. But you know how men are. Or you don't know. In any case, they can't see anything unless you point out to them where to look, and even then you can't guarantee that they see what you want them to see."

Edwin had indeed concealed part of his conversation with Ruyu from Celia, though for what reason? "Did you send him to check up on me again yesterday?" Ruyu asked.

"Yes, to look and to ask."

Ruyu sighed. "You could've asked me without going to all that trouble."

"You could've told me without my going to the trouble," Celia said. "I didn't want you to feel that I was intruding. On the other hand, I wanted to know what happened, and I thought it'd be best to have Edwin ask."

"Why?"

"Because he'd be okay if you didn't tell him anything," Celia said. "And since you know he doesn't care much, you might have chosen to tell him the truth—and I'm saying this not only about you but about everyone. Those who are lied to are the ones to whom truth matters, don't you think?"

Celia, by simply being herself, was sheltered from doubt, and Ruyu admired Celia for that: anything concealed from her was done so because she cared too much. In life we have all met those like Celia, and sometimes we have befriended one or two, but never too many: if they are not the sole reason for the events around them, they at least have a part in everything that happens or does not happen. Their commitment to life is to be indispensable, a link between one thing and another; what they cannot connect to themselves—inevitably someone, something, will fail them by falling out of their range—will stop existing in their world. But was this a bad arrangement for Celia, or for those around her? Without Celia, Edwin, who had no tentacles of his own, would perhaps have had a less solid grasp on many things, though what did Ruyu know about Edwin's marriage? What did she know about him while he had, at least for a few days, kept their conversation a secret?

The thought that at some moment she had been on his mind was alarming in itself. Ruyu's ease with the couple relied on Edwin's keeping an incurious distance and Celia's having enough drama in her life for Ruyu to watch; as much as Celia enjoyed the attention, Ruyu enjoyed watching, and at moments did not stop herself from imagining, as all audiences do at one time or another, being on stage. Without difficulty, Ruyu could see herself in Celia's position: at the hub of things, adding, expanding, until the bubble becomes the entire universe for its maker—a world as infinite as one's ego will allow.

Ruyu did not regret not choosing that position. If she had ever felt anything close to passion, it was a passion of the obliterating kind: any connection made by another human being, by accident or by intention, had to be erased; the void she maintained around herself was her only meaningful possession.

Ruyu had thought Celia, oblivious, would be safe from that erasing. Unlike Shaoai, who had deemed it both her right and her responsibility to teach Ruyu how to feel; unlike Moran, to whom Ruyu's happiness and unhappiness had taken on a burdensome weight; unlike Boyang and the men after him, who saw things in her that she did not care about—Celia did not mind Ruyu's being an anomaly. Or she had not minded before today. Impatiently, waiting for an explanation, today's Celia had dragged Ruyu off the spectator's seat. "I didn't think the dead woman was relevant to anything," Ruyu said.

"But you've been unsettled."

"Any death can do that," Ruyu said. She unwound her scarf and asked if they could sit down. She could use a cup of coffee, Ruyu said, sending Celia into the kitchen ahead of her.

Was Celia right that Ruyu had not bothered to lie to Edwin because he did not matter to her? On the walk up, she had run into him at the bottom of the hill. He had stopped his car and rolled down the window. Would she like a ride to the house, he asked, and she said no, she would walk. He looked at the sky, as though disappointed by Ruyu's decision to remain inconvenienced by the weather, so she added that she'd always liked to walk in the fog and rain. Why had she said that, Ruyu asked herself now: one does not talk about oneself without a motive. She liked the couple enough to have allowed some sort of permanency into her relationship with them, though Edwin— or Ruyu herself—had disturbed that balance, and in doing so had deprived her of what little luxury she had allowed herself in the Moorlands' house: exemption from participating in life.

Ruyu watched Celia operate the shiny coffeemaker, which hissed professionally. "I've been thinking—I know this is sudden," Ruyu said. "But what do you think of my going back to China?"

"Back to China? When? For how long?"

The thought of returning to Beijing—for what, Ruyu wondered, though that question could wait until later—had been on her mind since she had woken up this morning. "It's only a preliminary idea," Ruyu said.

"But why do you want to go to China now? Whom are you going to see there?"

A better question, Ruyu thought, was *what* she wanted to see. Over the years, she had given Celia some information about her history. With a vagueness that must have been taken as an unwillingness to stroll down memory lane, Ruyu had made Celia understand that she no longer had living parents in China; if she had friends or relatives, they were distant enough not to bind her to the place. "Not really anyone important," Ruyu said.

"Is this trip prompted by this mysterious death that you're not telling me about?"

One could never avoid having a history. Ruyu thought about how much truth she could give away without actually giving away anything. Such calculations had become second nature to her because she did not like to lie. Lying, like living, needs motives, however obtuse they may be. With Paul, she had had to make up stories, both about her parents' deaths and about a childhood she'd never had: her parents had died in a traffic accident in Anhui Province, when a bus had missed a turn on a cliffside road and plunged into a river—a tragedy Ruyu had stolen from a newspaper article she'd read in college; her experience of being an only daughter she had borrowed from Moran, and a couple of childhood friends were modeled on Moran and Boyang—though naturally, Ruyu had told Paul, she had lost contact with them after so many years. What she could not produce as evidence—family pictures, snapshots of herself at different ages—she had explained as a natural and necessary loss resulting from emigration and a difficult divorce.

If Celia was right, the lies she had told Paul must have meant, somehow, that he had had meaning to Ruyu, at least more than the other men in her past. With her first husband, she had not needed to make up anything: he had known she was an orphan, which he had welcomed as a bonus because he would be free from in-laws; he had met her grandaunts—that is, he had met with their disapproval, though long before that, they had, without withdrawing their financial support of Ruyu in high school and college, made it clear to her that she had let them down. They had not questioned Ruyu about Shaoai's case. What they had heard, they said, had been enough, though for them the unforgivable was not that Ruyu had stolen, but that the crime was motivated by the sinful thought of suicide; it was the latter that had made them shake their heads and say that she was, after all, not related to them by blood, and they had no way to understand her. That Ruyu had decided to marry at nineteen—no doubt another violation of their vision for her—they had accepted with resignation; to marry at all constituted a betrayal of them, though betrayal caused less damage than sin. What would be less redeemable: to take one's own life, or to take another's life? It occurred to Ruyu that she had never really known the answer. She turned to Celia. "What is more sinful in Catholicism—suicide or murder?"

"Where did that question come from?" Celia said. "Is it inspired by this woman's death?"

"I don't think it's particularly this person, or her death. I suppose I've always been puzzled," Ruyu said. "Well, let's forget about it."

"Let's not, yet. Is this why you want to go back now, to find out if she was murdered or she killed herself?"

"No, it has nothing to do with her," Ruyu said.

"Then why China? Why now?"

"It's just a mood. It's been quite a long time since I last saw the country."

"When was your last visit?"

"I haven't been back since coming to America."

"That's what I remembered you told me," Celia said. "And how long ago was that?"

"I came in '92."

"What a shame!" Celia exclaimed. Ruyu wondered what the shame was, exactly—to be gone for so long, or to be gone for so long yet still not thoroughly gone.

Celia handed a mug to Ruyu, and they carried their coffee to the table. "Now, you must say something good about this coffee. Edwin roasted the beans himself, the first batch."

"When did he start getting into coffee?"

"Only about two weeks ago."

"What happened to beer making?" Ruyu asked. For the past two years, Edwin had been experimenting in the basement with his home-brewing kit; there were a couple of bootlegging tales about his granduncles he liked to tell at parties, and Ruyu was certain she was not the only one to have heard them more than once. She had wondered why no one ever told him not to repeat the tales, but perhaps others, kinder than herself, believed that having anything to say was better than having nothing to say.

"Going well," Celia said, "though a man is always in need of new things. Or else he'll feel stale. A man is not like a cat that you can leave to its own entertainment. You have to help him find things to do. Speaking of cats, where's Scooter?"

"He was by the garage door when I came in."

"I just warned him this morning not to bring another dead bird into the house, though I'd bet ten dollars he didn't hear me. Sometimes I think my problem is that I'm outnumbered in this household," Celia said with an exasperated glance at the framed family pictures on the sideboard—a look that could only belong to a contented woman. "Technically speaking, Scooter can't be called a man anymore, but he's in every sense your average male. And how they can make you talk all the time without hearing a word you say. If you decide to stay quiet just for one moment, they say, Mom, you didn't tell me where my gym clothes were, or, You didn't say the violin lesson was rescheduled. Or, like last night, Edwin said you looked terrible. I said, Oh, did she, and he said it surprised him that I hadn't noticed your mood, or asked you more about your friend's death. What friend, I said, and he said you told him yesterday that a friend in China died. He said he thought I had heard all about it, but wouldn't I have told him if that had been the case?"

Ruyu sipped the coffee. It occurred to her that she would one day miss Celia's company—or perhaps she had already begun to miss Celia, and the time sitting at this table, listening to Celia talk about her family trips and this or that complication with her sister and parents. Scenery that Ruyu had not seen with her own eyes she had seen through Celia's; people Ruyu did not know—and did not mind not knowing—she had met in Celia's tales. But all the same, the thought of leave-taking, once formed, pointed in one direction only; she had left plenty of people behind, and it did not bother her to add Celia and her family to that roster. Though Celia, the most unsuspicious one among them, gave Ruyu an odd feeling that she was burying something alive.

Celia observed Ruyu's expression. "Is the coffee not so good?"

"It's good."

"You don't look like you're impressed."

"You can't rely on me for any judgment," Ruyu said.

"That I already know," Celia said and leaned closer, propping her head on her hand. "Seriously, is the dead woman an enemy of yours or something?"

Ruyu thought about it. "Not really. I don't think I care enough about the world for anyone to be my enemy," she said honestly.

Celia shuddered—or was it only Ruyu's imagination?—and at once recovered. "But with her gone, are things going to be easier in China for you? Is that why you want to go back now?"

"What do you mean?"

Celia sat up abruptly, as if she could not contain her excitement. "So, this is my hypothesis—and you can correct me if I'm wrong, but this is the most reasonable version of the story Edwin and I could come up with."

"Whose story?"

"Yours. But before I start, you have to know I'm not the judgmental kind, so you don't have to feel uncomfortable. For all I care, you could be anyone, or anything, and I would be your friend."

Ruyu looked at Celia curiously. "For all I know, I've always been nobody and nothing."

Celia ignored Ruyu's words. "I've read in the newspapers that rich people and high-ranking officials in China keep their mistresses in California—have you heard of such a practice?" Celia said, looking into Ruyu's eyes.

"Or New Jersey," Ruyu said. "Yes, I've heard of it. But carry on."

"You're not uncomfortable where I'm going."

"No."

Celia nodded and said she was only making sure. "So my guess is that, however it happened, you met a married man when you were young—eighteen? nineteen?—and got yourself involved, but when things became complicated, he arranged for you to come here. And now, this woman—whoever she was, the wife most likely—died, and the hurdle is gone."

"Did you and Edwin come up with this last night?"

"No, I always wondered, but Edwin never bought my theory until he saw you yesterday. I suppose what you said about the dead woman convinced him that I was right. Why, which part doesn't make sense?"

"It all makes sense," Ruyu said. "Except, how do you fit my two ex-husbands into the story?"

"Were you really married twice?"

"I see that you have started to question everything I've said."

"We only have your word about the marriages."

Ruyu sighed. "Why did you help me move if I looked so suspicious in the first place?"

"I didn't know then!" Celia said. "But I wouldn't have minded helping in any case. I thought you were only trying to move out. That arrangement with your former employer did look suspicious to me, though."

"So how do you fit that part into your story?"

"That seems to make more sense than your marriages. I would say, unless you show me evidence, I prefer to believe that your marriages are not real."

"Why? Do I look like the kind of woman who could only be a mistress?"

Celia laughed.

"No, I meant it as a serious question," Ruyu said.

"What does a mistress look like?" Celia asked and studied Ruyu. "I don't know, but I do think you look like someone who doesn't know she deserves better."

Ruyu wondered if part of her problem was that she could not imagine herself as a wife. Moran, for instance, always had that wifely look about her—she would never become anyone's lover; she was born to be someone's wife. "Carry on with your detective work. How do you explain the man in Twin Valley?"

"I thought the man in China stopped supporting you, so you needed to find someone else to support you, but Edwin said that the man might be a business partner of your man in China and only served as a guardian. But I would prefer that you'd moved on from the man in China—am I not closer than Edwin?"

"From the kept woman of a Chinese official to the kept woman of an American politician?"

"Is that what the man was, a politician?"

"He didn't end up having a bright career in politics," Ruyu said. "Though at one time, he seemed to think he would."

"See, I was right! Is he someone we've heard of?"

Ruyu shook her head. There was no need to bring Eric's name into the story.

"How did you meet him?"

"Who?"

"The failed politician. What's his name?"

"John Doe," Ruyu said. "I did a bit of bookkeeping for one of his businesses. And then he hired me as a housekeeper. No, Celia, you don't have to sit there dying of curiosity. If you want to know more, ask."

"What happened between you and him?"

"Nothing much. I suppose we tried to see if we could settle into each other's lives, but it didn't quite work out."

"Why not?"

"Not enough love, I think."

"On your side, or his?"

"On both sides," Ruyu said. At least Eric had had the patience to put up with her for three years, though they had been the same three years he had gone through the legal battle for his divorce. Ruyu preferred to believe that he had offered her the cottage in the first place because he had needed convenience without complication. How he had chosen Ruyu—chosen wisely, both of them had later agreed— she had not asked; she had moved in because there had not been a better—or worse—place for her to be, then or ever. In a sense, they had enjoyed each other's company, though something that had begun with a contract could only end within the terms, written or unwritten. Ruyu wondered now if either of them, at any moment, had been waiting for the other person to propose an amendment— though what difference would it have made? Neither had wanted to blunder, and, in the end, neither had been willing to give up his or her mildly sarcastic view of the relationship; it was as though they had been two business competitors who had admired each other, but had to laugh at themselves for that admiration, or else they would've embarrassed themselves. They had parted ways amiably, both agreeing not to stay in touch.

"So," Ruyu said, and glanced at the clock. "That's all about my former employer."

"Did you . . . not love him because of the man in China?"

Ruyu smiled. "You really do believe there's someone in China."

"Why else . . ." Celia said, and then caught herself.

"Why else what?"

"Why else do you want to go back to China now?"

Ruyu studied Celia. "Is that what you were going to say before you stopped yourself?"

Celia sighed. "Why else do you not want to have a real life?"

Perhaps Celia's version was better: a story of loyalty and betrayal, of scheming and innocence. For a moment, Ruyu could see herself in Celia's—and Edwin's—eyes: a life lived under the spell of a first encounter, if not a first love; years spent, or misspent, waiting for another woman to die. The romance and the tragedy would be perfect footnotes for her insubstantial life; without such drama and mystery, she would have been too commonplace. Yet how could she explain that being on her own—and not someone's property—was the only thing she had wanted? Once upon a time, she had been her parents' possession, however momentarily, and after that she had belonged to her grandaunts, in whose minds she had belonged more to their god than to them; all sorts of people had since tried to claim her, but to stay unclaimed was to be never disowned again.

"Hello," Celia said. "Hellooo."

Ruyu looked at the clock again and finished her coffee. "I don't mean to interrupt our conversation, but I need to leave soon for the shop."

"There's still time," Celia said. "I'll drive you down. Now, don't look so rattled. As your friends, we are genuinely concerned about you. That's why we're asking these questions."

"I know," Ruyu said.

"And however you feel at this moment, don't rush into a decision," Celia said, and when Ruyu did not seem to understand, Celia leaned closer. "Don't go back to China."

"Why?"

"Don't you feel you deserve something better than what you've had? Why do you want to return to some bastard who has kept you in limbo for twenty years?"

Ruyu wondered if she should acquiesce to the story, take ownership of something that did not belong to her, so that when she vanished from their world, Celia and Edwin could go on imagining her living that heroic tale of love and stupidity. But stupidity was easier to live with than love, and if Celia and Edwin ever thought about her in the future, she would prefer not to have anyone connected to her. Perhaps she was more egotistic than she realized: she could not stand sharing even the space of someone's imagination with another person. "Very wise advice, Celia, but my life has been much more boring than your version. There is no person in China as you thought," Ruyu said. "I don't have a family. I don't travel. I don't eat at restaurants. I don't go to movies. There were two marriages, and both failed. And there is no one now, in this or another country. You may be tickled to know that I don't have health insurance. What do you Americans call a person like me? A loser, no?"

"You don't have health insurance?"

"I can't afford it, Celia. Do you really believe selling chocolates and dog-sitting are my hobbies?"

"But you don't look like you're struggling," Celia said. "I mean, financially."

"So there must be someone secretly funneling money into my bank account?"

Celia looked painfully baffled. To be a mistress in hiding, Ruyu thought, was certainly to be somebody; her being nobody must be a disappointment for Celia.

"But why don't you want to have a life?" Celia said after a moment. "For all I know, you could have many things if you wanted them."

What if, Ruyu could not help thinking cruelly, she wanted Edwin? She stood up abruptly. "Seriously, we have to leave now—and thank you in advance for the ride, as I do need it."

Celia was quiet as she backed the car out of the driveway. She must feel deceived, though people always cast Ruyu this or that way; it was not Ruyu's fate to play the proffered part, and she saw no reason to apologize. In a lighter tone, she asked Celia about her upcoming trip—a Caribbean retreat with Edwin's company, for which Celia had bemoaned her less-than-ideal skin tone and the loss of her perfect bikini body.

"Speaking of that," Celia said, her grip on the steering wheel loosening a little. "You do remember that you've promised to take care of my children while we're gone."

"Are you worried that I'll take off and leave you stranded at the last minute?"

"How would I know?" Celia said. "With all your talk about going back to China."

"I'll let you in on a secret so you don't worry: I don't even have a passport to travel on."

"The more you tell me about yourself, the less I feel I know you. Who knows? You may even be a secret agent for North Korea."

So rarely did Ruyu laugh that when she did now, Celia turned to look at her for a prolonged moment before returning her attention to the road. "Seriously, are you a Chinese citizen or American, or both?"

"American," Ruyu said. "I can show you my naturalization papers if you want to see them."

Celia sighed as she pulled into the small parking lot behind the shop. "The thing is," she said, turning to look at Ruyu, "it feels odd now to think that we don't know a lot about you."

"You certainly know more about me than most people do. And the things you don't know are not worth knowing," Ruyu said, feeling all of a sudden melancholy. To have an identity—to be known—required one to possess an ego, yet so much more, too: a collection of people, a continuous narrative from one day to the next, a traceable track linking one place to another—all these had to be added to that ego for one to have any kind of identity. "Well, many thanks for the ride, and do tell Edwin I loved his coffee."

"Are you sure you don't want me to call Rebecca and tell her you don't feel well?" Celia asked. "You look awful."

"Maybe I'm coming down with something, but I should be fine."

"If you need to talk more, you know I'm always around," Celia said. "And don't think I haven't noticed that you didn't really tell me the story of the dead woman."

"Maybe another time?"

"In fact, why don't you come to our Thanksgiving dinner?"

"Your parents will be here," Ruyu said.

"The more reason for you to come. They're harmless if there is another guest present. I think Edwin would be happy to have someone to distract them."

Ruyu turned to look at Celia, feeling a strange sensation that this was the last time they would be seeing each other. Of course it would not be so, Ruyu thought, trying to shake off the fatalistic shadow. Normally she would have found an excuse to decline the invitation, but today, as if to prove to herself that there was no finality in anything, she said yes.

The thought of leaving, though, began to take a more definite shape. Ruyu saw little point in resisting, just as she had found it natural to answer an ad for a nanny position when she had needed a reason to withdraw from Eric's life. The next day, she sent off an application for a passport. Flights between Beijing and San Francisco were booked—the only reason she purchased a round-trip ticket was that it was cheaper than a one-way ticket. The return date, which she had chosen randomly, offered her a sort of comfort, as if the decision to vacate her present life was reversible, though that illusion was easily overridden by the concreteness of the steps leading up to the exit: the acquisition of a passport that lawfully identified her; the stamping of her visa, which categorized her as a traveler in her home country; the assigning of a seat on the plane, one next to a window—nothing could be undone now.

The loose ends that she could not neatly tie up she had to accept as her debt, mostly to Celia, which would confirm her belief that those who mattered would be owed, just as they would be lied to. Ruyu could not give Rebecca advance notice of her resignation, but Rebecca would easily find someone else to install in the shop. The lease to the cottage would have to be broken, but Ruyu would leave an extra month's rent, and that, along with her security deposit, should be enough compensation for her landlords, who were Celia's friends, and who might not be in a hurry to rent the place out again. Various women for whom Ruyu did babysitting or pet-sitting would have to wait to hear the news from Celia, but none of them would consider Ruyu irreplaceable.

But Celia—and Edwin too—belonged to a different category; their curiosity toward her, like their kindness, Ruyu could not return with any curiosity or kindness of her own. When she saw them again it was at their Thanksgiving dinner, and Ruyu, without Celia's prompting, took on the role as the audience to Celia's parents, who talked at length about their other daughter, a high-powered attorney in Dallas. Jittery, fearful of any detail that could go wrong with the dinner, Celia looked exhausted when it was time for her parents to withdraw to the guest room. The older couple, having artfully praised everything about the evening, nevertheless managed to leave a critical imprint before turning in for the night: Jake, who had just turned sixteen and obtained a driver's license, was planning to leave the house before midnight and participate in the Black Friday shopping craze with a few friends; Celia's mother good-humoredly commented, reaching for the rail on the staircase, that she wondered if such an adventure would be of any use to Jake's getting into Stanford, and

Celia's father chuckled before placing a hand on his wife's elbow and guiding her upstairs.

"Touché," Edwin said when the older couple was out of hearing.

Celia moaned and poured herself a drink before asking Edwin if he needed one, too, and he said yes at once. He turned to Ruyu and said she should join them, even though he knew Ruyu never touched alcohol.

She declined the offer and said it was time for her to go. Edwin placed the drink on the counter. "I'll drive you back," he said.

Ruyu said no, a little too harshly, so she tried to soften the tone by adding that he should relax and have a drink with Celia. If he found Ruyu's voice unnatural, he did not show it. Celia, having spent much of the evening watching her parents' every move, was in a daze, ready to be left alone perhaps, even though being left alone was the last thing she wanted from life.

"Think of the Caribbean next week as your reward," Ruyu said at the door, with copies of the keys to the house and Celia's car in her purse. The mention of their upcoming trip brought a whiff of tropical air to the cold, drizzly night. The couple looked momentarily cheered up, as though it was only their husks that had to endure a few more days of the visiting parents.

Celia said she would leave detailed instructions about the boys' schedules, and Edwin promised to send pictures. Ruyu, wishing them a fun time and giving each of them a good-bye hug, felt as though she were a mother feigning a smile, lest her children detect any abnormality. In first grade, she had seen a film at school—the first film of her life, as her grandaunts had not believed in the merit of going to the movies—about how life had been bad before the Communist era. At the end of the film, a mother, who had lost her job in a fabric factory and who had no hope left, gave her last few coppers to her two young children. She told them to buy a bun to share, and when they returned, they found that she had drowned herself in the river.

On the way back to her cottage, looking through unpulled curtains at other Thanksgiving dinners that were still lingering, Ruyu felt an urge to go back, to say a proper farewell to Celia and Edwin. Her flight to Beijing, on the same day as their flight back home, would be preparing to take off as they were landing at SFO.

But what could she say to the couple? Be brave, and be happy, you orphans with parents, you parents to future orphans.

18

Against his better judgment, Boyang did not stop pursuing Sizhuo. He recognized the peril of his persistence. What did a man want when he courted a woman? With his ex-wife, he had believed in a fresh start, that they could bring what they liked from their separate pasts and build a new world with only those good things; he had not realized that in choosing what to contribute, he had already cordoned off part of his life. Having erred age-befittingly, his only guilt was that the divorce had affected his ex-wife more; but that should be expected, as it was always a greater risk to be a woman than to be a man.

What about Sizhuo and himself, though? Boyang could not see their transaction with clarity. Her impertinence, her scrutiny of her surroundings, and her unsmiling expression at times reminded him of Ruyu, but Sizhuo's heart was too affectionate, her view of the world too moral, her dreams too many. Or was he only grafting some of Moran's qualities onto a person that he wished to be his first love? Boyang recognized the absurdity of this possibility: if he did not watch out, one day he would become one of those dotty old men who looked in every young woman's face for his dead wife or his lost first love.

Once upon a time, Boyang had thought that he had fallen in love with Ruyu, but what he had wanted, he understood now, was to be seen by her, not only in that moment but also in those moments before and after. Call it youthful conceit, but to be seen—and to be seen as someone with a past and a future—is that not our most sincere design for love? Our greediest, too: in wishing for such continuity, one places oneself—with arrogance and delusion—beyond the erosion of time.

The wish to be seen by Sizhuo, however, baffled Boyang more: he was torn between the desire for her to see him in his world, in which he could flirt with a business partner's lover (just as he would allow Coco to be flirted with, all within mutually acceptable terms), and the desire for Sizhuo to know nothing about that part of his life. Certainly he could not singlehandedly protect her from this already corrupt world, which he had felt no aversion to, except when it threatened that strange unworldliness in Sizhuo. In a sense, what he wanted from her was impossible: he wanted her to stay unchanged, to remain the only resident in her impracticable habitat, which he alone would have the right to guard—and perhaps to taint—with his own worldliness. He wanted to be a good person for her, and he wanted only her to know that he was a good person. If she noticed any discrepancy between his behavior and his intentions, she should understand it, because in his design, she was there to see him not as who he was, but who he could have been.

These thoughts, not having an audience—all his friends were the convenient kind—took on a life of their own. If only he could say these ridiculous things aloud and get them over with: any kind of reception—whether understanding or derisive—would be better than the silence. Boyang was not a person used to silence.

Sizhuo's ease with that silence perplexed him. What they were to each other seemed to her either irrelevant or settled, though if it were settled, he did not know on what terms.

In not wanting to bring Sizhuo into the world his friends and Coco occupied, Boyang had to carve out a space for Sizhuo in his life. This turned out to be not too difficult: she was fond of the old parts of the city, some of which had not been touched by tourists or developments for the past thirty years. Fewer and fewer of these places were left, Sizhuo explained to Boyang, as though it had not been his city to begin with.

Once a week—often on Saturday, but sometimes on Friday afternoon if he could not free himself on Saturday—he took her to one of the city neighborhoods or a village outside the city that had stayed behind the times. *Authentic* was the word Sizhuo used to describe these places; coming from another person, the word would have made Boyang sneer, though he felt forgiving toward Sizhuo: she was too young to immunize herself to the vocabulary of her time.

Sizhuo had an old Seagull camera that used 120 film, an ancient machine requiring one to look down on a glass plate to see through the lens, turn several knobs to adjust the focus, and crank a handle after taking each picture to advance the film. Boyang remembered these antiques from his childhood, though they had represented a different status then, owned by people who could afford a bit of luxury. In others' eyes, Boyang could see the absurdity of these outings: a middle-aged man with a receding hairline parking his BMW in a rundown alley, a young woman photographing the cracks in the walls and the dust accumulated on a discarded bamboo stroller. He wondered if it had occurred to Sizhuo that they were both impersonators of some sort: he played the indulgent provider and keeper of a young woman, and she, having little to claim as her own, presented herself as a nostalgic soul in search of a time long lost.

They did not discuss any specific topic when they took these walks, partly because Sizhuo constantly had to pause and look through the camera's viewfinder. She liked to show him the things she saw: a rusty bicycle lock with cobwebs; an old slogan haphazardly printed on a brick wall, calling for a Communist leap; a booth selling cigarettes and soda water that had been constructed from an old pickup truck.

The things that interested her did not interest Boyang at all. They were part of his past, which was not distant enough for them to take on any beauty in his eyes. But he liked to watch her, climbing up on an overturned handcart or getting down on her elbows to read a childish curse that must have been carved fifty years ago on the corner of a door. If she was aware of his watching, she did not alter her behavior out of self-consciousness.

At times he desired to be in her viewfinder, but he knew better than to place himself in any position that could endanger his status. If he was a sugar daddy, he was the chastest of his kind—he had not touched the girl with a single finger. He had stopped calling himself her suitor, and she did not seem to fret over the change. Were they playing a game together? Both were patient, or worse, calculating, though Boyang preferred to think that the ambiguity would sort itself out. He was not in a hurry, as he rather enjoyed these weekly outings that did not come with any burden of responsibility. For him, at least, this side project—what else could he call it?—made him more tolerant of Coco, as the vulgar straightforwardness of the latter could be refreshing, too.

One thing that Boyang noticed, not without alarm, was that his mind often wandered to Aunt, to Shaoai's death, and to the silence of Ruyu and Moran, when he was watching Sizhuo take pictures. He had stopped by twice to see how Aunt was doing, though he had not pressed to know more when she put up a brave show of independence in her isolated apartment. He had given an additional three months' pay to the woman who used to come every other day to watch Shaoai so Aunt could go grocery shopping or take a walk for fresh air. The woman, middle-aged and laid off from a state-owned factory, had been appreciative of his generosity, which had turned her into a friend of sorts for Aunt. It was too late, he knew, for Aunt to make new friends or get in touch with her old ones.

He had not heard from Ruyu or Moran. He wondered how much it would cost to hire someone to track them down—surely he could find someone inexpensive in Chinatown in New York City, or Los Angeles.

"What are you thinking about?" Sizhuo asked, and Boyang realized that he was particularly quiet today. They were near an old village where a stretch of abandoned railway lay among tall, dry weeds. The December sun had begun to set behind the poplar trees, a few unshed leaves shivering in the wind. Earlier, Sizhuo had turned the camera upward toward half a torn kite caught between the branches; he had even made a joke about the kite having introduced them to each other, though it had not dispelled his moodiness.

"How to be a good man," Boyang said.

"Are you a good man?"

"I'm trying to be," he said.

Sizhuo closed the faux-leather cover of the camera, and he handed her gloves to her, which he carried for her when she maneuvered the camera's buttons and knobs. "Do you mean that these things you do for me are part of your trying to be a good man?" she asked.

"What kinds of things?"

"Driving me around, carrying my gloves, making sure no one abducts me . . ."

"You may not believe it, but I do much more for others than I do for you."

"Then shouldn't you already be a good man?"

Sometimes Sizhuo's questions sounded as though she were flirting with him. He wished that were the case.

"I wonder how boring this is for you," Sizhuo said when he did not speak.

"I'm more cold than bored," Boyang said. "Do you want to stop by a pub? Ten minutes down that road there's one that's relatively clean."

"How do you know?"

"I know this area pretty well," Boyang said, though he did not explain that he had helped a business contact close a deal that turned the land outside the village into a holiday resort with a vineyard, winemaking being part of the newest trend. At the last minute, the contract had not gone through, though it was just as well. Boyang would have hated for the city to lose another patch of bleakness to prosperity.

"Do you know all the places you bring me to?"

"More or less," Boyang said. "Generally speaking, I want to know what I'm doing."

"Then what are you doing here?"

"Enjoying an outing with you."

"But why do you agree to come, when it's cold and boring like this? It can't be hard for you to find a more exciting way to spend your afternoons."

"If you mean to kill time—yes, I have other ways, but I wouldn't call this misspent time," Boyang said, and opened the car door for Sizhuo.

She ungloved her hands and put them in front of the heater when he started the car. "Don't do that," he said. "You could get chilblains."

She looked at him oddly and put her gloves back on without saying a word.

"What? Did I say something wrong?"

"Nobody gets chilblains these days."

Boyang wondered if that was true. He remembered the winters in grade school, when the boys all had swollen red fingers, and sometimes the girls, too, though Moran had never had them. She had been the one who had reminded Boyang, every time they entered a room, not to go right away to the heater but to rub his hands first. Always the one to offer a solution to any problem, Boyang thought; always there, always, counting a hundred before letting him go to the heater. What kind of comfort does a good person like that offer? Less than she has imagined, alas.

"You look annoyed," Sizhuo said.

"Why don't kids have chilblains now?" he asked.

"Why should they? The world is enough of a bad place without chilblains."

Boyang looked at Sizhuo, who only looked down at the fingertips of her gloves. He wondered what had brought on her mood today. "The world would be a good place if all we had to worry about were chilblains," he said.

"That must make you feel good, then?"

"What?"

"That your only concern about me today is that I don't get chilblains."

"How do you know that's my only concern?"

"Why do I want to know?" Sizhuo said.

"It's natural for a person to want to know another person's thoughts," Boyang said. "That is, if they're next to each other."

"Natural?" Sizhuo pointed to a giant crow spreading its wings and hopping to the other side of the road, to make way rather than fly away. "That," she said, "is a perfect example that nothing is natural in this city."

"Where did that criticism come from?"

"Shouldn't a bird take flight when a car comes?" Sizhuo asked. Somewhere she had read, she said, that the only emotion birds felt was fear.

"Maybe the crows are used to the cars."

"Does that mean they can't feel fear anymore? That they have been robbed of their only emotion?"

Boyang turned down a narrow lane. He had a sense that something had gone awry. He thought back to the afternoon—she had looked calmly engaged when she had photographed the kite; she had not shown any sign of listlessness when he had picked her up that afternoon. His comment on chilblains ought to have been taken as both considerate and innocuous. "I don't know if you're only talking about the birds or about something else," he said.

"There's always something else, no?"

What he thought of her, which he hated even to sort out in his mind, and what she thought of him, which he had no way of knowing—these questions were their companions on their outings, though they had never stopped and faced their silent followers. "And what's that *something* in this case?" Boyang asked.

Sizhuo stared ahead—the car was coming to the end of the lane, which was blocked by metal chains. On the other side of the chains was an open lot. Boyang honked, and someone looked out a window of a bungalow, and then unlocked a door. It was an older man, whose face showed no expression when he walked across the lot and told them that the place was not open. "Not open?" Boyang said. "It's almost five o'clock."

"Not open," repeated the old man, turning around the cardboard sign hanging on the chain so they could see it. Sold, it said.

Boyang leaned over and apologized to Sizhuo, who sat straighter to make room for him as he felt around in the glove compartment. Finally he located the right pack of cigarettes, half-full—he kept three packs of different brands, which, depending on whom he was speaking with, he would choose from accordingly. "Sold to whom, Uncle?" he said, handing over a cigarette.

The old man sniffed the cigarette—the least expensive brand Boyang carried in the car—and nodded to himself. "City Ocean," he said.

City Ocean, Boyang thought to himself. "Not by any chance Metropolitan Ocean?" he asked.

The old man said yes, indeed it was Metropolitan Ocean. Boyang asked a few other questions, which the old man waved off. "Ask my son," the old man said and turned away. Boyang wondered if the old man was playing dumb, but there was little else he could do, so he backed the car out of the lane.

They stopped at another eatery a few kilometers down the road. When the waitress came with their menus, Sizhuo said she only wanted a pot of hot tea. "Did you get a chill?" Boyang asked. He would have made an effort to cheer her up if he hadn't just discovered the sale of the land around the old pub to Metropolitan Ocean.

Distracted more than distressed, he ordered a pot of tea for Sizhuo and some dumplings to go.

"Why don't you eat?" Sizhuo said. "You said earlier you were hungry."

"If you're not feeling well, I'd prefer to get back to the city as soon as we can," Boyang said.

"Or you need to get back for a business reason, and my not feeling well provides a perfect excuse."

"I don't work on Saturdays."

The waitress brought the tea, and Sizhuo asked if she could order the peasant stew on the menu. "That'll take some time," the waitress, a middle-aged woman who no doubt recognized Boyang's role, replied with her face turned to him. He said they had plenty of time.

"I see someone is moody today," Boyang said when the waitress left.

"Is that part of your being a good man, catering to every mood of mine?"

"You're the least moody woman I've met."

"So you've had your share of women with bad moods?" Sizhuo said. "How many of them have you known?"

"Why do you ask?"

"Do I not have a right to be curious?"

In her eyes he saw defiance mixed with resignation; it was a look he hadn't seen before. Could it be that she, being the less experienced of the two, had finally cracked, as he had feared would happen to himself? He felt a surge of satisfaction—until that moment, he had not caught any sign that he existed in her world as more than a chauffeur and a walking companion, and had been both amused and puzzled by her patience. "Of course you have every right to be curious," he said, pouring the tea for her. "But what I don't understand is this: my comment about the chilblains seemed to upset you."

"What does it matter to you if I get chilblains or not?"

"Now, that is childish."

"I don't understand why, week after week, we meet for a walk, sit down and talk about trivial matters, and then disappear from each other's worlds for the rest of the week as though nothing happened. You don't like my photography. You have better ways to entertain yourself. Why do you humor me?"

"I've never had a chance to see the final prints. How do you know I don't like them?"

"You'd have asked if you were interested."

"Is it too late to ask now?"

Sizhuo looked at Boyang, and he could see the confusion in her eyes. "Listen," he said and glanced at her hands on the table. He calculated the effect of covering her hands with his, but decided against it. "You must know I like you. A lot. So however we spend time together makes me happy." Or was it a misstep to say "happy," when he did not really believe in happiness? "I never got the sense that you hated these outings, but if that's the case, I will certainly leave you alone."

"I didn't say I hated them," Sizhuo said.

"Then what's upsetting you?"

"I don't know what we are to each other. Perhaps this is never a problem for you, but it's unnatural."

"What's unnatural about being friendly?"

"We're not meant to be friends."

"So we should either be lovers," he said, and watched Sizhuo blush—"or strangers. Are those the only two options? Is there not space in between for us to be genuinely affectionate toward each other?"

Sizhuo looked agonized, cornered by a mind more lucid than hers, though what could his lucidity do but confirm the distance between them? The truth was, wherever they were at this moment—no, before this moment, before she laid out in the open the questions they both must have been asking themselves—whatever they had been then was better. Why, thought Boyang with a weary sadness, couldn't people stay in a place they could not name, rather than wanting to know, always wanting to know, more of the truth? Everything comes to an end when explained, rightly or wrongly.

"Can I tell you a story?" Sizhuo asked.

Don't, his heart cried out. Do not tell your story to me; I'm not one to whom you should entrust your secret. When you hand it to me, you will either expect me to hold it as something precious, or, in exchange, you will expect me to offer you a story of my own. Can't you see that I'm going to fail you on both accounts? "Certainly," Boyang said. He had known that sooner or later one of them would have to take a step to make things go one way or another. At least he should be glad that he was not the one who'd lost his poise first. "Do tell."

"Yet you don't want to hear it."

"Of course I do," Boyang said, turning his eyes away from Sizhuo's stare. This was going to be the end of something that had not begun properly; would that make everything easier for him, and for her?

"I know you're lying, but I don't mind being lied to today," Sizhuo said. "It's time to stop this silliness of seeing you every week and pretending all is happy and normal."

"I haven't been pretending."

Sizhuo ignored Boyang's words, and when she spoke again there was a note of abandonment in her voice. Do not lose your composure over the past, Boyang wanted to advise the girl; what you think of as tragic will one day make you laugh.

The story, as he had guessed, featured a boy and a girl—Sizhuo herself—and would no doubt turn out to be a failed love story of the most heartbreaking kind. He braced himself for the moment when he was expected to offer something—comfort, wisdom, forgiveness.

The two had been playmates, Sizhuo said, having known each other all their lives. The boy, three months older, had taken on the role of big brother—the one to provide and to protect. When their parents could not offer enough food, there had been sparrows killed by a homemade slingshot, cicadas caught with glue attached to the top of a bamboo pole, frogs, hedgehogs, grasshoppers, all roasted in hot ash. The boy had not been interested in education and had failed school early on; nevertheless, he had been called a smart boy, too smart for his own good in the eyes of his elders. When her parents' income could not satisfy her need for more books, he had invested his intelligence in stealing: copper wires dug out of the ground, wild ginseng and rare dried mushrooms swiped from the packing factory, small items that people had left around their yards. She had not asked to whom he brought these things—at age ten he was already connected to dubious people out in the world. She had not approved of these misdemeanors, yet neither had she declined the offerings. When she had left her hometown for college in Beijing, he had followed her, discarding a network of friends that could have made his life more convenient in the provincial town. In Beijing he had become an illegal transient, working odd jobs and living a life that did not cross paths with her college life. They met once a month far from campus to take a walk, and always, before parting ways, he would put an envelope of money into her hands and tell her to buy the name-brand clothes that the other girls in the city were wearing.

"What are you thinking?" Sizhuo stopped and asked.

"I was thinking that in everyone's heart, there's a graveyard for first love."

"Of course to you there's nothing special about the boy's love."

"I didn't say that. He was in love with you, but the question is: were you—or are you—in love with him?"

Sizhuo looked at him strangely. "You can't be in love with a dead person."

Boyang felt a pang. How do you, he asked himself, compete with a young man in the grave for a woman's heart?

The story that followed belonged to the metro section of the evening newspaper, one of those tales in which a young man, having no legal residency in Beijing, brought nothing to the city but chaos and danger. One night he had broken into a rental shared by three young women. He had thought they were out of town for the Lunar New Year, not realizing that one had returned early. Out of panic, he had stabbed and killed the woman, a journalist whose next assignment was to interview a rising star in local politics.

No doubt the young man's execution would forever be the pinnacle of a tragedy that Sizhuo thought she could have prevented. Yet he—uneducated, without any connections or means—stood no chance in this city. Apart from some perfunctory sympathy for a life lost, Boyang felt little for the young man. Any premature death could be called a tragedy, but how many tragedies would one be willing to admit into one's thoughts? There were worse losses: Shaoai, for instance, locked in her own body for twenty-one years. The life she could have made—a brilliant career, a successful family, influences on many lives, good use of her time on earth. Could he explain to Sizhuo that sometimes death was a mercy—that it was worse for the dead to go on living? In an ideal world, death should be the end of the story, but in this world, where they had to make do with muddles, death never ended anything neatly. "Your friend made a mistake," Boyang said. "And yes, a pricey one. But if I were you, I wouldn't burden myself with unnecessary guilt."

"But you are not me."

"You wouldn't have changed many things in his life."

"At least I could have let him believe he had a chance."

"At what? Your love, or a better life in this city?"

"Either," Sizhuo said hesitantly. "Or both."

"But you were not in love with him, and you know that. You couldn't have gotten him a better job, and you know that, too. What's the point of regretting something you haven't done wrong? The same misfortune could have befallen him all the same, and you would be sitting here feeling guilty for having lied to him about your love."

Sizhuo looked a little dazed. "But in his mind, he must have thought part of his misfortune my responsibility."

"Did he say that to you?"

"He always asked me why I hadn't been like the other girls and found a sugar daddy in this city."

Boyang cringed. That she had no trouble saying the words *sugar daddy* made him sad.

"He considered all men who were richer and older his enemies. He considered the young men whose parents had already bought them apartments in Beijing, and who already had the best jobs lined up for them, his enemies. But you must admit that he was not wrong. What did he have but his wish to make a better case for his love?"

Boyang felt an icy tingling on his back. Somewhere, the ghost of the young man must be glaring at him, resenting him, because he possessed what the young man would never be able to have.

"He always said he knew what I was going to do," said Sizhuo. "He said that I would sell out in exchange for a comfortable life."

"But you didn't."

"Does that mean that I haven't thought about it, or I won't ever? What am I doing here with you if I am not considering that possibility? If I were a better person, I would have said no to you right away because everything in connection with you proves him right."

"Why not look at it this way? You didn't say no because I didn't come simply to propose that I become your sugar daddy."

"But what do you call what we've been doing?"

"We're trying to get to know each other."

"Is that what we're doing? Do we know each other better than we did four weeks ago?" Sizhuo said. "Or are we just avoiding getting to know each other, because it's too much of a risk for you?"

Again Boyang was frightened by the abandonment in her tone. "But not a risk for you?" he asked.

"What do I have to lose?" Sizhuo said.

Her childlike defiance unnerved him. He had never asked himself if she was worth his effort because to ask was to admit that this was more than a game. He had believed that at any moment he could leave, but what he hadn't realized was that she had, without his know-ing it, taken his deposit—of what?—his honor, his peace, or even his hope of building something called a life with her. How could he ex-plain to her that she had too much to lose, not only on her own be-half, but on his, too? "What," he said with some difficulty, "can I do to make things better?"

"It's not what you can *do*, don't you see?" Sizhuo said. "It's what kind of person you are, but I don't know who you are, or what you are. Sometimes I think maybe I did make the mistake of never commit-ting to any position—had I chosen to be practical, had I chosen to be like some of my classmates from freshman year, my friend might have lost hope in this city and might not have stayed. So why didn't I? Did I think I deserved great love, when other girls like me had re-signed themselves to reality? But if I didn't want to sell out, I should've been stronger. I should've believed in building a future with him in this place, however hard it would have been; I should've received his presents and returned with . . ."

Abruptly Sizhuo broke off. The waitress was coming with a steam-ing pot but had stopped a couple of steps away, lest it was not the right time. Sizhuo looked away with a flushed face, and Boyang motioned for the waitress to bring the stew over. She ladled the soup into two bowls and told them to enjoy. The moment before she turned away, Boyang caught a slight mocking smile on the face of the middle-aged woman.

"Well, eat something hot," Boyang said.

Sizhuo made no movement to touch the food. "I was thinking before you picked me up today that we should stop this nonsense."

"Why do you call it nonsense, when it seems to me to be the most sensible thing for two people to get to know each other?"

"It won't work out in the end."

"You don't know that if we haven't tried."

Sizhuo looked at him sadly. "You know what's the only thing that could absolve me? To fall in love with you, to have you fall in love with me—no, not you, but any man who is in a better position than my friend. Only love can absolve me, can't you see? If only I could prove to my friend that a man richer and older than he can love as he did—do you see?"

Could he, or anyone, love as the dead boy had?

"You look hesitant. And you're right to hesitate. You don't feel up to the challenge, or perhaps it's not even fair to ask you to try, because you would always suspect that I would compare you to him, or else I would use you. Sometimes I thought it would be better if I found another boy like him, who had nothing to his name, and we would support each other in our struggling. No, you're laughing, and you're right that however honorable that sounds, we would not get very far. Yes, I know that, but it isn't for that reason that I'm not dating another boy like him," Sizhuo said, looking into Boyang's eyes, the tears she had been holding back now rolling down without inhibition. "But this: if I could make a life with someone *like* him, why not with him in the first place?"

Sizhuo stood abruptly and said she would be right back. For a moment Boyang worried that she would leave without him—he could see her do that, sneaking out of the restaurant and walking to the nearest bus stop, asking a passerby the bus schedule, playing hide-and-seek when he went to hunt for her. But to allow himself to panic was to surrender to a situation where he should have control. To distract himself, he took out his phone to see if anyone had contacted him in the past few hours.

An email from Ruyu was waiting for him, in his regular account, and only later did he figure out that it must not have been difficult for her to find that address. He had registered with that email on a few social media websites, and he had a microblog connected to the email.

The message was short: Ruyu gave the address of a hotel and the telephone number, and said that she would like to meet. There was no mention of how long she would stay, or when would be a good time for her.

Boyang felt sweat on his palms. The most sensible thing would be to call now rather than later, though Sizhuo would be back any minute. He looked around and signaled for the waitress to bring the check. "To-go containers?" she asked, looking at the untouched food.

"No, just bring me the bill."

The waitress gave him an I-knew-it look. As she walked to the counter, she looked at Sizhuo, who had come out of the ladies' room with slightly swollen eyes, without hiding her interest. With so many people coming and going through her restaurant, Boyang thought, the waitress must need to find a way to score points over the customers, morally or in another manner, but don't we all do that? "I hope you don't mind that I asked for the check," he said when Sizhuo sat down.

She shook her head and said she was ready to leave.

He drove faster than usual on the way back, honking at the slower cars and cursing under his breath at the trucks. He was aware that Sizhuo watched him critically, and he wondered whether this behavior would be misunderstood—though did it really matter now if he was misunderstood by her? As they approached the city, traffic slowed to a worm's speed, and he could not help but press his upper body against the steering wheel from time to time and join the chorus of honking. The fourth time he did this, Sizhuo looked at him coolly and said, "Do you think that's going to change anything?"

"I'm not doing it to change anything."

"Complaining?"

"Protesting."

"What's the difference between the two?"

"Protesting makes one feel a better person," he said. "Though there's really not any difference, if you ask me."

"Do you protest often?"

"No," he said. "I often don't see the point."

"Then what's the point today?"

He turned to look at her. "What do you mean?"

"I think something I said put you into this protesting mood. What was it? Did I overstep and share too much information? Did I disappoint you because I've decided to stop playing your game?"

He sighed. "I've not been playing a game with you."

"How do I know that?"

How does anyone know anything about another person? Our mind, a slate that does not begin as large as we wish, grows smaller with what we believe to be experience: anything we put down has to be erasable, one passion making way for another, one connection replaced by an equally precarious one. Once and again we lie to ourselves about starting with a clean slate, but even the most diligent wiping leaves streaks—fears, distrusts, the necessity of forever questioning the motives of others.

Later, as Boyang sat in the hotel lobby, he tried to focus his thoughts on Sizhuo; his standing with her in the immediate future— the next day, the next week—provided solid footing for him as he waited for Ruyu. Sizhuo had been quiet when he dropped her off; he had promised to call soon. He would have to say something when he saw her again—what, though? She had given him an ultimatum; in laying her past open, she had demanded from him a kind of honesty he did not believe he had in him.

He looked up at the clock—ten past seven, not far enough into the hour to think of Ruyu as being late, but what if she had had a change of heart and would never show up? He brought out a handkerchief and wiped his forehead. He wondered if he should go to the receptionist and announce himself, though that would indicate impatience, and worse, loss of faith in the eventuality of their meeting. He crossed and uncrossed his legs. This, he told himself, was not a first date, nor an illicit rendezvous.

The elevator door opened, releasing Ruyu among a few other guests. He recognized her at once. Her body was no longer a girl's but remained slim; her face was serene with an expression closest to contentment. He wished, against logic, that she were attached to one of the other guests and would disappear in a moment, but they quickly dispersed, leaving Ruyu, who met his eyes but did not move closer. He stood up and stepped forward. Having neither the proper gesture nor the right words for a greeting, he felt caught again, underprepared. "Here we are," he said finally.

Ruyu studied him with an unequivocal gaze. "I imagine you know a quiet place nearby, where we can sit down and talk?"

Of course, he said, and added that he had called to reserve a private room at a nearby restaurant. "It's Sichuan-style. I'm not sure if you eat spicy food, but they have good non-spicy choices, too. It's just across the street, and it's quite clean there. But if you prefer somewhere else, we could find another place."

She said that sounded fine, and he led the way. Neither spoke until they were shown to the reserved room, the glass door of which bore the name "Reuters" and was a one-way mirror, allowing those eating inside to view the restaurant without being observed. Ruyu pointed that out to him and asked if this was a place for foreign journalists to gather, and he said that he doubted that was why the room was named as it was. There were other rooms in the restaurant that had names like CNN, BBC, Agence. Not Xinhua? she asked, and he said no, no one wanted to dine in a room named after a news agency they could not trust. Ruyu said she could not see how any of the foreign agencies were more trustworthy. "They are all the same," she said.

"Surely that can't be," he said.

"They are the same the way people are the same," she said. "Would you look for a better person in a foreign country if you couldn't find one at home?"

"To you, perhaps, but not many people have seen the world as you have. You've got to allow people the hope for something better."

The waitress brought tea and started to recite the restaurant's Saturday special. Boyang stopped her and told her to leave the menu with them and wait outside the door. The waitress readily gave up her post.

Through the glass, Ruyu watched the waitress standing straight next to the door. "I haven't seen the world as you think," she said, turning her attention to Boyang. "But that's all right, as I don't see the point in doing that. But you, what is your life like these days? To get away from whatever engagement you have for a Saturday night at such short notice—you must be in a good position to be able to do that."

Her words had an undertone that he could not read well, or perhaps he'd forgotten how she always seemed to be asking for more than an answer. "There's nothing more important than seeing you," he said.

"Why?"

"You don't happen to be in town often. Or at least I don't happen to hear from you often."

"You've heard from me *and* seen me in person. Now what? You can go home to your wife and child with one thing ticked off your list, no?"

"I have neither of those, as a matter of fact."

"Why not? Isn't that bad news for a man your age? Or you prefer the freedom of a diamond bachelor?"

"I was married once. It didn't work out."

"You don't want to try again?"

"Once bitten by a snake, one has to be cautious around ropes for ten years," he said, feeling momentarily apologetic toward his ex-wife. Though she had been the who had betrayed the marriage, what was wrong with his playing the victim for now? "And you? Are you visiting the country by yourself?"

"I suppose it's only fair that you get a chance to ask me about my personal life, too," Ruyu said. "I had two marriages. Neither worked, of course, as you can very well imagine."

"I can't imagine."

"That I could fail at not one but two marriages?"

"That you would ever be married."

"But you knew I left the university to get married."

"You left the university to go to America was how I looked at it," Boyang said. "I don't count that marriage as a real one. And the second—was it a better . . . a different kind of marriage?"

She shook her head. "As pointless as the first one."

"Why get married at all, then?"

"Why not? You got married, too."

"Mine was a real marriage," he said. At least for a while; at least he preferred to think so.

Ruyu smiled. The expression seemed a new addition; it occurred to Boyang that he had never seen her smile. "I can't, of course, defend my marriages. I would have preferred not to use marriage to solve my problems, but there are issues of practicality. And I don't think I'm good at figuring them out."

"So marrying yourself off was the only option?" Boyang said, and realized that he sounded more bitter than he meant to. Selling yourself off, Sizhuo would say.

"Certainly not the only one."

"But the easiest one?"

"Let's not get into these arguments," Ruyu said. "I'm not back here to discuss my marriages with you, and I'm sure there is little I can say about yours."

"What are you here for?"

"To see you, of course."

"That's it?"

"Who else? There are not many people for me to see in this country."

"Your grandaunts, are they still . . . around?"

"They are with their god now."

"When did that happen?"

"Maybe nine, ten years ago?" Ruyu said. "You don't have to look at me that way. I know how ungrateful I must sound to you. To be honest, I only got the news afterward. No, I didn't come back for either of them."

"Typical of you not to return for a funeral."

Ruyu opened her mouth as though she had something to say, and then smiled forgivingly. Boyang apologized for his unfriendly tone.

"You don't have to apologize. I'm as heartless as everyone thinks," she said. "Though my grandaunts would not have liked me to come back either. They disowned me when I left China for the marriage, you see."

"Why?"

"I didn't turn out as they wished, and then they also found out that their little brother was alive in Taiwan, with a full family of children and grandchildren. So everything worked out just fine."

"For whom?"

"For them, and for me too," she said. "They didn't raise me to be someone's wife, nor did they raise me to defy God's will by speaking of suicide. But then they didn't expect to find their brother, so I suppose they were two happy women in the end. Perhaps their god did see how much they sacrificed to raise me and grant them something better than me as a reward. Who knows? They might have told each other that God had other plans for me, and it was good for them to wash their hands of me."

Boyang shifted in his seat. He had once wanted so much to ask Ruyu about her grandaunts, but being young then, he had not found the courage or the right words, and now the women were just two anecdotal names in her life. If he asked about her ex-husbands, would she shrug and say there was little to tell? Did everyone in her life end up like that—had he himself already been in that position? No, he denied this violently: she would not have come back to see him if he had already become a fossil.

"Does this make you uncomfortable?" Ruyu asked. "Shall we order something so the poor girl doesn't have to stand there all night?"

He ignored her prompting. "Did you . . . love them?"

"My grandaunts?"

"Yes," he said. "Did they love you?"

"I'm afraid that was beyond their capacity. I don't think they loved me more than one would love a pig one raises as a sacrifice. Why? Do you think I'm unfairly harsh toward them? Perhaps I should withdraw that comment. No, they might have loved me in a way I didn't understand. As for me, they were the only family I had, but I wasn't raised to love them, or any mortal."

"That must be a difficult place to be in."

"I would say there's no better place for anyone."

"Do you really believe that?" Boyang asked, looking into Ruyu's eyes.

She did not avert her eyes from his gaze. "At least I want to believe it."

"Have you ever wondered if that's unnatural?" *Unnatural*—Sizhuo's word, but what could he use to protect himself but the younger woman's willfulness?

"Nothing," Ruyu said, "is natural with my life."

"Including coming back?" he said.

"In fact—you don't have to believe it—but coming back seems the most natural thing that has happened to me."

"Did you come back because Sister Shaoai died?"

Ruyu's eyes looked strangely out of focus for a brief moment. "No," she said. "I'd have come back earlier, in time for her funeral, if it were for her."

"Her ashes are not buried yet."

"Why not?"

"I don't know. Perhaps Aunt is not ready to bury her yet."

"How is Aunt?"

"I can take you to see her tonight," he said. "Or tomorrow. Or anytime."

"I think we should order now," Ruyu said and leaned over to tap the window. The waitress came in right away. Ruyu, without consulting Boyang, asked for enough food for two.

"Why change the subject?" Boyang said, watching the waitress close the door behind her. "You don't like to hear about how Aunt has been struggling all these years?"

"I've not seen one person in this world who's not struggling," Ruyu said.

"That is quite a coldhearted comment," Boyang said.

"Yet it is true. You're implying that I'm responsible for Aunt's struggling and should feel some sort of guilt. But the thing is, if it weren't this struggle, it would have been another. If Shaoai had not taken ill, she would have turned out to be a pain for Aunt still."

"Shaoai did not take ill. She was poisoned."

Ruyu remained silent, her expression frosty—a more familiar face to Boyang.

"What? You don't like me to remind you of that fact?"

"What," Ruyu said, turning her eyes to Boyang and for the first time looking baffled, "do you want me to say?"

"Did you poison Shaoai?"

"Is that all you want to know?"

"I suppose, in a way, everyone wanted to know," Boyang said. "I've never stopped wanting to know."

"Who is everyone?"

"Me, my parents, Aunt and Uncle, the neighbors."

"Moran, too?"

Boyang had been wondering when and how this would happen—he had not had the courage to bring Moran's name into the conversation. "I suppose she must want to know, too," he said.

"How is she doing these days? Where is she?"

"I don't know."

"You don't keep in touch with her?"

"The way I've kept in touch with you, yes, but I've never heard from her."

"Are you not curious about how she is? Are her parents still around?"

"Yes, but I've never asked them about her. I haven't talked to them for years."

"Why not?"

"She has a right to stay away."

Ruyu smiled. "How sad for her."

"Why?"

"If she mattered to you more than she does, you'd have sought her out," Ruyu said. "It's not as though this is a world where a person can hide away forever."

"Perhaps I have reasons not to seek her out."

"That's why I feel sad for her."

"Why?"

"She was quite smitten with you, wasn't she?"

"Everyone has an adolescent crush. But that's not a reason for me to continue being in her world," Boyang said.

"I remember that Shaoai once said Moran was only a child," Ruyu said, the expression on her face turning hazy. "Poor child."

"What do you mean?"

"She really was a child when we knew her, no?" Ruyu said. "I always feel bad about all those things happening to her."

"To her only?" Boyang said, feeling a sudden rage. "But was I not a child? For heaven's sake, Shaoai was only twenty-two. Was she not still a child, in a way?"

Ruyu looked at Boyang as though amused by his anger. "Oh, don't look like your life's been destroyed. I imagine you've come through with little harm—right?"

He wanted to argue that that was not the case. He wanted to list the years of care he had dedicated to Shaoai, watching her deteriorate and hiding her from his ex-wife and friends, separating his life into two compartments, neither of them real enough. But whatever he said would only amuse Ruyu more. "So you did poison Shaoai, didn't you?" he said. He had only that question as a weapon.

"I didn't mean to kill her," Ruyu said. "Though I should say, I didn't mean to *not* kill her and leave her as a burden for you and the others. But is either statement true? No, I would say no. I didn't even know if I wanted her to take the poisonous drink or not. She had drunk it before I made up my mind."

"What do you mean?"

"If there was a cup of orange juice in a room that she shared with another person, she would think she had the claim to it. Why didn't she ask me first if I wanted it? She felt entitled to everything."

"So it was the Tang you used," he said. "I always wondered."

The door was pushed open, and the waitress wheeled in their dishes. Boyang looked at the food; it occurred to him that this would be the second meal of the day that he would pay for without touching. Ruyu signaled to the dishes, and he shook his head.

"I didn't put poison in them," she said with a smile.

Boyang felt an urge to hit her, to make her repent, but more than that: to make her cry, to make her feel the pain, to leave her wounded and never healed.

"Go ahead," Ruyu said, watching him calmly. "If it would make you feel better."

"What?"

"You look as though you want to slap me."

Boyang felt a pang. It was the same indestructible Ruyu no matter where their encounter occurred in life. Could it be that his youthful love for her had been a desire to weaken her so that she would need him? His desire to hurt her now—could it be his only way to love her? "I don't hit women," he said.

"Or perhaps you want to kill me," Ruyu said. "Which is understandable, too."

"Why would I want to kill you?"

"That's one way to destroy me," Ruyu said. "There aren't many ways. If I were a real killer—you see, I'm not defending myself in any way, but I can say with absolute honesty that it was partly an accident with Shaoai due to my indecision—but if I were a real killer, I would seek out someone like me. Shaoai was not that kind of person. Yes, I despised her, and I pitied her, but you have to know that neither would be a sufficient reason for one to kill a person."

"You mean you'd kill yourself? Didn't you use that once as your defense?"

"You could call that a lie. I've never been suicidal. You either have that in you, or you don't," Ruyu said. "I don't have that. All I'm saying is, I would have been much less lenient if I'd found someone like myself."

"Have you ever found anyone like yourself?"

"People in general are kinder than I," Ruyu said.

"But have you ever felt guilty?"

"About what?"

"About Shaoai," Boyang said. And about Moran, and himself, all these people left behind.

"All I wanted to do was to mind my own business. If there was a poisonous drink I mixed up and left on my desk, it was my own business," Ruyu said. "Shaoai's problem, like many people's, was not knowing how *not* to mind other people's business."

"Yes, she could be bossy. She could be unfriendly. But was that enough for her to suffer the way she did?"

Ruyu paused. "That, I have to say, was her bad luck."

"Do you have a heart? Do you not have any remorse in you?"

"Point out to me one person who could benefit from my having a heart."

Boyang stared at Ruyu. Her look, candid, without animosity, could have belonged to the most innocent person.

"Would you feel better if I lied, and said I felt some remorse?" Ruyu asked gently.

"I don't know."

"That's what I thought," Ruyu said. "No, nothing can be changed. You asked me to go visit Aunt. Do you think seeing me would do her any good? No, I don't think so. What people deserve is peace, and I'm afraid I am not a person who can leave anyone in peace."

"Then why did you come back to see me? Do I not deserve peace?"

"Would you prefer that I hadn't come back?" Ruyu said, her voice softened. "Have you already found peace? Have I disturbed it by coming back to look for you?"

Boyang shook his head. Peace, he knew, was the last thing he wanted at the moment.

19

"It's a good story, Moran," Josef said.

"But?"

He sighed. "It's a very good story," he said. "It's romantic and melancholy. But it's not a real story."

They were sitting on a lakeside bench. An early heat wave had confused all the trees and flowers into blossoms. Wait until the next snow, people kept warning one another, as though they needed to remind themselves, before hope was taken away, that it would not last. Yet the daffodils and tulips did not heed the warnings. There is no point in waiting, as every moment is the right moment.

"Why does it matter?" Moran asked. She had told Josef the story of Grazia, of her childhood in Italy, of her cold death—too early, too quiet—in Switzerland. It was the details she liked to describe to Josef: the dolls Grazia's nanny had made for her; her French governess's face, small and heart-shaped; the German musician who came to the house to give piano lessons to her and ended each encounter with a severe bow. In the days and weeks to come she would tell Josef other stories, too, of the Parisian cobbler and the Bavarian peasant, of the Russian maid riding in a coach with her mistress to Baden-Baden. "I like the stories."

"I like them, too, but I would like it more if you could tell me something else."

"About what?"

"Things I don't know about you. Your parents, for instance. Your traveling with them."

When they had gotten married she had told him that her parents had not been able to get visas; her father worked for a government ministry, which made traveling to the States complicated for him. Later, still in the marriage, the 9/11 attack made their traveling even less practical. She would not want them to go through stringent security checks, she had explained. Josef had agreed because it had seemed as though there would be plenty of time.

"But there is little to say about them," she said.

"That must not be true," Josef protested mildly.

Moran thought about it, and told Josef about when she and her parents were on a tour in Central Europe. In the old town of Zagreb a man was playing a Soviet song on the accordion, and her parents had come over to sing along, her father in Russian, her mother in Chinese, and the musician in a language none of them understood. "The Night in the Suburb of Moscow," she said, a most romantic song that her parents had sung when they had been in their early twenties.

Josef waited for more, and Moran smiled apologetically. "This doesn't work. I don't think I can make up a good story about real people."

"I'm not asking you to make up a story."

"But I like myself more when I make up those stories," Moran said. They were not her stories. They were not about her time, or her people, but what she had once found in these stories—escape—would eventually become her wisdom. Perhaps if she kept these tales going Josef would one day forgive her stubbornness in choosing solitude, because he, kinder than solitude, was always here for her.

20

On an overcast afternoon in late March, Sizhuo stood in front of the shop and watched a pair of swallows fixing their nest under the eave. Swallows were monogamous birds, she remembered reading, and a couple would return to their old nest year after year.

Stubborn creatures, she thought. Why come back to this polluted city when there must be a better place—fresher air, bluer sky—for their offspring? Yet at least they were bound to an old home. She herself had not grown up here, and she had little to claim in this place; still, she resisted decamping, struggling to make this unkind city her home.

A couple walked close. Sizhuo turned, and her face paled momentarily before she regained her composure. Boyang, accompanied by a middle-aged woman, had stopped a few steps away, both studying Sizhuo.

"Are you closed today?" Boyang said.

"No," Sizhuo said.

A few months ago, after their disastrous meal at a countryside pub, she had sent him a text message, saying she had decided that it would be best for them not to see each other again. She had thought that he would call or stop by, to plead for himself, and she had been disappointed when he had sent a one-word reply: "agreed." She had refused to believe that he had hurt her feelings, but now, facing him, she felt the coldness in her fingertips.

Boyang introduced the woman as an old friend, Ruyu, who had lived in America but who had come back to settle down. They had taken a walk around the Back Sea, he said, and he thought he would bring her to see if there was a new exhibition here.

There was, Sizhuo replied, and led the way back to the shop. She pointed out to Boyang and the woman the collection of minute crystal vases, with miniature still lifes of butterflies and orchids painted inside. She did not ask if they needed a tour, and they did not request one. From the way they walked together Sizhuo could see that they must have an intimate connection. If she herself had ever occupied any space in Boyang's heart, she knew it was no longer there.

They did not stay in the shop for long, and before leaving, the woman looked into Sizhuo's eyes and wished her good luck. Why, Sizhuo thought after they left; what would she need good luck for? She did not know that Boyang had presented her to the woman as a girl he might have loved; he could have made a life with the girl, Boyang had admitted.

Not anymore? Ruyu had asked.

Not now that Ruyu had come back, Boyang had answered.

Out of curiosity Ruyu had requested to meet the girl, and afterward they walked along the lakefront, not saying much. There would be a time when the girl's face would come back to them, as every one of us has to unearth, at times, a face or two from the past—that of an earlier love, of a lost friend, or of ourselves from a bygone time, when we hadn't learned that our faces could haunt others' hearts, too.

He was wise not to fall in love with the girl, Ruyu said eventually. The girl deserved a happier life, and he was right to leave her alone.

Acknowledgments

I am grateful to Cressida Leyshon, Sarah Chalfant, Jin Auh, Kate Medina, and Andris Skuja for their support, and to Mona Simpson and Tom Drury for reading the manuscript.

This novel could not have been written without Brigid Hughes and Amy Leach.

About the Author

YIYUN LI is the recipient of numerous awards, including the PEN/Hemingway Award, the Frank O'Connor International Short Story Award, the *Guardian* First Book Award, and a MacArthur fellowship. Many of her stories have appeared in *The New Yorker*, which named her one of the top twenty writers under forty. She teaches at the University of California, Davis, and lives with her husband and two sons.

About the Type

This book was set in Sabon, a typeface designed by the well-known German typographer Jan Tschichold (1902–74). Sabon's design is based upon the original letter forms of sixteenth-century French type designer Claude Garamond and was created specifically to be used for three sources: foundry type for hand composition, Linotype, and Monotype. Tschichold named his typeface for the famous Frankfurt typefounder Jacques Sabon (c. 1520–80).

MAR -- 2014